Satan R
Daught

curated by

James H Longmore

A HellBound Books® LLC Publication

Cover design by Kevin Enhart for
HellBound Books® Publishing LLC

www.hellboundbookspublishing.com

Printed in the United States of America

CONTENTS

Satan Rides Your Daughter Again

The Saving of Agatha MacMillan

R.D. Tyler

"Experience daily proves how loath they are to confess without torture." - King James, *Daemonologie* (1597)

***

Agatha huddled in the cell, damp, cold, and alone. There was a small window, high on the one stone wall, far out of reach and barred besides. Barely any light shone through during the day. Only cold seeped through at night, or the occasional rain. A stone slab protruded from the wall directly below the window with a threadbare woolen blanket providing meager protection from the chill. The only other thing in the cell was a chamber pot. Bars of rusty iron made up the other three walls of her cage.

There were other cells down here, but no one else was in them. The quiet was oppressive. She had lost track of how long she had been down here. A guard brought her stale bread and watery gruel, but she wasn't sure how often. He never answered any of her questions or said even as much as a single word to her. He barely even looked at her. Probably afraid.

No one came and visited her. Not her family, nor friends. She hadn't seen anyone since she had been accused.

She didn't understand. She didn't understand how no one could come see her, check on her. She didn't understand how anyone could believe any of those charges, that she could do any of those heinous, ungodly things.

The boredom was the worst of it. Just waiting for something, anything to happen. She tried praying. Agatha called out to God over and over, but there was never any answer. Just the darkness of her prison and the silence of the stones and iron.

Would they just forget her down here? Would she even get a trial? A chance to defend herself? None of the terrible accusations were true. She just needed the chance to prove it. A chance she wasn't sure she would get.

She huddled in the dark and damp and cried quietly to herself.

***

It had been a perfect day when they came for her. She remembered it because it had been raining so hard the whole week before. Runoff had washed out the roads and a wagon had gotten stuck in the mud. Some posts in the wooden fence that formed the sheep pen at her papa's farm had fallen, and a few had used the resulting gap for their daring escape.

She had been rounding up the wayward lambs, enjoying the sunlight bathing her in warmth when they came, men armed with halberds and wearing steel cuirasses. These were full men-at-arms, coming up the road, approaching her with weapons pointed at her. A few even had muskets aimed at her. Muskets? She was a slender thing, no more dangerous than a mouse.

She had no idea why they were coming after her at all. She lived a quiet life, helping tend her papa's farm. The only thing she ever got in trouble for was dreaming too much. Her mother had died three or four winters back. Her sister, a few years younger, had just recently married, her husband moving her to a village a few miles away. Her brother was not yet ten. Agatha had no husband, nor any man of her own, and she much preferred it that way. She kept to herself and kept herself out of trouble.

But here they were, half a dozen armed men, come for her. One was carrying manacles, another held a black hood, ready to cover her head. One of them, clearly an officer or sergeant of some kind, stepped forward. His wide brim hat shielded his eyes as he read charges from a parchment, his voice booming with authoritative formality.

"Agatha MacMillan, you stand on this day accused and charged with witchcraft most foul. You are accused of providing the method by which to abort unborn Christian babies, of having done such a procedure yourself. You are accused of seducing, charming, and hexing the married men of this village. You are accused of committing mischief upon the village. Of comporting yourself with the Devil and being a servant of Satan.

"You will be remanded to the prison at Dirleton Castle, by order of Magistrate Bartholomew Williamson. You will remain there, until your trial, where you will be judged. May God have mercy upon your soul."

He finished his pronouncement and stood back to let the others bind her. He never looked at her. The others approached her, fear obvious in their tense movements, preparing to take her into their custody.

Agatha was confused. She had no idea what was going on. If this was a jest, it was most unfunny. She couldn't form a reply. It must be some error, some grave mistake. She didn't talk to any man in the village. She was no midwife, offered no treatment. It wasn't real. This couldn't be real.

Her father had come out to see why there were so many armed men on his farm. He couldn't believe those charges, could he? He knew she was a good and pious girl; she never comported with men. Why did he look so ashamed? He didn't believe it, did he? *Papa don't believe it, it's not true.*

Agatha couldn't protest any of this, say anything at all. Her mouth was bound, her hands were chained. Then there was darkness as a hood covered her eyes. It clung to her nose and mouth as she tried to breathe. It smelled of mildew and sweat, and she couldn't stop herself from imagining the fate of the last person who had worn it. Her mama had always said her imagination would get her in trouble.

She was no fighter, avoided conflict when she could, so she went along obediently and quietly. Still the men took no chances. She didn't even know what curse they thought she could cast. She knew no magic, no spells. Six grown men terrified of a sprig of a girl.

God. God would save her. Agatha prayed, though she had the presence of mind to just pray in her mind and not aloud, in case these men thought her muffled words were some unholy incantation. God would know her thoughts and hear her prayers.

God, help these men recognize I have done nothing of that which they accuse me. Please help them to find me innocent and let me go. Please help your faithful servant. May Jesus watch over me and give me faith while you show these men the truth. Please, O Lord, deliver me.

Agatha knew it wasn't likely the Heavenly Father would just send an angel to free her right then and there, but she still had hoped he might. A prod from a musket stock and a yank on her chains sent her walking. Each step was a step into an abyss, a void. Each hidden rock clawed at her feet, threatening to bring her to ground.

She walked for many miles. None of the guards said a word to her, but she could hear the heavy crunch of their steps, the slight clang of some armor or weapon. The sun beat down on her and she was drenched in sweat. The sweat and heat built up in the hood, and she struggled to breathe through the humidity. She was so tired and thirsty it made her dizzy. Her feet were blistered and bleeding, aching with each step.

She had fallen more than a few times. Each time she was quickly jerked to her feet by the chains around her wrists. That hurt her ankles (and wrists) as much as the falls had. It didn't take long for her to start walking with a limp.

Finally, mercifully, they came to a stop. They gave her some water from a canteen but only lifted her hood enough to lower the gag and have a few sips without letting her see anything. The water inside was tepid and stale, but she gulped it down. She would have kept going but they took it from her mid gulp. They replaced the gag and lowered the hood, not bothering with the water that had spilled over her.

Agatha wasn't sure how long they stopped for. Not being able to see completely threw off her sense of time. The others had chatted amongst themselves. She couldn't make any of it out. They sounded far away. They must have taken their rest away from her. So much fear and caution against something she couldn't even do.

Eventually they started their trek again. After another indeterminate length of time, they stopped again. This time, they removed her manacles and hood, leaving her mouth bound. Momentary blindness at the sudden light took her, before her eyes adjusted and she saw it wasn't even that bright. In fact, it was fairly dark.

She was in the cell. They had arrived.

***

Agatha had been a small child when the last Great Witch Hunt had gripped the county only 16 years prior, but she had heard tales of what indignities accused witches went through. She wondered why they hadn't happened to her yet.

Or if the waiting was part of it. To build up the stress and fear in her mind.

She paced. Her cell was 6 and a half paces from the stone wall to the iron bars. It was just shy of five full paces from iron bar to iron bar. It was a small distance, and too many rounds eventually made her dizzy, but she had very little to occupy her, and so before long she paced again.

She prayed. Even the perpetual silence didn't deter her. This was a test of faith. God is just, and she would see justice. But she only had so many ways and words to ask for help.

Sarah! She missed her Sarah. Sarah was her dearest friend, who lived in the village proper. They were constant companions, and one of the few whose company Agatha ever sought out. It hurt not being able to see Sarah. It hurt even more thinking she might believe the nasty charges. She couldn't though; she knew Agatha better than anyone. Knew her soul. Agatha would get through this, and Sarah would be there afterwards.

Why didn't Sarah come, though? Why didn't her father, or her sister?

Where were they? Agatha thought maybe they weren't allowed to. Maybe they didn't care, a small voice in her head told her. They were ashamed, afraid of the witch. Her imagination was getting out of hand again.

Too much darkness. Too much alone. She couldn't keep her mind from picturing terrible, terrible things. Terrible things in the darkness, when there was a noise in the gloom. Terrible things that were going to happen to her. Terrible things that were happening to her family. She couldn't stop herself from picturing them.

That became her life. Pacing. Praying. Imagining. Day after uncountable day. She didn't start hearing the voice though, until the torture started.

***

Agatha was brought before the Kirk Council after what she imagined was years. They told her the date. It had only been a few weeks.

Men in black robes, framed in white wigs stared down at her from large wooden stands. The wood was dark, as was the rest of the chamber. She stood in what reminded her of a pulpit from church, high, exposed to all. Armed men were there, ready to intercede were she to utter any curses. There was a small crowd of onlookers. She didn't recognize anyone. No one from her village came for her trial.

They re-read her the charges. A man who looked like he had never smiled or known laughter intoned them gravely. He extolled on the seriousness of her crimes, expressed how many had come forward to bear witness against this faithless maiden, this bride of Lucifer. If Agatha hadn't been so terrified, she would have found it funny how silly all this ceremony was. It was all ridiculous. Silly, little wigs and silly, little robes and silly, little proclamations.

They asked her to confess. The Lord would forgive her, and she could be saved, if she would but confess.

Agatha said, "I cannot confess because it is a lie and there is nothing to confess to."

They asked her to confess again, on her mortal soul. She could be spared this trial. She could return to her home.

Again, Agatha responded with the truth, that she was no witch.

With unanimity, the council ruled to torture her until she confessed.

And so, Agatha found a new routine to supplement her pacing, praying, imagining. In the morning testimony was provided against her. In the afternoon, she was tortured. At night, they sent someone to wake her and keep her from sleeping.

The first day a man she had never met or seen in her life accused her of cursing him with an erection that wouldn't recede. His wife testified he was so engorged it was painful, and he would not lie with her anymore, because she could not satisfy him, and it was all Agatha's fault.

Agatha stood there, listening to them speak, utterly flabbergasted. Her face was flushed with embarrassment. This was clearly insane. She had never met this man, nor his untouched wife. She certainly had no interest in his member. She had never lain with a man, nor known one in that fashion. No one would believe her though, nor would anyone vouch for her.

The first day's torture has an examination. In front of the crowd, they stripped her naked and searched her body for the Devil's mark. They looked for the spot where Satan had supposedly set his claw, marking her as his own. Of course, there wasn't one, because she had made no such covenant, but it didn't stop men from pawing at her body. She felt ashamed and humiliated.

The first night without sleep was a shock. They had not disturbed her during her first few weeks in the stone and iron cell, and she went to lie down on her slab after the day's trials without a thought. She couldn't have had her eyes closed more than a few moments when she was splashed with cold water. She jolted awake.

Even without constant prodding from the guards, the shivering from the water would have kept her up. The first night felt longer than the week before.

The second night, she started to feel delirious. She was exhausted in a way she had never known before. There was no trial the second day, nor any torture. Just a horrible denial of sleep. Nothing felt real. Her head bobbed, constantly trying to find rest. These men were relentless in preventing it.

The third night is when she first heard the voice of the demon. It started by calling her name. Softly, barely audible, she heard its call. A scratchy, hoarse voice. She didn't see anything in the shadows. The current guard on duty didn't react, didn't seem to notice anything. She didn't answer the voice in the darkness. She prayed as hard as she could. Heaven and her cell were silent.

The fourth day brought more "witnesses"; more torture. A man claimed that Agatha cast a spell to transfer the pain of childbirth from his wife to himself. It was unnatural because God had designated women for suffering that burden. She at least knew this man, from dealings with her papa. But she had no idea who his wife was, nor had even known they had a child. Where were all these accusations coming from? Why were people believing them?

She could barely stand, barely speak. She tried to defend herself, to explain how none of this was possible, none of it true. How she bore no ill will to any of the witnesses. How she knew no spell nor formula, nor magics of any kind. Her words might as well have been the voice of the Almighty for all they listened.

They gave her the boots in the afternoon.

Large straps of rawhide were soaked in water and wrapped around her feet, ankles, up her calves. They bound them with cordage as tight as they could. They set her feet over a low fire, the heat warming up the water and shrinking the rawhide. She screamed, but she could hear her bones creak and dislocate over her own shrieks. The pain was awful. She wanted to die just to stop the suffering.

At the height of agony, they asked her to confess again. She could not, her heart would not let her lie. God saw all, she would not sin to save herself pain. The flesh would fail; her resolve would not.

It lasted all afternoon, the heating of the boots and the calls to admit to her crimes and true nature. As evening fell, they decided not to press further, not out of mercy, but fear of her losing her ability to confess.

Agatha could not walk, so they had to carry her to her cell. They had to cut the rawhide boots off of her feet, they had shrunken so tight. Her feet and shins were purple and swollen, misshapen. They throbbed in time with her heartbeat and each throb sent shooting pain up her legs.

The demon spoke to her again that night.

"You don't have to suffer, you know," it whispered. The voice was right in her ear. It was across the room. She saw nothing, but a shudder rolled up her spine. She shivered and that sent more pain up her legs.

"God will save me. Get ye gone, fiend," Agatha said through clenched teeth. The guard looked at her, dismissed it as ravings and continued ignoring her. As long as she didn't sleep.

"God?" A cold, callous laugh reverberated in the darkness. It sounded like a hiss. "God does nothing. God watches. You pray and pray, and He offers what? Pain, humiliation. Death. I offer Freedom. Escape. Life."

"Lies! Keep your poisoned gifts, deceiver." Agatha prayed as loud and as deliberately as she could manage, words catching in her mouth as often as not.

The demon chuckled softly but said no more. She couldn't see it, but she was certain she could feel its presence, still haunting her.

The fifth day brought no trial or torture, but a fever instead. A barber was called in to set her feet. They held her down, as she raved and screamed, bones grinding audibly as they were pushed into place. She was given a draught and finally allowed to sleep. She slept all day and all night.

She dreamed of a creature with many spider-like legs and three heads. One was a frog, one was a cat, and the middle one had the face of her father. All three opened their mouths wide, far too wide, and spewed insects, vermin, and all the crawling things onto her.

She woke up with a rat on her chest, sniffing aggressively, looking for food. She flung it from her as far as she could. It squeaked and scurried off into the darkness, searching somewhere else for a meal.

The seventh day brought the witch pricker. John Kincaid

was a famed witch finder, known for rooting out dozens of witches. It had taken him a few days to get the notice, and then a few more to ride in from Tranent for the trial. Since her Devil's mark wasn't found in the last inspection, it must be invisible. It would feel no pain and draw no blood when pricked. Kincaid was famed for his ability to find this spot on a suspected witch in no more than two hundred pricks.

He was a pompous man, well-dressed and arrogant, playing the crowd more like a showman than a soldier against evil. Agatha didn't believe any of the women he uncovered had ever performed a single act of sorcery.

She was undressed again, the crowd allowed to gawk at her nakedness. Kincaid made a demonstration of pulling out his pricking devices, needles with elaborately carved handles. He organized them on a table in front of them. At great length and much carefully pantomimed deliberation, he selected one of the longer, thinner pins, and with the pride of a parent, displayed it to the audience. He then presented it to Agatha, as if she would enjoy seeing it. She did not.

He dragged it across the skin of her belly as a lover might, teasing her. A few of the gathered laughed. She failed to see the humor. Indeed, he was not acting in any manner appropriate to an official of the Kirk and court. Her lack of appreciation did nothing to deter his performance. If anything, it seemed to encourage him.

A hungry fire overcame his eyes. Agatha would have shied away from the man if she hadn't been bound. The first prick came to her shoulder, a flash of pain and a drip of blood. Then her forearm, her thigh, her calf. With each jab, Kincaid would carefully watch her face, making sure she winced or reacted to the pain. Then, with a dramatic flourish he'd reveal needle and wound to the crowd, showing that she was bleeding.

Agatha hated the display of it all. This was her life, not entertainment. Her shame and pain and fear shouldn't be making people laugh. She rankled at the injustice of it all.

The pricks and pokes lasted for hours. Each of the toys on Kincaid's table had blood all over them. Agatha was reeling. She had lost count of how many times she had been stabbed. Thin streams of crimson dripped from everywhere. There was a pool gathering at her mangled feet.

Kincaid must have noticed the attention of the audience starting to wane, because he exclaimed he was certain he found it. He looked for a specific prod on his table, grabbed it, polished it with a tenderness. He put it against the skin of her innermost thigh and smirked at her.

He pushed. She felt nothing. Even with being so exhausted, she had felt each of them, so the shock made her look down in surprise. His hand held the tool delicately, making sure where it made contact with her skin was visible to most of the crowd. Her skin clearly was pushed in, the steel prod shorter. It appeared to everyone to have pierced her skin.

He pulled it away. There was no new blood. On cue, someone among the crowd gasped. Everyone focused on her thigh. Only Agatha looked at the witch-pricker. It was a subtle thing, but she saw the needle had gone inside the handle. It was a deception! The tool was a fake!

She screamed out. Her protestations were ignored. Mr. Kincaid was an honorable and righteous witch finder, dedicated to eradicating evil. She was an accused witch, bride of the Father of Lies. The evidence was now irrefutable. All that was left was to confess.

Either fortunately or unfortunately for Agatha, she was in no state to confess. Her body had given out. She lost consciousness and darkness took her.

***

Agatha woke up in the darkness. She was aching all over. Her wounds were crusted over. Her feet were throbbing. She huddled on her slab, the only familiar thing in her life offering her small comfort. She cried.

Despair and loneliness crushed her. There was no overcoming the injustice done to her, no hope for anyone to believe her. How could she stand against such powerful men, so already convinced of her guilt? It was not fair.

The demon came to her then. There was no strength left in her to resist. She still was afraid for her soul, but loneliness at least made her listen.

"Poor, poor child. Such evils thrown against you." Its harsh voice was surprisingly comforting, far less hostile to her than anyone else. Agatha felt more than saw something stir in the shadows. She squeezed her eyes shut. She didn't want to see any more horror today.

"You don't have to suffer through this. I can give you the power to save yourself. Not the feeble magics they accuse you of, but true power. Control. Of your life. Of the natural world."

Agatha scoffed. "You offer to save my flesh and damn my soul."

"Be not obstinate. Your soul is already forfeit. The false father has abandoned you. Heaven is denied to you. Why endure such pain for a reward that won't come?

"You can be great, a lord unto yourself. Do not resist needlessly, clinging to childish dreams sold to you by the very men punishing you for nothing more than threatening their grasp. Let me help you."

"So I can serve the Devil for all time? No thank you." Agatha had no desire to serve anyone. If she survived this trial, she would never listen to or trust another man again.

"I do not offer slavery, but freedom. I do not want your obedience but your liberation. I recognize no master, and I would not have you recognize one either."

Agatha didn't know why she was still talking. She should be praying. At least the demon wasn't hurting her. Kindness after so much pain and hate goes a long way.

"What do you want from me then?"

The demon said, "I require nothing. Ask nothing. Consider it a gift. Recompense for the injustice delivered by these men of false faith."

Agatha couldn't believe it. "You offer me such power for nothing? No promises of favor? No proffering my soul? No signing my name in your book."

The demon chuckled, the sound of snakes coughing. "Such fantasies your kind tell of me. No, I am not so transactional as your tales would have you believe. MY grace has no requirements." The demon's emphasis left no doubt in Agatha's mind on what the creature was implying.

"You lie." Agatha couldn't trust it. It was a demon.

Impatience snuck into its voice for the first time. "Never." It practically spat the word.

"Do you enjoy when those condemning you deny the truth you speak so plainly as lies without listening to you?"

Agatha stubbornly said nothing but saw its point. Always being accused of speaking falsehoods had indeed weighed on her. But how could you trust a demon, known for being nothing but a liar? But what if all the stories themselves were lies? Agatha felt conflicted. Could she afford to give the demon the benefit of the doubt?

The being continued, "Though there is no oath I can give you that you will accept, know that I will never lie to you. Unlike that book you cling to, filled with lies, half-truths and treacherous slander."

Agatha finally opened her eyes. There was a formless patch of darkness, darker than the rest of the cell, but that was all she could see. Agatha couldn't fight against her curiosity. Her imagination was going wild. She had to know.

"Do you have a form? A physical being?" she asked.

"I do." If voices could twinkle with mischief, it did.

"Might…might I see you?"

The dark patch shimmered and contracted, pulling itself in, condensing into the form of a bipedal creature. She couldn't quite call it man-shaped, because it was most obviously not a man. The lower legs were like a chicken, scaly and ending in a three-clawed foot. The thighs, instead of having feathers, were coated with long, wiry brownish fur. The fur continued up the roughly humanoid torso.

She couldn't tell what its gender was, if it even had a gender. It wore no clothes, but large bat-like wings protruded from its back and wrapped around its frame like a robe. A long, thin tail twitched playfully between its legs. Its arms were also scaly and clawed but were more lizard-like than bird-like.

The head and face reminded Agatha of a greyhound dog with a narrow, long snout and swept back ears. Thin goat horns erupted above the ears and wrapped back around the head. A tarnished crown sat awkwardly on the horns, a crack running through the whole of the face of the crown.

Agatha felt she should be afraid, that she should find this thing horrifying, but she wasn't. It wasn't that the countenance wasn't monstrous, because it was. It was just that that monstrousness wasn't frightening. She felt less threatened by its physical appearance than when it was just a voice in the dark at least.

The demon allowed her to take in its form for a moment, then introduced itself, quite formally and politely.

"I am Lord Belial, sixty-eighth of the Seventy-Two, Lord of the Unworthy and Unyoked, Angel of that which is considered unlawfulness; Belial, whose name is Matanbuchus." The demon finished with a deep bow.

Agatha curtsied back as best she could, lying on the stone with her injured feet. "My name is Agatha MacMillan. Pleased to make your acquaintance, Lord Belial."

"Please, call me Matan, my friends all do."

She giggled. The whole thing was surreal.

The giggle was ill-timed. A guard had opened the door to the bank of cells to bring her meager rations for the evening just as the last of the laugh echoed through the stone walls.

"You talking to yourself, or conjuring the devil, eh

girlie?" The man was a brute, rougher than any of the other guards. Agatha had caught him several times eyeing her unsavorily, his hands lingering a bit too long on her body. He didn't seem to notice the demon in the cell with her.

She didn't say anything. She wouldn't give him anything to work with. He slid the food through a slot on the floor, then leaned on the iron bars.

"Oh, you don't look so pretty now with all 'em holes in ya, but I bet I could still make you scream better'n the devil'd."

Even now, with all the humiliation she endured, Agatha still couldn't help but blush. Being called a whore and being offered sex in the same breath was too much. She kept silent, lips pursed tight.

Matan glowered at the man, but the guard continued to ignore his presence. Instead, he said, "It's only a matter o' time. This trial is almost over. Ya gonna miss yer chance wi' me."

He reached a hand through the bars, fingers outstretched to reach for her hair. Agatha instinctively withdrew further into her cell.

The demon roared in rage and rushed the bars. The guard's eyes doubled in size. He tried retreating, but his feet got tangled. He fell on his arse, the wind knocked out of him.

"What the bloody hell was that? What did you do?" The man blamed Agatha for whatever he had seen. Fear painted his features. He ran off and out of the prison.

Matan sighed. "That might have been…ill-considered of me. I fear I might have made it worse for you." The demon turned to her.

"I beseech you, accept my power. Save yourself before they come back."

Agatha considered for longer than she should have. She was committed though. She would do what is right.

"I cannot. I must stay the course."

The being shifted its stance and Agatha read the

movement as disappointment.

"As you wish. I must resign for now." It bowed deep again. It then shimmered again, this time in reverse. It became formless darkness and then was gone.

Agatha was alone again.

***

For the next few days, they kept her awake again. They wanted her exhausted and disarmed for the final round of interrogation. With the "discovery" of the witch's mark and the new witness in the form of the guard, it was inevitable she would be sentenced soon, with or without a confession. But a confession was preferred.

So, they didn't let her sleep. She was more heavily guarded now that she had allegedly sent a familiar after the guard, right after he brought her food even! She wasn't left alone nearly so often.

Matanbuchus or Belial, whatever the creature called itself, did not come to her except for a few times in the deepest of her exhaustion, when she was nearly hysterical with delirium. It encouraged her to hold on and be strong. And as always, to accept its gift of power. She didn't accept, but she couldn't deny she appreciated the company, even from a demon.

The world didn't feel real anymore. She didn't feel real anymore. She wasn't sure if the demon was real. She missed Sarah. She missed her father, her brother.

She tried to pray, but she couldn't find the words anymore. They were jumbled in her mind and jumbled when she spoke the words. Maybe the demon was right; she was already damned. She just wanted to let go. She wanted it all to stop. *God, why won't you make it stop?*

***

They brought her before the council one last time. They didn't bother asking her anything or give her a chance to counter the accusations. She was silent, only allowed to listen to each new testimony.

First John Kincaid gave his account of finding the witch's mark. The placement of the mark being significant, as such an intimate location made it assured she was the Devil's favorite bride. There could be no doubt she was a witch. Kincaid had found hundreds of witches, and this case was the one he was most certain of.

Then came the guard. The man recounted his experience in the prison. He spoke of how he had brought her meal and offered her compassion. Like a spider, she took advantage of that and tried to seduce him. When he denied her like a good Christian man, she grew rageful and summoned a familiar to attack him. It was a monstrous dog-like creature. He barely escaped with his life.

With such reputable testimonies, it was utterly clear this woman was a witch, the council declared. Before her punishment, she would be given one last chance to confess. And by chance to confess, she would be tortured until she admitted being a witch or couldn't continue.

Because she was a whore who seduced men to steal their seed for the Devil, she would be given the chair treatment.

Apparently, everything about being a witch required nudity, because they stripped her again. A large iron chair was brought out and she was bound to it with several large iron bands. Embedded in the chair's back, armrests, and seat were hundreds of metal pyramids, wide spikes that dug into her. The bands that restrained her could be tightened, so as to drive the points deeper into her flesh.

A fire was built behind the chair, low but hot. The men began pushing the chair towards the fire. Inch by inch, she grew closer to the heat.

They paused, the chair at the edge of the fire. They asked her to confess to being a witch. She wouldn't. They tightened the bands. The spikes bit her flesh. She gasped.

She was so tired. She was so afraid. It hurt, how it hurt. She couldn't resist much longer. God forgive her and show mercy. Let this end. Where was God? Where was her father? Where was Sarah? Where was her demon?

They asked her how many men she had seduced. She told them there were no men. She had been with no men. She couldn't think straight. Terror poisoned her mind; pain wracked her body. She screamed out for Sarah.

"Who is Sarah?" the interrogators asked.

"My love," was all she could reply.

Obviously only a witch would love another woman. They pushed her farther into the flames.

It took a few moments for the metal to heat up, but once it did it seared her skin quickly. Agatha could not stop from screaming. The smell of her own flesh burning overwhelmed her. She instinctively squirmed in the chair, but the bonds held tight. The spikes dug further still. Trickles of blood ran in the spaces between spikes and began to steam immediately.

It was agony. She cried out to God. She cried out to Sarah. She cried out that she was no witch.

The men all laughed. They mocked her pain. They accused her of selling her body to the Devil and now the devil wouldn't, couldn't make love to her with her womanly bits all cooked.

"The Devil does come to me!" The words escaped her lips before she could stop herself.

The laughter died. Instantly, there was a hunger in the air, as they sensed the long-awaited confession was near. They pulled her away from the fire to give her a chance to speak. And so she didn't burn too fast.

"Are you ready to confess?" the lead interrogator inquired, almost sweetly as if talking to a misbehaving child.

Agatha took a moment to compose herself, as much as she could. Her body was failing. Her spirit might too. But she spoke the truth.

"I have been with no man, nor no devil. But a demon comes and talks with me in my cell, in the darkness. On my soul, I do not acquiesce! I do not submit!"

"What does it say to you child?" The man hovered eagerly.

Agatha panted, trying to focus through the searing pain. She was delirious. "It offers to give me power. It offers to free me from this place."

She described the demon and its visits to them. Their entire demeanor changed. They were caring, listening, hanging on every word. She was no longer the evil temptress, but the victim, the unwitting prey of infernal forces. Oh, they even believed her that she had denied the demon.

And that's why they sentenced her to burn anyway. She needed to be purified and sent to Heaven. It was the only way to save her soul.

***

They took her back to her cell for the last time. It would be the final night she would spend in the prison. They would put her on the pyre in the morning. They told her it would guarantee her reward in heaven and prevent the demon from visiting anyone else. Remove the corruption. Deny the temptation for further evil.

She lay down on the slab, sobbing. Her skin was torn and blistered. She could not bear to stand, nor to sit. The mere act of existing in a physical space was suffering. At least being immolated tomorrow meant infection wouldn't have time to set in. Small comforts.

"If you will not accept power, will you at least accept aid with the pain?" came a voice in the gloom. The shadows stirred, and the demon returned. Agatha couldn't be sure, but its inhuman face looked to be what she thought was concerned. Its tone certainly sounded so.

"I'm certain that can't possibly be a sin, could it?" a weak smile crossed her face.

"I will lay a hand on you, with your permission?"

She nodded, a slight movement. She had no strength for much else.

The demon stepped forward and placed its clawed hand gently on her back. She didn't know why, but she expected the scaled thing to be cold, but it was warm. A gentle comforting warmth, like when she cuddled under a blanket or drank hot soup. It spread through her, radiating out and erasing the ache. The pain dulled and for just a sweet, small moment, she felt better.

Matan kept its hand on her, and said, rather wryly, "I will make a small note to point out that while you have cried out to God and Heaven for aid many a time, it is Hell who has answered, each time."

Agatha was drifting, exhaustion staking its claim on her above all others. "Well, demons are a girl's best friend," she said, half asleep. The warmth was lulling her to sleep.

A thought jolted her awake. "Will you be there tomorrow? When they…?"

"Be there as in to rescue you or be there as in to watch?"

"As in I don't want to be alone," she said, voice small.

"You will not be alone."

***

She woke up alone in her cell, the dawn's light barely breaking through the high window. She felt surprisingly well rested. Even her wounds seemed far more healed, as if it had been days, not hours.

Fear and anger warred in her mind. Fear for the pain to come, anger at the senseless injustice of it all. She realized, no matter what she had said or done, the outcome would have always been the same. She would have been burned as a witch or tortured to death for a confession that wouldn't come. All these men, willing to condemn innocent women out of fear and hatred. Their petty control and petty rule. They have the power and so they make the rules. There was no justice.

There was no justice.

They came.

They put her in a fine linen dress, clean and white. They offered her a strong wine, to calm the nerves and dull the senses. She declined. They marched her out of the prison, through the village, to a clearing at the edge of town.

A large pole had been driven into the ground. A metal collar and chain had been pinned to the pole, just above her height. A stool sat below the collar. Bundles of wood and barrels of pitch were gathered around the pole. Gathered around that was the entire village, come to watch.

They locked her into the collar, had her stand on the stool. Her feet screamed out and she could barely support herself. They began to intone a recounting of her supposed many crimes. She didn't listen. She closed her eyes, prayed one last time. Still nothing.

She looked at the crowd, searching for Sarah or her family. She wasn't sure if she wanted to see them there or not. She didn't find them. She thought of Sarah, and the last time she had seen her. They had lain in a field, daydreaming. Tears filled her eyes.

She saw a curiously familiar greyhound in the crowd, watching her. She tilted her head; the dog did the same. Heaven is silent, Hell answers.

This was it. She was going to die.

They kicked the stool from under her. She dangled, legs kicking, unable to find purchase. The weight of her body pulled on the collar, choking her, but slowly. Her hands grasped at the ring, her body instinctively fighting to keep living. She gasped for air. Each ragged breath was weaker than the last.

Darkness swam in her eyes, closing off her vision until all she could see was the dog. As everything became blurry, it shimmered into the form of the demon.

She said the words without thinking. Her voice was barely above a whisper, her throat so strained against the collar. "Belial, save me."

In the very last moments of her vision, she saw an outstretched hand.

"Take my hand, accept my power. Save yourself."

She let go of the collar, choking faster. Seconds left. Her fingers reached out. She missed. Tried again. Took its hand.

Fire consumed her, but she did not burn. She WAS the fire. She was power unleashed. The chain broke, the collar fell away. She did not touch the earth but floated above it.

She spoke and it was her voice and Belial's voice, speaking as one. "Behold, Heaven has turned a blind eye to injustice. Heaven ignored the suffering of its children. And so, Hell has risen to protect its own. Hell denies no one their justice! Witness the cleansing fire!"

She pointed her hands, fingers outspread. Flames shot from each digit. Each member of the council burned, incinerated in hellfire. The town caught fire and was soon an inferno, every building ablaze.

Chaos broke out. The townsfolk ran, screaming, trampling each other in their attempt to escape unholy retribution. Smoke filled the air, blocking out the sun, blackening the sky. The only light was the smoldering buildings. It was pandemonium. Hell was on earth.

Many hours later, the fires subsided and the smoke cleared. The survivors had gathered soldiers and priests and went back to the pyre to exorcize the witch and demon in full. Agatha was nowhere to be found. There was no body, no tracks, nothing. Only the charred remnants of the men who had found her guilty. Hell had saved Agatha MacMillan.

Moloch and Mammon Limited

Dan Bolden

Albion Hightower clicked his gold pen on the marble desktop as he eyed the brick housing project below him. It had been there since the last century: a festering red sore in the heart of a downtown otherwise replete with the chrome and reflective glass of skyscrapers. Civilization in other words. As Albion stared and imagined what animals inhabited the red barn, he caught sight of the shiny, winged black hair that outlined his narrow visage. His face was red. The damn barn had been spiking his blood pressure since his promotion had landed him in the corner office. If only he could convince the city to knock the project down and put up something sensible like a hotel or some luxury condominiums. It would be even better if the name Hightower was on the side.

His desk intercom sounded. “Mr. Hightower, your father is in the conference room. He says it’s urgent.”

“Thanks, Gabby,” Hightower said. He picked up his other pen and blew out an icicle of vape smoke, appreciating the snaps of his neurons as the smoke traveled through his body. “Tell him I’ll be right in. He tell you why it’s urgent?”

"Um, he mentioned something about 'actually getting your ass in gear for once,' apologies for the phrase, sir. His words, not mine." Hightower inhaled again, neurons snapping like the lobster claws he had just eaten at the business lunch an hour ago. Clifton Hightower would no doubt want his pound of flesh for his son's promotion to this corner office. Albion knew what to promise his dad, he just didn't know how to make it happen. Yet.

Fortified by the vape hits, Hightower stood up and smoothed the wrinkles in his navy worsted suit. He would give his dad the brick projects below to add to the Hightower Real Estate Portfolio; he would do it come hell or high water.

After five minutes had elapsed, Albion Hightower found himself back in his office staring down at the buildings below. Yes, his father wanted that brick monstrosity gone but, no, he found the idea that Albion could make it happen laughable. The feds had it protected and nothing could touch it. Didn't Albion realize that this was a project his dear old man had already tried? Many times before?

It was the tone that made him determined, cemented his decision. Albion Hightower would raze that red brick project to the ground no matter what it took. He just needed to figure out how.

The electric fireplace clicked. Hightower watched red and orange flames sluice up behind the glass protective plate. Sitting back in his office chair, Hightower crossed his legs and puffed on his vape pen. Minutes passed, maybe an hour. Still, no answer came to him. That brick project would stand forever, a reminder waiting for him just outside his window of how much of a disappointment he was to his father. "I'd sell my soul to send that piece of shit building and all of its worthless fucks to hell," he said, his lips smacking on a scotch glass.

The electric flames shimmered and then went out. Hightower waited a moment for the flames to come back. They did this, sometimes. After a minute, he growled. Then he chucked his scotch glass against the glass protective plate. The glass shattered. The plate remained, perfect.

"Temper, temper, Albion," a voice whispered to him from next to the faux fireplace. Hightower sat silent, waiting for the voice to continue. Or for his mind to tell him he was being a dumbass for hearing voices. "Do you feel better now?"

"No."

"Nor should you," the voice replied.

"Am I talking to myself? Have I finally lost it?"

"Au contraire, my earthly friend," the voice said. "I am here to make you an offer, one I hope you can't refuse. Forgive me if that's an old line. We don't get out much where I come from."

"And where do you come from?" Hightower asked.

"Hell, of course."

"Fuck you," Hightower said. The flames in the electric fireplace sparked to life like they never had before. A napalm orgy that brought with it the smell of a car crash that Hightower had passed by a couple of years ago. Four fatalities, their bodies charred worse than any forgotten marshmallow on a campfire. Hightower gagged, then vomited. The lobster meat from lunch was now a yellow mishmash on his tiled office floor.

"Have I upset you, my officious friend?" Hightower wiped his mouth and sat up. The overhead lights were hazy now, casting the world as he knew it into a misshapen spell of shapes and colors. The vape pen was gone; his scotch bottle was gone. He felt alone. The voice remained. "Now, now, don't be sad. My offer still stands."

"Does your offer have to smell so bad?" Burned flesh and rubber turned into pungent whisky and sandalwood. Footsteps turned Hightower's attention to the corner of the office. A skinny man in a blue suit stood next to the fireplace with steepled hands and a gleaming face. The face was collegiate, almost pre-pubescent. The trace of a goatee was visible. "Okay, funny guy, the magician convention is a couple of blocks away. Try there."

"I already did, no buyers," came the reply. "They said they didn't need any smoke and mirrors to help them."

"Great, but you think you can help me?" Hightower said.

"Of course, my friend; you have no idea the powers I have. Just ask and you shall receive," the man in the blue suit said.

"I need that brick shithouse to disappear. Think you can do that?" Hightower said.

"Absolutely. With some friends and your faith in us, we can make that become a black hole or the next Metropolitan Museum of Art. It's up to you." The narrow face smiled to reveal perfect little teeth, all except for the sharp incisors.

"And what would it cost me?" Hightower asked.

"Just your soul, of course. I am the irrefutable Mephistopheles in case you were wondering."

"Oh, you're the devil's genie dude, then?" Hightower said.

"If a wish granted means a soul taken, then yes, I am your 'genie'," the figure said. Hightower guffawed and looked out the window at the red blemish that stood between him and the recognition that he deserved from his father and the company men that had deemed him an incapable kid since he had joined the company a year ago. He thought about what it could mean if he was the one to remove that miasma from the city skyline. Possible success? Possible fatherly love?

"Yes," he said to Mephistopheles. He realized he was ready to surrender it all. "Tell me what I need to do to get the vermin out and that building gone."

Mephistopheles laughed and said one thing: "Let's see what Mammon says."

"Mammon?" Hightower asked.

"God of greed; god of money, you know that green stuff that makes the world go round," Mephistopheles said. "I must consult with him before any offer of this nature can be finalized."

"You mean you don't have the power to just grant deals?"

"Afraid not, my avaricious avatar of ambition," Mephistopheles said. "Mammon oversees finances and…if that brick 'shithouse', as you say, has families, then we may need to also consult good old Moloch."

"Moloch?"

"Funny fellow. You'll love him. His idea of a good time is snapping a child's neck off like cracking open a breath mint, then drinking the blood from the open wound. He makes your Dracula look like the Kool-Aid Man." Hightower stared at the clean-shaven face a beat too long. "Second thoughts?"

"You expect me to deliver a school bus load of children to this guy?" Hightower asked.

"Oh, goodness, no," Mephistopheles said. "Only one. Moloch is an aficionado in this sort of thing. Just one little tyke, but the child must be perfect. The prime rib of tots." In the haze and smoke of his office, Hightower located his vape pen and scotch glass.

After two sips and a long drag, he looked at the narrow face of Mephistopheles. "Let's do it," Hightower said.

"I'll go find Mammon and Moloch then, my greedy Gus with gumption. Be back in a jiffy; don't get too drunk." The smoke and haze cleared as Mephistopheles vanished.

Back in his office as it was before his visitor, Hightower took stock of his surroundings and circumstances. After another two drags and a pull from a new scotch glass, he figured he had probably had an out-of-body experience, like those idiots he had seen on a documentary recently who had drunk Iowaska. But if that preppy bastard and his offer were real, then all the better. How did a soul compare to wealthy domination on earth?

He was casting a vacant smile out the window at the red blemish below when the electric fireplace snapped, and the smoke and haze returned. The dapper Mephistopheles appeared. Behind him were a toad-man and a humanoid figure composed of obsidian. The sunlight cut through the haze and bounced off the reflective slime of the toad-man and the gloss of the obsidian figure. The effect was blinding. Hightower felt nearly giddy with booze and power.

Mephistopheles presented a weighty contract and placed it on Hightower's desk. Flies crawled and buzzed along the blood red font of the document. One of the flies landed in the dregs of Hightower's scotch with a plop. "What the hell is with these things," he said as he swatted at an errant fly by his eye.

"That's the way of Beelzebub, our lord," Mephistopheles said. "He has a thing for flies; they're kind of like his unofficial emissaries." Hightower nodded, looking for a pen to sign his name with.

"Um, so sorry, my newfound friend, but all documents between us must be signed in blood. Here, allow me." Mephistopheles leaned over and pricked Hightower's right index finger with a small pin. He handed the contract to Hightower.

At the feel of the leathery paper, Hightower raised an eyebrow. The obsidian man stepped forward with a startling array of light shimmers.

"Moloch, forgive his lack of speech, the last thing he said drove an old man in Munich insane. He wants you to know that he picked out this specimen especially for you," Mephistopheles said.

"Specimen for me?" Hightower said. The obsidian figure stepped forward again and lowed sibilantly in Hightower's direction.

"Moloch wants me to inform you that he personally retrieved the canvas for the document you are about to sign back in 1705. He thinks you have promise." Hightower dropped the rough-hewn document on his desk and stood up, second thoughts springing to mind. Mephistopheles continued as if he had read Hightower's mind. "No, it's not a child's skin. It's the hindquarters of a drunk father who dared to stand before the great Moloch himself and a small girl of five. Out of respect for the drunk father's bravery, Moloch left that child alone." Hightower breathed a sigh of relief.

"For a year, then he went back and got the girl, too." Nausea crept up Hightower's throat. Second thoughts were a dime-a-dozen in his mind now. "Relax, he doesn't make so many house calls anymore. Recently, there has been an uptick in the kinds of activities that make Moloch happy."

Mammon, the toad-man, jumped in front of Hightower wearing an old tan trench-coat and fedora. With a foreign, croaky voice he told Hightower his plan: "We take the place by the front, you see. Yeah? Then we go room by room and tell those little vermin to get out. Then Moloch picks a prize, he'll want your input, though. Every initiate is expected to help him with his process. Then we torch the place."

"Help with the process? We?" Hightower asked. Mammon produced an old-time Tommy gun and slapped a cigar into his amphibian wedge of a mouth.

"You come with us on this run. Moloch and Mammon Limited, that's what the big guy downstairs calls us." Mephistopheles rolled his eyes. "Come with us. Then we can complete the transaction. Deal, or no?" Mammon said. Hightower glanced at Mephistopheles. The dapper man with the narrow face shrugged and raised his eyebrows.

"It's the way of all deals, my newfound comrade. First, you prove your mettle, then we give you the keys to the kingdom." Albion Hightower hesitated a moment, his eyes locked on the brick building below. He found his eyes refocusing on the portrait of his father above the fireplace. Smug bastard.

"Let's go," he said. Mammon chomped his cigar; Moloch uttered nonsense and raised his obsidian arm in an arc that encompassed the window. Hightower noticed the jagged daggers that were Moloch's teeth, sharp as ritual knives ready for a sacrifice. He was still staring at the teeth, recalling something a high school history teacher had mentioned about the Aztecs and their sun god, when Mephistopheles sidled over and placed his slender hands on Hightower's shoulders. He guided him back to the flesh parchment on his desk.

"The contract. Sign, please," Mephistopheles said. Hightower used his pricked finger to sign on the dotted line. Moloch clapped his back. "He must really like you, Mr. Hightower. I haven't seen him this jazzed in a century."

"Let's get the show on the road, yeah," Mammon said. His toad hand reached out with a handgun. "Cover me in there while I do the heavy lifting." Moloch grunted. "Big man says he's counting on you to find that prime rib for him." Hightower nodded, his sense of place and time fuzzing up on him.

"What about you?" Hightower said to Mephistopheles.

"Me? Why I think I'll explore this building here. I'm sure I can find another person as fine as yourself looking to strike up a deal." With a squelch of smoke, the dapper fiend disappeared.

"We'll meet you there, kid, yeah," Mammon said. Hightower watched as the squat toad man reached up with his long arm, tugged the massive figure of Moloch, and walked out the door of Hightower's office. When he checked the hallway, Hightower saw no one. He looked down at the gun in his hand, feeling its weight. He shifted it and looked down the black hole of its barrel. With the gun in his sport coat pocket, Hightower walked down the sterile office hallway colored an immaculate ivory.

In the elevator, Gabby, one of his father's innumerable secretaries, stood listless in the corner. Her eyes flickered with mild amusement when Albion entered. "Albie, you look like you've seen a ghost."

"Try a demon." Hightower smirked at his own quip.

"Oh, poor baby," Gabby said. "Was Clifton really that upset with you?" She had seen him leave his dad's office earlier. She had most likely heard the yelling, too. "No fires, I hope, Albie."

"Only sparks, Gabby." The ding announced their arrival at the lobby. Hightower let Gabby out first before filing out and heading for the exit. Gabby was almost out of earshot: "I'm going to set his world on fire now, though." Gabby looked back at him.

"Break a leg, Albie," she said. She offered a kind smile that Hightower returned. Outside, he patted his sport coat pocket, still in awe at the heft of the pistol. People decked out in either business wear or casual attire swarmed the avenue around him, encasing him in a protective mesh of anonymity. He joined the sea of humanity and headed towards the brick building.

After three blocks, the crowds began to thin. When he turned down an alley, glass crunched under his boat shoes, and he could count the cigarette filters by the dozen. The electricity of the crowd's movement gave way to the heavy air and uncertainty. An old man watched him from the stoop of an apartment building. Hightower lowered his gaze and walked faster.

The heaviness of the air broke when Hightower came to the street across from the brick complex. The sun shined down in the gaps between the complex and the rest of the city. Crossing the street, Hightower couldn't shake the feeling he was entering another world. A world separate from the rest of the city's rhythms and movements.

He didn't see any signs of life. But at near 3 PM on a Wednesday he figured most of the residents would be working or at school, unless they were the types to draw a check from the state and stay home. That had to be common in a place like this, he thought. He hoped one of those deadbeats had a child for Moloch, a beautiful child.

The building was ten stories high and had a locked front

entrance. Mammon and Moloch were nowhere to be seen. But they didn't have to use doors, did they? They were probably inside already. Hightower scanned the side of the building and saw a red fire exit door lined with rust. It looked ajar.

Hightower traipsed towards the door with his hand on his sport coat pocket. He peeked in the doorway. Nothing but a worn stairwell with broken tiling along the steps. He walked with the intent to go up all ten flights. His shirt was soaked through by the third floor, the smell of Johnny Walker and burnt salt pouring out of the pores of his skin. He decided to continue for as long as he could. He stopped after he was sure his shirt would never dry again. The sign next to the door read '5'. Shaking his head as much in disbelief as to also get the cobwebs out, Hightower produced the gun from his pocket and twisted the doorknob.

Locked. He laughed. Three pulls of the trigger and the doorknob came off, leaving an uneven hole in the door which now swung open. A woman with two grocery bags in her hands screamed at Hightower's appearance. He raised the gun. No thinking necessary.

"Get the hell out of here," he said. The bags fell to the ground and Hightower saw egg yolk staining the already discolored carpet of the hallway. Muffling her sob, the woman turned for the elevators. "No, behind me, lady. Go down the stairs and don't look back." She nodded her head in exaggerated motions as she took off past Hightower and sprinted down the stone stairs. As the echoes from her flight faded, an acrid scent filled the air.

"Nice entrance, kid, yeah," Mammon said. The plumes of smoke from his cigar curled around him. Hightower watched the smoke creep closer and closer to a smoke alarm. Mammon caught him looking. "You just fired a gun three times and you're afraid of the smoke alarm going off?" Mammon let loose a throaty chuckle. His toad tongue lolled out along the length of his cigar. "The people ain't leaving their room after the gunfire, kid. We're gonna smoke 'em out, yeah." A moment later, the overhead lights caught the iridescence of Moloch's obsidian skin as the demon materialized. The cigar smoke was now next to the smoke alarm.

"When the alarm goes off, the elevator shuts down. All these people gotta go down the escape," Mammon said. "You couldn't make it to the top floor, so I'll go. Here are the rules: 1. Check every room and get the people out, 2. Find that kid for big man here, and 3. No fatalities." Hightower stared.

"No fatalities? I thought you guys would be all about that," Hightower said.

"I whack too many people, and the guy upstairs sends some jackass like Michael or Gabriel down here to jam up the works. It's no good," Mammon said. The smoke alarm went off. Doors started to open as the alarm's piercing shriek of ten-thousand birds drove sound waves straight into Hightower's brainstem. Mammon laughed. "You'll be fine, kid. Remember the three rules. And Moloch will be right behind you." Mammon vanished.

Moloch tapped Hightower on the shoulders and waved at him when Hightower looked up at him. Trampling feet and a sudden pull on his shoulder redirected Hightower's attention. A skinny man was wrenching Hightower's gun away. Hightower was going to lose the gun.

Moloch squeezed the man's shoulder and then reached into the man's sternum with his other hand. The hard glass of Moloch's fingers sliced open the man's midsection and Hightower heard a terrible snap. Moloch produced a broken rib bone and held it aloft for the man to see. On his knees, the man blubbered with clasped hands. Moloch swung the hand holding the bone in an arc and hooked the man in the fleshy part of his jaw. The man went silent; Hightower saw the tip of the bone sticking out from the top of the man's hair.

"No fatalities, Moloch," Hightower said. Moloch

shrugged his shoulders and then held up one finger and rolled his black eyes. Hightower thought he saw him mouth the words: "No big deal." Hightower looked around the hallway. Except for the dead man lying in a pool of blood, everyone else had made for the stairs. Hightower went to check all the rooms.

He lingered in the kitchen of the last room at the end of the hall. The kitchen window faced his father's office building. The view from the other side. From here it looked as if Hightower Corporation headquarters ascended all the way to heaven. The sound of heavy feet informed him that Moloch had entered. Hightower watched as the giant form bent down and picked up a fire extinguisher from beneath the sink. Moloch hit some buttons on the oven and then opened the oven door. He placed the extinguisher inside and shut the door again. Homemade bomb.

Next, Moloch got some rubbing alcohol from the bathroom and dumped it all over the couch. With some deft flicks of his fingers, his obsidian hands produced sparks that ignited the couch. Hightower leapt back into the hallway. Moloch sauntered past him to the other end of the hallway. Hightower got the sense that he was on kid patrol now. Above him came the sounds of gunfire and screams. Were Mammon's rules on no fatalities as flexible as Moloch's?

Hightower hoofed it to the fourth floor. The fire alarms must have done the job. Every room he checked was empty. He went down to the third floor. Empty. On the second floor, he waved the gun at an old man in the hallway until he headed for the stairs. He was heading for the first floor when he saw a flash of movement from the room on his left.

Albion Hightower burst into the room and overturned the couch in the living room. A little yelp escaped the mouth of, yes, indeed, a child. He had done it, found a little one on a school day. He hid the gun behind his back and instead proffered a breath mint that had been in his pocket for some ungodly amount of time.

The child's body unfolded from the defensive ball it had wound itself into to reveal long black hair and a toothy mouth. When she grabbed the mint from Hightower and smiled thanks, he knew that he had found the prime rib of children for Moloch. He crouched down next to her and gave her his most sympathetic stare.

"Hey, you like that mint? I got a lot more that I can give you if you come with me."

"Really?"

"Absolutely," Hightower said. He held out his hand. The child took it. "What's your name?"

"Rosie," she said. "What's yours?" As Hightower was about to make up a name, Rosie caught sight of the gun he was holding behind his back. The child tried to wrestle out of Hightower's grip.

"My daddy said to never trust strangers," she said.

"While if your dad cared, he'd be here to protect you, idiot," he said. The toilet flushed in the bathroom down the hall. A man emerged and caught sight of Hightower. It was too late.

Hightower had the gun leveled and pulled the trigger. Searing pain enveloped his right wrist. Rosie had latched onto him like a pitbull. He shook his hand left and right until Rosie flew into the wall. The gun fell and went off, its bullet entering Hightower's left shin, shattering the bone. Hightower looked up in time to see the man, blood streaming down his shoulder, pick up Rosie and run out of the apartment.

Hightower shimmied onto his elbows and went to stand. He promptly passed out from the pain. "Break a leg, Albie," he heard Gabby say in the distance. In his delirium, he imagined flames licking his scalp, singing his hair, and filling his nostrils with ash and dead skin.

When he came to, Mephistopheles stood above him holding the contract. "Great news, my money-hungry merchant of useless merchandise: that building is gone.

Hightower smiled; the pain was incredible.

"Where am I?"

"Hell, of course. You died, little Albie. Burned to death nursing a gunshot wound after failing to capture a child for Moloch. Oh, he is very angry with you. And Mammon is upset he put so much effort in when you were quite lazy. He says you couldn't even be bothered to make it to the top floor. Yes, they very much want to speak to you. I hear they have quite the torture regimen for you. Some skin flaying followed by some tooth removal using a hammer and file. Such fun." From the corner of the darkened room, a belch of flames gave way to the toad figure of Mammon and the giant, glinting form of Moloch. Hightower realized he had an eternity to think things over.

The End

Don't Break The Circle

K A Douglas

From the desk of Joseph Stephens
Doctor of Psychiatry
Eloise Psychiatric Hospital
Westland, MI

I sat down to write this note with the intention of it being my last. My 357 Colt revolver lay within arms reach, and I planned to use it to end my life upon completing this explanation of my recent actions. But, as I gathered my thoughts, I quickly changed my mind. For now, for the first time in my life, I believe in hell. Because I know that demons do exist. And they must have an abode to dwell in when they are not working their evils here on earth. Evils, which I have not only witnessed, but to which I have also been an accomplice. Although I have sealed my earthly fate, perhaps I can avoid damnation or at least the deepest, most torturous levels of hell.

With my remaining time being limited, my priority now is to document the events that happened, as they are responsible for the current world crisis. I suspect the likelihood is high that this statement will be considered the ranting of a madman and will be destroyed outright or locked away once it is found. If not, I pray that it will convince some that such evil truly exists and will serve as a warning. Not only to those foolish enough to consider bargaining with such forces, but to those that associate with other people and organizations that engage in such practices.

It started with the case of James and Lydia Felix. It received extensive coverage in the media. Government scandal and murder dominated the headlines. In summary: Lydia worked for the office of a United States senator and had witnessed his assassination. Shortly following her statement to police, the son of a mobster and the brother of the mayor were arrested. That night she was assaulted in her home. She was shot multiple times and left for dead. She entered into a coma and died several weeks later. Immediately, all charges against the accused were dropped. Officials denied any major conspiracies and the entire incident abruptly disappeared from the media, at least for a short time.

A month after her death, the police, for reasons never explained, raided Mr. Felix's house. Body cameras on the officers captured a bizarre and horrifying site as they entered the basement. Through flames and a cloud of toxic smoke, Mr. Felix and another man could be seen. They had been engaged in some occult ritual. The other man was hunched over on the ground and Mr. Felix struck him with a sword, killing him.

A few months later, the vast conspiracy between organized crime and our government was revealed. The chaos that followed has since swept across the globe.

After being declared unfit for trial due to insanity, Mr. Felix was brought to my hospital.

Offered here, as an explanation of current events, is his story. Pieced together from statements by Mr. Felix to the police, and my personal notes.

***

One week after the attack on Mrs. Felix.

The formal part of the lodge meeting was over. The budget for the remainder of the year had been approved; the Christmas party and the next meeting had been scheduled. The members split off into their usual groups, some heading to the card tables and others toward the bar. Phil headed toward the latter and James Felix followed. Seeing his friend coming, Phil poured two glasses and handed one to James as he walked up.

"Thanks Phil," said James.

"Hey James. I didn't expect to see you tonight."

"I needed to get out of that hospital. Plus, I was hoping to run into you. I need your help," replied James.

"Anything. What do you need?"

"Didn't you used to belong to another society before joining the lodge? One that devoted itself to more …esoteric studies?" asked James.

"Yes. It was very fascinating," replied Phil. "The members were brilliant and very willing to pass their wisdom down to me. But I had to leave. It became obvious that it wasn't compatible with my faith. It requires more pluralistic religious beliefs and a gnostic ideology."

"Did you learn anything that could help Lydia?" asked James.

"No, and to be blunt, with the condition she is in, it would take some high-level stuff."

"I'm willing to pay, a lot," said James.

Phil let out a nervous laugh which confused James. There wasn't anything funny about his situation or his request. But when Phil was young, he would jokingly accuse his dad of summoning demons at his lodge functions. The irony was a bit too much. "James, I'm not going to be part of this," replied Phil. "I'm far from a saint. But I've never engaged in sorcery. And that's what you need at this point."

"Please, Phil, for Lydia's sake. There must be something."

He turned and stared at James. The desperation and exhaustion were painful to see in his friend's face. Phil replied, "I still keep in touch with a few of the members. I know of one that can do what you want. But I strongly advise against it."

Phil pulled out his phone. After a minute of tapping, James' phone chimed. "His name is Simon," said Phil. "Tell him I sent you."

James stood up. "I won't forget this, Phil. I owe you one." They shook hands. James set down his glass and turned to head towards the door.

Phil grabbed James's arm. "Wait. James, I seem to remember that there is a demon that has great healing power. I think he has the head of a lion."

James raised an eyebrow. "Thanks," he replied.

***

James called Simon as soon as he got home. They talked briefly and arranged to meet the following morning. The next day, after visiting his wife and stopping at the bank, he drove to Simon's estate. He lived in a relatively close suburb that was noticeably more upscale than his own. Under different circumstances James enjoyed travelling down these streets, admiring the old architecture and the large estates. Today he was simply focused on the business at hand.

James drove past the open gate and onto the large horseshoe driveway. He parked near to the door. The house was a large two-story home that reminded him of a miniature plantation home, complete with half a dozen pillars used to support the overhanging roof and wrap around porch. After grabbing his briefcase, he climbed the steps and rang the doorbell. The door opened quickly. An elderly man, at least in his seventies, stood in the doorway. He was tall, thin and clean-shaven. A full head of wavy white hair adorned his head. He reached out his right hand. "Hello, you must be James?" he said.

"Yes, are you Simon?" asked James.

"Yes. I'm sorry about your circumstances but I believe I can help. Please come in."

Passing through hallways filled with expressionist paintings and Baroque sculptures, Simon led him to the library. It was a huge room, each wall lined from floor to ceiling with packed bookshelves. In the middle of the room sat a large oaken desk. Tall stacks of books and papers littered the top and spilled onto the keyboard of an antiquated computer.

"Sit down please. Lets' get down to business," said Simon. "You mentioned your wife needs healing. The ideal time to do this would be next week. How soon do you need this done?"

"As soon as possible. Last night she took a turn for the worse. The doctors told me…she might not recover," said James as he choked back some tears. "They said I should be prepared."

"I understand," replied Simon. "The soonest I can do this is tomorrow. It's not ideal but since time is an issue I have no choice. You understand the terms we discussed? Half today, the remainder the day of the ceremony, which is now tomorrow. There is a small chance it will fail and from this point forward there are no refunds for any reason."

"I understand. Phil wouldn't have sent me here if he didn't think this would be worth trying." James handed Simon his briefcase. "I'll bring the balance tomorrow morning."

"Perfect," replied Simon.

"What exactly are you going to do?" asked James. "Phil mentioned a lion headed demon. Why would a demon heal someone?"

"Do you really want to know?"

James nodded.

Simon answered, "There are many demons that have a lion's head. The demon Phil referred to is named Buer. He often appears having the head of a lion. He has great power to heal. He will heal your wife because I will use a ritual to summon him and command him to do so."

"It's really that simple, huh?" asked James.

'There's nothing simple about it," replied Simon.

***

On his way home James received a call from the hospital. His wife's condition had deteriorated rapidly. He rushed to the hospital, and she died later that night.

***

James returned from the funeral to find his home had been ransacked. After the police came and investigated, James sat on his couch amidst the carnage and turned on the TV. The local news came on and the reporter stated, "The men accused of conspiring to kill the senator have just been released." The scene cut to a statement given by the district attorney. "With the death of Mrs. Felix, we no longer have a strong enough case to-" James turned off the TV. He knew the corruption that led to his wife's murder would also rob her of any justice.

***

The following evening, James drove back to Simon's house to deliver the final payment. Simon met him at the door. "Hello James, I'm sorry I wasn't able to help your wife. Please accept my condolences."

"Thank you," replied James. "I'm sorry this is so late; this last week has been so hectic. Also, on the way here, I think I was being followed."

"That's very disconcerting. Especially considering the break in of your home. Please come in."

Simon led him back to the library. James handed Simon the briefcase and said, "I'd hate to have a demon sent my way for lack of payment. You made it clear there would be no refunds."

"Yes, that is true," replied Simon, "but I can offer other services. I feel I owe you something. Perhaps protection from whomever is following you?"

James considered the offer. "I doubt you can deliver what I'm looking for."

"You'd be surprised," replied Simon. "Tell me exactly what you want."

"I want justice for my Lydia. I want their syndicate destroyed. I want those who ordered my wife's death dead and all those that were responsible to suffer. Suffer as much as she did!"

Simon considered his request. He replied, "There is a demon named Andras. He is known for instigating conflicts. He causes contention and strife between and within organizations. Many wars throughout history are to his credit. If you want to break up the mob and its influence on the government, he can make it happen. But I must warn you. It will grow into something much more and there will be a lot of innocent blood spilled. With respect to those responsible for your wife's death, there is a demon named Sabnock. Oddly enough he also has the head of a lion. He can afflict those responsible with sores that will fill up with worms and turn gangrenous. They will suffer a slow, horrible death."

James thought for a moment. Tears streaming down his face. "Do it. Make them pay for what they did to her."

"My work has doubled, and the price has tripled. In the unlikely event it doesn't work I'll refund half."

"Why triple?" asked James as he wiped his eyes.

Simon walked over to his bookshelf and pulled out a large, leather-bound book. He placed it on the lectern. "There are seventy-two demons listed in this book. Dealing with any one of them risks your life and your soul. Andras is the only one listed here that comes with an additional warning. Our lives will be at stake."

"Our?" asked James.

"You must assist," answered Simon, "your anger will increase the chance of success. It would be ideal if we could do it at your home where your wife was attacked. Do you have close neighbors?"

"No," replied James, "the nearest house is a few hundred feet away."

"Good."

"I'm not even sure that I believe in demons," mumbled James.

Simon grinned. "It doesn't matter if you believe in them. It doesn't even matter if they exist. These ceremonies, properly done, will invoke a desired result. Whether they are completed by demonic entities or simply by the power of our own wills is debatable." He paged through the book and stopped twice, each time adding notes to a notepad. Then he carefully returned the book to the shelf. Simon continued, "These rituals lead to results. In this case the slaughter of many. There will be blood on our hands, in large amounts and much of it may be innocent. If you can't live with that you need to say so now."

"When can we do this?" asked James.

"One moment and I'll let you know," replied Simon. He walked to his computer. After a few minutes of typing he replied, "Andras will be first. Ideal conditions would be two weeks from tomorrow, two a.m."

"You'll have full payment by the end of the week," stated James.

"I'll have some things for you when you drop it off. You must follow the directions I give you to the letter, no matter how bizarre. Do you understand?"

"Yes," responded James.

***

There were numerous times James considered cancelling the whole thing. The amount of money was substantial, even for him. The instructions from Simon were quite ridiculous. Including the recitation of numerous prayers, fasting and a ritual bath. Why would God ignore his prayers for Lydia but give him blessings to summon a murderous demon?

Simon arrived just after midnight. James went out to the van and helped Simon unload his wares. After a few trips everything was downstairs including a large lectern, two braziers with stands and a large duffle bag.

Simon began to carefully unpack the bag. Pulling out numerous things wrapped in silk onto the table, including a wand and a long, ornate sword with inscriptions on the pommel, hand guard and blade.

James picked up the sword and deftly swung it through the air a few times and said, "Balanced really well for a ceremonial sword."

He looked over to Simon who was clearly irritated. James carefully set the sword back down. Simon immediately picked it up. "Not purely ceremonial," said Simon, "it's blessed and sharp for a reason."

Simon continued perusing through his bag. After making sure he had everything he continued, "You followed my instructions?"

"Yes. To the letter."

"Do you understand your role?" asked Simon.

"Keep the fire in the brazier going and add the mixture to it when you tell me," recited James.

"Perfect. As I begin the conjuration I need you to think about what happened, and the justice you want for your wife. And whatever you do, don't leave your protective circle for any reason. He will try to trick you to leave it. If you stay in it you will remain protected. Otherwise, he will kill you. Do not leave until I tell you it's safe to do so. And don't be surprised if this takes multiple attempts. It's quite common. Have patience."

"OK," replied James.

I'm going to prepare the space for the ritual," said Simon. "Go back upstairs, pray and change into your robe. I'll call for you when it's time."

James returned upstairs and put on the long white robe. He looked at himself in the mirror and laughed. He picked up the paper with the prayer he was supposed to recite. He set it back down, shook his head and went to grab himself a stiff drink, or two.

A while later Simon called for James to join him downstairs. The basement had once been James's favorite part of the house. Lydia's insistence on keeping the living room upstairs pristine for visitors encouraged him to finish it. He did such a good job it ended up being the primary family room and place to entertain their friends. It hosted children's birthdays, holiday parties and countless get-togethers with friends and family. He had avoided it since the attack on Lydia. But Simon had insisted on using this space for his ritual. Now it was unrecognizable. They had already removed the bloodstained carpet, leaving a bare cement floor. All of the furniture had been removed, as was the drop ceiling. The knotty pine paneled walls were covered floor to ceiling with black drapes. Simon's additions, however, had completed the transformation from the memorable place it had been to the set of a bad seventy's horror movie, which oddly seemed appropriate to the whole situation.

The fluorescent lights were off, but the braziers and numerous candles had been lit and supplied sufficient illumination. Most of the floor was overlaid with numerous geometric shapes: stars, a triangle and two large circles.

Parts of which were brightly colored. The circles, simply drawn on the floor, supposedly would provide them protection from the wrath of an angry demon. The triangle, drawn a few feet outside the larger circle would be where Simon would command the demon to reside.

James stepped into his area of protection, two unfinished concentric circles. The area between them filled with Hebrew and Greek letters. Simon took the chalk and completed the circles. He then stepped into his area, a larger and far more elaborate space. The image of a snake spiraled around numerous times between the two circles. Filling the snake's outline was a long passage written in Hebrew. He indicated to James, who then opened a small box. Inside was a mixture of powders, dried leaves and wood shavings. He reached in and tossed some of it on the fire in the brazier. It gave off a cloud of smoke and filled the room with a strange odor. Simon began with a prayer. Then, using a stern and commanding voice he started the first conjuration attempt. Curious, James listened intently as Simon recited a strange mix of old English commands and nonsensical words.

"I conjure ye, and I command ye absolutely, Oh, Andras. In whatsoever part of the universe ye may be, by the virtue of all these holy names: ADONAI, I YAH, HOA, EL, ELOHA, ELOHINU, ELOHIM, EHEIEH, MARON, KAPHU, ESCH, INNON…"

It went on for several minutes. After Simon finished, he waited, looking about the room to see if it had been successful. A few minutes later they continued the experiment. Simon turned the page in his book and indicated to James who then added more of the fumigant to the fire. This time Simon raised his voice louder and he recited the conjuration in the form of a chant.

At this point James realized something. It was much like an exorcism. Robed men with their sanctified objects were performing a ritual to compel a demon. Beforehand, each one prays. They then command the demon in God's name.

Both men even use a book.

Simon finished. They waited. Again, there was nothing. Simon, unconcerned, turned the page again. Without Simon's prompting, James added more to the flames.

James was caught off guard when Simon started the third time. He was louder still, his voice making deep inflections, his arms making wild gestures. It was like watching a crazed televangelist on TV but instead of telling people to repent, he was threatening to curse the demon for not appearing. Sweat began to pour down Simon's face. James stifled a laugh. The fumes had made him lightheaded. The absurdity was just too much. It was a complete waste of time and money. What would Lydia say about it? He ignored Simon's ranting. He began to think about her, her violent murder and how the men that did it would never be punished for such a horrible act.

The intensity in Simon's voice quickly faded. Suddenly, he stuttered then stopped. James looked over at Simon. He was hunched over, breathing heavily with his hands gripping at his chest. Simon collapsed to one knee. James turned to go help, but noticed the flames of the candles had tipped as if a breeze had blown though the room. James paused.

"Stop!" moaned Simon. "Don't ...break ...the circle!"

James's motion to help Simon made him realize that he was quite dizzy from the fumes. He steadied himself. Then he heard a strange sound, like the tapping a dog's nails make when it walks across a hardwood floor. Within the triangle something began to materialize; a huge, black wolf. Riding it like a horse was a strange creature, a naked man with white angelic wings. Its head was that of a bird resembling an owl with black feathers. In its right hand a long, straight sword. The creature was terrifying but at the same time a thing of wonder. It filled James with awe. It looked over at Simon then down at the triangle made to contain it. Without hesitation it commanded its mount. Leaving the triangle, it began to ride around the room. It stopped first in front of Simon then it went over to James. The wolf paced from side to side but always remained facing James. The creature riding it leaned forward, staring straight through him, and then gave a loud, piercing shriek. James stumbled back but caught himself before falling out of the circle. He could feel the heat from its breath. It looked back at Simon then at James. It glanced around the room, closed its eyes and inhaled deeply. Then in a strange, hoarse voice, it spoke, "You have suffered much loss here."

Simon, using his sword, propped himself up and then pulled himself up using the lectern as a brace. "Don't talk to him. You must send him back … or … he'll destroy us both!" He turned a few pages in his book. Placed a bookmark and closed the book. Throwing the book towards James he collapsed face down to the ground. The book hit the floor and slid, stopping a few feet outside of James' protective circle. The demon looked down at the book then at James. "I am growing weary and angry. I have been summoned, and I cannot leave until I am dismissed. Grab your book and release me."

"I'm not leaving the circle. Throw it to me," countered James.

"Why have I been summoned? What do you want?" it asked.

James answered with a shaky voice, "My enemies. I need you to make them hate each other and destroy each other. That's what you do, right?"

Andras made a sound that could only have been a laugh. His feathers ruffled for an instant. "It is indeed."

James continued with fury, "I want the corruption my wife found exposed. I want the government to destroy the mob, not conspire with them or any other criminal organization. I want those responsible for my wife's death and who conspire against me dead. I want them all to suffer!"

The creatures tipped its head, and its eyes narrowed. It replied, "Everything comes with a price. What can you offer me as payment?"

James stood there, dumbfounded. He looked over to Simon as if he could give him the answer. All he heard was Simon's labored breathing.

"I have a proposition," said Andras. "Drag the sorcerer from his circle and I'll do as you wish. He's dying anyway. Otherwise, I'll take you both, body and soul."

James's head began to swim as he stared at the creature and considered his options. Its appearance varied from solid to translucent depending on the thickness of the smoke passing between them. For an instant he questioned its actual existence. But shear terror wouldn't let him act on that premise. He still had a handful of the concoction he was dumping onto the chaffing dish. Perhaps, he thought, he could ball it up and throw it and the wolf would give chase, giving him time to grab the book. Realizing how ridiculous that sounded, he dumped it all into the dish before dropping the box onto the floor. For a moment it seemed to douse the flame. But the cinder quickly rose back to a large flame and began billowing a dense cloud of smoke causing James to retch. He stumbled, knocking over the dish, which crashed to the floor. The mixture was aflame on the floor and filling the room with dark, noxious smoke.

James's eyes darted back and forth from the demon to the book. He carefully stepped outside his circle, careful not to disturb its border. He wasn't sure if it would retain its protective ability if he jumped back in, but it was worth the chance. He waited a moment, expecting an attack from the demon, but it simply sat on its mount watching. James grabbed the book and threw it into the center of his circle. Then he stumbled over to Simon. Grabbing him by the arm, he started dragging Simon out of the circle. Despite his condition Simon was able to resist. He clutched his sword and dug the hilt into the floor causing it to grind heavily.

James lifted Simon's arm, grabbed the sword and pulled Simon out of the circle.

James saw his chance. Using both hands he swung the sword hard in a wide arc hoping to generate enough force to catch the creature on its weak side and deliver a devastating blow. He barely felt his blade being parried but was jarred when the blade came to a sudden stop in Simon's neck. The blade stuck there. Andras burst into high-pitched laughter. James looked up as the demon faded from view. But he knew he would be seeing him again. Then he heard shouting and saw lights coming towards him through the heavy smoke. Then everything faded to black.

The police were able to get James out of the house before it burned to the ground. High levels of hallucinogens and alcohol, along with known toxins and some unknown substances were present in his bloodstream. Even after his blood chemistry had returned to normal it was evident that James's mind had not. And it continued to worsen over time.

***

Dr. Stephens saw James in a number of private sessions. Physically, James was healthy for his age, tall and stocky with no chronic conditions. His mental condition was difficult to assess. Permanent damage due to chemical exposure was suspected. In the last few weeks after the ritual he had become highly irrational and sometimes violent. After trying a number of drug combinations, they were able to achieve a suitable condition where Mr. Felix was calm yet reasonably lucid.

During their first session the doctor's goal was simple. To convince Mr. Felix that there was no demon. It seemed a reasonable objective based on James's previous statements and should provide substantial benefits.

The doctor began, "Mr. Felix, I'm glad we can finally have a sit-down conversation. How are you feeling today?"

James replied slowly with mumbled words, "Like I've been drugged!"

"Unfortunately, the sedation was necessary to calm you down. After today we'll see how you react using a smaller dose."

"I'll do fine from now on. I don't think I'll need any more," replied James.

"And why is that, Mr. Felix?" asked the doctor.

"I've come to accept my fate. I don't want it to happen, but I know I can't stop it."

"What exactly is your fate?" asked the doctor.

"The demon," replied James, "Andras. He'll be coming for me."

"You're an intelligent and educated man," said the doctor. "You're not the first to turn to … non-traditional means in desperation to save a loved one, but this insistence about your interaction with a demon is a bit hard for me to understand. Do you really think you interacted with an actual fallen angel?"

James looked up at the doctor. He knew this would be a waste of time, but he was more comfortable in the office than his cell. He considered lying but instead simply stated the truth. "I wish that were the case doctor, but I saw it. We had a conversation."

"The mixture you were burning contained known hallucinogens and several toxins. You had substantial levels in your bloodstream. It almost killed you. Tell me, why won't you even consider that your interaction was just a result of that? Why do you still insist it was real?"

"Have you watched the body cam footage Doctor?" asked James. "You can hear the blades strike. You can see the demon."

"I've watched it a number of times," replied the doctor. "Three police officers were running into a burning room screaming. It was a chaotic scene. I can't pick out the sound of two blades striking during that commotion."

"The demon. You can see him," repeated James.

"That's called pareidolia Mr. Felix. Like seeing shapes in a cloud. You expected to see something and were under the influence of hallucinogens. So to you, a faint outline in a smoke-filled room must have been the demon you tried to summon. In your statement you yourself admitted the fumes were affecting you. You questioned its existence even then. The next logical step is to admit to yourself that the demon was only in your mind."

James looked up with an eyebrow raised. "Perhaps you're right, doctor."

The doctor smiled for a moment. Perhaps he was making some progress, but then James continued, "But according to Simon it doesn't matter. I have set things in motion. And the proof is on the news every night. You can't deny he's kept his part of the pact. All of those people are dead because of me."

The doctor's frown returned. He replied, "So, you won't accept the responsibility for killing Simon, but you blame yourself for hundreds of deaths since?"

"Hundreds?" asked James. "Is it that high already?"

"Yes," replied the doctor, "it started with just the police and mobsters, many dying in agonizing ways. Then it spread to the politicians. Now all sorts of people are dying. Violence has spread to several states. There are riots nightly now. Most including arson and murder."

James let out a heavy sigh. Then replied, "Simon's death was an accident. But I was warned about the others. I just didn't believe it would actually happen. Not like this. My turn is coming soon."

The doctor paused. He needed to show James how ridiculous it sounded. There was no logic to it. "Why? If such a creature exists, why would he do as you ask and then come after you?"

"When I dragged Simon out of the circle I fulfilled my part of the bargain," said James. "Now he is fulfilling his.

My fate was never negotiated. Though I believe he would have left me alone had I not attacked him. I really don't know."

"Why not just destroy you then and there and be done? Why carry out your wishes?" asked the doctor.

James replied, "Because that is what he wanted to do all along. He didn't care about killing Simon. For him it was more of an opportunity than a duty. It's more like I gave him license to do it than a command he was compelled to follow."

The doctor realized that James had rationalized every aspect of the incident. His would be a difficult case. "Let's backup a moment. You said it didn't matter if the demon was only in your mind and that you had set things in motion. What did you mean?"

"I don't exactly know. Simon had mentioned something to that effect. That their existence didn't matter but that there would be results created by our wills."

The doctor quickly countered, "Scientists have understood that demons only exist in people's minds for a long time, the same for the perceived results of magic and witchcraft. Are you suggesting this demon exists and has caused this carnage because you and Simon created it in your minds by performing a ritual while under the influence of drugs?"

James's mind was foggy, but he didn't like the doctor's mocking tone, and his expression showed it. "I don't know," he said tersely.

"So, if this creature only exists because you willed it into being to accomplish this task why don't you just tell it to stop?"

"I don't know how," replied James.

"Of course you do," countered the doctor firmly, "just do it! Tell it to stop. Tell it to leave you alone!"

"That's not how it works!" replied James.

"Why not?" asked the doctor. "If you believe that you

willed it into existence then why not will it out of existence?"

"It won't work," shouted James.

"Why?"

James shook his head and began to mumble to himself.

After a pause the doctor continued in a lowered, calmer voice, "How are you so sure the recent events were caused by you?"

"Because that was the purpose of summoning him. He agreed to do it."

"Mr. Felix, your wife witnessed the murder of a United States senator. Her statement implicated a number of powerful people in organized crime and our government. This all happened before your ceremony. Is it not reasonable to expect that some bloodshed would follow?"

"It's reasonable. But it's not what happened," answered James.

"How can you be so sure?"

"I JUST KNOW!" screamed James. "And I know he's coming for me next!"

James Felix began to shake. At this point it was obvious that the effect of the drug cocktail was beginning to wear off. The doctor had James returned to his cell.

Later that afternoon two men unexpectedly walked into the doctor's office. "Dr. Stephens, we're from the FBI. We need to talk about your patient Mr. Felix."

***

Mr. Felix had responded well to a new drug regimen and was able to be transferred from his cell to a regular room and was allowed to interact with the general population. He remained persistent that a demon would soon be coming for him. The doctor decided to try a different approach. One evening he visited him in his room. "Mr. Felix, how are you finding your new accommodations?"

"Much better. Thank you," replied James.

"You still seem to be on edge," said the doctor.

"Haven't you been watching the news? There have been skirmishes in Eastern Europe, new unrest in the Middle East, assassinations in Asia. I'm responsible. On top of that I'm a condemned man, Doctor. Whether you believe it or not."

"I don't," replied the doctor, "but it matters that you believe it, Mr. Felix. So, I've talked to some colleagues and done some research." He handed James a box. "Here, take these."

James opened the box. Inside were a large silver crucifix, an amulet decorated in Hebrew letters with a small piece of parchment inside and a book on demonology. "What's this?" he asked.

"According to so called experts in the occult, these things will protect you from a demonic attack. That amulet is from some design found in a famous five-hundred-year-old magical tome. The book has prayers and things that are supposed to protect you from demons as well."

James looked up. For the first time he looked hopeful and trusting. "Thank you, Doctor."

"You're welcome. But James, you can't continue to blame yourself for all of this. Mankind doesn't need an excuse to murder or to go to war; certainly not demonic intervention. We'll talk again soon, when you feel safer."

A few days later Mr. Felix was escorted to the doctor's office. While James looked healthy and refreshed, the doctor had a more concerned look on his face.

Dr. Stephens began, "Toward the end of our last session I brought up the fact that this conflict began before your ceremony. But since then, I've realized that some things don't add up. Perhaps there is more to it."

James was encouraged that the doctor may believe his account of what happened. The doctor continued, "Why did they raid your house, Mr. Felix?"

"I think they were looking for something," replied James.

"What?" asked the doctor.

"My wife had gathered physical evidence of the conspiracy. It involved the senator and others high in the administration. They had ties with organized crime and many powerful and elite people in the world. Including bankers, businessmen and foreign leaders. She had emails, pictures and more."

"That was never discussed in the news! Why didn't she give it to the police or the FBI?"

"She didn't trust them," James answered. "The conspiracy was too extensive. She doubted there was even anyone she could give it to. I didn't think anyone knew about what she had. It has to be the reason."

"Was it all destroyed in the fire?" asked the doctor.

"Just the hard copies. She had a digital backup."

"Where?" asked the doctor.

"On a hard drive," said James, "hidden in a cabinet in the garage."

The doctor had learned what he needed from Mr. Felix. Information he was paid handsomely to get. He abruptly ended the session, and Mr. Felix was returned to his room.

Later that week Dr. Stephens received word from the FBI. He then had Mr. Felix taken from his room and placed back into a cell. His crucifix, amulet and book were taken from him. The doctor opened the small viewing door and called inside, "Mr. Felix?"

"Doctor, why are you doing this? You said I was getting better and that I could get out of here."

"I'm truly sorry Mr. Felix, but that won't be happening."

"I don't understand. Why?" asked James.

"I don't honestly know. Perhaps you know too much. Maybe, because we are now on the brink of a world war, and you have claimed responsibility."

The doctor reached into his pocket and pulled out a box cutter. He tossed it through the small door and into the center of the room. “Here, make things easy on yourself. You’ll either cheat that demon or some government assassin. Either way you won’t last the night.” The doctor closed and locked the small door, then headed back to his office. He sat with his head in his hands. Passing information was one thing but now he wondered if he could live with what he had just done. The explanation that it was important for the security of the nation was less believable than James’s bird headed demon riding a wolf.

Dr. Stephens sat at his desk and changed to the video feed from the security cameras to James's cell. He double checked to see the recording was turned off and was about to turn off the camera when he saw James reach into his pocket and pull out a piece of paper and marker. He studied the paper, and then he began drawing on the floor. In the end James sat in the middle of two crudely drawn concentric circles. The doctor recognized Greek and Hebrew words in the space between them. James knelt and prayed for a moment. Then he sat on the floor with his back to the camera, rocking back and forth. The doctor began to stand up and head to the cell when he heard James speaking in a strange sounding voice. “James, this circle is worthless. You lack the faith or the will to make it work. You never truly possessed the former and the latter has been shattered.”

James began to weep, and then responded in his usual voice, “Leave me alone. I don’t deserve this. You caused this. Not me.”

The doctor jumped back as the first voice burst into a strange sounding laughter, which filled the speaker. As it died down he could hear James sobbing, just under the continuing laughter.

The doctor quickly took control of the camera and panned the room looking for the source of the second voice. Seeing no one, he changed the feed to the camera outside of James’s room. Maybe someone from the federal government was the culprit, trying to drive James mad, but the hallway was empty.

The unearthly voice continued, “You convinced yourself that you had been wronged, and that violence was a justified response. You didn’t save or protect anyone. It was pure vengeance, which you knew would lead to further violence and death. The politicians and the mobsters deserved their fate, but most you’ve doomed were ignorant puppets mislead by others with their own agenda. Perpetrating violence and murder in the name of justice.” The demon’s voice changed from a calm monotone to one of excitement and elation, “And it’s rare for a man to repent of a sin he justifies in his own mind.”

A shadowy figure began to appear on the screen. The doctor stared at it, but it never became clearer. He thought perhaps it was an issue with the camera, but as the shadow moved about the room James’s head would turn and follow it. It stopped in front of James and the voice returned, speaking calmly again. “There was a time you pretended to be a religious man. Do you remember the parable of the sower? Well, you’ve provided me a vast, fertile field. I’ve sowed little but I will reap in abundance!”

The doctor heard the whistling sound of a blade slicing through the air. For an instant nothing happened. Then blood sprayed through the air and James Felix collapsed to the floor. A large pool of blood began to accumulate under his head.

The doctor sat frozen. Not knowing if he should hit the alarm or rush to check on James. He opened his desk drawer and grabbed his revolver. He pressed the button for the intercom to James’s room. “Mr. Felix! Are you all right? James, answer me!”

The response was not in James's voice. The outline of the shadowy figure became larger. As if it had moved closer to the camera. “Doctor, he is dead, thanks to you. Now my reckoning will continue, unabated. Enjoy your thirty pieces of silver, while you can.”

The doctor sat frozen in his office. His grip on the revolver causing his hand to turn white. Then he heard a sound. The clicking sound of a dog's nails walking across a floor. He looked up. A large shadow emerged behind the smoked glass of his office door. It remained for a few seconds and then continued down the hall. The clicking sound finally faded off into silence.

Then the phone rang. He picked it up with a shaking hand. "H-Hello, this is Dr. Stephens."

"Doctor, I showed your notes to our people at the highest level. There's been a change in plans. Our man has been told to stand down. Protect Mr. Felix at all costs. We need him alive. It's a long shot but he may be the only one who can put an end to this."

"He-he's dead, Mr. Felix is dead," replied the doctor.

"Dead? No!"

The doctor heard several screams in the background. Followed by a muffled, panicked voice. "He's found a way out of our pact. There's no stopping him now. After all we've done, he'll want revenge."

"I don't understand. What's wrong?" asked Dr. Stephens.

A moment later the man answered, "You don't know what you've done!"

"You said it had to be done," argued the doctor, "I did what you told me to do."

"Yes. Yes, Doctor you did. Welcome to the conspiracy."

The End.

Gifts of Autumn

Dylan Bosworth

Dry leaves drifted in waves across the old footpath that led through the field to the mouth of the forest. They crinkled under my feet like wasps' nests as I crept along under the dying light of the day, crumbling to dust and sodden flakes that seemed to melt into the mud that sculpted into my prints. As if they had never thrived in golden shades that bled into the sunlight – flickered in the wind, casting violent bursts of turbulent rays across the ground. Dancing in the late summer breezes, then left fallen into rot. Disintegrating into my footprints, it was as if they never lived at all.

I couldn't help but think of our similarities, the leaves and mine. How darkly things had turned for me.

For all of us.

Autumn was here again. The dying season. The time when I'd watch the grasses wilt after the trees had turned and shucked their branches clean. I felt the cold coming long before now. The snow would bring a bleakness and hatred of the gray—three months—days and nights filled with blackness, with the wind whistling through every crack in every seam of our homes.

I haven't mentioned the grief. I haven't mentioned the despair, the despair if *He* weren't to get his offering. The little ones that seemed to wink out of existence in the middle of the night. The howling and the screeching and the claw marks and the bright red splashes, splattered across the snow.

Sometimes, I wished I had never found him. Never fed him. Whatever I had done to deserve this life. I had this certainty at times, on the years where the cold hadn't run so long, and the children made it through the nights cozy in their bunks and beds—nobody missing in that gloomful, never-ending fucking blizzard of hate—I *knew,* without a doubt in my mind, that I had caused the calm. That the being in the woods had been satisfied.

That's what I had thought.

Tonight, Father hadn't known I left; God, how could he, and if he had caught me some other time going out or gone in the middle of the night, he'd have assumed the worst. And he would have made me pay.

I had felt alone with my father for so long now, me leaving didn't even matter. I was more alone at home than I was out in the dark, hugging my cloak tight around me.

The path approached the dark maw of the overreaching forest, and the field I trod upon turned from dying grasses to black mud. I crossed my arms tightly against my chest, with my chin down against the breeze, and tried to fight the heaviness weighing on my insides.

Beth hadn't woken as my boots clunked around the hard wood of our home. As usual, father was lying his head upon the dinner table, snoring so loudly the cup in front of him was vibrating against the wood.

He'd still be there when Beth woke in the morning, and he'd never know that I had left at all.

When I crept through the village to the field, only some lights still burned lowly in the windows of a few houses that had been far between, and no head had peered over a sill to see me slinking off. Nobody to witness.

Nobody to see the offering.

The creature in the woods was mine, in a way. I thought I shared some unholy kinship with it when we first met. One of our goats had given birth, and the creature she bore had mangled her insides.

Father had to grab the kid out of her, tugging until it came free with a slick, ripping sound. The creature already had his horns, black and twisted, and Lila's insides snaked out of her womb, speared on the head of her baby. The little goat was black as pitch, and upon his face he had three eyes, three eyes that were all open and staring at father and me as we looked upon it with horror.

I could never forget those eyes. They were as golden as the sun. The radiance of them; Lord, they almost seemed like they'd burn you through if you peered into them for too long. The three of them there, glowing and staring, always staring.

Still, throughout all the wretched seasons, I would see them in my dreams.

Those eyes, along with the crooked horns upon its head, had made father call it a living sin. A demon made flesh. He stormed from the pen, sickened, in search of his shovel for Lila, and he ordered me to take the little, malevolent goat to the woods.

I did as I was told, but as I held a rock above its little head ready to bash in its skull, I found I couldn't do it. For I had killed my mother, too—in much the same way as the three eyed devil there below me.

When I was born, my father said, my mother suffered deeply. Her labor was not short, and I came tearing out of her, wrapped in the umbilical, and covered with a caul. She bled for three days before she died, and with her fading breaths, Father said she cursed me, cursed me for ever being conceived.

I felt the resentment in my father as soon as I was old enough to understand the cold looks, and the sternness that bordered on cruelty. He talked of my mother often, and each word said to me was dripping with bitterness. I grew up alone in my house, an outcast from the start.

But when I was approaching womanhood, the looks my father gave—no longer cold and hateful, but deliberating and confused—had told me that that was not quite true, at least to him. I'd catch him watching me, his eyes glazed over like he was somewhere else, and soon, the cruelty he so often exerted had donned a much more becoming sort of grace. "You have your mother's eyes," he would say, or something of the like, and then he'd look away.

It wasn't until the night of that year's Harvest that his change in demeanor suddenly made sense. After the village feast, I had tossed and turned in my bed, unable to sleep with the commotion of the inebriated town, but at some point, into the early hours of the morning, I had drifted off.

I awoke to the down of my mattress compressing next to me with a quiet creak of the bed frame that followed. As my consciousness formed around the darkness of the room, I felt a hand cover my mouth. A voice whispered in my ear, breathy, and heavy with the scent of spirits. "Shh. Mary, shh—Don't make a fuss," he slurred. "Have I ever told you, Mary? Just how much you look like her?"

It would be a long time before my father could look at me again, and longer still for me to speak to him more than a word. I worried each day that I'd end up with his creature growing inside me, and for years after, I had fantasies of taking my life—of taking his for what he'd done.

So instead of crushing the billy's head in, deep within the woods, I laid him on a soft bed of weeds and went back to the house for the milk of another goat.

I fed the little three eyed goat as often as I could, and I'd hold him as he stared up at me, milk trickling from his mouth. I fed him until winter came, and with it, the snow.

Before the frost and the blizzards and the ice, I dug my creature a small den, and filled it with hay, and set him inside. I whispered to him, telling him that I couldn't come back—that it was no longer safe. Soon, my prints in the deep snow would betray me, and the village would follow and find the poor baby, and they'd bash his head in or cut his throat and throw him to the pigs.

His blinking eyes made me think he understood, but as winter thickened, my dreams, my very thoughts, were drowning in his bleating. He cried for me out there each day and each night until the silence came, and after the silence came the storm.

That was the winter the twins had died, as the snow blew and fell, covering and adding to the drifts up to the roofs. The piled snow tipped and dropped into the Edwards' chimney, dousing their fire in the night. Mr. and Mrs. Edwards awoke screaming. Freezing. And the twins in their wooden crib were as blue as the ice on the lake.

These thoughts—the regrets and the guilt, the resentment, swarmed in my head like flies. The memories piled atop one another until their weight was crushing against the seams of my skull. But still, I pressed on.

The entrance to the woods yawned before me, and with a warm silence, guided me into it. The dying grasses of the field behind me whispered their secrets in the forlorn wind. Telling the night the things they'd seen.

The trail was almost nonexistent. So overgrown, it was hard to tell apart from the rest of the forest floor with its bed of leaves and fallen brush. Even without a lantern, with only the vague luminescence of the moon, I could find every crook. I knew this place like I knew my own heart, for I had traveled this path nearly as much as I'd traveled my rooms.

After the first winter of howling storms, the wan, gray skies like endless dusk; after the Edwards' twins had frozen to death in their beds, the spring rains had finally birthed the warmth of the summer sun.

I had nearly forgotten my goat left alone in the woods for the wolves, but just as fall had announced itself with the turning of the leaves, and the cold had edged the wind, his golden, three-eyed stare had again penetrated my dreams.

One morning while father was asleep on the rug in front of the fireplace, I had ventured out to the forest before beginning my chores. When I entered the darkness of the trees, much like this night, the sounds behind me from the field to the village had stopped. I had expected the normalcy of birds singing and the chipmunks and squirrels skittering about, but there was nothing. The silence seemed to ebb and flow, like the waxing and waning of the moon.

It wasn't long before I found him. The forest floor and its lush fauna, the wildflowers and fungi, had given way to blackness and rot. I stood before a large circle of nothing but decay; even the leaves that had fallen should have held their color but instead had crinkled and blackened. It was a circle of death, and in the middle, stood my goat.

He was larger now. The misshapen and nodulous horns that adorned his head had grown so long and deadly, I was surprised the thing could hold his head up at all. His resplendent eyes seemed to vibrate as he stared at me, his thoughts—not words or even sounds, really—were pushed from him into my head.

He was hungry.

Back in the village, I checked on father, who, of course, was still face down on the floor. Beth was out hanging wet clothing upon the line.

"Where've you been?" she said, tinged with indignation. "Goats have been asking about you." She gave me a smile, more of a smirk, like she was trying to imply some sort of secret between us, and for this brief interaction, I was terrified she could read my thoughts.

As if my thoughts then had any rational or logical reasoning to them in that moment.

I told her a lie. "One of the kid's got itself out of the pen. I'm going to need to go after it."

Beth's face went slack, and she dropped the sheet she was hanging. "Bring it back, Mary. We'll need 'em all if this winter's bad as the last." She grabbed her stick and began to beat the sheets, harder than she needed. "Bring it back, fool girl."

I often wondered if Beth had lay awake in her own bed on that harvest night and had listened to father as he did what he had done to me. What had she felt then? Jealousy that I'd had the looks of my mother while she, herself, was left so plain? Did she curse me like my mother had as she died? I knew she blamed me. Just like everyone else.

But it didn't matter anymore.

I stole a nannie named Maggie from her pen and led her with a rope. Under my coats, I tucked one of her suckling kids to sneak with me so Beth would have less questions to ask if she were to go and investigate the lie I had told her.

As we entered the woods what seems like a lifetime ago, Maggie reared up on her hind legs and kicked the air in front of her. She screamed and thrashed, the rope around her neck choking her, and I was petrified that she would break my grip and run away.

Instead, the baby goat under my arm bit me in the side, and in my pain, I opened my coat, and down he went. The little goat bounced back down the path we had walked, fleeing toward the village like he was being hunted down.

Maggie tried to turn, tried to follow, but without her baby under my coats twisting and contorting, I was stronger. I dragged her down the path toward the circle of death and decay, and she screamed, and she screamed.

My little billy was waiting just as he had when I had left to get his gift. His eyes met mine, and then went down to where Maggie stood, yanking and snorting beside me. When their gazes locked together, Maggie stopped struggling. I dropped the rope that bound her, and she walked forward into the black circle of rot of her own volition. She nuzzled her face against my billy's, and then she lay down on the ground.

The billy sniffed her, running his nose along her body. He lay down with her, and began to suckle from her, and I couldn't look away. Something inside of me was telling me to run, to get as far away from this forest, from father and everything else as fast as my legs would carry me, but there was a tug that stilled me in place. It was as if I were tethered to this goat, our fates intertwined, and I was meant to witness him there in his putrid den.

Maggie's eyes rolled back in her head as the billy drank from her, and she started showing her teeth. When the black goat had pulled away from her, Maggie's white underbelly was covered in blood—spattered red with white foam diluting it into her fur. Her milk sac was nearly ripped away, the billy slurping ferociously at the ragged strips of flesh that hung from her underside.

Then he mounted her. I watched through my fingers as he buried his teeth into the back of Maggie's neck, as she opened her mouth to cry out, but couldn't make a sound. Those three golden eyes of my little billy locked with mine, and he never looked away—thrusting into Maggie as she died.

That image, that memory, was fresh in my mind as the day it had happened, as I walked the path through the woods again. The way that he had torn into Maggie had caused dreams I hadn't wanted to remember. Although I had reared him from milk and this gift and that offering over the seasons—practically raised him—I feared that he may one day treat me with the same apathetic ferocity which he had shown Maggie.

After a calm winter, I'd dreamt of his eyes peering at me in the darkness again, their emotionless gaze, radiant in their goldenness sunk deep within my soul. Through that stare, through my dream, my billy goat had again talked to me, and his thoughts were filled with hunger once more.

I had brought then another goat to his decaying patch of woods, and for the first time witnessed the beginnings of his metamorphosis.

The young lactating goat I had brought for him screamed and bucked and thrashed at my leash as Billy approached the edge of his rotten garden. He was still mostly goat, but he walked upright on his hind legs and towered over us. His head was massive, the twisted, violent horns curving up and outward atop his head, devilish, and glistening ebon. He had the chest and the arms of a man—the skin so slick and black, it appeared to be made of oil, and just below his bare chest, his black fur began again—everything below, that of the goat he had once been.

He snatched the goat from where she stood, and in one fluid motion, ripped her head off and tossed it at my feet. His three eyes gazed longingly into mine, and somewhere deep inside me, I knew what he had wanted. How his hunger must be slaked. I ran out of the woods, tears streaking down my face.

I came back to him a day later, after the dreams of his hunger had kept me up all night, and this time, I brought with me a girl.

Her name was Lorna. She was a new mother in the village, unwed, and thus the talk of all sorts of rumors. People had whispered their theories of who the father was, ranging from quaint possibilities, to fantastic; some said her child was put inside her by the devil himself. Oh, the irony! She was shunned. Turned away.

Like Billy.

Like me.

I took no joy in lying to her. I had found Lorna by chance, walking alone to the market by herself, the new babe at home being sat by her disinclined mother, I'd found out later. I say *by chance*, but even then, I was beginning to wonder if there was such a thing. Or if this were all meant to be.

I ran to the girl and grabbed her wrist, almost all of it feeling slightly like a dream, like in some way, it wasn't me controlling my actions. I begged her, pleading that I needed her help *now*, emergently. She sputtered loose words of resistance, but I was too fast for her to refuse, too persistent.

"The forest," I cried, "Please help me."

As we ran together, she tried to formulate her words into questions, now imploring me to tell her what, where, who! She spoke of her babe needing to feed.

I gave her no response, and we ran until we were out of breath, taking the edge of the field behind the hill. I never asked her where her baby was. If she were to speak of the child again, I wasn't sure I could keep the quiver from my voice.

We slowed to a slight jog, and then down to just whispered steps as we entered the maw of the woods that arched above the footpath. The silence there was as imposing as ever, and fear crept across the girl's face like a shadow.

She no longer spoke, and beneath her fear, now there was a look of curiousness. I could only imagine the thoughts going through her head, as once, I had been in similar boots as hers. The silence was something unnatural. Something impossible to behold.

We approached the black ring. The spread of decay had grown considerably, even since the night before when he had ripped the head off my offering. What he would do with this one, I could only guess.

Lorna's panicked breaths slowed as the power of the place gripped her. She walked on as if entranced, with her arms lying limply by her sides, eyes glossy and looking straight ahead. I wondered, why had the bewitchment never mesmerized me so? Why had I been immune to the will of the creatures luring?

I felt like a caretaker. A loyal servant.

My breath quickened as my billy stood and approached the edge of the ring of his corruption, and I wiped my slick palms on my coat.

The beast loomed before us, and Lorna looked upon him as if seeing a God. She trembled where she stood, her eyes wide with majesty and a gasp escaped her lips as the half-human, half-goat held his hand out for her to come.

I watched as they knelt together in a tender embrace as she undid the buttons of her blouse. I stood staring, my heart racing within my chest, unable to breathe, as my billy creature bent to feed from Lorna's bosom. I waited for the screams as I remembered how he had torn into Maggie's udder, but they never came. She stroked the coarse black hair of the top of his head as he fed from her.

When he was done drinking of her, I left—my pace quickening the further I traveled from the pair. He had looked *into* me after feeding, and the three eyes had a hunger in them, still. When Lorna had stood and began to button her blouse, the lure of the beast wearing thinner, the creature reached up and grabbed her by the throat, his eyes never unlocking with my own.

Behind me as I ran through the forest and into the field, Lorna's screams butchered the quiet of the evening.

Fall passed and winter came, and Lorna never emerged from the woods. I cried often over her, over what I had done. I saw her baby grow over the next few months, wriggling in Grandmother's arms as she took on Lorna's duties in the village. The child had his mother's eyes, and he would never know. I alone had altered the entire course of the babe's life. And I had ended his mother's.

How had I been so stupid? So cruel? I had left her with *him*. *God*, I thought, what had I done?

But with the quietness, and the absence of the dreams of eyes and longing, came a willed forgetfulness shoving down and packing away of the guilt that had felt consuming. And with the dissolution of my worst regrets, came the bane of that year's winter.

The freezing temperatures and the snows came early, with flakes large as summer moths. It snowed, and it snowed, for weeks on end, until nearly all the village was buried and everything left outside was dead.

Father had killed the rest of the goats and salted and dried their meat. He traded it for all the alcohol in town he could scrounge, so while most of the other villagers had cupboards and ice boxes full of meat and grain, ours was sparse and bare, except for the drink.

Our living space was full of cords of wood, and father sat at the table most days barren of care. He sipped his bottles and glasses, and Beth and I spent the days knitting with what yarns we could find, and both fearing the night.

Early in the winter that year, as the snows locked us in our own private hells, the nights were full of howling. The wolves cried from the forest, and with each cry unanswered, they crept closer to the village, until one night, we could hear them on our rooftop. They dug at the shingles and sniffed at the chimney, little piles of snow tumbling down to sizzle on the fire that we kept as hot and as high as we could in remembrance of the Edwards twins.

Every now and then, after the long howls began in the early dusk, and the scratching came to our roofs and shutters, screams would fill the air. Someone cried, out there, cold and alone, “My babies! Oh my God, they took my babies!” and we knew that voice to be June, three houses over from our own, and we cried.

Some nights, we’d hear people yell out in quick horrified yelps, cut off and left echoing in the dark. If you listened hard enough, you could hear the snarling, and the yipping, and your mind would reel with visions of teeth rending flesh and snapping bone.

But other nights, there were things much worse lurking in the darkness than the wolves outside.

As father burned through his store of alcohol, as he stumbled and slurred and drooled his way through the winter, his leering, and his curling lips grew oppressively. I kept my eyes averted and donned the drabbest of clothes—things that couldn't possibly show a curve of a hip or breast, or a glimmer of flesh. In the night, I propped a chair in front of our bedroom door and slept in swaddles of clothes packed tight around me with burdensome covers.

Still, he crept in.

And in those torturous nights with a hand clamped over my mouth so I couldn't scream, through tear-glazed eyes, I watched as Beth stared back from her bed, watching father—watching me, and her face had no expression at all, no glimmer of sadness or anger, no fire to get up and help me from that purgatorial imprisonment. She watched, and she did nothing at all.

The winter went on like that, and it felt like it'd lasted a million years. By the time the snows had slowed and begun to melt, and when my moon cycle had failed to appear for two moons in a row, and by the time my belly began to show the waxing bump of forming life, my father had lost interest in me and moved on to my poor sister.

And I hate that this admittance comes forefront to my mind when I think back on that night, but I must confess, that all I felt was *glad.* It was her turn to endure, at least, for a while.

When the snows were finally gone and the warmer months had come, I made my bed each night in the abandoned goat pen under the leaning shed that smelled of mold and shit. On some nights, I could hear Beth scream, but I felt immobile, and more than that, I felt hurt. I wanted to run in, to topple my drunken father and stick a fire poker down his throat until it burst from his backside, but I couldn't get her slacken, uncaring face out of my head as I looked over at her during my molestations. Why hadn't she helped me? Why hadn't she cared?

In the dreams I'd had in the pen of the dead goats, the nightmares of my sister's empty, doll-like face faded away, and with the coming fall, my dreams were once again tortured by a burning, three-eyed stare, calling me to come to him once more.

And so, I walked on, my belly heavy, contracting rhythmically, but I bore down on myself, step after step, moving forward with my swollen feet and aching knees.

Behind my back, out the cavernous gorge of the yawning woods and over the field with its sweeping, dying grasses that creaked and whispered and shamed me with the nightlong wind; inside the quiet houses of my sleeping village, weeping mothers mourned their missing young.

Although the snow had long passed, and the summer's heat and bouts of rain had withered to this night of brittle grains and biting gusts, the blood—good God, the blood—had left its stain upon the dirt.

If you were to look upon the drifts of snow that long, last winter— to open a frozen shutter and peer heedlessly toward the forest—the streets to the field and again to the woods, covered in white like a drawn-down sheet, would have been flecked, spattered, sprayed awash in crimson gore, painted by the torn ragged necks of the children ripped nightly from their cozy beds.

I had left a town deep in mourning, and a sister alone in her blood-stained sheets. I walked out my door, to here, to this place, where devils lurk, and I left my father lying still with his head upon the table—his neck opened and an ocean of blood around his feet, and his bastard child contorting in my womb.

The feeling of the heavy wooden knife handle was still itching ghostly upon my palm.

Father would not wake when Beth walked down the stairs from her sleepless bed. Our father would never wake again—a small parting gift for the sisterhood we'd both abandoned in our months of quiet torment.

This night was full of gifts, it seemed.

Now the farther I wandered into the woods, the more twisted its trees became, and the rotting limbs reached to scratch at my face as if they were the pleading arms of lepers. Where my bootheels sunk into the earth with sucking sounds from the mud, or the crumpling of dried leaves, the ground now snapped and popped underneath my feet as if I were treading on a pathway of eggs.

I looked down, and through the light that emanated through the dead twigs and branches of the forest canopy, I could see that what I walked upon were bones, and the baby inside my womb began to push hard against my insides as if it had wanted to see them, too.

I was forced to kneel to the forest floor as my contractions hobbled my legs. Tears began to trickle from my eyes, but I forced them to stay open. I needed to press on.

I steadied myself to stand and sliced my fingers on the broken bits of bone that littered the forest. There were swaths of tiny, straw-like bones, fitting together in archaic puzzles, larger bones, like leg bones of some creatures I couldn't even fathom, mixed and piled together, guiding the way onward.

Ahead on the path lay a ribcage of some fair-boned, four-legged creature, such as a deer or something of the sort, and next to it in the dirt, was a large, bright white bulbous object. I saw that it was a skull, with two dark voids where its eyes would have been. It was such a little thing; the body it had rested upon must have been no larger than a child of two or three years old.

Somewhere in the night, a wolf released a mourning howl, and the baby within me stirred. My belly tightened again, pain surging from the back toward the front of my abdomen, and I couldn't breathe until it stopped. I felt a small popping sensation within me, and a trickle down my thigh like I had wet myself and wasn't able to stop.

When I could breathe again, I looked up and there were two sets of golden eyes staring at me ahead on the trail of shattered bone, swaying up and down, coming closer to where I knelt. Two great black wolves appeared out of the darkness and trotted toward me with their tongues hanging from their salivating mouths, eyes bright and full of radiant gold, and I did not feel afraid.

One of them circled me, smelling at my skirts, and the other licked and nuzzled my wounded hand where I had sliced it on the bone shard. Both wolves flanked me at my sides and squeezed into me as they moved forward down the trail, herding me it seemed, and I let them, running my fingers through their thick, coarse hair.

I could smell their breath and see it shape itself as mist in the cool air like ghosts in the breeze, and I thought of the children and the long winter nights, and the endless screams.

The trail grew heavier with bones the farther we walked, now fully hiding the dirt underneath. The wolves at my sides delicately leapt over large femurs and hip bones of something that could have been a moose or even a mammoth, and my mind began to construct all manner of malformed creatures within my head.

The air I breathed was thicker, it felt. Filled with something, like it wasn't the atmosphere I'd breathed before. Now, the gaseous wind seemed to teem with life itself—spectral in a way I couldn't explain. As I looked overhead, the constellations were none I had ever seen in any of the skies I'd dreamt upon in all the years of my life. They were closer, I could swear it, and they were brighter, too; poised just above me, one burned red as embers sometimes do when they are about to die.

Around me throughout the wood, no longer was the silence a figure wholly itself, a character in whatever dream this had seemed—but now, full of the scrambling and clawing of creatures following our course. Whatever lurked beyond the edge of the trail, whatever beast scampered and climbed, they chittered and screeched and reached to grab my wrists. The wolves nipped their fingers away.

I trembled, and the wolves pressed into my sides.

Soon, I smelled the scent of burning wood and could see yellow and orange flickers dancing upon the bark and falling leaves. Bones snapped like dead branches under my feet as the wolves led me on without making a sound. The skeletal path led to the fire, massive, as it raged in the night, and as my eyes adjusted, Billy walked around the fire's side.

The wolves left me, and I watched them go to a woman sitting on a boulder at the other edge of the fire. Lorna was naked and covered in dirt and grime, but she smiled at me with a loving grace, and the wolves lay down beside her. Her hair was wild and filled with beauty and bones. It flowed over her like water. She stroked the head of a baby wolf that lay feeding from her breast.

From the darkness beyond the light's reach, four more wolves walked in, heads low and eyes reflecting fire. They went to their siblings at Lorna's feet and all humphed down to the dirt with a groan.

Flames licked at my Billy, but the heat seemed not to reach him. He towered over me, and now, almost all the goat he had been, had been cast off as he'd fully grown. He had the body of a man, but his skin still held the blackness his coarse coat had once shone. On top of his head, those jagged twisted horns glimmered in the firelight.

His three golden eyes peered into mine, and I could feel his thoughts course through my soul, deeper, and deeper, connecting themselves to, and becoming part of every fiber beneath my flesh.

Mother, he said, and the baby within me writhed.

I removed my cloak and tossed it in the fire as I laid myself bare at the feet of the creature I had reared. Crying now, pain, immeasurable pain, tearing me apart, I spread my legs and pushed.

I pushed and stopped and breathed, and Billy knelt to hold my hand. I gripped his oily flesh and dug my nails into his palm as another wave of hardening, squeezing pain bore down upon my insides.

The wolves rose to their feet and began to howl, their midnight song raising the hair upon my arms, and tears streaked hot across my face. I felt a sloshing rip, an emptying, like my innards had come undone, and relief—relief like I had just choked in air after a lifetime of drowning. I laid my head back and I smiled as howls and snarling ripped open the very night.

The baby I birthed kicked between my legs and began his little gasps and cries. Billy scooped the kid up and placed it on my chest. I caressed the coarse hair between my baby's jagged horns as he bleated quietly, held tightly against my flesh.

End

The Last Dance at the Bunny Ranch

Conor O'Brian Barnes

I

Sheri didn't know why she could never say no to Harold, why she always went eagerly with him to their favorite motel in the depths of the desert where they would fuck like rabbits and plot out their intricate plans, but she knew that a force beyond all human power had brought them together, and that she never wanted to be apart from him again.

His kisses were steak tartare soft, filet-mignon tender, and her nipples swelled with eagerness as he caressed them with his swirling fingertips. To be is to be vulnerable, she thought, and to be female is to be especially so. The weaker is always in thrall to the stronger. Always. That's celestial mechanics in a nutshell.

Harold was forty, Sheri, thirty-five. They decided to leave California to get away from Norm and Kay -- her husband, his wife -- and move to Bullhead City to start a new life. The lovers were meticulous in planning their schemes. They'd gathered their fortunes and treasures and forged fake identities -- Harold and Sheri's new names would soon be Paul and Glenda Hendrickson, for they planned to live happily ever after under these aliases after they went to Vegas and murdered their spouses.

"I need you, baby," Harold said, holding Sheri in his arms that fateful dawn.

"I need you too, my love," Sheri whispered, running her soft fingertips through the tufts of chestnut hair on Harold's chest. "The past has passed. It's done with us. Let's be done with it. Let's never speak our old names again. Let's forget yesterday and start anew in Bullhead City."

"That's what we're gonna do, baby," Harold said, "we'll be in Bullhead City soon. After we bury the past in Vegas, we can begin our new lives as Paul and Glenda Hendrickson."

"Norm's staying at Caesar's," Sheri said, "what about Kay?"

"She'll be at the Mandalay," Harold said, "she's flying in from California this afternoon, and she's eager to see the construction site. When I told her I was interested in buying a strip of land my political connections had arranged for a bargain, a few acres next to the future Interstate 11, she wanted in."

"Norm wants in too," Sheri said, tenderly stroking Harold's cheek with her petal-soft fingers. "He thinks the strip of land next to Interstate 11 is a great investment, and he's eager to see the site."

"He'll see it today, and soon thereafter, he'll see no more."

"Has their deathbed been dug, my love?"

"Yes, baby, a pit has been dug for them," Harold whispered, kissing her forehead, "their grave awaits them in the strip of land just off the 11. There's a Bobcat excavator there, and I have the key. A cowboy has set up the scene for me. He's friends with my political connections -- state senators and whatnot; he's in construction, mostly concrete.

He's overseeing the site. He said no work would be done there for the next few days, it's just too hot, so there will be no witnesses when we go there with Norm and Kay."

"What if the workers dig up the bodies when they get back to work?" Sheri asked.

"They won't. The pit's deep. After we throw Norm and Kay into it and fill it in, a parking lot will be paved over it, and no one will ever know what's buried beneath the sheet of cement."

II

The Mojave sizzled and steamed like a flank of ham in a frying pan as the adulterous lovers traversed the scorched earth in their moving van. Reaching Vegas by noon, they parked their treasure-laden U-Haul in a guarded garage before taking cabs to their respective spouses. Sheri went to Norm at Caesar's and Harold went to the Mandalay to get Kay. Norm thought that Sheri had just arrived from the airport after a brief business trip to Denver, and Kay thought that Harold had been in Vegas for the last few days finalizing his Interstate 11 deal, but, of course, the secret lovers had gathered their treasures and run away together to their favorite motel in the depths of the desert.

When the two couples were riding in Norm and Sheri's rental car, heading by back roads to the abandoned construction site in the desert between Henderson and Boulder City, a tawny nimbus crowned the horizon. Neither Norm nor Kay seemed to sense anything dangerous or sinister lurking behind the treacherous lovers' placid exteriors. As gazelles see not the crocs that take them in their jaws until it's too late, Norm and Kay were blind to the stealthy evil coming their way.

When they arrived at the site, Sheri was pleased to see the Bobcat excavator and a deep pit with a pile of dirt stacked like a pyramid next to it. The strip of land was just a couple of hundred feet from Interstate 11, which was nearing the end of its construction.

"It's like a ghost town out here," Norm said, climbing out of the car and shielding his brow with the edge of his hand. "It's just too hot. I can see why the workers take lots of summer days off."

"I know it's hot, Norm, and we don't have to stay long. I just wanted to show you the strip of land and give you some idea of how close it will be to the freeway," Harold said, wrapping his arm around Kay and leading her through the desert heat toward the Bobcat excavator. "In less than a year, after the Bunny Ranch brothel and titty bar moves in -- and the contract is already in place, mind you, my political connections have confirmed that -- this strip of land will be worth a fortune."

"It's ideally situated just off Interstate 11," Sheri said, taking Norm by the hand and leading him toward the pit behind Harold and Kay.

"Ideally situated indeed," Harold said, turning back to Norm and Sheri. "We can buy this land beneath our feet for less than three hundred grand -- two hundred ninety-three grand exactly. It'll be worth millions in a few years. Like I said, my political connections have already arranged for the Bunny Ranch to move in, the contract is already in place."

"Why don't your political connections buy the land themselves, Harold?" Norm asked. "Why are they letting you in on this sweet deal, and allowing you to take in other investors? What's in it for them? What do they want from you?"

"My political connections would prefer that regular fellas with good reputations like us owned the land, Norm, at least on paper. That way, they can remain anonymous and run the operation behind us. You know the deal, Norm. You know the way the game is played. My political connections are going to make a killing off the Bunny Ranch -- and we'll get a steady cut of that, Norm, no doubt about it!"

"It sounds like this could be a great opportunity," Sheri said as she and Norm stood next to Harold and Kay at the edge of the pit.

"Seems like a random place for a hole, Harold," Kay said.

"Go into it, Kay," Harold said nudging his wife until she had to slide on the heels of her shoes down the pit's steep ramp to its nadir.

"Why is this hole here?" Norm asked as Kay playfully laughed.

"This hole is where the parking lot will be. I don't know why the Bobcat dug it at this exact spot. Maybe to get a better idea of the earth's solidity, or something like that." Harold said.

"What on earth are you doing down there in that hole, Kay, digging your grave?" Sheri said with a laugh, taking her husband's hand and leading him to the edge of the great gash. "Go get her, Norm. Reach down and grab her. It's hotter than hell out here. Let's head back to Vegas and eat. I'm starving."

"You're right, Sheri. It's just too hot," Norm said gingerly sliding into the pit and extending his sweaty hand out to Kay. "Let's head back to town and finalize this sweet deal over some cold beers and hot steaks!"

"Let's do it, Norm. Let's fucking do it!" Harold cried, kicking Norm's meaty ass, causing him to tumble down the steep ramp into the hole.

Kay looked up at her husband as pale as a ghost, stunned and horrified by the magnitude of his betrayal.

"Shoot them, Harold, shoot them, shoot them now!" Sheri cried as Kay recoiled in terror and Norm rolled in the dirt.

"No, Harold, don't do it, for God's sake, don't!" Kay screamed as Harold drew a pistol from a hidden holster.

"Do it, Harold, do it!" Sheri screeched. "Do it at once!"

"God no, Harold, God no, God no!" Kay screamed at the

top of her lungs, but to no avail. Harold fired his pistol into her skull.

"You're a pair of devils!" Norm cried, and Harold shot him in the heart and watched him bleed out at the bottom of the shaded hole.

"Without devils," Sheri said, blushing with arousal, "there'd be no greatness in angels, and no need for heroes in the world."

Climbing into the Bobcat excavator, Harold put the key in the ignition and turned on the mighty rumbling and humming mechanism. Pulling on the right lever lifted the boom, and pulling on the left one lowered it, and Harold soon mastered the machine, swiftly filling the pit with the pyramid of dirt sitting next to it.

"What's done is done," Harold said after rolling the Bobcat over the tightly packed earth and parking it above the buried bodies, "now we can begin our new lives under our aliases -- Paul and Glenda Hendrickson."

III

As the years passed, Paul and Glenda Hendrickson -- enriched by their wise and prudent investments, especially in the Bunny Ranch -- rejoiced in the bounty of their good fortune behind the high adobe walls of their sprawling desert estate on the outskirts of Bullhead City. One day, while Paul was collecting his kickback at the Bunny Ranch, a cowboy sidled up to him at the titty bar, his craggy face shaded by the brim of a black Stetson.

"Hello Paul, or should I say, Harold," the cowboy said, "you remember me, don't you, your old friend, Buckaroo? I bet you were hoping I was long gone, huh? Well, I ain't... I suppose that up til this minute you thought you got away with it, killing Norm and Kay, that is, but you didn't… You can never truly get away with killing a husband, killing a wife... There's always a price to pay for the taking of life."

"Who the hell do you think you are?" Paul said, gulping down a whiskey sour.

"You know who the hell I am, and what I'm here for," Buckaroo said as his rugged visage contorted with dark delight. "You should've known that this day would come, Mr. -- what is it now -- Hendrickson? You should've known that I'm relentless, insatiable. When I set up the scene for the slaughter of your spouses, digging the hole and leaving the Bobcat excavator for you to fill in with the pyramid of dirt, you should've known that I'd come asking for something in return."

"You are insatiable, Buckaroo." Paul said. "How much do you want from me? What price do I have to pay to make you go away?"

"Oh, Mr. Hendrickson," the cowboy said with a laugh, "I don't want your money. I have all the money in the world. What I want from you transcends this mortal veil, and I own it already. I'm just here to claim it, for you gave me your deathless soul when we met at the crossroads…"

"The crossroads… What do you mean? I thought our meeting at the crossroads was just a fevered dream… If such a thing were possible, that you could be the devil, and that you could take possession of my deathless soul and bring it down to hell with you, could it also be possible for me to back out of the deal, I mean, take a Mulligan?" Paul inquired, glancing at the svelte girl with an angel's halo dancing enticingly on the titty bar's stage. "Could I do something for you that could save my soul, and maybe even help me cheat my way into Heaven?"

"You know that I'm not just theoretical," the cowboy said, "I'm so much more than a symbol, an antagonist in fiction, or a philosophical abstraction. I exist in blood, flesh, and spirit. I'm the real deal, the devil, the Lord and Master of the infernal Nether Realms."

"The real deal, you say?"

"I'm the very shadow haunting being, Paul, the dank

underbelly of reality. You knew who I was when we made our deal at the crossroads. I made that explicitly clear to you during our negotiations; you knew that I wanted your soul, and that there would be a price to pay for my assistance in helping you conceal the corpses of your victims."

"Yes, I knew it was my soul you sought," said Paul, gazing even more intently at the svelte angel dancing wistfully to *Friend of the Devil*, "but I didn't think I'd ever actually have to give it up to you. I thought you'd forget about it or give me a chance to win it back. Double or nothing, or something like that. Is that even possible? Is there any way I can back out of the deal, is there anything I can offer as a surrogate for my immortal jewel?"

"I'm intrigued… Double or nothing, you say? I tell you what, Paul, I'll give your soul back if you help me win Sheri's soul, er, I mean, Glenda's, as a replacement. What do you think of that, Paul? Does that sound like a good deal?"

"You can't cheat your way into Heaven," the topless, buxom bartender said, sliding another whiskey sour to Paul. "Don't trust Buckaroo. He's the father of lies, you know, the devil."

"Now, now, my little Bunny," said Buckaroo, "it's not your place to scare off my quarry. Of course, I only want what's best for Paul… I'll even help him cheat his way into Heaven after he helps me win his wife's soul."

"You can't cheat your way into Heaven." the buxom bartender said, leaning against the bar. "Remember that, Paul, and if the devil wants to help you, it's only to help you into hell."

"As I said before, my lovely Bunny, I bring hell with me wherever I go," said Buckaroo, "and Hell's not a place of pitchforks and torments, it's the state of purest freedom, the kingdom where you yourself are total sovereign. Hell is simply the condition of being your own master, not a slave to the tyranny of an inscrutable God."

"God's not inscrutable," the Bunny said, "God's nature

is comprehensible. God is the perfection of the Good, the Beautiful, and the True."

"Who the hell do you think you are, little girl -- Plato, Plotinus, or another bullshitter like that?" said Buckaroo, "Get back to mixing drinks, sugar tits. None of these hallucinatory categories -- the "good," the "beautiful," the "true," are objectively real. All human hopes, thoughts, and dreams, are chimerical."

"I don't listen to your nonsense, Buckaroo, because I'm a believer and I know you're the deceiver… I'll get back to mixing drinks… I just wanted to give you my two cents and let Paul know that he can't cheat his way into Heaven."

"With all due respect, I think you're mistaken, my lovely Bunny, Paul indeed can cheat his way into Heaven," said Buckaroo, "he'll win back his soul this very night if he helps me convince his wife to surrender her soul to me like he did at the crossroads."

"I'll help you win my wife's soul," said Paul. "If betraying Glenda gets my soul back, hers can be damned -- I'll miss her, but there are plenty of Bunnies to replace her at the Bunny Ranch!"

"That's splendid, Paul! Soon our trap will be sprung, and our quarry caught. Glenda's fallen soul will be mine, and your soul will sprout angel wings and soar to Heaven… Where on earth is Glenda anyway, Paul? I know it's a very special day for you both… That's why you ventured into the depths of the desert to celebrate at your favorite motel, is it not?"

"It is indeed. Six years ago today, we did away with Norm and Kay." Paul said. "When I stopped here at the Bunny Ranch on the way to our favorite motel to collect my monthly kickback, Glenda went to the parlor to help primp some of the Bunnies -- rouge their cheeks and paint their lips, do whatever she thought would help them be more appealing to the powerful politicians they'll be servicing this evening. The Bunnies are expecting the Governor and a dozen state senators tonight, so they're very excited, hoping to make bank."

"The girls will make plenty, I'm sure, for the Governor and state senators are generous tippers," Buckaroo said, "and you'll be rewarded as well, Paul, when you help me win Glenda's soul."

"I'll help you, I promise, Buckaroo," Paul said, "but I must know the plan... What tricks do you have in your diabolical repertoire? How can I help you capture Glenda's soul and win mine back again?"

"My plan's simple," said Buckaroo. "We'll convince Glenda that it's good to give her soul to the devil, and you're the proof; for we'll tell her that when you gave me your soul, I gave you many blessings -- wealth, health, and freedom from death."

"If Glenda believes that my soul is yours forever, that it can never be won back," Paul said, "I think she'll give you her soul to keep us together. To love, and to love being loved, is woman's basic nature."

"We'll tell Glenda that wealth, health and life itself will be hers forever if she gives me her soul and partakes in her trial by ordeal."

"What will Glenda's trial by ordeal involve?"

"Descending into another dimension, Paul. In the parlor of the Bunny Ranch there's a portal to the Under World. You and Glenda, the Governor, and state senators, will cross through the portal and partake in Glenda's trial by ordeal. Glenda must murder Norm and Kay to prove she's every inch a killer, just like you are. She must shoot Norm in the heart and Kay in the head, just like you did, Paul, when you were Harold."

"I thought this was Glenda's trial by ordeal," said Paul, "why do I have to participate?"

"Because if you don't play along with the ruse, Glenda won't fall for it, and she'll withhold her soul from me, meaning I'll have to keep yours everlastingly."

“But what if I don’t make it out of the Under World? What if I’m buried alive?” Paul said. “What’s the point of winning back my soul if I lose my life?”

“Death -- the cessation of existence in the physical, temporal world -- is not actually real, Paul,” Buckaroo said. “No soul that comes into being ever ceases to be. Whatever is, is forever. Existence exists eternally.”

IV

When Glenda swept into the titty bar, resplendent in her scarlet Dolce and Gabbana floral-print cropped shirt, she was surprised to see her husband sitting with a strange cowboy.

“Whiskey sour?” the buxom Bunny bartender asked Glenda as she sat on the stool to Paul’s right, gently wrapping her arm around him and resting her head on his shoulder.

“Don’t think so,” Glenda said. “Paul and I are good to go, right Paul? It’s still a three-hour drive to our favorite motel.”

“I think we may stay a little while longer, baby,” Paul said, as the dancing haloed angel skipped off the stage. “I’ve run into an old friend, Buckaroo, and he wanted to meet you.”

“I did indeed want to meet you, Glenda,” the cowboy said with his dark eyes glowing beneath the brim of his black Stetson, “but it feels like I know you already. Paul and I have been buddies since he went by Harold, and you, by Sheri.”

Glenda stiffened atop her stool and glanced at Paul with alarm. “Is this the cowboy who dug Norm and Kay’s grave for us?” she tersely asked.

“Yes, he’s the one who dug it with the Bobcat excavator; Norm and Kay’s corpses are still there, just feet from where we’re sitting, rotting under the pavement,” Paul said motioning toward the parking lot with his thumb. “Now the cowboy's come to us for payment."

"I see that this is an extortion plot, Buckaroo." Glenda said squinting at the sinister vaquero. "How much do you want? What's the price to get rid of you?"

"Oh, my dear girl, I'm afraid you just don't understand," Buckaroo said with a laugh, "I'm not making any monetary demands. I don't want your money; I have all the money in the world. What I want, dear Glenda, is your deathless soul. Paul has given me his already, we met at the crossroads not long ago, and if you want to be with him in hell, you must give me your soul."

"But I don't want to burn in hell," Glenda said.

"That's not what hell is, kid; hell's a hell of a lot better than what you think it is. Hell is whatever you make of it."

"Oh yeah, is that so? How the hell would you know?"

"Because I'm the devil, and I take hell with me wherever I go."

"I don't believe that Paul gave his soul to you, Buckaroo. Why would he be so stupid?" Glenda said.

"Guilt, perhaps, for killing his wife, and your husband…"

"We did what we had to, Buckaroo. Norm and Kay were in our way… We knew we'd have to get rid of them to be together... We sinned, abysmally, yes, that can't be denied, but a force beyond all human power made us fall in love with each other, and that force compels us to share the same eternal fate. We'll always be together, come hell or high water."

"I am that force, Glenda," said Buckaroo, "I am that force beyond all human power that brought you and Paul together when you were still Harold and Sheri, and I intend to keep you together always, but you can't remain with Paul unless you give me your soul, like he did."

"That's right," said Paul, "I've already given Buckaroo my soul, and I'm none the worse for it."

"But I'll burn in hell if I give my soul to the devil."

Glenda said.

"Like I said, kid, hell's a hell of a lot better than what you think it is." Buckaroo replied. "I think you've been brainwashed. Hoodwinked. All that one-sided divine propaganda, all that religious hocus-pocus, that 'Life is a morality play' nonsense… yeah, it's really sad; all that jazz has really done a number on you, it's distorted your perception of reality, to tell you the truth…"

"He's right, baby," said Paul. "Hell is just one side of an eternal, all-embracing whole; half of the taoistic duality that sustains the vitality of the world. There are two sides to divinity, the dark, and the light, and just because Buckaroo is on the dark side doesn't mean that he's any less divine than the god of the light. Sadly, it seems that human superstition has lacquered many imaginary and exotic accretions on to the concept of hell -- fire, brimstone, excruciating physical torment, stuff like that, but the truth is quite different. Hell is a place, a psychic and spiritual space, where the noblest and boldest souls go to declare their independence from God's despotic control."

"What do you mean, Paul," Glenda asked, "are you saying that hell is where those who want pure freedom go, that hell is not a pit for punishment, but a sphere of freedom beyond good and evil?"

"That's what I'm saying, baby. To be truly free, you have to ascend beyond God's Law and become a law of your own… Give Buckaroo your soul and break free from the false dichotomy between good and evil!"

"But I don't want to be a slave of the devil!"

"Buckaroo doesn't want to control you," said Paul, "he wants to liberate you from your bondage to an inscrutable God's incomprehensible Law. Now come on, baby, give him your soul! Be a friend of the devil, not a slave to God."

"He's right, Glenda," Buckaroo said, "if you want to be free from God's Law, like Paul, you must give me your soul… listen to me, Glenda, shhhh… Just listen… If you give me your soul, and embrace the dark side of divinity, I'll give you blessings and treasures to honor and empower you beyond your wildest dreams."

"He's right, Glenda," said Paul, "when I gave Buckaroo my soul, he put an end to our money troubles; he also gave me perfect health, I haven't even had the sniffles for ages, and I'll never grow old. No older than fifty -- that's what I was told. I'll be forever young, like that Rod Stewart song -- always immune to senescence, decay, and death; and if you give your soul to Buckaroo, baby, you'll be forever young too."

"Very well, Buckaroo," Glenda said, "I'll give you my soul if that means I'll always be with Paul. I'd rather be in hell with my man than in Heaven without him."

"That's great, Glenda, wonderful news!" exclaimed Buckaroo. "But I'm afraid it's not that simple. You see, you'll have to pass a trial by ordeal. You must earn your way into hell, you know, you can't just declare your allegiance to the abstract idea of the devil and automatically gain membership to his VIP club. If you want to give your soul to me, you'll have to kill Norm and Kay. That's your trial by ordeal. They're now waiting for you in the brothel's parlor."

"Norm and Kay, waiting in the parlor? That's impossible!" Glenda exclaimed, clutching Paul's wrist in a panic. "Have you dug them from their grave and breathed life into them again?"

"I guess you could say that, yes. I reanimated them. They're zombies." Buckaroo said. "Like I told Paul, the cessation of existence in the physical, temporal world is not actually real; no soul that comes into being ever ceases to be. Whatever is, is forever. Existence exists eternally."

"I don't know if I can believe you," Glenda said.

"You don't have to believe me, Glenda; you can see Norm and Kay with your own eyes, at least Norm and Kay as zombies. Let's go to the parlor where Norm and Kay await;they'll be crucial players in the trial by ordeal that'll determine your fate -- whether I'll accept your soul and let you live happily ever after with Harold, er, I mean Paul."

V

Paul and Glenda bid adieu to the buxom Bunny bartender and followed Buckaroo out of the titty bar's swinging doors and into the still scorching dusk sun. The compound consisted of several hot pink Googie buildings. The main structure, reminiscent of a Malibu Barbie dollhouse, had "Bunny Ranch" spelled out on its roof in cursive aqua lettering. Making their way down a dusty path, the trio entered the dollhouse's air-conditioned, checkerboard-tiled parlor where dozens of topless Bunnies sat on a semicircle of red velvet sofas quaffing cocktails with the tuxedoed Governor and assemblage of state senators.

Glenda had thickly rouged the faces of the plump and youthful girls; their lips were cranberry red, and their eyelids, huckleberry blue. Facing the sofas, the image of an antique Victorian fireplace with a cast iron mantle burned on the screen of an 86-inch Samsung smart TV. When the Governor, a corpulent, middle-aged fellow with a foppish, Neronian mop of ginger tendrils, saw Buckaroo coming in, he gave his Cosmopolitan to the Bunny reclining beside him, and hurried over to the cowboy to shake his hand.

"Oh, Buckaroo, my dear, dear friend," the Governor said, bowing obsequiously, "it's so nice to see you again! Welcome back to the Bunny Ranch! The state senators and I are going to have an orgy with the Bunnies shortly, and you're welcome to join, as are your friends, if they're so inclined… By the way, what are their names?"

"Glenda and Paul," Buckaroo said, gesturing to the handsome couple. "They're not here for the orgy, though, but for the trial by ordeal. Tonight, Governor, Glenda will give me what you and the state senators gave me long ago, her immortal soul!"

"Well, that's magnificent!" the Governor exclaimed, turning to Glenda, and clasping her delicate hands. "Just magnificent! When you give your soul to Buckaroo, you'll be born again, saved by the power of Satan! I gave the cowboy my soul when I was merely an ambitious state senator, and then, Abracadabra, he fixed the gubernatorial election, making me Nevada's most powerful man! You're gonna be born again after you pass your trial by ordeal, Glenda, I sure as hell know I was when I passed mine. Born again hardcore! When does her trial begin, Buckaroo? What time?"

"Now's as good a time as any," Buckaroo said, "in fact, now's the only time there is, for the past is dead and the future is still unborn, so neither really exist."

From the antique Victorian fireplace burning on the 86-inch screen of the Samsung smart TV, two hazy figures slowly came into focus, and Norm and Kay made their reappearance. The zombies standing in the licking flames seemed to be real, living beings, not two-dimensional figures on a screen. Norm had a crusty circle of dried blood on the left chest of his dirty white Izod shirt where he'd been shot, and Kay still had a bullet hole in her skull, just above her right eyebrow, and a thick streak of dark blood ran down her cheek and chin, splotching her cream blouse. The flesh of the slaughtered spouses was grayish and rotting in places, but they still had their ears, noses, and lips, and their limbs and digits remained intact.

"Are they real, or just apparitions?!" Glenda exclaimed. "Are Norm and Kay actual physical entities, or simply images on a screen?"

"Oh, they're real, as real as real can be," said Buckaroo, "I dug them out of their graves, enfleshed their skeletons, and breathed air into their lungs just this morning, making them zombies so they could participate in the ceremony."

"What does the trial by ordeal entail, Buckaroo?" Glenda asked.

"You must murder your betrayed spouses, like Paul did when he was Harold," Buckaroo whispered in Glenda's ear, "you must shoot Norm in the heart, and Kay in the head."

"But why?" Glenda said.

"You have to remove them from the spiritual realm as I removed them from the physical one," Paul quietly counseled, "if you don't, you can't be with me, and I can't be with you… Don't be afraid, baby. After you kill the zombies, your soul will belong to the devil, like mine, and we'll enjoy Buckaroo's blessings for all time. I'll always stand by your side, baby… Like Buckaroo said, there really is no such thing as death…"

"Come to us. Leap through the screen and enter our domain," Norm called from the fireplace onscreen.

"Come to us, all of you, Harold, Sheri, Buckaroo; come to us, Mr. Governor and esteemed state senators!" cried Kay.

"Follow me through the portal that leads to the Under World!" Buckaroo exclaimed, leaping like a sprite into the fireplace and vanishing with Norm and Kay behind the onscreen flames.

In obedience to their master, the tuxedoed Governor and state senators left the lovely Bunnies on the red velvet sofas and jumped through the portal leading to the Under World. After they vanished into the fire, Glenda leaned within inches of the Samsung smart TV screen, straining her eyes in vain to see anything beyond the flames.

"I'm scared, Paul, scared of the devil," Glenda said.

"That's understandable, baby," said Paul, "it's normal to be nervous before your trial by ordeal, but as you know, we can't be together forever unless you give the devil your soul."

"If that's what I have to do to be with you, my precious love, my steely man, that's what I'll do!" Glenda said, clasping Paul's hand.

"The devil is the monarch of the world, the devil is the monarch of the world, The devil is the monarch of the world," the lovely Bunnies on the red velvet sofas solemnly intoned, and the lovers took a deep breath and jumped through the screen of flames. Finding themselves in pitch blackness after passing through the fire's radiance, they slid down an unseen slide before slipping through a small point of light and landing softly on a patch of sand in the desert just off the 11 where Buckaroo, the Governor, state senators, and the zombies of Norm and Kay, of course, were milling about next to a Bobcat excavator by a deep hole and a pyramid of dirt.

VI

Crawling into the gleaming Bobcat and sitting on its bright orange seat, Buckaroo pointed at the hole, and said: "Go into the pit, Norm and Kay, lead your treacherous spouses into it so that the trial by ordeal can commence."

"God damn you, Buckaroo," Kay exploded with the vein in her forehead bulging, "why'd you dig us out of the pit if you just wanted to throw us back into it?"

"Yeah Buckaroo," said Norm, "our souls aren't yours to do with as you wish. Kay and I are innocent. Our sinful spouses should be buried in the pit, not us; we're victims. We've suffered enough. If there's any justice, and perhaps there isn't, we deserve to be paroled from the Under World, not condemned to rot in it."

"Oh, come on now, Norm and Kay," Buckaroo said, "where's your faith? Don't you know that I'm one half of the divine whole? God and I are collaborators, we work together, you know; everything I do has God's imprimatur."

"We don't believe you," said Kay, "and we know there's no equality, no collaboration, between God and the devil. You and God aren't two halves of a divine whole. You're not one with God, Buckaroo. God is one, and you're nothing; you're a negation, the antithesis of the Good, the Beautiful, and the True."

"I think you're hysterical, Kay, truly, I do," the cowboy said, shaking his head with disappointment, "but it doesn't matter because Sheri's gonna shoot you. She's gonna put a bullet in Norm's heart and another in your head, Kay, just like Harold did. When the deed's done, you and Norm will cease being zombies, and your souls will at last be free. The greatest burden will soon lift from your shoulders. The greatest blessing is not having to be."

"But that's not true," cried Kay. "Life's the greatest blessing, despite its pain!"

"But death wins in the end," Buckaroo said. "Epicurus was right about that. Death's the eternal condition. Life's but a blip."

"Your trial by ordeal will be relatively simple," the Governor whispered to Glenda, drawing a Luger pistol from a holster hidden in the waistband of his tuxedo and offering it to the elegant woman in the scarlet Dolce and Gabbana floral-print cropped shirt. "I had to torture and murder toddlers and harvest their pineal glands for adrenochrome before Buckaroo accepted the offer of my soul, so be thankful that all you'll have to do is remove Norm and Kay from the spiritual realm as your husband removed them from the physical one. Take this pistol, Glenda, please; be firm, bold, and resolute; take this pistol, and shoot the zombies; after they vanish, crawl into the pit, and let Buckaroo bury you in it. When you dig yourself out of the deep and dark hole, the cowboy will take your soul, and you and Paul can be together forever, beyond good and evil, free from God's control."

Glenda grabbed the gun from the Governor and pointed it at Kay's head. "Go into the hole," she commanded the zombies, but Norm and Kay refused to budge from where they were standing at the edge of the pit.

"Didn't you hear what she said?" Paul demanded of the zombies. "Go into the hole so my baby can pass her trial by ordeal!"

"We won't go," said Norm, "our souls are pure, unlike yours, so if there's any justice, at death we'll ascend to the Lord!"

"Very well then, I'll send you to the Lord this instant, unless this is a universe with no justice in it!" Glenda roared, firing the pistol through Kay's skull where Harold had shot her. When Kay's body crumpled and she tumbled into the hole, Norm charged Glenda and seized her by the throat, wrestling her to the ground, but the Governor and state senators swiftly pulled him off her and restrained him on the hot dirt.

"Do it now, Glenda," said the Governor, pointing his chubby finger at Norm's heart as the state senators pried the zombie's arms apart, "fire a bullet into the hole in his chest where the bloodstain blotches his breast!"

"You're all devils doomed to burn in hell's most fetid bowels!" Norm gasped. "Go ahead, Sheri, do the deed. I don't want to live in the Under World anymore -- do the deed, evil, fallen woman; do the deed, vile, vicious whore!"

"Hell's where those who want pure freedom go, it's not a pit for punishment, but a sphere of freedom beyond good and evil," Glenda said, pulling the trigger.

As the bright blood flowed from the bullet hole just under the alligator on his dirty white Izod shirt, the Governor and state senators tossed Norm's ashen body into the pit with Kay's, and the corpses of the twice-murdered victims vanished.

"They've gone to the beyond, where there are no devils, no angels, nothing at all," said Paul, looking down into the empty hole.

"Go into the hole, Glenda and Paul," Buckaroo said, "so I can bury you both in its depths. When you dig yourselves out from the pit, you'll pass the trial by ordeal, having proven the power of your conjugal bond; and Glenda, I'll accept the offer of your soul after you and Paul dig yourselves out of the hole!"

VII

Paul and Glenda slid down the steep incline and sat Indian style at the bottom of the pit. Looking up at the Governor and state senators who were standing in a semi-circle at the edge of the trench, the sinful lovers kissed each other, and Buckaroo removed his key and started the Bobcat excavating machine.

Guiding the boom so that the bucket deftly lifted a huge bucketful of soil from the pile, the cowboy dropped it on the couple, covering them completely in the desert's gravelly powder. In time, Paul and Glenda could hear the humming and rumbling Bobcat busily packing the dirt above their heads, but soon, all went silent, and they knew they had to escape the pit. Trying not to panic, they slowly dug their way out of the dirt by swimming through it like skiers swimming through the snow after an avalanche.

Breaking through the surface and pulling themselves out of the hole into a realm of pitch black, they saw a small point of light flashing in the distance, and they clasped hands and hurried in the direction of the flickering beacon. Where the Bunny Ranch's parlor should've been, a fire was burning, and when Paul and Glenda reached it, they saw it was the image of an antique Victorian fireplace glowing on the screen of an 86-inch Samsung smart TV. Realizing it was the portal they had crossed through to get to the Under World, the lovers put their noses to the screen and looked through it.

Beyond the flickering flames, Paul and Glenda could see the naked Governor and state senators in the parlor thrusting fiercely into the splayed Bunnies, making their pink titties jiggle like Jello on the red velvet sofas. When Paul tried to climb through the portal to escape the Under World, he found that the screen was impenetrable, and he and Glenda scratched their fingers and pounded their fists against it frantically, but to no avail. Suddenly, Buckaroo and the buxom Bunny bartender appeared on the opposite side of the screen, glaring at Paul and Glenda almost mockingly from the comforts of the brothel's parlor. "You can't cheat your way into Heaven," the big-breasted barkeep bellowed, "every soul goes where it deserves to in the end!"

"But Buckaroo, you said you'd return my soul if I helped trick Glenda into giving you hers as a replacement!" Paul screamed, scratching in terror at the screen.

"We're trapped! We're trapped!" Glenda cried, turning away from the flames, but finding nothing behind her but infinite darkness. "Damn you, Paul!" she wailed, slapping and scratching the lover who had fatally betrayed her. "You've doomed us both, trapped us in hell forever! You tried to leave me here alone, you devil, so you could save your soul and cheat your way into Heaven; but you were betrayed as well, you fool, by Buckaroo! And now, the hell you'll be trapped in with me will be especially hellish for you, for my love has turned to hate— pure vitriolic venom, and the torments I'll inflict on you will remind you always that we're in hell, and not in Heaven!"

"Maybe you shouldn't have let Glenda know about our little deal, Paul the one to swap your soul for hers, that is; especially since I never had any intention of honoring it," Buckaroo said with wicked delight. "You wagered double or nothing, and lost the bet, so another soul will always afflict you with her torments. Hell hath no fury like a woman scorned, right? Well, soon that female fury will be pegging you good and hard; it'll be excruciating being stuck with Glenda forever behind this screen, never able to escape through the portal that leads out of the Under World."

Buckaroo and the buxom Bunny turned their backs on Paul and Glenda, who screamed silently behind the screen as the orgy pulsated on the red velvet sofas. "I think we may join your orgy after all, Mr. Governor," Buckaroo said to the copulating politician. "The barkeep and I are two sides of the same whole, you know, the yin and the yang that make the world roll."

"There's no point visiting the Bunny Ranch if you're not gonna pound some ass," the Governor grunted as his fat, mole-speckled belly jiggled above the cranberry-lipped Bunny he was fucking.

The craggy-faced cowboy drew the buxom Bunny bartender close, kissed her softly on the neck, squeezed her fleshy ass, and caressed her hardening nipples with his swirling fingertips.

"You can't cheat your way into Heaven, but you can bust your way in," the lovely Bunny moaned, laying back on the red velvet sofa next to the Governor and spreading her legs wide so the cowboy could see her moist axe wound glistening with the dew of a slut's lust.

High School Is Hell

Dan Muenzer

There's a portal to hell in my bedroom and I hope Grandma doesn't see it. I laid the chicken bones correctly, and the butcher promised me that the pig's blood wasn't more than a day old. Still, something seems wrong. Maybe I shouldn't have broken with the Infernal Brotherhood of Mayfield. Opening a portal is no laughing matter, and not to be assayed by a neophyte of the brood. I've been studying for years and was confident in my ability to channel the darkness; though, in retrospect, the preparations may have been a little rushed. Rob stole Kelly-Ann right from under me, after all – and just a week before prom. I wanted to open the portal while the blood he pounded from my nose was still fresh, and before my heart had had any chance to heal or forgive. Rob's a quarterback on the football team with the physique of Absalom, if not of King David himself. Kelly-Ann has blinding beauty and the power of privilege and wealth. And me? All I have is the patronage of Satan.

Where is he, anyway? I keep gazing through the portal but right now all I see are people with halos. Have I made a miscalculation, punched right through hell and landed in heaven? I don't think I'll have the power to keep the portal open much longer. Most of all, I want to tell Satan what I've learned about love.

My grandma is a strong person but very religious. I hope she doesn't come home early and catch me in the infernal act again. As a Black woman of a certain age, she's lived through things I can only imagine, and that she can still smile so sweetly at the world is a miracle in itself. I don't want to add to her burden. I think she's really a satanist at heart and that if she could get past some misconceptions, she'd embrace darkness utterly. But it's a hard sell for someone her age, who has lived through a lifetime of misinformation and is set in her ways. A satanist would never come bearing a book and a brand. As Moses says, love God with all your soul and let worship be as a free offering to the Lord. So we do, except directed to omnipotent Lucifer, when we crack turtle shells and chant the litany of flies.

I don't believe in fate, since satanism is all about autonomy of the will, but I do think that things have a way of working out, if you want them to. It's been a lot of hard studying to climb to this rank in the pestilential hierarchy. Our middle school library was just a storage closet with a half a set of ancient encyclopedias and whatever had been donated at the deaths of a few local aunties. The collection was heavy on romance novels and Reader's Digest editions. No one thought it strange that fifth graders should be checking out books like *Ribald is the Wind* and *The Stablehand's Whip*. I stuck to the masterworks, and because they were heavily edited, I had a chance to read many of them. By the end of eighth grade, I could tell Dos Passos from Hemingway and thought both inferior to Hawthorne, whose stories provided the first taste of the sweet fruits of darkness, even headier for being couched in allegory and an atmosphere of moral ambiguity. (They also helped me ace the SAT.)

There was another book, though, with a title unlike the

others: *Unlocking the Daimon: Ancient Mysteries for Modern Problems*. It fell off the shelf as I was reaching for a copy of *Little Dorritt*. On the cover an elegant looking man in a cape gestured to a distant fire, seeming a little cheesy but that's partly why I liked it: he wore his ascot without diffidence or shame. Inside the book he talked about how over millennia the real forces of darkness have hidden themselves in light, and that what we stigmatize as darkness is actually the source of creation. By scapegoating what is black, independent, and free we mutilate our own potential and damn ourselves to live under a burden of shame.

It made sense to me.

One former student had marked the passages he or she liked best with a pentagram, and another had decorated the margins with demons. Another, showing admirable respect for the forces of generation, had drawn a huge phallus on the flyleaf, more or less anatomically correct. The week before eighth grade graduation I was tempted to borrow the book and never return it, but I thought that would be ungenerous to future acolytes. It still makes me happy, sometimes, to imagine them opening it for the first time, thrilling, as I did, to damnation's dialectic and enraptured by the bloodletting rituals of stygian Thule.

I didn't have access to a lot of the codices in middle school. I couldn't use the computers, since the lab monitor always paced up and down and seemed to know what you were looking at even from across the room. Still, my appetite had been whetted, and I felt pretty sulky until I realized I already had a demon's bounty at home. I'm now glad that I didn't start with the secondary literature, and that my satanic education began with the Bible. It's always best to start with classics. I could be seen reading it everywhere and gained a reputation for piety.

Grandma praised the Lord when I was accepted into Hollybrook high. She took me to town to buy some new shirts and a backpack. She said it would be hard but that the

Lord was on my side, and the law was on my side, and history, too. She said that mother and father were looking down on me, supporting me with all the force of their love. They're proud of you, she said, they're looking down at you from heaven.

Some might explain my satanism as a reaction to the fact that my parents perished under a flaming cross, but I don't deal in such reductive psychology. The investigators still say the famous Wooden Cross conflagration wasn't arson, and I'm still not convinced. Either way, Grandmother takes me every year to pay my respects, since it's all been rebuilt. There wasn't much left afterwards, of either the church or the people, and the community stoically banded together not only to refashion the church, but also to install a large memorial to the deceased. My parents were among the lucky ones: they were able to find a way into the yard before the doorways collapsed, so at least they expired under the stars. By the time they escaped, though, the roof beams were blazing and the giant cross had caught: it fell on my father, pinning him to the ground, and my mother died of the burns she sustained while failing to rescue him. When the community rebuilt the cross later, they made it five feet higher than before. I enjoy memorial trips with my grandmother. They let me reflect on my parents, and on life in general, and the gruesome, inevitable death that awaits us all. I always take a pocketful of dirt from the courtyard so I can spit on it later and pronounce the anathema. It's nothing personal, and I have nothing against the church. I spit to show my freedom from superstition, and from the chains that have bound my race and all of mankind.

The first year at Hollybrook, I was exhausted by having to make everyone proud all the time, including whatever ghostly entities might be looking on expectantly. It was especially embarrassing to have everyone pairing me and Regina, the only other Black student – but I took heart from the bravery of Elisius, the mad monk who, after Martin

Luther had posted his 95 theses, went to a church door opposite and posted just one, calling for the abolition of all organized religion. He didn't try to hide but just kept singing the Agnus Dei backwards until they pounded a stake into his head. He didn't mind a staring crowd.

Has it already been almost four years since then? The college acceptance letters have already come in the mail and all that's left to surmount is senior prom – that ridiculous ritual to which I foolishly thought I might have secured a date until reality shattered my illusions. I wish I were still in contact with the Infernal Brotherhood of Mayfield. They'd probably help me get some perspective on the whole thing. It was they who oversaw my matriculation into the dark arts, after all.

I didn't have many friends at Hollybrook that first year, except the inevitable Regina (whom I really do esteem). I am Black and a geek, and if someone can look past one, they usually take exception to the other. I haven't faced too much outward hostility and violence, at least nothing compared to what my grandmother's gone through, so I tell myself not to complain. The teachers are friendly, and white, and do their best to create a learning environment in which everyone feels safe. But a teacher's not always there in the hallway, or the bathroom, or on the walk home. There have been one or two contretemps, but I've survived them all right without help from anyone. I meditate on Diagoras, sinister Pythagorean who, rather than eat the forced offering of Apollo, bit off his own tongue. The priests beat him with reeds and sent him into exile. He went with joyful heart, an island unto himself.

Still, I'm thankful I found support in The Brotherhood, despite their aesthetically questionable website, which is kind of hard to read because it is all white text on a black background, and every spare corner has a strobing gif of a pentagram or a goblet of blood or a skull with a snake coming out of its eye. I knew the conclave was all white even without any pictures, though sometimes someone would post a closeup of a succubus tattoo or summoning injury. I don't mean to stereotype, but avatars in honor of bosomy elves, or perverted Knights Templar, or hair metal bands are highly suggestive of melanin deficiency.

But then again, I've not met anyone, White or Black, who shares my passion for Lucius the Heterast. It seemed unimportant that anyone know my racial admixture, since everyone is equally capable of spawning for Satan. All of us were somehow isolated in our own communities, and the message board was a place where we could share our problems and get advice. They were surprised to learn that "BlackAspergillium" was only fourteen years old. They'd expected much older from my grammar and sense of poise. I think it's on account of having spent so much time reading the Bible. I write in complete sentences and always double-check my spelling, nor do I ever include an acronym or emoticon. Satanism, I find, enjoins a clarity of expression: the fires of hell may be murky, but their syntax is not.

The Brotherhood helped me through many crises. For example, I was very nervous before attempting the road test for my license, and the message board supported me with friendly advice. The archon suggested I park the car in a cemetery and spend the night among the graves. I would ask the support of all those who died on the road, and the reminder of mortality would sharpen my focus. It worked. I dedicated my new license to the glory of Satan, and the whole Brotherhood wanted to meet me in person. I'd become well known for my intuitive grasp of the canonical sources, and I was looked on as a kind of prodigy. At first, we were going to meet in an abandoned church, or a mortuary, or in the shade of a blasted tree. We eventually settled on a Denny's by the highway. The archon ordered pancakes with a glass of orange juice, and I had scrambled eggs. Our archon was a scrawny man in a big leather jacket who must have had at least twenty piercings. There were about a half dozen others of various sizes and shapes, and it was nice to meet my digital comrades in person.

I learned a lot from them, and I'm sorry things ended the way they did. Maybe I was too sensitive. I was worried about being singled out on account of my appearance. My fears weren't for nothing, but in a way I didn't expect. They started treating me with even more respect than ever before. A few even said outright that they were jealous of me, and that the darkness loves the one that resembles itself. The archon encouraged me to take up Vodou, which he said was a great source of necromantic power, and as yet underrepresented among the regional practitioners. It was not a bad suggestion. Vodou is a noble tradition, and I'll admit to still being a little Euro-centric in my tastes: I see hell through the portal that was first opened to me, and I hope, in my progress toward a more inclusive damnation, to further my acquaintance with world cultures. The death men of ancient Assyria, for example, have much to teach a Western practitioner, and the Sufi gnostics yield nothing in subtlety to Keingott the Faustian. Still, I want to earn my esteem, rather than inherit it, and eventually I posted less frequently.

I may have been overly sensitive, as well, due to something strange that was happening at school. Someone had started slipping love letters into my locker. I say "love letters" as a euphemism: these things were pretty filthy. Mostly in the first-person and present tense, they described all the things the writer would do with me if I happened to be missing my clothes. There were some pretty old stereotypes involved, too. Particularly noteworthy were the occasional illustrations, which betrayed a humorously fantastical understanding of my anatomy.

When I showed the letters to Regina, she couldn't help but laugh. Then she got angry and said I was dealing with either a pervert or a bigot or both. Of course, we assumed that the letters were meant as a kind of bullying, but the descriptions were so creatively lurid they couldn't have been written by an average member of the football team. As an aside, I told Regina that I didn't need anyone to get angry on my behalf, since I prefer to transmute my fate within the alembic of my own noble spirit.

Could that obstinacy be part of the problem? Was it foolish of me to open a portal to hell all on my own, merely in the service of my own pride and a broken heart? But maybe that's why my spell was so powerful, more powerful than any ever reported in modern times: the portal exploded with a great belch of light, knocked me on my ass, and flashed a light right into the afterworld clear as a mirror. The gate is shrinking now, though slowly. I have to say, hell looks much different than I imagined. Who knew that the damned wore blue, silky togas? Everything is so clean and bright I can hardly see a thing. I still haven't spied Lucifer. I want to thank him, and complain, and vow vengeance on my enemies. But Satan would probably say something about living well being the best revenge. Besides, I wouldn't want anything bad to happen to Kelly-Ann, not really. She already has torment enough in the form of her prejudiced and craven heart.

Kelly-Ann first caught my eye at a tenth grade Jesus camp. In between singing and sermons (which I turned to my own account by fingering a cursed talon that I held in my pocket), the leader had us play a game called "Look up." We all stood looking at our feet, and when given the cue, we had to direct our gaze to someone else in the circle, and if that someone else also happened to be looking at you, you had to shout before the other or be expelled from the game. I've never liked looking at people directly since grandma's always told me that it's not polite, and sometimes not safe either. I figured out that in the first rounds, at least, I could get away with looking at the space between people's heads. But as the group got smaller it would be pretty obvious if someone was cheating, so I had to summon the power of my eldritch master. I dug the talon into my finger until I drew a little drop of blood, as a sign of self-overcoming, and used it to draw a pentagram on my palm. I uttered the diabolus under my breath and when the leader next said look up, I let my eyes rest on someone across the circle. A cold shiver shot through me and went all the way to my stomach. She was staring back at me with the wide blue eyes, not hesitating or drawing away, but pouring all of her soul onto me, with a little smile and with the light shining off her golden hair. I thought of the time that Aeneas was visited by Persephone in the night and woke in a fright with the taste of pomegranate on his lips. One of us was supposed to scream but neither of us did. I don't think I could have made a sound if I tried, and she just kept staring at me with those blue eyes, and her red lips smiling.

I now suspect that that was the moment the demonic influence took hold of us both – though it took over a year for the spell to fully ripen.

Whenever I saw her in the halls, or stood behind her in line at the cafeteria, she'd nod and sometimes even say hello. The power of the diabolus usually deserted me, and all I could do was hang my head and mumble. Kelly-Ann is as popular as a girl can be without being a cheerleader or an athlete. First, she dated a star on the basketball team, then a hotshot wrestler. You could always tell when she'd broken up, because she'd stop putting her makeup on and wander between classes looking distraught and her girlfriends would always be hugging her and cooing over her like she was a puppy dog who'd stepped on a thorn. I didn't know anything about her, really. We'd never had a conversation. But as I sat in the evening in unholy meditation, breaching the astral plane and making contact with Azathoth, her lips would float before me in the dark and spoil my mantra. I couldn't make any headway in the Summa Infernium. I tried to get excited about the sixty-six categories of damnation, and the sins primary to each, and their secondary qualities - but it all seemed so academic compared to the fire I already felt in my heart. I re-read *The Scarlet Letter*, instead, and suffered along with Dimsdale. At the end, when he tears back his cloak to reveal the brand on his chest, I felt my own scarlet mark burning within me. Part of me wanted to beg the forces of darkness to wipe it away. But the other, stronger part knew that a stymied libido is worth a thousand black cats and purposefully agitated my torment to the glory of the wicked one.

My summonings became veritable orgies of adolescent yearning and angst. Some teenagers learn to play the guitar, or drive fast cars, or smash heads on the playing field to alleviate the burgeoning frustration: I redoubled my worship of the dark mothers and burnt paper effigies. My efforts became so desperately enamored I even let my grandmother catch me in a summoning.

Maybe I'd become too complacent, as well. I had a lot more freedom after getting my driver's license and could buy the materials I needed without worrying about intercepting the mail before my grandmother awoke from her nap. It's a pretty Christian area, so there are no Wiccan stores or anything, but between the Halloween Super Outlet, the Home Depot, and Bed, Bath, and Beyond I am able to find what I need, or at least a close enough approximation. This is one difference between a Catholic and a satanist: the Catholic needs to believe that the wine actually is the blood, and the host the body of Christ. For a satanist, the important thing is will. A plastic beetle is as good as a live one; a red candle burns as infernally even if it's scented with cinnamon and holiday spice.

It's the nightmare of every teenager – to be caught in an intimate, willful act. For me, that act just happened to be invoking the shade of spurned Lilith from the center of a bright red pentagram. When I opened my eyes from my mantra and spied my grandma standing in the door looking rather alarmed, I felt a wash of shame about my chosen allegiance for the first time in my life. For a moment I saw the thing as she would see it, as just the crazy rebellion of a church-raised orphan – as merely the desperate loneliness of one who felt abandoned by man and thus became distrustful of God. She wouldn't see the libertarian principle that motivated my action, and wouldn't understand that my evil, derived from self-sufficiency, had nothing to do with the wickedness that needs to prey upon others. I couldn't very well explain all that at the moment, however, so all I said was, "Hi Grandma, what are you doing up?" My voice shook: my heart was still pounding, after all, from having overcome the seraphim of the third choir of God.

"What is it exactly you're doing up here, son?" Grandma sounded tired and confused, as though she'd just stumbled upon some secret of adolescence better left unseen.

"I'm praying," I said. The pentagram of which I was the focus was drawn in strawberry-scented bath salts. Six red candles sputtered at strategic points around the circumference making eerie shadows on the ceiling. "It's a kind of prayer labyrinth like we do on retreat."

My grandmother nodded. "And what's the purpose of that?" She pointed to the grinning plastic skull that rested in my lap. I'd painted it with inscriptions in medieval church Latin.

"A memento mori," I said. "You see it in old paintings."

She just nodded again and started to turn, as though considering it were best to just shut the door, shuffle to bed, and forget the whole thing. But then she stopped, fixed her spectacles, and looked me straight in the eye. "And why," she said slowly, "are you naked as sin?"

The sweat filmed over my chest and back. I felt a fat drop of it slide from my temple to my jaw. I was feeling pretty thankful for the skull in my lap.

"I'm naked," I said, wiping my hand over my brow, "because it's hot as Hades in here."

And it was, on account of the hovering ifrit.

My grandma never said anything more about it, but for months I could hardly talk to her without feeling a deep sense of shame. Even now the thought of it makes me a little queasy, though shame, I know, is the antithesis of freedom.

After waiting a week or two I tried the summons again, but Lilith didn't come. I had been hoping to ask for her advice about Kelly-Ann. Too bad - if anyone knows how to win the heart of a woman without resorting to love spells or other misogynist tricks, it's Lilith.

Grandma understandably thought I was spending too much time alone and suggested I spend more time with Regina. She knows Regina's parents through the Three Pines Bible groups, and she and they never tire of talking about how brilliant we are, and how blessed by the Lord. I have nothing against Regina. She's a friend of mine. She's smart, and pretty, and wants to be a gastroenterologist: but I just don't feel carnally inclined, though I wish sometimes I did.

The archon, when we still were in touch, had a theory about it. He said my inamoration with someone of a different race was a blow against injustice, and my libido's way of asserting the autonomy of desire in the face of oppression. I told him I didn't know my libido was so enlightened and he said that the dichotomy between feeling and thought is a false one set up by the minions of Yahweh. Either way, my stomach still churned when I passed Kelly-Ann in the halls, and my heart would pitter-patter when I smelled her perfume –a floral bouquet similar to that which now gusts from the portal, fresh as if it blew from fields of asphodel and thyme. The distant damned sing a song that sounds a lot like "Amazing Grace," and the whole place looks, and smells, surprisingly like an advert for fabric softener. I continue to suspect something went wrong with the pig's blood. I summoned Lucifer specifically. Why hasn't he come? There's so much I want to tell him, and the portal's now shrunk to the size of a suitcase.

All through the sophomore year I kept my distance from

her, trusting only to the chance that would occasionally have us pass each other in a hall, or sit in the same section at religious assembly. Junior year she and Rob were going steady, and at Homecoming I convinced Regina to chaperone me to the game. I just wanted to observe their world from a distance: a distance so great that no jealousy could traverse it. For it wasn't jealousy I felt when, game over, and the band blowing from the sidelines, and the cheerleaders scrambling up into their pyramid, she rushed to the field, lifted off his helmet, and kissed his forehead with the tenderness of Ruth for Boaz. It wasn't jealousy, just the feeling Hawthorne felt when, sitting in the custom house, he watched the world slipping by: a placeless nostalgia and contemplative hollowness.

I never would have believed that someday those lips would press my own. The fact that it all ended in disaster – well, that, at least, might have appeased my incredulity.

Summers are long enough for pregnancies, piercings, and religious conversations, so it shouldn't have surprised me that Kelly-Ann entered senior year unattached and in studied dishabille. Something beyond the temporal must have occurred, however, since mere succession of linear time couldn't have explained what happened next. With hair unbound she approached me in the hall and told me the date and the time of a party – one of those beginning of senior year orgies of sentiment wherein everyone swears friendship forever, even with those who have spent four years being methodically ostracized. Me, invited to a party! Such a thing had never happened before. A strange energy emanated from her, a confusing melange of nervousness and aggression. It was as though this moment, for me entirely unanticipated, had squeezed itself into being through an immense, months-long pressure campaign.

She had never been directly cruel to me, and she must have noticed those pathetic stares I hadn't managed to terminate in time. Premature nostalgia had generated an unwonted moment of kindness to one whose lowliness had reflected well on her glory – or so I thought at the time.

The truth turned out to be stranger. And so began the greatest test my dark faith has yet endured, one that would harden me in the fire or shatter me utterly.

The party was one of those Christian bacchanals that lacks all pagan integrity: a self-conscious escape rather than an active rebellion, and a dilettantish orgy followed only by guilt. I probably would have left had Kelly-Ann not stepped onto the porch and taken a seat next to where I'd isolated myself on the porch swing. Her cheeks were flushed, and I almost fainted with the pleasure of her body near mine. Beyond the porchlights the yard was blue with the dark, and the trees across the road a veil that bristled with mystery. The dark obscured the world and hid me from myself; even time lost itself in its folds, and the moment hung motionless and pure, like a squid wrapped in its ink. The din of revelry created a pocket of sound in the night.

Kelly-Ann was the first to speak, and if I hadn't known better, I would have thought she was nervous – she, for whom the future was strewn with conquests, nervous before me, who was a virgin for Beelzebub.

"I don't blame you for being sick of their faces," she said, rocking in an atmosphere of booze and perfume. She moved closer beside me. In her voice had been a note of genuine disgust mingled with something that sounded almost sensual. "You, in particular, must wish most of them were dead."

"No," I said. "If they're going where I suspect, I might almost be envious."

"Really? You should hear the things they say about you."

"They'd say worse things about my master, if they knew him."

Kelly-Ann sat brooding for a moment, smoothing her hands along her thighs. "Let's play a game," she said. "Let's walk in together and see how they react. I'll go first and you follow behind. I'll act like I don't see you, and you'll act like my beauty has driven you crazy, so you can only follow and stare and not say a word."

She led me one circuit through the house and around the back. I was too drunk with her presence to notice what anyone else was doing or to question the indignity of my position. All I could do was follow. Her golden figure passed before me and all the other people might as well have been shades of the damned. I found myself back on the patio, alone. A few minutes later she reappeared and sat down beside me. In my confusion, I thought I was finally living the life I was meant to live.

Then she bent over to uncouple one of her shoes. Her aura radiated a fervid mixture of self-abasement and excitement. Pink and pointy, her shoes were made of some velvety material and looked very expensive. A strand of golden hair spilled over my thigh as she bent. "You're not the only one who's different," she said. When her heel broke free with a pluck and a chuff, she slid out her bare foot. The toes at the end were all welded together, as though only half-way notched from a block of marble. A clubfoot, though all the nails had been carefully painted.

Then without another word she slid on her shoe and drifted back into the house, her long white legs swishing over the click of her heels.

I was left feeling bewildered, aroused, and somewhat offended at her likening my race to a congenital deformity: not at all prepared for Rob's sudden entrance.

He stumbled out the door and collapsed next to me on the stairs. I had the sense he would have cracked his knuckles or pounded his fist were it not for his fingers being duct taped to two bottles of malt liquor. Rob had never talked to me before. Now we sat in awkward silence as he drank. His energy was almost a relief from Kelly-Ann's mottled intensity – it was thick, flat, and shiny like a tensed muscle. A toad croaked and hopped out of the bushes.

"I used to collect these in jars," he finally slurred.

"A toad is a noble beast."

"I'd collect them, and lizards, and snakes," he continued. "I'd show them to my grandfather. He used to be an expert on the things and wrote a book about it they still cite at the schools. You know what they call someone who studies frogs and lizards and snakes?" Rob rolled bright blue eyes clouded with red lightning. They flashed at me, vacant as a dormant storm.

"I don't know."

"You don't know? I figured with all the books you read you would know." His voice was smeared and broken with small, sharp hiccups. "A herpetologist. That's what they're called. And Kelly-Ann's a herpetologist, too. She collects trouser snakes."

"Is that so."

"And an exotic one would suit her just fine." He brought one of his bottles down hard on my thigh, sloshing booze into my lap. The frog stared up at me, gentle and ugly.

"This thing of darkness I acknowledge my own."

"And you better make sure," he continued, "your own snake don't get bitten by the one that studies it. She's a herpetologist for more than one reason. Herpetologist, get it? Herpe. Herpes. From one bro to another." He pushed up out of the chair, spilling cheap liquor everywhere and stumbled into the yard, trying to reach for his fly and not having much success on account of his fingers being taped to two bottles of malt liquor. Then he mumbled an obscenity and tripped, hitting his head hard against the ground. A dark stain spread on his trousers.

I thought about what Kelly-Ann had said about wanting everyone dead – but that's not your way, Lucifer, you worshiper of the living. Was that you watching me that night in the form of a toad to see how I would bear it? The portal's even smaller now, about the size of a moderately sized television. My eyes have pretty much adjusted to the light and I'm more convinced than ever that I've got the wrong address. A crowd of sober venerables in white and blue and pink are gathering around a dais erected on a cloudbank. The dais is set with lapis lazuli and seems to be made of solid gold. Seventy-two virgins are proceeding back and forth across the stage, waving palm fronds. Everyone has an air of expectation, as though someone important were about to arrive. If this is hell, it isn't nearly as dusky as I'd imagined, and its people are more deeply enamored of orderly queuing. Yes, if I didn't know better, I'd say I'd opened a portal to heaven instead. But since when did God respond to chicken bones and anathemas? If you don't come soon, Lucifer, I just might have to tell my tale to an unfallen angel.

But most of those other angels are too busy watching over others, including the people who set the fire that killed my parents, and the man who busted my grandma's "uppity" eye, and Rob sprawling with his pants bepissed in the middle of the lawn – all go unpunished. The angels always arrive for such people, and right on time. The police car rolled up with dimmed lights and the officers shut their doors softly as though planning a surprise attack. They were armed and one clicked on a flashlight. It rippled over Rob, where he curled in the grass, and then hit me in the eye.

"Is he bothering you, young lady?"

I turned around and noticed that Kelly-Ann had at some point sidled up behind. She just shook her head, looked blankly at Rob and stepped away, her pink shoes like sunsets at the ends of her legs. She'd left me with the police just like she'd left me with Rob.

"And what's going on here?" one of the officers asked me.

"Nothing, sir."

"Nothing?" He lowered the beam to where it reflected off Rob's varsity letter. "Don't look like nothing. This young man's stone drunk." He crouched down. "Underaged, too. Passed out on the lawn. Look here: he's done already soiled himself. And you." He blinded me again. "You just set there on the porch while he's liable to choke to death. What kind of Christian are you?"

The other officer shifted in his blues and spat into the lawn. "Practically seems like manslaughter to me."

"Get over here," the first said. "Come on, get."

I thought of Raoul the heretic, and how instead of suffering the ignominy of baptism, he anointed his own forehead with burning hot oil. But he was beyond my power. I felt a deep sense of shame.

"Yes, sir."

"You gotta do it like this." The officer cradled Rob in his arms and flipped him over gently as an omelet in a pan. "Like this, you see."

"Sorry, sir. That's how I'll do it next time."

The officer looked at me kind of funny and then the two of them went into the house. Someone in the living room was playing the opening riff to "Stairway to Heaven."

They had just wanted to put a scare in everyone. The officers wouldn't do anything too serious, since it was Brad's father's house, and he owned the only big factory still left in the town. I still don't know how I managed to drive home. When I got there I tried casting knucklebones, but it didn't make me feel any better. Then I threw up in the toilet even though I hadn't had anything to drink.

Someone given to sociology might understand my satanism to be an understandable rebellion against those so-called forces of light that, in my experience, serve only to perpetuate unjust systems of oppression. In assimilating God to the tyranny of his most objectionable supporters, I have reified injustice so that I might have the pleasure of shaking its throne. That might be partly true, and in itself would serve as ample justification for belief: but it neglects the more universal aspects of my creed, together with the fact that Lucifer needs little help from me to fortify his own existence, as can be seen by the efficacy of his minions throughout all of recorded history.

Over the coming weeks, Kelly-Ann continued to approach me when no one else was around – as we both happened to be passing through the hallway in the middle of the period, or as I fumbled for the keys to my old Chevy Aveo. It was as though her first approach to me had punctured some great taboo and now she visited the wound in secret. Each time I saw her she seemed harried, or in some golden disarray: if I didn't know better, I would have said she was possessed. It was only after she'd disappeared that my lust could be excited: while she was present, her staring blue eyes had an intensity that made me almost fearful, as though I were being challenged in a way I couldn't quite conceive. I thought back to the circle at camp and my subsequent frenzy. It occurred to me that somewhere an incantation might have backfired, that my desire might have summoned a brain worm that had made itself parasitical on Kelly-Ann's will – an abruption from everything I held dear about satanism, with its emphasis on mutual autonomy. In a way, it was like the Brotherhood's unhealthy obsession with my skin – though Kelly-Ann was far more beautiful.

She'd emerge in empty parking lots or in hallways while class was in session. Her banter grew more flirtatious. She'd stand very close with her arm against me only to step away when saw someone rounding the hall. Once, she even drove me out to Fairville, and the whole car ride there she talked about how she couldn't wait to leave town, to finally see something of the world.

"I'm sick of all these people," she said. "Do you think they'd still like me if I dyed my hair brown? Or if I had a big scar on my whole face? You'd still like me, wouldn't you?"

When we arrived, we sat in the food court of the Fairville mall, miles away from anyone who might know us or care. She sat beside me then, and under the table she laid her hand on my leg. Due to her family's wealth, she knew just about all the most powerful people in town. As we sat there eating our fast-food hamburgers, she anathematized them all. It was as though she'd fashioned me into a receptacle for all the bitterness she had accumulated over the years. Driving back, she swore me to secrecy, and I was in no position to withhold whatever she might desire. It was just as well that she dropped me off several blocks from home, since my vanity didn't want her to see how poor we actually were.

Another memorable afternoon, she crept up to me as I studied Paracelsus beneath the tree behind the gym. She looked as though she'd been crying, but she wouldn't tell me about what. She sat beside me and slipped off her shoe. Then she laid my hand on her misshapen foot as her golden hair spilled into my lap. I wanted to extol to her the virtues of a cloven hoof, but thankfully I didn't have the presence of mind.

It continued like that for a couple months. I stopped hanging out with Regina, instead choosing to spend my time in places I knew Kelly-Ann might pass. It was entirely undignified, but it was as though I were possessed. I'd spend hours waiting for her to arrive at the mall or show up at the coffee shop. If she were with other people, I'd immediately retreat, but if she were alone I'd stay where she might see me. I never took the initiative but let her come to me. She never requested it, of course, but somehow I knew that those were the terms. Somehow, I knew that a single misstep would deprive me of even those scraps of attention she was now willing to spare.

The new semester arrived, and Kelly-Ann and I were placed in the same Scriptures class, so I no longer needed to sneak to be admitted to her presence. Once again I thought my infernal prayers were being answered. Everywhere I went the good book was under my arm: people started saying that I was preparing to become a priest, and it was on account of this rumor, I think, that Kelly-Ann and I were able to stay study partners for as long as we did.

For it turned out that Kelly-Ann, despite possessing what

she imagined to be the requisite qualifications – she was popular, Christian, and white – understood very little about the Bible. After being paired together by Mr. Goldsmith for a group project, we continued to study together before tests. We'd meet in the library, a damp, brown room overlooking the football field. The collection wasn't much better than the middle school's: no *Unlocking the Daimon*, of course, but neither did they have pseudo-Dionysius or St. Thomas Aquinas. The semester was near its midpoint, and we were studying the book of Revelation when Kelly-Ann admitted that she feared going to hell.

She'd arrived a bit early and was flipping through a paperback called *Let Jesus Pull Your Tractor*, just looking at the illustrations and glancing out the window to where a football would arc against the blue of the sky. Her grades had improved since we'd started our sessions. Her hair now was only half unbound, and she'd resumed using lipstick, if not eye shadow. That afternoon she was distracted, but not nearly distracted as I by the golden hair that would occasionally brush my arm, or the scoop of her dress when she'd bend over the Gospels. I knew there was no future in it and that the present was dangerous, but the intoxication of her presence overpowered my fear.

"Do you think hell is real?" Two angel wings, golden bangles, dangled from her ears, catching light.

"I know that it is," I said.

"Of course. I know it is, too." She blushed. She looked at me through battering lashes. "I'm afraid of going there. It's so black and scary."

Then she kissed me for the first time. It wasn't a chaste little kiss either – I felt her whole tongue invading my mouth. The library was empty, and no one could see us from behind the shelves.

"Hell," I said, "is nothing to be afraid of." My stomach churned and I didn't know what I was saying but I just kept talking. Finally, I said that St Thomas claimed that one of the pleasures of heaven is being able to see your brothers and sisters being tortured in hell. "But vision's a road with two lanes," I said. "And the damned can look back." And I did. I looked right into those blue and staring eyes. Then we kissed again.

Was it all a dream? For the next two weeks that little alcove in the library became my mecca of esoteric Venus. We'd arrive separately during free period then make our way back to our nook. I'd run my hand down her leg, and she'd unclasp her shoe.

"Do you think the people around here would still like me," she said, "if my eye were gouged out or I was missing an ear?"

"I'd still like you," I said.

It only lasted for two weeks, but in my memory it gets jumbled up, expands into an eternity or shrinks into a single burning point. Whenever I wasn't near her, I was awash in the confusion of the compromised bounty that had befallen me. Whenever I wasn't thinking of her, I was laying careful hecatombs of praise to the dark powers that had seen fit to bless the end of my high school career.

Occasionally she would say something that would almost spoil the mood, but my lust remained unbridled by any ethical scruples – even grew stronger on every questionable word that fell from her mouth. "I wish I could make them go blind from looking at me," she would say. Or "Would you still let me touch you if I were as diseased as Rob says?"

I hardly even paid any attention to scholarships and admissions offers that started arriving in the mail, and I survived my course work only through the pure inertia of what I already knew: I was closed to anything that didn't further my entrapment, and all my paths seemed to lead only to that single hidden angle of the library, where my will dirempted itself and became both master and slave.

"Would they still like me if they knew I did this?" Her hand made its way down my pants and rested between my legs.

I didn't know what was going on with her or with myself. Satanism, being eminently rational, has no basis in psychosis. If I were true to my principles, I would have looked with pity on the both of us: a pity that doesn't demean, but that cures through the strengthening of self-control. Instead, I neglected my friends, spoke coldly to Regina, and resented anything that might restore me to sanity.

Then I did something really crazy, which is just what I needed. Reality aroused and gave me a firm slap, a blow that I can still feel and whose salubrious effects I accept with both gratitude and resentment.

I asked Kelly-Ann if she wanted to go with me to prom.

"I know you and Rob aren't back together," I said. "You're not seeing anyone."

"No," she said. "But I'm through seeing people. Now I just want to know them. I thought you knew that."

"I'll buy you a new pair of open-toed shoes."

She clouded over for a moment. It was the first time I had addressed her with anything other than meek adoration. Then she laughed.

"If Rob said that, it would be cruel. From you it's something else, I'm not sure better or worse. Anyway, it's over now, I got what I wanted."

"Something exotic to add to your collection?"

"No. Something to punish myself with."

I didn't know when, but the golden aura about her had begun to tarnish. Cramped over one of those worm-eaten study desks she looked a little like a corn husk doll, vegetal and smudged. Even I, who had been so wrapped up in my own mania, had noticed that old friends had stopped greeting her in the halls. In previous years, it wouldn't have been nearly as easy to catch her alone.

We closed our books. On the way out of the library Kelly-Ann promised of her own accord not to tell anyone I had asked her, not Rob or anyone and that I should do the same.

"I still have my pride," she said, "which is also why I will never speak to you again."

The old lady at the front desk stopped us as we passed. She leaned forward conspiratorially. "You know," she said, her voice low in a librarian's whisper, "I think it's really sweet." She laid her wrinkled hand on Kelly-Ann's arm. "It's really kind of you to help the boy with his studies."

Kelly-Ann just nodded and walked out the door.

True to her promise, she never did speak to me again. But her car pulled up one cool afternoon and we drove in silence to the part of town where the houses get big golden fences. No other cars were in the drive, but despite the availability of that full, furnished house, she led me to a tool shed. There we had sex surrounded by soil and various gardening implements. When it was over, I nestled against her back and asked her again if she wanted to go to prom. Her whole body shuddered, and she pulled her clothes around her. With a look of pained self-control, she led me back to the car and drove me home – all without saying a word.

That was three weeks ago, Lord Lucifer. I could have borne the rebuff. What was prom to me anyway? I don't need the affirmation of society, and it's not as though I imagined any future with Kelly-Ann. I could have swallowed the toxic concoction of pity and disgust she had poured out for me. Graduation is almost here, with its miniature apocalypse: anything can be endured until then. The beautiful girl whose eyes I could barely meet sophomore year had had sex with me on her own property– that was something, indeed. It almost seemed incumbent upon me to teach her, in recompense, that dark art of transubstantiation – how to spiritualize shame until it became an offering to self-will sweeter than wormwood.

But I wasn't in the mood for teaching. Something in me felt ashamed and dirty – and not dirty in a good way, either. I have no hang-ups about human sexuality, Lord Lucifer, since I know that Eros is a double-agent, and serves both you and the Good with equal alacrity. That's not what I was ashamed of, but the cover-up. I was ashamed of the cringing gratitude that I felt. I was ashamed of the months of self-abasement just to get near her in the shadows. I was even ashamed of being so polite to the police officers that night at Brad's. True, my obsequiousness had paid off – I will remember those kisses for the rest of my life – but I felt I had to atone for the way in which I'd earned them. I had yet to sanctify them to you, lord of darkness: I had to pay the full price. You always demand it be the full price. The devil refuses to take the easy way to salvation, and it's up to the acolyte to follow in his hoofprints. Only then would I be able to graduate with pride. With tears, I thought back to *Unlocking the Daimon*. He had worn that ascot with such daring and panache: where did I go wrong?

Earlier this afternoon I found them beyond the football field – Rob and Kelly-Ann. They were spread beneath that same tree I'd been reading under when she laid my hand on her foot. They were smoking and eating peanut butter crackers and passing back and forth a two-liter bottle of grape soda. The dappled light fell on Kelly-Ann picking highlights in her hair. I didn't need to ask the cause of their sudden reunion or invoke the general spirit of an ending that rebinds old unities: suffice it to say, the angels of light always watch out for their own. When they spied me approaching from halfway across the field, their conversation ceased, and I continued my journey under their silent scrutiny. When I arrived, I stood before them unhurried. I tried to meet Kelly-Ann's gaze, but she was staring at her feet, which were shod in moccasins dotted with pompoms. She was once more fully herself, beautiful and poised.

For the past four years I had made myself small and thought it some infernal incognito, but it had been cowardice all along. No one knew I consorted with powerful demons by night. No one knew that mighty presences bowed at my feet. No one knew that I could outstare the darkest horrors of night. They may even have mistaken my reserve for Christian humility.

"Greetings from the lord of the flies and my Tartarean master," I said. "We just wanted to see if you've reconsidered. Would you like to go to prom with Legion and me?"

Rob and Kelly-Ann stood silent.

"If you take me," I continued, "I promise not to get drunk and pee my pants. That's more than some people can manage."

"What are you talking about?" Rob said.

"Get out of here," Kelly-Ann said.

"That's okay, you can have time to think about it. Rob, has she ever shown you her drawings? She has a real knack for anatomy. I just might have an old example somewhere around here."

"Rob, get him out."

"Are you sure you don't want to give me another kiss?" I bent toward her, but Rob moved quickly and shoved me to the ground.

"Not cool, dude," he said. He crouched over me and I could see the sun glint off his class ring. For a moment we hung there in tableau, victor and vanquished. "I don't know what the hell you've been talking about."

"But hell knows you, Rob Anderson. Hell knows you very well. Some day your angels will abandon you. Darkness will cover the sun and everything that lives in caves will devour your pets. Jacob's ladder will fall to pieces and the full forces of Goetia will assemble. Then you will cower, Rob Anderson, the urine running down your legs once more, and your God will stand by helplessly as a big flaming brand descends, pinning you to the earth, and your mother will –"

I lost my train of thought due to the punch he gave me in

the eye. And then I couldn't speak because he stomped me in the gut. And then, to better show the strength of his cleats, he kicked me a couple of times in the shins.

"I'm so sick of all this, so so sick of it all," I heard Kelly-Ann say, and it was the last thing I heard from her.

I made my way back to the car without anyone trying to stop me. It felt like my right eye was outshining the sun and a thin needle of blood spilled from my nose; but still, it was the others who looked away, who coughed into their arms as I passed, or looked down at their shoes.

I'm a good driver, thanks to the Brotherhood. In addition to his advice about the graves, the archon taught me to never drive angry and to not trust the rear-view mirrors, but always to turn and see the traffic myself. It wasn't anger I felt as I passed Wooden Cross, turned right on Elm and pulled up in our drive. It was the noble pride of Hester retreated to the wilderness, resewing her brand and treasuring her Pearl.

I opened this portal using the most powerful magic at my disposal. I wanted to offer up my sufferings to all the legion of the damned. Who knew breaching the afterworld would be so easy? Grandma's still at work, thank Belial, but the portal's closing so slowly. All it took was blood and a brush and an inverted pentagram; a mobile of chicken bones and a bundle of twine; an infernal apothegm in ancient Sumerian; and the freshly smashed shards of a first broken heart.

When a man screams in the wastes he doesn't expect a reply, only an echo that duplicates him across distance. The cloven hoof, neatly turned; the glossy horns and forked tail; the pitchfork with which he humbles the hubris of the tyrant: I couldn't have actually expected to see them, except with the vision that surpasses the mundane, with the imagination that, as Theseus so aptly puts it, "sees more demons that great hell can contain," and that is the wisdom of the madman and the folly of the wise.

The portal's about the size of a lemon now. I press my unpunched eye to the narrowing gate.

They're all gathered together - red men and brown men, and women and children, and yellow men and black men. The virgins have returned from the stage and the great, effervescing mass is raising a scaffold from cloudbank to sky, pulling on great golden ropes. Little boys with wings lend their pitiful assistance. It must stand at least a hundred feet tall and its crossbeam shines with rubies and decorative scrollwork. A man soars above their rapt faces, arcing like a watermelon seed and trailing a rainbow behind him. His robe flaps its folds, and he spreads out his hands. The wind whistles through the wounds, sounding the keynote for a hymn, and the crowd erupts into a musical hosanna.

Something is awry. Did I lay the chicken bones wrong? Where is the one to whom I dedicate the rebellion and the blood?

The man's on the dais now. The great cross shimmers behind him. He gestures for silence and then summons his elect. First all the infallible popes mount the dais and kneel reverently before him, even the ones who poisoned their rivals and damned all the infants. Then I see John Calvin, who called gentle Lucretius a dirty pagan dog, and King James the persecutor with the *Daemonologie* under his arm, and St. Ambrose with his scourge, and many more beside. Each is wrapped in a golden robe and tended by ministering angels. The crowd erupts in ecstatic cheers and raises hands to the light. The Lord makes the manna rain and pours out honey and milk. It looks like a clam bake that never will end.

Kelly-Ann will fit right in, and her foot will be healed.

I squint to see if I can catch sight of my parents, not sure if I want to see them there or not, but the crowd is too full.

But there, on the periphery, forking through the cloud, with blue metallic coils and a sleek, noble head... Could it be? All the host is distracted by their pious elation. He curls along the perimeter, a blue slithering seam. Then he rears his head like a midnight flower uncurling on a frond— and looks directly at me.

Great power is there, and energy is there, and noble intent. The Galilean spins his miracles in the service of Yahweh: the Holy Dove sharpens its claws, on hunt for the snake.

Lucifer blinks and darts out his tongue.

“Congratulations,” he says, “on your full ride to Stanford.”

The portal seals up.

We’ll storm heaven, yet.

White Angel

Josh Darling

With the tide out and so close to the water line, Reardon was reminded of all death and shit he'd seen over the years it was the stink that did it. The wind blew the low tide fragrance into the dunes lifting it into the sky. The walk from the road to the dunes to this muddy side of the thin island was minutes. Lazaro turned, half facing Reardon. Reardon gestured with his gun for Lazaro to keep walking through the reeds extending over their heads.

"This mud is fucking up my shoes, I spent two thousand dollars on them, they were hand made," Lazaro said.

"That should be the least of your worries."

"Fucking…"

"Keep walking."

"If I'm going to die, what's the incentive?"

"I thought it was important to you Italians to have open casket funerals."

Lazaro started moving.

"You don't have to do this; this has to be a fucking joke."

"I do have to do this, I'm into Pauly too for a lot of

money, this gets me square."

"Reardon, that's a mick name? The organization ain't what it used to be. I don't even get the courtesy of a proper death at the hands of an Italian. Whatever he's paying you I can double it."

Reardon reached into his jacket, pulled a silencer, and screwed it to the barrel of his Glock.

"I want you to think about what you're doing. You clip someone and that's it, you go to hell forever. What you're doing is not just a mortal sin, but think about it, you have to live with it."

"I have to live with paying the vig on a fifty large debt cause the Yankees couldn't cover the point spread."

"I'm dying at the hands of a fucking degenerate, and why? Because I punched a made man who was fucking drunk at a party. He was talking about how my wife, the mother of my children has dick sucking lips, and I'm supposed to do nothing about that?"

They reached where the black marsh mud terminated into water. It was The Great South Bay between Gilgo Beach and Long Island. Across the water, the lights of million-dollar vacation homes twinkled in the dull of twilight.

Lazaro faced Reardon.

Reardon exhaled, "You've been a shitty earner, and they don't like how disrespectful you are. Keep in mind, if you were pulling in more money they'd let the punch slide. That and they know you're considering snitching."

"Bullshit, I never talked to a cop in my l--"

Reardon pulled the trigger.

The bullet split Lazaro's kneecap and exited the back of his leg.

He went down on his opposing knee.

Lazaro made a hoarse guttural scream. His fingers splayed and tensed hovering inches from his wounded leg. The agony a vibration of sensation gone wild. He couldn't stop making the noise. The nerve endings destroyed, everything below his knee he couldn't feel. Everything above his shattered kneecap sizzled with the raw electrical spark of hateful feeling.

His pants leg darkened with wetness above his shin.

"Jesus Christ it fucking hurts, why did you do that? Just fucking kill me you piece of shit."

"Fat Pauly said he wanted you to feel how much this pains him, that you should have apologized. On the bright side, be happy I'm shooting you in the knees and not in the balls."

"Please," Lazaro's voice was hoarse from its volume.

"Oh yeah, I forgot…"

Reardon shot Lazaro's other leg above the kneecap.

Tears mixed with sweat on his face. He screamed again, "Please, you piece of shit!"

"Let you live? You're never going to walk again; you really want that?"

"Kill me you fucking asshole, this hurts so much!"

"Oh that, yeah, I'm just taking it in, enjoying your screams."

"Fuck you, fucking shoot me you fucking cocksucker!"

"You know, when I was younger, all I wanted to do was good. It's people like you, the predators, that made me see the world as shit. There is no justice, so yeah, I'm going to enjoy you crying like a little bitch."

"Heeeeeeeeeeeeeeeeeeeeeeeeeeeeeeeeeeeelp, he's trying to kill me, heeeeeeeeeeeelp."

"You don't know where you are? This is Gilgo Beach. Multiple serial killers have dumped over thirty bodies here. The place is totally inaccessible, there are no cameras here and no one can hear anything happening in the reeds here. You're fucked, anyway--" Reardon raised the gun and shot Lazaro through the head.

Lazaro splayed backward, his calves folding under his legs. His hands twitched, he farted and shit himself.

Reardon tossed his gun into the water. Behind him there

was a flash of bright white light.

He spun.

He blocked the light from the sphere of brilliance with his hands.

The light dimmed.

In the center of the light, a naked woman with white wings twice the length of her body appeared. Horizontal, her eyes were closed; she seemed unconscious.

The light faded to nothingness.

She dropped to the earth.

The world was a shade darker as his eyes adjusted.

Reardon rushed to the woman.

He'd seen people with vitiligo and albinos, but her skin was a different kind of white. She was a box of crayons white. Wax white. Snow white. Paper white. Milk white.

Growing up in Queens, his parent spent extra money to send him to St. Mary's Catholic School on Long Island. He knew this was a divine being.

"Fuck shit, are you okay?"

She didn't respond.

She was tiny, 5'2" at the most. Her white flesh was rippled with muscle. He checked her pulse at her neck; it was fast and strong. He slid an arm under her and lifted her. She weighed maybe eighty pounds –wings and all. If she was injured he'd have to risk moving her. He couldn't have an angel at a murder scene. He carried her to his car on the side of the road.

Opening the back door of his black Ford Mustang Mach-E, he folded her wings and lay her on the seat. Her hair was white. He felt ashamed noticing her white nipples and her white hairless vagina. While her frame was tiny, she had the face of a woman in her thirties.

When she wakes, will she visit God's vengeance upon me?

Angels were God's hit men.

He got into the driver's seat. The car started with a

smooth hum to life. He'd left the radio on, and the DJ announced, "You're listening to WFAN one-oh-one point nine, the home of New York sports talk--" he shut off the radio before he could find out if the Yankees took the Sox. God didn't like gambling. The game ended hours ago but getting Lazaro to Gilgo Beach took hours.

He pulled onto the empty highway.

"Dear God, who art in heaven…" he said.

She moaned.

He turned onto the Ocean Pkwy and got the car up to seventy.

"Are you okay? Listen, I'm sorry for all the horrible shit I've done in my life, if you're here to kill me?"

"Where am I?" she slurred.

Angels should be all knowing.

"We're near Gilgo Beach. You're an angel?"

"What is an angel?"

"They are a creature that serves God."

"God is the ruler of this planet?"

"No, God is the creator of all things?"

"He built this planet?"

"He created it out of nothing."

"Oh," she rubbed her eyes with her palms. "Has this planet harnessed all of it's potential energy?"

"I don't understand the question."

"Does this planet have…" she closed her white eyelids, then opened them. Her eyes were white, with white irises and white pupils. "Sorry, I had to remember the word. Does this planet still have war?"

"Yes, isn't that everywhere?"

"Do you still use money?"

"All the time."

"Have you developed weapons based on splitting atomic nuclei?"

"I don't know what that is."

"Energy weapons?"

"Like an atomic bomb?"

"Can you see your God? Is that one of your people, or has no one seen him?"

"Weren't you there when they killed him?"

"Oh? Was that a long time ago?"

"Two thousand years ago. You must have had your bell rung."

She huffed, "What did your people evolve from?"

"Monkeys if you believe the science."

She grabbed her stomach and rocked forward.

Red and blue illuminated the vehicle. Reardon pulled over. She said, "This is a super primitive planet."

"Depends on who you ask?" Reardon rolled down his window and waited for the officer.

She started mumbling to herself, *why did I do it? Why did I do it?*

The officer at the window shined a light into the car.

"License and registration?"

Reardon reached into his jacket's breast pocket. Pulling his wallet open, he flipped it over, displaying his badge.

"I've got a messed-up raver in the back who saw some shit go down, so how about some professional courtesy?"

The Patrolman shined his flashlight on the badge.

"Sorry, detective."

"My question is, why didn't you call this in? You should have run my plates before making your way up here? That's some shitty police work. I should write you up for that."

"My bad, sir."

The creature in the back sobbed.

"Mistakes like that can get you killed," Reardon said.

***

The drive to his home in Massapequa took twenty minutes give or take. For the duration of the car ride the Angel in the back cried milk like tears. He parked his car inside his garage. The house was bought and paid for. Gambling problem or not, he made the right bets – sometimes. There were also pay offs. When he was a patrolman in Queens, he took more payoffs before moving up to homicide. Patrolmen got free meals and were paid off by drug dealers and pimps seeking to maintain their turf. When he was lonely, he fucked prostitutes in exchange for not busting them. There were a few women he'd loved over the years but none worth making a real connection with. He'd seen too many of his friends marry, get divorced, and lose half of their stuff.

As the garage door closed, he got out of the car.

He opened the back door of the Mustang. He half expected to carry the Angel. She gestured his hands away as he reached for her.

"Don't," she said.

He backed up from the car.

She followed him into his house.

Entering his home, she examined the walls. The photos of him with his dad and brothers. His Mom and Dad in front of a barbeque grille. His graduation from police academy. An award for 15 years of service on the force. Him holding an AR15, wearing fatigues, with Iraqi desert behind him. There were signed baseballs. Framed Mets and Yankee's jerseys. Photos of him as a kid at ball games.

She spread her wings and flapped them. She stumbled forward, landing on her palms and knees. She struggled to her feet.

"Your gravity… it didn't occur to me."

He went to his bedroom and returned with a T-shirt that fit him and would be huge on her.

He held out the shirt to her. "What's God's plan for you on earth?"

"God doesn't exist."

"You're an angel."

"I'm not. . . you won't get this, but I'm from another

dimension. You evolved from monkeys; we, in a parallel dimension, evolved from birds. The bulk of our language is crossing over. Your planet, this time, this place, is primitive. I am a scientist; I was trying to create a time portal. Instead, the portal delivered me here. I'm here because of a miscalculation."

Reardon tucked the shirt under his armpit. He pulled out his phone and started tapping the screen.

"I don't know what to do with you, but this might make things easier for you." He handed her his phone. "You push up the front of it with your fingers."

She scrolled up the image search of angels on his phone.

"I see why you think I'm a monster."

"No, angels are good, they serve God."

"Fictitious creature?"

"You're here, aren't you?"

"I'm not an angel."

"You're not fictitious either. Here put this on."

He handed her a t-shirt.

"Why?"

"You're naked."

"Does that bother you? We only wear clothes when the climate requires."

There was a knock at the door.

The game. The Yankees vs. The Sox, shit. The Yankees must have taken a dive if they were here only hours after to collect.

"I need you to go to the bedroom and not come out."

"Primitives. Your people wouldn't make peaceful contact. I am grateful for what you're doing. Where do I go?"

"Through that door."

She went into the bedroom and closed the door.

Reardon opened the front door.

Christopher was beefy, mid-twenties. Reardon had seen dozens of guys like him before. They all wore track suits and gold chains. They spent their days at the gym. They lived to impress capos. A lot of it was watching too many mob movies as a kid and buying into gangsta rap lyrics without realizing the lifestyle sucks. Some of them came up through family.

Reardon owed money to Christopher's boss Fat Pauly, who was a lower-level loan shark for Georgino Salvatore.

"What the fuck are you doing here?" Reardon held onto the door handle.

"You owe Fat Pauly fifty large as of two hours ago."

"That still doesn't answer my question. I just did some work for him; we should be clear, and I'll settle with him when I have the money."

"You didn't have the money last time and you did a job for us, that I assume is complete—"

"And that kind of job should let you know, I'm not to be fucked with."

Reardon didn't see the jab. His head recoiled but he was still functioning when the right cross caught him in the face, putting him down.

Reardon gained consciousness to the sound of screaming.

Christopher was a blur, pulling the angel out of the bedroom by her wrists. She'd spread her wings, using them to grab onto the door frame.

Reardon got to his feet. His guns we're in the safe in his bedroom. There was no way to get past Christopher. Instead, he headed for the kitchen. He grabbed the cook's knife from the magnetic strip over the stove.

He pressed the back of the blade to Christopher's neck.

Christopher put his hands up and froze.

"I wasn't trying to do anything to her, I just wanted her to meet my bosses, they value things like this."

"Yeah, you're going to get the fuck out of here and if I see you again, I'll kill you and it won't be pretty when I do."

With the knife against his neck, Reardon lead

Christopher out of his house.

***

Reardon wrapped ice cubes in paper towels and pressed them to his eye.

"I'm sorry this is where you landed," he said. His phone vibrated.

He put the bundled ice cubes on his counter freeing his hands for his phone.

Unregistered Number

"Reardon," he said.

"Listen to the sound of my voice, even though we've never met, you should know who I am. Don't speak my name."

"Yes sir, I do sir," Reardon knew it was Georgino. He didn't want to be identified on the phone.

"I was told that you have access to something divine."

"She's not what you think, she's--"

"What you think doesn't matter. You are in debt to me. You can clear that debt if you bring me what I want."

Despite the hour, there was the distant sound of car engines off the main drag of the town. Long Island is too close to New York City to come to a complete stop.

"I can work off this debt like in the past."

"Don't frustrate me. I will say this so you understand. I get what I want. That will happen. You're not much of a family man. The last time you saw father and brothers was memorial day. You called your mother on Mother's Day, before that, New Year's Eve. I think you care about them more than you let on. Bring it to me now. Do we have an understanding?"

"Yes sir, we do."

The line disconnected. Reardon put his phone back in his pocket.

"I heard all of it. Things like debt and ownership we're

taught them as part of our primitive studies. They're really not my thing. This person who wants to see me, he believes in God?"

"If he were any more Catholic he'd be The Pope."

"I don't know what that means."

"Yeah, he goes to church every Sunday. He super believes in God."

Reardon sighed, he'd need to get another gun from his safe.

***

The ride from Massapequa to Georgino's estate in the East Hampton village of Wainscott was almost an hour long run down the Sunrise Highway. In a few hours, the sun would rise above the road as per its name. It complicated driving having one hand on the steering wheel and the other pressing ice wrapped in paper towels to his eye. Over time, the ice melted and the papers towels became a wet sopping mess.

He threw the soaked towels out the window before the East Hampton exit.

When it was purchased it was called a compound. Georgino didn't like the sound of that. Calling it a compound made it sound cultish.

Reardon couldn't identify the guy working in the guardhouse but the man recognized him.

Gate opened, he proceeded down the road, creeping along at 10-MPH. Georgino didn't like people speeding down his private road.

The size of the house reminded Reardon of a four story office building.

Christopher opened the front door.

"How'd you get the shiner? You get poked in the eye sucking cocks in a truck stop bathroom?"

"Fuck you, you piece of shit."

"Fuck me, oh, no sir?" Christopher reached behind his back for the gun tucked into his pants.

"Stop it," Georgino spoke and the men listened. "I want to see it."

Reardon had never seen Georgino in person. He wasn't just big, but muscular, his bespoke suit couldn't hide his gut or massive biceps. He extending a hand to shake. His hand was rough and engulfed Reardon's. His handshake was an oppressive display of primitive power.

"No more waiting," Georgino said.

Reardon opened the rear door of his car.

Naked, the creature stepped from the vehicle.

"The time is upon us, truly a sign," Georgino said. "Please, enter my home, and what is your name servant of God?"

"Azixazelle."

"Azixazelle," Georgino said, letting her name move through his mouth. "Is that Hebrew or Aramaic?"

"It is divine."

Reardon realized in the two hours or so since he'd met her, he never asker her name. This was her plan to mess with Georgeinio, and with a little knowledge of angels and this planet she was jumping in and playing the part.

They entered the expansive house. Reardon expected lots of Rococo statutes for the decor, something like the interior of a Cheesecake factory. Instead, everything was simple and handmade from stone or wood with the occasional painting on the walls. It was far more Spartan than the stereotype of a man who'd stolen everything in life.

"We need to talk of the future," Azixazelle said.

"Yes creature, follow me as we discuss things, I have a room below I'd like to show you."

Georgino pressed a panel on the wall which sprung toward him. It was a hidden door. It opened to a stairway with soft while light illuminating the steps and oak banister.

Georgino lead, Azixazelle was next, Reardon followed.

Christopher pulled the door shut behind them.

Halfway down the stairs, Georgino, pulled off his tie. He stuffed it into the breast pocket of his jacket. At the bottom of the stairs, he turned opening a door.

When Reardon got to the room, it hit him like a bolt of electricity. The walls were lined with whips, paddles, dildos, anal pears, butt plugs, breast rippers, thumb screws, knives, scalpels, violet wands… Throughout the room there were bondage chairs, a stockade, cages, a rack. The center of the room was cleared out. There were nine other men in robes in the room. Reardon couldn't make out their shadowed faces.

By the door a red satin robe hung flaccid.

The air started feeling slippery, Reardon breathed in, but ever breath felt like a half breath.

He'd seen an angel, who said she was not an angel. This was not a room for an angel. These were not the men of God.

"Azixazelle, stop," Reardon said.

"You don't command me lower being."

"You don't understand."

Georgino removed his jacket. He draped it over a wooden stretching rack. He unbuttoned his shirt, he tossed it on top of his jacket. His salt and pepper chest hair turned white over his sternum. His chest and gut were covered in scars. The pink lines faded by the distance in time between his rough upbringing and his current luxury existence.

"No, Reardon she doesn't understand, The Great Satan has brought her here to be sacrificed."

"I thought all you Italian mobbed up types are Catholic?" Reardon said.

"The greatest lesson Lucifer imparts is the lesson of corruption. The greatest skill Lucifer gifts his disciples is that of deception. The commodity soul, falsifies faith and shows devotion to the light while serving the darkness."

"Azixazelle, come clean, tell them you're from another dimension, they're not going to listen to reason."

Gerogino slipped out of his loafers and unbuckled his

pants.

Reardon focused on Azixazelle's stomach over Georgino's small penis jiggling under his gut. He pulled the red robe over his head –signifying he was in control of the black robes.

"At best, they're going to kill you, these people believe in the enemy of God," Reardon said.

"Reardon, take a seat, you shall bear witness to his Satanic Majesty," Georgino said.

The only chair in the room was made from 4 x 4 beams. A toilet seat replaced anything traditional to sit on. Under it was a bucket.

"We make snitches sit there with a gun to their heads. When they finally spill their guts we make them eat up," Christopher chortled.

"I assure you it's been bleached," Georgino said.

The seat and everything else felt like a pressing weight of intrusion on Reardon. He wanted to pull his gun and kill them all. They were scum. That's why taking out a wiseguy didn't matter to him. As far as he concerned that was taking out the trash. Reardon knew why these assholes didn't check him for a weapon. Killing one of them wouldn't mean just death. They'd come for his Mom, Dad, and brothers. It wouldn't be simple executions either. It would be something awful. His mother raped and shooting her in the asshole letting her die slow of internal bleeding. His dad and brothers' dicks cut off and they'd forced to swallow them before having their hearts ripped out. It would be humiliating, too disgusting for the mainstream media to carry, and so horrifically bombastic no one on the street would forget: You don't kill bosses.

Reardon expected to see a pentagram on the floor. It's what all the midnight movie Satanists did their shtick inside of, but none of the symbols on the floor looked familiar. They were brown –painted with blood dried long ago.

"Bring her forth," Georgino said from the center of the

floor.

Christopher grabber Azixazelle by the arm and dragged her to Georgino. Less than half his weight she was easy to pull.

"I command you to release me," Azixazelle said.

Christopher threw her to the floor. She spread her wings lessening the force of the push.

"Get the machete," Georgino said.

Christopher headed for the wall of torture devices.

"You understand, whatever you do is meaningless. There is no God or the Devil, she's not a supernatural creature, she's from another dimension," Reardon didn't know if he believed his words, or if he believed in anything at this point.

Georgino held his palms up and mumbled to himself. He enunciated, "Hail Satan," returned to mumbling, then another "Hail Satan." His speech continued in waves, with the same demonic crescendo.

Azixazelle got to her feet.

"I strike thee down creature of God," Georgino backhanded her so hard he lifted her off her feet.

She landed on her wings.

The other men in the room closed in on her.

"None of you touch it, this belongs to me," Georgino held up a hand.

"You said we'd taste of its flesh and know infinite power and immortality," one of the men in the black robes said.

"And you shall, but I am executioner of Satan's rites, it is by my will and my power that she shall be crushed under the hoof of our dark lord."

"You fucking idiot, there is no Satan, she's not an angel," Reardon said, he whispered *fuck,* to himself.

Georgino approached Reardon at a snails pace. Georgino never moved fast for anyone. He wound up the punch, striking Reardon's black eye. The pain blossomed trough his head until it over took everything. It was a pain that controlled everything. A pain that was singular. There were no thoughts or rational. There was the pressing and real suffering –the truth of the moment: Agony.

Georgino spat in Reardon's face "Don't clean it, remain like that for your blasphemy against Satan."

Georgino sauntered back to his place on the floor.

Christopher stood next to him with the machete at his side.

Azixazelle was on her knees. Her wings quivered.

After more mumbling and more of Georgino shouting "Hail Satan," he punched Azixazelle in the face. She wavered back and forth then toppled forward. Georgino stood over her, his legs straddling her ass. He pulled up his robe. Spitting in his hand, he jerked his cock hard. Kneeling down he aimed it between Azixazelle's butt cheeks.

"In the name of Lucifer, my dark lord, I defile this creature of god."

Driving his erection into her asshole she screamed punching the floor. Her wings batted.

Worming her body she tried to escape.

His massive frame pinned her.

"Praise Satan," he yelled thrusting inside her, "You're a tight little piece of shit."

Azixazelle's face twisting in anguish hit Reardon in the guts. There was a time in his life when he helped people. *How did it come to this? How could he have brought this creature so much suffering?*

Georgino pulled his throbbing penis out of Azixazelle's ass.

"You wanted a piece of the power, you, come get what is yours."

A man in a black robe approached as Georgino circled to Azixazelle's face. He smacked her mouth. Georgino grabbed her by the bottom of her jaw. The man in the black robe grabbed her by her hips. As The Black Robe force himself up her ass, Georgino forced his dick streaked with her porcelain white shit into her mouth.

She punched Georgino's hips.

"Oh, that's good, resist, you're going to make me cum, fight harder."

Reardon knew in that moment, there was no God or Devil. God wouldn't stop this and The Devil wasn't showing up to collect his due. He didn't know if there was good in the world either. He was certain there was evil.

Evil didn't need good to exist. Chaos is the natural order of things...

He was watching it.

"Fight harder you cunt," Georgino moaned.

Azixazelle punch his gut, his hips, his thighs, his balls, her fighting made him fuck her faster.

He grabbed the back of her head clutching her white hair.

She beat her fists against his gut while choking on his ejaculate.

Georgino spit in her face.

He huffed for a few minutes catching his breath then stood.

"Christopher," Georgino gestured *come hither* with an open hand. He took the machete from him then pointed it at another black robe, "You come here and fuck her in mouth."

The Black Robe did as he was told. While the men raped Azixazelle, Georgino grabbed one of her wings.

"Hold her tight," Georgino said.

Lifting the wing, he turned it, she made an awful noise – even with her mouth full.

Georgino raised the blade high.

Bringing the blade down the machete stuck in the bones and cartilage connecting the wing to her body.

Azixazelle screeched.

Reardon felt her sounds of anguish in his chest. He wanted to cry.

This room would not allow weakness.

"Fuck, she bit me," The Black Robe said.

The machete was jerked free from the bone.

White blood flowed from the wound on her back.

Georgino raised machete.

The Black Robe took his erection out of Azixazelle's mouth.

"Please, stop. Stop, I can teach you things--" Her pleading cut short by the next strike of the machete that took her wing off. Lifting it, Georgino examined the amputated appendage. White fluid spurted from her back.

He tossed it to the floor.

As she wailed, Georgino grabbed her other wing.

It took three hard chops for him to get the second wing off. He discarded it alongside the other one. He tossed the machete, it clanged on the floor.

Azixazelle's cries were cut short as the black robe shoved himself in her mouth.

Georgino got on his his knees. Leaning over, he sucked the white blood from the wing stumps.

He swallowed.

He teethed her ribs.

Getting on his hands and knees, he pulled her breast to the side, and put a nipple in his mouth. Using a sawing motion and his front teeth he clenched down. Her arms and legs frenzied until the black robes dicks were out and they were restraining her. Georgino tore her nipple off with his teeth.

The portion of her flesh rested in his mouth.

He swallowed.

She vomited chunky white fluid. Then was put back in position and fucked in the mouth and ass.

Reardon looked at his hands on the armrests. There were straps there. Open restraints used to torture people –but he was free. Fear held him back from being the good person he once was.

Georgino stood.

With the creature that was not an angel getting pushed back and forth between to the two men violating her,

Georgino pissed into her open wounds.

It was more of the same, the horrible voiced sounds of suffering.

Reardon did the math. There were nine men in the room. When he got the gun out of his safe it had a full clip plus. Fourteen shots. He kept the chamber empty.

"Let it be known, I have committed the ultimate blasphemy against God by defiling his creations and his servants. Oh Lucifer, grant me eternal life in exchange for my damnation. Strike my name from The Book of Life and write it in the indelible blood of this angel in The Book of Death among those who would do your bidding."

"Hurry it up, I'm about to nut," The Black Robe said.

"Silence! We are on the cusp of immort--"

The bullet through the back of Georgino's neck blew his teeth out of his mouth. His viscera mixed with the pooling white on the floor.

Reardon shot more of the black robes.

He didn't know how many he'd killed but there were bodies on the floor.

The first black robe to speak said, "Do you know who the fuck I am?" before Reardon shot him through the eye.

With each shot, Reardon took his time and aimed. The black robes would run, put their hands up, beg, curse him. None of it mattered, they were easy targets.

Reardon had four bullets left when Christopher ran for the corner of the room. He was the only one of them to get to their guns. Christopher pointed it in Reardon's direction firing twice. Missing both times before Reardon clipped him in the throat.

Piss, shit, blood, cum, and gun smoke hung in the air.

Reardon's ears rang.

He holstered his weapon.

On her knees and clutching her breast, Azixazelle coughed and sobbed.

Could white tears speckled the floor.

He knelt beside her.

"Do you think you can get up?"

She moaned.

"Can you stand?"

She whimpered, "Yes."

"I'm going to help you get to your feet, is it okay if I touch you?"

"Yes…"

"We're going to have to get out of here. They'll come for us soon. We're going to have to run."

Reardon slid an arm under Azixazelle, carefully, he raised her to her feet.

She stood on shaking legs.

Wobbling, she came to her wings on the floor. Reaching down, she grabbed the machete.

"At least it'll be a bit easier to hide you without your wings. You're going to have to get used to wearing clothes and--"

Ramming the machete under his ribs, she caught him in the heart.

"Your species is awful."

The Karma Colt

Barend Nieuwstraten III

I sit on top of the rainwater tower, or at least the platform that holds the giant tank as I'm too scared to climb any higher. I watch the train arrive, blasting its steam out like it rolled in on a cloud. Folks are getting off it, carrying their bags out with them. The closer they are to the engine, the more bags they have, bigger, and nicer. The men are wearing suits, and the women are wearing those dresses that look like giant bells. I slowly look down the train until I see those at the back getting out in more regular looking clothing carrying old moth-bitten sacks, if anything at all.

One man stands out to me. He's wearing a red shirt under a black vest, both scuffed and full of holes and tears, caked in patches of dry dirt. He's packing an iron on his hip and he's carrying three nice-looking bags. Bags you might expect from near the front of the train, though. Something ain't right about that picture.

"Pa," I call out, as I start climbing down. "Pa."

"What do you see, son?" my father calls back. He lifts me off the ladder and puts me back on the ground. I'm nearly thirteen but impressively, he can still carry me.

"There's a fella in some beat-up clothes, carrying some pretty nice bags," I tell him.

"Well, well," my father says, stroking his whiskery chin with an excited grin. "Nice bags carried by rich folk may very well be full of fancy, frilly rubbish that ain't worth squat to the likes of us. But a poor man carrying rich folks' bags probably has something in them worth relieving them of, seeing as he likely relieved *them* himself." My father cocks an eyebrow. "You're sure he wasn't carrying them for rich folk."

"No, sir," I tell him. "He walked away from the train like he had somewhere to be."

He puts his hand on my back, pushing me to start leading the way. "Sounds like the same place I reckon *we* ought to be."

We follow the stranger through the main street, then into the back streets of town, and out past the outhouses, bathhouses, and storehouses. My father puts his hand on my chest to stop me. "He's heading clear out of town. Probably planning to hide those bags full of wonder somewhere quiet."

"Shouldn't we keep following him, then?"

"We are, son. We are. Just got to give him a little head start. We've run out of buildings to hide behind or pretend to be visiting if he turns around. Don't want to spook him. At least not this close to town where the law's still in earshot."

I nod. My father leans on the wall of an outhouse for a few minutes. At least until an old man comes shuffling bow-legged out the back of somewhere, unpinning his overalls. "Oh, Lord have mercy," he says, rushing into the narrow structure and slamming the door shut behind him.

My father gets up as terrible noises immediately start blasting from within the small wooden booth.

"Alright," my father says. "Maybe that's time, then. Let's go see where Captain No-beard's burying his treasure."

***

We follow the red-shirt stranger at least a mile out of town, hiding behind small mounds and the odd patch of bush.

"The very fact that he's dragging those bags through the dirt means he don't care much about 'em," my father explains. "Which means they ain't his bags."

"Do you think he's going to bury 'em, Pa?" I ask.

"He ain't got a shovel, so I reckon not. Maybe he's just coming all the way out here just to count what's inside. Away from prying eyes."

"All but ours, right, Pa?"

My father smiles at me and ruffles my hair. "That's right, son."

The stranger dumps his bags in a pile together, then starts looking about. My father pushes me down and gets low himself to hide behind what little cover a small rise in the ground ahead provides. My father puts his finger over his own lips to instruct me to be quiet.

I can hear the stranger stepping about, then eventually I can hear scraping in the dirt. I manage to sneak a peek and see the stranger walking with a stick he's dragging hard on the ground. He walks in a big circle. I stay low when he faces our general direction, then I peek again. He makes the big circle several times, circling the luggage wide as he drags the stick hard into the ground, really carving his big round mark into the dirt. Then he starts crisscrossing lines, back and forth, inside the circle.

"Wait here," my father whispers to me. "I better mosey on over." He gets up and approaches the man as I lay low and watch. "What you up to, there, stranger?"

The man keeps carving up his lines in the dirt with his stick, paying my father little mind. Doesn't even flinch when he hears him. "Oh..." he says, casually. "You know, just making a little deposit."

"Looks like you overshot the bank by about a mile, stranger."

"That bank lacks the facilities to make the type of transfer I require."

"Is that a fact? Maybe I could help."

"Maybe you could, and…" he huffs amused, "I suspect you will."

"Well, I can help you make a withdrawal," my father says, slowly drawing his gun on the stranger.

"If you want any of this money, I'm afraid I'm not really the person you need to be talking to. I *can* help get you in touch with them, though."

"What say we cut out the middleman," my father suggests.

The stranger stops scraping his stick in the dirt. "You're not the first man to have that thought. And, despite the saying to the contrary, the Lord does *not* help those who help themselves. There's only one way you can help move this stuff and I'm afraid you wouldn't like it. So, put away your iron, and go back to town while you still can."

"I'm not going back empty-handed after you dragged me all the way out here."

The stranger tosses his stick. "Oh? *I* dragged *you* out here. I don't remember inviting you to follow me, but I *am* glad you came. You see, I need to make a little withdrawal of my own. I got something you *wan*t; you got something I *need*." He turns around. "The question is… who's going to take which first."

My father waggles his gun, still pointing it at the stranger. "I think you'll find that's already been settled, mister."

The stranger smiles. "The only way you're getting this big pile of money is literally over my dead body. I'm not handing it to you, and I'm not going to stand here and let you take it. So, the question is whether you're the type of stray mangy mutt that just barks a bunch, or are you the type that actually puts his flapping jaw to use and bites?"

"I suppose I'm the biting type, stranger," my father says, before shooting the stranger in the foot.

"Woo," the stranger howls in pain as the shot echoes out into the dry plains. "Hot damn, a shot in the foot." He hops and shakes his foot in pain before limping about in a circle. "You're the kind of mangy little rat-dog that bites feet, huh? Thought as much as soon I saw you."

My father looks angry and shoots the stranger again. This time in the shin. The stranger buckles where he stands, struggling to stay up as he grunts, shaking his head. "Ooh-whee.... Graduated from rat-dog to some kind of pigdog. Good for you, stranger. Good for you."

"Pigdog?" my father says. "You did *not* just call me a pigdog."

I can hear a strange rattling and scraping noise somewhere, like someone's shaking a couple of iron rivets in a small tin or something.

"Oh, I think you'll find that's exactly what I did just call you," he says. A defiant look comes across his face that scares me. "You going to do something about that, Mister Pigdog?"

My father shoots him in the thigh of the other leg.

The stranger flails his arms to maintain his balance as he buckles from the shot. "Oh, ooh. Three shots, all below the belt. Bit me in the thigh, now. Looks like you made it up to a purebred pig after all. Oink, oink. You going to straighten out that curly little tail of yours?"

My father shoots him in the belly. The stranger hunches forward and clutches his belly but straightens back up.

"How do you like that, then?" my father asks the surprisingly tough stranger.

"Gut shot?" the stranger hisses in pain. He peels off his hand from his belly to look down at the damage my father's done to him. "Four shots and all still south of the vitals. I had you wrong mister, and I apologize. That's not the work of four-legged creature at all."

"Damn right," my father says.

"That the work of a god damned chicken." He smiles at

my father who raises the barrel of his gun an inch.

"I'm warning you, fool. Choose your next words carefully. You call a man a chicken with two bullets left in his gun, your next words better be damned profound."

The stranger smiles at him. I've never seen anyone take this much punishment and still find the will to smile. "I got just two words left for your two last bullets."

My father's eyes widen angrily. "What are they?"

The stranger smiles sharply. "Cluck… cluck."

My father shoots him twice in the chest, sending the stranger back. Once the echoes of the shots move out across the dry plains a mile from town, I can hear more rattling as the stranger pulls his own gun out. It's a much older pistol.

"That's six I owe you," the stranger says, as my father quickly pulls out his knife and rushes the stranger who should already be lying in the dirt.

The stranger fires six shots off, really fast, and a red cloud puffs out behind my father as all six bullets go through his neck. I put both my hands over my mouth to stop myself from crying out while the stranger casually walks over to him. Blood's pouring out of my father as he drops to his knees. The stranger drags him to his circle and dumps him, choking and gargling on the ground. My father's lying face down in the dirt, bleeding fast from what's left of his neck and sucking in dirt.

"Thank you for your contribution, mister," the stranger says. "Much obliged." He stands looking down at the ground while I look on in shock.

My father fired six rounds first and still somehow lost. The stranger was definitely hurt, but he seems fine now. Like nothing happened at all. With his back to me, I dare to rise a little to get a better look. A red circle forms in the ground and lines begin to fill with my father's blood. It's a big star inside the circle and the bags are sitting right in the middle of it all.

When the pattern is complete, the stranger steps outside

of it, pulling my father away and tossing him aside like some useless junk. Like a coyote he caught going through his provisions or something. Like he's nothing. My mean, tough old dad. Kicked aside. The callousness of it feels like a punch in my belly but I'm distracted by what I see next. The bags slowly sink into the hard, dry ground like it's quicksand. Once it's gone, the stranger crouches by my father's side and takes his knife and hat and starts walking back towards town.

When he's far enough away I run to my father, but he's dead. His head barely attached. His eyes are half closed and when I touch his pale and bloodstained face, he feels cold. I sit there and do the only thing I really can: cry.

***

Eventually, I walk back into town. My father always said that if anything ever went wrong to go to my Uncle Clayton's house. Just a little way south of town. I walk there. Not much more than a shack by a creek. He's sitting on the porch with a couple of his and my father's friends, sharing a drink from a clay jug.

"Well, little Caleb. What brings you out here?" he asks, happy to see me. He can immediately tell something's wrong, especially after he realizes I'm alone.

I have to tell the whole story without shedding a tear – which is why I cried myself dry before coming back to town. Story already sounds crazy enough. I can't be sobbing while telling a man his brother's dead through my own runny snot and tears.

"That's the craziest horse crap I ever heard," he says angrily, at the end of the story.

He makes me take him out to the spot where it happened, bringing his friends and some shovels. Sure enough, my father's still there next to his empty gun, missing his knife and hat. The wind's blown a lot of dirt into the blood-filled grooves of the scratched-out circle and star. Uncle Clayton looks confused and disgusted. "Bobby," he says to one of his friends. "Go get the sheriff. But don't tell him Caleb's story. Tell him the stranger killed Clifford for his hat and knife. Don't say nothing about Clifford shooting first or the like. Just keep it simple."

Bobby agrees and runs back into town. Uncle Clayton reloads my father's gun and pockets the used shells, while he gets Frank to kick dirt over the star and circle of blood to make it look like it was never there. He goes over and jabs a stick in the ground where the centre had been. "Best keep that marked, just in case those bags *are* buried here," Uncle Clayton says. "We'll check on that a little later when it's time to dig a hole for my brother."

My father always said Uncle Clayton was the smartest man he knew. I have to trust he knows what he's doing.

Frank eventually comes back with Sheriff Bridges and Uncle Clayton tells a very different story to the events I saw. He keeps talking about how my father was killed right in front of me, robbed for his hat and knife. I describe the stranger as best I can, when sheriff asks.

"Can you point him out to me, if you see him?" Sheriff Bridges asks.

I nod.

"Best you come back to town with me, while your uncle buries your Pa."

I look to my uncle who nods in agreement. "Don't worry, boy, we'll be along soon enough."

***

The Sheriff takes me from building to building in town until I spot the man in the red shirt and my father's hat drinking at the bar in the White Whistle Saloon near the train station. "Hello there, stranger," the Sheriff says.

The man who killed my father looks in the mirror of the

whisky shelf behind the bar at the sheriff's reflection. "Don't tell me you've come to run me out of town already, Sheriff."

"No inclination to go down that path. Mind telling me your name?"

"Traditionally, the introducer starts the introductions, not the introducee, but I'll break with tradition if you're so inclined. The name's Szoji."

"Well, I'm Sheriff Bridges, and this little boy tells me you're wearing his father's hat and carrying his father's knife, there on your belt."

"Well, that can't be, Sheriff. I don't have a son."

"Boy's not claiming you're his father, he's saying you murdered him and took his hat and knife."

Szoji puts down his drink and turns around on his stool. "Is that *all* he says?"

"That's all he says. What about you? You got something to say to that?"

"Yeah, I've got plenty to say that. First and foremost being that that's not how things went down at all. Not even slightly."

"You calling this boy a liar?"

"He's calling me a thief *and* a murderer and I'm not either of those, so if you have a better label for someone who says things that don't tally with the truth…"

"Did you kill this boy's father or not?"

"I do recall a man following me out of town, demanding things that didn't belong to him, pulling a gun on me, and shooting six shots before I even drew to defend myself. He didn't say anything about a boy, though. He also pulled a knife which, once our paths finished crossing, I figured he no longer really needed, along with his hat."

The other people sitting in the saloon are all listening.

"Well, I found his father with six bullets gone through his neck. His own shooter was still in his holster and still filled with six bullets still waiting to be shot."

Szoji smiles at me before looking back to the sheriff.

"Sounds like someone did a little housekeeping before coming to get you, lawman."

"You calling the boy a liar and suggesting he tampered with the evidence?"

"Well, it's either that or *I* put the fresh bullets in his gun and the gun back in its holster to make it look like I'm the only one who did any shooting just to incriminate myself, for some messed up reason. Why? Just so you'd interrupt my drink to arrest me? Which of the two sounds more reasonable?"

"I think I'm sticking with the idea I first walked in with, rather than those two options."

"Well, that's mighty uncharitable of you Sheriff."

"Even if things happened the way you say, the law doesn't let you just take what you want. Looting's still illegal."

"Oh? What if I give the kid the hat and the knife back?" Szoji says as he looks to me. "Will that smooth things over, kid?"

"For killing his father?" the Sheriff asks.

"His father killed himself," the stranger says, taking off the hat and tossing it to me. "Go check the bullets in his neck. They came from *his* gun, not mine."

"What?"

"You want to talk evidence? Then forget *everything* anyone said. Look at the piece by my side. Old civil war iron. Doesn't take the same bullets that fit into the boy's Pa's six-gun."

I look to the gun by his hip and realise the cylinder's turning by itself, scraping against the frame of the gun and the worn leather holster holding it.

"His father's being buried as we speak."

"Along with all the evidence, eh?" Szoji says, giving the sheriff my father's sheathed knife. "Better go stop them then."

"Either way I think you should surrender your piece and

wait in a cell."

"Here's what I'll agree to. I'll wait in a cell, provided I can keep my piece."

"That's not how we do things here," the Sheriff says.

"If how you do things here is to listen to lying children while the evidence is tampered with and buried, I'm afraid I'm not terribly keen on doing things how they're done here."

"Hand over the piece, or there's going to be trouble."

"Sheriff, you don't want the kind of trouble I dabble in."

The Sheriff puts his hand on his gun. "I don't want *any* kind of trouble."

"Yet here you are about to draw on a man, who's giving you none."

"You already admitted you killed his father."

"Hinted it maybe, just to justify taking the hat and knife from a man who killed himself. Maybe the kid just said I murdered him because he couldn't handle the shock of seeing his dad shoot himself like that."

"Six times in the neck?"

"Man was clearly no doctor," Szoji says. "Maybe you need to ask the kid why he said what he said." Szoji looks right at me. "Go on kid. If whatever you told the sheriff's true, you shouldn't have any trouble telling me. Go on. Say it to my face. Look me in the eyes and say I bushwhacked your dad. Swear it… on your *soul*."

I want to say what my uncle told me to say, but something about that 'soul' remark sends a shiver up my back. When I look into his eyes, it's like looking out into the wilds beyond town in the middle of the night. Only, I feel like I can see a hundred times further. There's something behind those eyes that feels like forever. I feel like if I swear anything false, I'm going to lose something important.

"Well, kid?" Szoji asks. "Did I murder your father or not? You can tell whatever story you want, but I'm only asking you *that*. Tell this lawman I murdered your father without provocation or warning and swear it, so that if you lie, the devil will take your soul forever to burn for all eternity."

"That's enough, you're scaring the boy," the sheriff says, gripping his pistol at his side tighter.

My heart is pounding so loud I can hear nothing else. Except for the scraping of that ever-turning bullet wheel in the stranger's old gun. "I…" is all I can say. I'm frozen with fear. There's just something about those eyes. They've seen things I don't ever want to see.

"I'm facing my accuser, but it seems he has nothing to say," Szoji says, looking back to the sheriff. "I think the boy saw something terrible that upset him, and his mind got confused. Maybe, if someone's out there putting his father in the ground, you need to go check what part *they* played in this. Hell, I'll even come out with you, just to see what's going on."

"Goddamn it," Sheriff Bridges says, pulling his gun out. "Lead the way, then."

Szoji, not frightened of the gun pointed at him, casually finishes his drink and gets up.

***

After walking a mile with the sheriff's gun pointed at him, Szoji follows me to the place where he killed my father. My uncle and his friends are still digging when we get to them. They're deep in the ground in the middle of where the circle and star were. Where the bags sank into the ground.

"You burying him in China?" Szoji asks them, with the sheriff's gun still pointed at him.

"Is this the man?" Uncle Clayton asks, looking to me.

I nod and he climbs out. "Come on, this is the bastard," he says, and the others follow. "You killed my brother, you son of a bitch."

"Your pockets were jingling when you climbed out of that hole, mister," Szoji says.

Uncle Clayton squints at Szoji. "Sounds like *your* pockets are jingling too."

Even though there's a clinking sound coming from him, Szoji reaches into his pockets and pulls them inside out to reveal nothing. "Your turn."

"Sheriff, this man murdered my brother," Uncle Clayton says. "Ain't you going to arrest him?"

"I got him at gunpoint, don't I?" the sheriff says. "But I sure would like to see those pockets turned out, all the same," the sheriff says.

Uncle Clayton looks at me. "*What* did you say?" he demands, accusingly.

"Nothing," I say, shaking my head.

He turns his pockets out and six shells fall to the ground. As they do, he draws his gun and there's shooting. Loud bangs go off, back and forth, fast. Frank and Bobby draw their guns as my uncle and the sheriff fall to their knees with several shots about their bellies and chests. The smell of gun smoke and blood spray hang in the air. I can taste it, and my ears are ringing.

"Quite a predicament," Szoji says, with his gun out. "See, the way my gun works - the Karma Colt, as a nice man in the last town called it - I can only shoot what gets shot at me, as Clayton's brother learned. But just now, no one had the courtesy to shoot at me. So… after you, gentlemen."

Uncle Clayton slumps to the ground groaning while the sheriff coughs up some blood, still sitting up, resting on his own legs folded under him.

"Come now, don't be shy boys, take your free shot," Szoji invites.

"That's why you let Pa shoot you till his gun was empty," I say, now understanding what happened. Not the how nor why, but at least the idea. "The bullets hurt him but not for long. I don't think you can kill him. He's something else. But he can't shoot until *you* do," I explain to Bobby and Frank.

"He's right," Szoji says with a sigh. "Only thing is, in the last town, someone else shot the last guy to put a couple of bullets in me, so…" With a couple of loud bangs, he puts a bullet in each of their heads. Frank and Bobby hit the dirt hard. "So, I had a couple in reserve."

"What the hell?" the sheriff manages to say.

"Hell indeed," Szoji says. "Those boys would have had to dig all the way to hell to get what the boy told them I'd buried out here. You see… when a man makes a deal with the devil, I'm the one who delivers the goods. And when things go sour, I'm the one who collects. To maintain balance, I'm only allowed to shoot those who shoot me first."

I can no longer hear the rattling coming from his old colt, but the cylinder is still rotating in place as he puts it away.

"Killed those last two with a loophole," Szoji says. "Sins of man, yadda, yadda. Anyway…" He crouches by the sheriff. "I don't think you're going to make it back to town, Sheriff. If there was ever a time to make the kind of deal I typically facilitate, now would be a good time."

The sheriff shakes his head. "And send my soul to hell for all eternity?"

"Your call, lawman," Szoji says, drumming his fingers on the sheriff's shoulder. "Of course, *you* could save him," he says to me instead. "Given the role models you had, and that you lied to the law the way you did, I'm pretty sure you're sitting on a southbound soul anyway."

Sheriff Bridges looks to me, shaking his head again.

Szoji smiles at him. "Well, now, who knows? Selling his soul to save you might be just the magnanimous gesture he needs to get *out* of hell. Loopholes being what they are and all." He winks at me. "Can't guarantee it, kid, but it's worth a shot. Whichever way your life goes, it should be handy to have a sheriff who owes you his. So, what do you say kid? Want to roll the dice?"

I think about it a moment. I shrug and nod.

Szoji smiles as I suddenly notice a man standing some

distance behind him in a dark red hat and matching leather overcoat. Even though he's facing the sun, his face is silhouetted like it's behind him. He has a roll of paper in one hand and pen in the other. As he approaches, I can't bring my self to even look at him.

He stands behind Szoji who raises both hands to receive each item without looking back. He unfurls the scroll of paper filled with old looking writing on it.

"I can't read," I confess.

"The words tend to escape those who can, so it probably doesn't matter anyway," Szoji says, dipping the pen in one of the sheriff's bullet holes. The sheriff is too busy fighting for each breath and bulging his eyes at the red figure to wince in pain. Szoji holds the blood dipped pen at the bottom of the document. "If you don't read, you probably don't write, but it's really all about the action. Just make a scribble of some kind on this spot, and the sheriff gets to survive this particular encounter."

I take the pen and make a few loops that sort of resembles the kind of thing I think I've seen people write. I do my best.

Szoji takes the pen and lifts the paper that rolls back into a scroll and holds them above his shoulders again for the figure in the coat to take back. "That's a deal then," the man who killed my father says.

I look to the sheriff and his wounds are gone. He looks down to his own chest and fingers the bloody holes in his clothes to feel no wounds. I look back to the figure who took my signature and there's no sign of him, like he was never there. I look around, but he's nowhere.

The sheriff breathes easy for a moment but looks to me with regret. "Oh, Caleb…" he says, mournfully. "What have you done?"

"Helped a small gang of thieves, liars, and murderers for most of his short life so far," Szoji says. "But on this day? He saved a man's life." Szoji helps him to his feet. "But now that all those men have gone, he's in need of a better father figure. You fancy the task? Maybe guide him in a better direction?"

"To what end?" Sheriff Bridges asks. "He signed away his soul."

"You want another villain in your town? Or do you want to help this boy that gave you his eternity to let you live another day? There's some good in him. Maybe you could do something with *that*, and maybe my previous employer will be so impressed he nullifies that contract signed by an illiterate child. I've seen him let worse things slide."

The Sheriff looks at me and nods.

The Antechamber

Matthew Fryer

"You! Pit-fiend!"

"Master?"

"I have a task for you in the Antechamber."

"But… inflicting pain and physical violation is forbidden there."

"So?"

"I am a pit-fiend. Physical torture is my specialty. I was commended for my advances in the science of nerve-shaving, and I hold the record for both the loudest and longest screams ever extracted from a soul."

"That may be so, but any pit-fiend must learn the craft without having to rely on needles and bone nibblers."

"I understand, Master. Who is the victim?"

"Max Winters, a staunch atheist who has been in a coma for two months."

"What happened to him?"

"He was walking to a restaurant with his girlfriend and suffered a brain haemorrhage. He was about to ask for her hand in marriage. It was the anniversary of their first date."

"How wonderfully tragic."

"Stop masturbating."

"Sorry, master. I will go and make his purgatory a misery."

"But remember the Law."

"I will."

"Once the doctors terminate his life support, his nerves are all yours to shave."

***

"Hi Max," Anya said. "Sorry I've been a while; the traffic was a nightmare. Are they looking after you okay?"

The lack of any response seemed exaggerated by the pull and release of the ventilator and the steady rhythm of the ECG on the screen beside his bed.

Anya walked across, jeans hanging low from her scrawny hips. She took a tissue from the bedside unit and wiped a crust of saliva from Max's lips, careful not to nudge the endotracheal tube. She leaned over and kissed his cool, dry forehead.

"I thought we could try music therapy again," she said, sitting on the chair beside the bed. "I've put some old favourites of yours together on a playlist and thought we might as well give it another shot. Mr. Mirza said not to get my hopes up, but hey, we've got nothing to lose. They're…" She swallowed a lump. "They're going to do the tests this afternoon, after all."

Mr. Mirza's words rolled ominously through her head.

"If Max no longer has any brain stem functions, he will have permanently lost the potential for consciousness."

The bitter grief rose, taking Anya by surprise and pinching her throat shut. She closed her eyes and took a long, deep breath as a tear spilled down her cheek. "So, if you *are* gonna make a miracle recovery, big guy, then you need it to do it quick." She turned her head away. She'd never been comfortable crying in front of Max, and bizarrely that shame persisted even now.

Anya spun the engagement ring on her finger. It was nice to think they were engaged, even though Max had never been allowed the chance to ask.

The hospital staff had given her the ring, still nestled in its luxurious, silk-lined box, when they stripped Max for emergency surgery. A rose-cut diamond, it must've cost him a fortune; no wonder he'd been working so much overtime for the last few months. Only then had Anya realised why he'd booked seats at Picasso's for their anniversary. A pricey but charming seafood restaurant, it had been the location of their first date. She also discovered that Max had arranged a lush bouquet of oriental lilies – her absolute favourite - and a ludicrously expensive bottle of Cristal champagne.

Anya rubbed her eyes, wanting to continue with the one-sided conversation. It tempered Max's eternal silence and kept her vaguely sane, but she knew that if she spoke now, her voice would crack.

Instead, she turned back to Max and clasped his limp hand, wondering if he was dreaming somewhere in there. And if so, was he dreaming about her?

***

Max jumped as a face leered from the darkness. He squeaked, sitting bolt upright in bed as the image – a rictus of malevolent glee – mercifully vanished.

Just a bad dream.

He frowned as his sleep-clogged eyes focussed on a small room with spearmint walls and a stack of medical machinery at the bedside. There was nobody else here.

He looked down at his body to see it was draped in a thin hospital gown. He didn't seem to have any wounds and other than a general fatigue, nothing actually hurt. Good. He *hated* hospitals with a passion, and the sooner he was out of here the better.

The last thing he remembered was walking along the

street with Anya. It was their anniversary. She'd been telling him about a cheap holiday to Cancun she'd found online when a sudden thunderclap shocked deep in his skull. He couldn't remember anything after that. Perhaps something had fallen on his head?

He touched his scalp with tentative fingers but couldn't feel any dressings.

It was supposed to have been the perfect evening. Gourmet food, music, flowers and even a posh bottle of champagne. The ring had bled him dry too, but Anya was worth it. She was worth the whole world.

Max pushed back the blankets and rose from his bed. This wasn't right. The machinery at his bedside was dead: no lights, no bleeping. Nausea rinsed over his brain as he walked across to the window and scraped aside a crooked blind.

"Jesus *Christ!*"

Wrecked cars were strewn across the road beneath pyres of chemical smoke that coiled up into the sky. The surrounding buildings were ruins of scorched brickwork, skeletal girders poking up from great dunes of ash. Shredded corpses lay everywhere, smeared across the ground like trodden-on fruit.

What the hell had happened here? Some kind of terrorist attack? It had to be!

Max shook his head. He *knew* this was coming one day. Sure, the government was always banging on about the terror threat, but he bet they didn't expect something of this scale. His friends, and indeed Anya, would always humour him when he vented about how the world would come to a horrific end this way, but they never took him seriously.

His bowels flushed cold as he stared at the scattered victims. They weren't just damaged by whatever blast had ravaged the city; they'd been mutilated. Tortured. And most of them were still alive.

He saw a woman, a police officer, draped across the

bonnet of a car. A broken railing was stabbed between her legs, emerging from her shoulder, and her eye-sockets were just black wounds, but still she writhed gently in extremis. Nearby, another victim was crucified upon a buckled metal stanchion. Max couldn't even tell the victim's gender: much of its skin and muscle had been hacked away leaving a vaguely humanoid skeleton of crimson tissue that grinned up at the dead sky. It twitched and pulled weakly at its bonds.

And there were countless more.

"No!"

Max whirled. The voice was female, piercing the sinister quiet of the hospital.

"No! Please!"

That sounded like Anya!

Max staggered from the window, shoved open the door and burst out into the shadowed ward. He immediately froze, raising a hand to his mouth.

The walls were decorated with leaking bodies, strung up like grisly tinsel. Some were staff, still half-draped in ragged nursing uniforms and surgeon's greens; others were fellow patients, their gowns stained deep scarlet. Blood drenched the scene as though somebody had sprayed it through a hosepipe, splashed thickly up the walls and clotting in gelatinous puddles on the floor.

As with the carnage outside, they were alive. Countless febrile eyes turned towards Max, blinking through the gore-flecked air. As he stared, a young doctor - lashed to the ceiling above the nursing station by slippery loops of his own intestines - began to sob. An oily tract of offal slithered from his abdomen and smacked down onto the desk, scattering a pile of paperwork.

Max hunched and vomited, spattering his bare toes with bile.

"Somebody please, make it *stop!*"

"Anya!" Max lurched in the direction of her voice, through the ward exit and into a dim corridor. She shrieked:

a guttural sound of agony that came from a doorway to his left.

Without hesitation, Max burst inside.

It was an operating room. A naked woman – not Anya, thank fuck, but strikingly similar with short blonde hair and freckled shoulders – was strapped face-down to a gurney. A vulture-thin figure, dressed entirely in black and wearing a balaclava, hunched over a tray of surgical instruments. His victim's buttocks and back were slashed to wet ribbons, quivering in the shadows as she sobbed and begged.

The man turned towards Max, a feline hunch to his poise. He held a bone saw in each hand, and an enormous erection protruded from his trousers like a bloody spike.

Max should've attacked the sick bastard right then. He should've grabbed one of the scalpels off the tray and given this monster a taste of his own vile medicine, but the expected rage at this atrocity didn't come. Instead, there was just fear. It scrunched Max's guts tight and spun his head. He turned and ran.

The faceless figure screeched in delight and tore after him.

***

Anya stroked Max's arm, watching as always for any hint of recognition on his face. While ever she had hope, anything was possible.

She reached up and touched the crucifix around her neck: the legacy of a deeply Christian upbringing. Max didn't buy the philosophy, but as long as she stayed clear of fundamentalism – he was quite vocal about religious extremists – he didn't begrudge Anya settling her own theological conundrums. Live and let live, he always said.

She squeezed his hand, and the engagement ring rolled loose on her finger. If she lost any more weight it would slip off altogether.

"Anya?"

She looked up to see Samira standing in the doorway. She hadn't even heard the nurse come in; an oddly timid girl with a fragile whisper of a voice.

"Mr Mirza will be along to see you shortly."

"Okay. Thanks."

Samira offered a sympathetic half-smile, then slipped silently back into the murmur of the Intensive Care Unit.

Mr Mirza was reportedly the best consultant neurosurgeon in the region and had conducted Max's initial surgery and post-operative treatment personally. But he'd decided it was time to do the final and conclusive tests for brain stem death. This was the big one. If Max didn't react to a series of stimuli when they conducted the tests this afternoon, he was never going to wake up.

"Mr. Mirza's on his way," Anya said, taking her earbuds from their case and gently pressing them into Max's ears. Setting the volume low, she tapped at her phone and selected the playlist she'd made of his favourite indie and grunge-rock classics. "This might be your last chance."

She stared at his sleeping, restful face and prayed.

***

"Kneel, pit-fiend."

"Yes, Master."

"I assume you know why your torment of Max Winters was interrupted?"

"Sorry, Master. I was lost to the thrill of the hunt."

"You must learn restraint. Until he leaves the Antechamber, dead in both spirit and body, he is not ours to violate. The Law is very clear."

"Yes, Master."

"Why not have him bear witness to the defilement of his fiancée?"

"I attempted that. He didn't recognise my image of her."

"Creating the likeness of a soul's loved one from their memory is very difficult. But you will improve with practice."

"Yes, Master. I suppose I am to be punished."

"Not this time. I understand and approve of your enthusiasm. But disregard The Law again, and I will rape you myself."

"Yes, Master."

"Now go and finish what you started. And stop masturbating."

***

Max crept through the grim corridors of the hospital a hunted man.

He wasn't sure what had happened. That demonic freak had chased him down then tackled him to the floor, giggling like a kid on Christmas morning. But just as he'd felt that sharp, engorged cock jabbing at his buttocks, his assailant had vanished.

Perhaps he'd gone back to the victim strapped to the gurney. Christ alone knew what was happening to the poor girl now.

Max had at least managed to arm himself. He'd found a long, serrated knife protruding from the eye of a midwife he'd assumed was dead, but she'd shrieked as he yanked the blade free, and he'd thrown up over her head.

Shamed by his cowardice, he was trying to retrace his steps back to the operating room but soon found himself lost in a ghastly maze of corridors with only the girl's occasional screams to crank up the guilt another notch. He should've stayed and fought while he'd had the chance to save her, but he'd bolted like a terrified rabbit.

Clutching the weapon, Max tried to ignore the dying that littered the corridors. Their moans sounded almost pornographic en-masse, but at least they were helping to drown out the music.

Somewhere in the hospital, one of Max's favourite songs was playing.

It was an old Nirvana track that took him back to times when life was free and easy. It reminded him of raucous nights with his friends in the pub, of jumping around on the dance floor of sweaty rock nightclubs, of snuggling with Anya on the couch with a Chinese takeaway and a bottle of red wine. But there was no time for memories now.

He spat a gob of thick saliva, accidentally splattering the face of a toddler mewling in the corner beside the corpse of a semi-flayed woman in a maternity dress.

"We can SEE you!"

Max froze as the mocking, sing-song voice echoed along the low ceiling of the corridor. He spun around, but there was nobody there except the dying.

His pulse raced as he spotted the gun, clutched in the hand of a bearded man lying against the wall. Somebody had forced an entire oxygen cylinder into his mouth, his jaw fractured wide like a feeding python.

Max rushed forward and tore the weapon from the man's grip, who stirred and began to gag, his teeth squeaking and splintering on the impossibly thick metal that invaded his throat. How were these people still *alive?*

Clutching the gun, Max ran. He skidded around a corner, but the corridor ended with a single windowless door. He pulled it open and stopped dead.

"Shit…"

It was a small storeroom, stacked with cardboard boxes and dusty medical equipment, but nowhere to hide. Max was about to turn back when he heard footsteps. Light and insectile, they skittered towards him from around the corner.

Max dropped the knife and stepped into the shadows. Pulling the door shut, he backed against the far wall, holding the gun in both trembling hands.

He could hear music again, louder now without the

groaning of the mutilated masses.

"You've gotta be kidding me," he mumbled. Somebody was playing their song.

It was "There Is a Light That Never Goes Out" by The Smiths. Anya and himself had danced to it in the Boiler Room nightclub on her birthday earlier this year, and her delighted grin had lit up his world. It was the only truly dreamlike moment of his life so far, slightly drunk and deliriously happy as they whirled in the clouds of dry ice, belting out the lyrics as though the rest of the world had ceased to exist and it was just the two of them, lost in a dizzy vortex of happiness. It had been exactly during that moment that he decided to propose.

Don't go there.

Max cocked the gun and aimed at the door.

***

"Are you finished with Max Winters already?"

"No, Master. I thought I'd let him squirm for a while."

"I'm impressed. Anticipation is an effective means of torture."

"His fiancée is also attempting music therapy, and it is a song that clearly inspires unbearable emotion. I saw fit to prolong the agony."

"A good decision, pit-fiend. It amuses me when loved ones try to help with such maudlin devices. Nostalgia is crippling to the damned, and their good intentions only inflame the suffering."

"How long before they terminate his life support? The restrictions are very frustrating."

"Indeed, but you have exploited his personal fears of terrorism, hospitalisation, cowardice and physical torture very well so far. Perhaps you should involve his fiancée again."

"Yes, Master. This time, I will perfect the likeness. I just

wish they would switch him off and let me get started. I have hypothesised some new nerve-shaving techniques that I cannot wait to test on a fresh soul."

"Patience. His doctors will deliver him to us very soon. But pit-fiend?"

"I know, stop masturbating. Sorry, Master."

***

"Hello, Anya."

"Hi." She rose to her feet as Mr Mirza stepped into the room.

The consultant had prematurely silver hair and wore half-moon spectacles that made him look somewhat austere, but his eyes were caring. A young, pale woman hovered in his wake.

"This is Dr. Mitchell, a colleague of mine."

Anya nodded in acknowledgement, then carefully took the buds from Max's ears. As she switched off the music, she noticed it was playing their song. She smiled at the bittersweet memories, trying not to let them be ruined by the hurt that swung in her chest like an anchor. She remembered her last birthday. It had been the best day of her life, culminating in an ecstatic whirlwind of beer and music and dancing. She'd decided that very night that she wanted to spend the rest of her life with Max. She wished she'd told him that back then. While she had the chance.

"If you're ready," Mr. Mirza began. "Dr. Mitchell and myself will carry out the tests that I explained."

Anya took a deep breath, looking back at Max. It was time to discover if the ventilators, the drips and medication were wasting everyone's time.

"Do you have any questions?"

"No, thanks," she said. "I'd rather just get this over with."

"Of course."

Gripping the ring on her finger as if it were a protective

talisman, Anya left the two doctors to their work.

***

The handle turned.

"Come on. Come on you pencil-necked little…"

The door of the storeroom burst open, and a scrawny shadow loomed in the corridor. Max pulled the trigger, jumping as the report shocked off the walls and the figure in the doorway squealed and spun round. It toppled into the room in a half-pirouette and fell to the ground with a bony clatter.

"Yes!"

Max exhaled as the body spasmed, heels drumming the floor. He leaned forward to look.

"Anya!"

Short, awkward gasps jerked from her lips.

"No, no, no, Jesus fucking Christ NO!" Max pulled her against him as hot blood pumped against his naked skin, both of them immediately soaked from the wound his bullet had torn through her heart.

He moaned – a hideous, alien sound - as Anya's gaze rolled round to focus on his. They bloomed with recognition.

"Max . . ." she wheezed. "I found. . . you. . . at last…"

Max felt her muscles relax against him. Her eyes gleamed, love shining through the pain. Her ragged breathing slowed. Then stopped.

"Please," Max squeaked. She couldn't have survived armageddon only to die like this in his arms. And by his very hand. "Don't leave me…"

But she was already staring through him.

"Anya, no… I'm sorry…"

Max clutched her hand and noticed the engagement ring on her finger. She must have found it after the accident and assumed his intentions. She'd kept the ring and put it on. She would've said yes.

Of course she would. They were meant to be, there was never any doubt.

Burying his face into the softness of her hair, Max howled.

***

Anya sat in the relative's room beside the Intensive Care Unit, staring at a framed picture of a sunrise. Unlike the rest of the hospital, the walls were a soothing pale blue, decorated with blossom wall art.

"Please God, let him be okay," she whispered. Max didn't believe in God and applauded positive action, not praying for help from some divine nanny of the universe. But just as with the music therapy, she had nothing to lose. And maybe God was the only thing that could bring him back into her arms.

"Anya?"

Startled, she looked up. It was Mr. Mirza, and his expression told the complete story.

"He's dead, isn't he."

"I'm sorry. We've done all we could."

Anya looked down as her whole world fell away from beneath her. Tears fell on the faded denim of her jeans. "Could I see him?"

"Of course." Mr. Mirza turned, and she rose stiffly to her feet and followed him from the relative's room and through the unit in a shell-shocked trance.

She stepped back into the side-room that had pretty much become her second home, aware that it might be the very last time. As always, Max's chest rose and fell with the ventilator, the ECG displayed the rhythm of his heart, but now it was different. It was simply the mechanics of a body whose soul had departed.

She walked across to the bed. For the first time, she no longer had to force herself to hope, to stay strong, or keep believing despite the odds. The limbo was over. Max looked peaceful, his face relaxed with dreams and hints of an otherworld bliss.

"We won't discontinue Max's treatment until you're ready," Mr Mirza said. "Samira will help you with everything. If you'd like to…"

"Just give me two minutes."

Mr Mirza nodded respectfully and stepped from the room.

The grief rose, slamming through her. She sucked in breath and closed her eyes reverently. "Dear God," she croaked. "I know he didn't believe. But he was a good man, a wonderful man." She touched the crucifix around her neck. "Please look after him."

Perhaps they would be together again one day. She imagined Max waiting for her on the other side. Maybe they could be married after all. In heaven. It seemed a saccharine and frankly ridiculous notion, even to someone with faith, but it was all she had. Max would probably think it absurd.

No, he wouldn't. He would understand. Completely.

"I love you so much," she said to his unresponsive face, taking hold of his hand and squeezing tight.

***

Max gently lay Anya's corpse on the floor. His head spun, tears dripping into the blood that drenched them both.

You killed her.

He fumbled for the gun and pressed the barrel to his temple as more footsteps approached from outside the room. It was probably the bone-saw wielding psycho, and he had no intention of being another victim. With Anya gone, hopefully happy in the afterlife she so desperately wanted to believe in, he might as well join her. There was nothing left for him in this hellish nightmare of a world. Nothing but horror, crushing grief and guilt.

Gritting his teeth, Max pulled the trigger, but nothing happened. His hearing thickened, vision turning to static. The gun slipped from his grip but didn't hit the floor. He was suddenly floating, his brain fuzzing yellow with pain.

Max Winters...

The voice seemed to speak directly into his head and it frosted the blood in his arteries. If he was a man who believed in such things, he would have said it was the deepest, blackest voice of hell. It spoke again, engulfing him like an ice-cold fog.

Welcome to the Pit.

For the first and last time in his entire life, Max began to pray.

***

"Pit-fiend. You seem very pleased with yourself."

"I am, Master. Max Winters is finally where he belongs, despite imploring God to save him."

"They always do that. But if redemption was allowed at the actual point of death, Hell would be a very empty and barren dominion. Did you deliver him personally to the Pit?"

"Yes. To its darkest and most Godless depths."

"So, I assume his real torment is now underway."

"He lost his voice from screaming within the first thirty seconds. His nerves are ripe for shaving."

"Good. If only his fiancée knew. She believes in a God of mercy."

"It's funny that you should mention her."

"Oh?"

"I'd barely got started before he tried to offer us Anya's soul in exchange for his own."

Well, The Bible Says…

Kevin L. Kennel

"So, do you think Shirley Peterson will be found?" Simon Evans asked Darla as they left the church.

"I hope so."

"Who else is missing?"

"Janet Henderson and Ronald Spencer."

"Who?"

"The man who owns the hardware store. He wears his hair in a ponytail."

"Oh, yeah. Him. Okay." Simon wondered if Shirley, Janet, and Ronald had their reasons for leaving the church and didn't want to discuss them.

"If they don't find Shirley, I can play the church organ. It can't be that different from a piano."

"It shouldn't be." The piano would be a better salve for her pain than the time she spent at church, he thought.

They stopped at KFC for drive thru then went home. Darla set out the good China her parents gave them as a wedding gift that was white with a gold band etched into it. Just because they ordered fast food for lunch didn't mean they couldn't eat elegantly on Sunday. Simon rolled his eyes since he preferred eating from paper plates. Less clean up that way.

"Well, we weren't as late for church today as we usually are," Darla said. "Good thing the spare car keys were in my purse."

"Yep, good thing."

"But we weren't as late as you hoped we would be."

"What are you talking about?" Simon asked as he reached for the gravy.

"Every week you find a reason for us to be late," Darla said and bit her lip.

"That's not true…" Simon began.

"A couple of weeks ago, you couldn't find your glasses when they were in the case all along. Or last Sunday when the car was low on gas, so we filled up after we left ten minutes later than usual since the alarm didn't go off. Please honey, if you are reluctant to go to church, tell me why."

"Sorry, I didn't know it bothered you so much. I promise we'll be on time next week. Okay?" Simon said and hoped she believed him.

"Okay." Darla forked a small bit of mashed potatoes into her mouth and chewed deliberately. "Does the reason you don't want to go to church have anything to do with my brothers?"

"I don't think you gave yourself enough time to grieve Donald. And I want you to be sure that church is the right decision to help you get over losing him."

"Why wouldn't it be the right decision? It gives me peace."

"But do you think Donald deserves to be dead?" Simon asked, before patting his lips with a napkin.

Darla didn't look at him. "You know how my brother chose to live," she said as she got up from the table to clear the food containers.

Simon watched in silence as she put them into the trash one at a time, then put the glasses and silverware in the dishwasher. She closed the door as if doing so would break the dishes that were in there.

"People don't choose to be gay, Darla. They are either born that way or not."

"I wish you'd understand how going to church helps Brandon and I cope with losing him. But since you'll do anything to get out of doing that, tell me how you cope with it."

"Well, I lose myself in my writing. Or sometimes I take a walk to clear my head. Even though I prefer to be alone downstairs so I can write, I could make an exception, and we can take a walk later if you'd like."

"No, I'm good. Go write."

"All right. I'll come back up later."

"Hold on, I have one question, though."

"What is it?"

"You aren't drinking and smoking again, are you?"

Simon crossed his arms over his chest and tried not to look away. "What? No, of course not."

Darla raised her eyebrows and fondled her cross necklace. "Good to know. I'll call you when dinner's ready."

"Sounds good," he said, then headed downstairs feeling some guilt about lying to her.

He waited until Darla began her warm-up exercises on the piano before opening the third drawer on the file cabinet. She'd be at the keyboard for at least an hour, so he could take out the Pall Mall reds and a lighter, then indulge. Sliding the basement door open as quietly as possible, he stepped outside and felt grateful there weren't any windows on the wall above to let the sight or smell of intoxicating smoke into the house.

"Hello Simon," a deep but mischievous voice said.

"Who's there?" Simon asked, feeling ridiculous for talking aloud.

"I am."

Simon turned around, and a man stood on the lawn about eighteen feet away from him, smelling Darla's rose bushes. He wore a black Italian double-breasted pinstripe suit with matching slacks and a red bow tie, black exotic Croco print shoes adorned his feet and his face was angular, with a chin that looked like a perfect rectangle. A small cigar sat clenched between his teeth. Removing the cigar, the man tapped ash into the rose bushes and gave Simon a smile full of cold sunshine. His slick backed black hair, tied into a ponytail, completed the look.

"Taking a break from the writing?" the man asked, opening a book made of cracked black leather that looked like something he stole from a museum. Simon caught a musty smell from it.

"I'm sorry, do I know you?" Simon asked.

Extinguishing his cigar, the man approached Simon. "Your wife's name is Darla, and she has two brothers. One is named Donald, who died a little over six months ago from AIDS, and the other one is Brandon. Because of Donald's death, Darla and Brandon have 'found Jesus, Hallelujah!' But you feel church is a waste of time even though Darla insisted you go too. So, you hide in the basement where you write, drink, and smoke to deal with it all." His smile grew more expansive. "Is that pretty much it?"

"How long have you spied on us?" Simon asked, as his shoulders tightened, and his mouth went dry.

"I haven't. In fact, I'm here to help you. But first, let me convince you I'm not lying." The man pointed at the pack of Pall Malls. "Can I bum a smoke from you?"

Simon clutched the pack closer, as though the man would grab them. "I only have one left."

"Really? Check again."

Simon did and saw the pack was full, despite the one dangling from his lips even now. "How the hell did you do that?" he asked.

"Some people do loaves and fishes. I do cigarettes. Credit where credit is due. We both do wine."

"What are you talking about? Who are you?"

"My name is Robert Bealzer and I think there's no reason

you should sneak your alcohol and cigarettes."

"How do you know I sneak them?" Simon said, handing Robert a cigarette.

"You'll find out," Robert said and lit up.

"I'll find out?" Simon asked, shaking his head. "Whoever you are, you sure as hell aren't a good salesperson."

"Interesting choice of words. But I'm not a salesperson. I'm someone who helps people like you set themselves free from what binds them. And since Brandon and Darla have you bound into going to church, why not let me help you by taking one of them away? Or I could take you."

"What do you mean 'take one of us away'? I don't want anyone to be kidnapped."

"Well, do you have a better plan? Besides, I'll let you decide who goes with me. How does that sound? I'll give you a few minutes to think about it and how much you enjoy drinking."

Simon looked at Robert like he told him a dirty joke, then remembered the night that forced him to get sober. The bottle of Jack and how hard he hit Darla. Her mouth bleeding when she bit her tongue from the shock. How she slammed the bathroom door, and he passed out on the couch. The next morning when he stumbled into the kitchen while his head throbbed, and his mouth tasted like a muddy tire. The bruise on Darla's left cheek and how she looked like she forgot who he was. He glanced at her, then dumped the beer he kept in the fridge and bottles of liquor that were in a cupboard down the sink.

"Good start, but not enough," she said and handed him a slip of paper with the number to Alcoholics Anonymous on it. He nodded and went to his first meeting that night, knowing no amount of flowers or chocolate could undo this damage. But with each meeting and day of sobriety, she slowly forgave him.

He stood in the middle of the senior center meeting room

six months after that horrid night and held his dark blue chip as the other recovering alcoholics applauded. "This is for my wife. I thank her for this chance to set things right and recover from my addiction." He sat down and when he returned home, Darla congratulated him with a candlelit dinner.

They made love that night and when she fell asleep in his arms, Simon knew he didn't need AA anymore. *I will never drink again, Darla. Not for the harm it caused,* he thought. But he'd pretend to go for a while to maintain the illusion and keep her happy until he had a legitimate reason to stop going. Something he could show her that wasn't based on emotion.

He went to his last meeting a week later and when the usual meeting night and time came around the next week; he drove to a cinema in the next town, twenty minutes away, to watch a horror film. This went on for a few weeks as he either went to a library to write on his phone, browse the Internet, or read. The reason to stop going happened the next week.

"Don't you have your meeting tonight?" Darla asked.

"Nope, they're canceled for now," Simon said and showed her his phone. On it, a headline read the senior center had closed indefinitely for a termite problem. "My sponsor called this afternoon and said they don't have a place for any future meetings. Do you want me to find a different AA group?"

"I want to say 'yes' but you haven't drunk for seven months now and as long as you stay that way, I don't see why you have to."

And that was it. He maintained his sobriety until he bought a half pint of Jim Beam when Donald died hoping it was something he did once then forgot about it. When Brandon convinced Darla they should attend church to help them handle their grief, the half pints became fifths.

Shuddering as the memories subsided, Simon noticed

Robert looked at him like he wet his pants.

"Nice to see you back," Robert said, rubbing his hands in anticipation. "Do we have a deal? Who am I taking?"

"Before I decide, don't I deserve to know what happens to whichever of us goes?"

"Usually, yes, but your fate might differ from Darla's or Brandon's. So, I'll tell you what happens when you choose who goes."

"Can I have some time to think about it?" Simon asked, even though he almost told Robert to take Brandon. Then he could convince Darla to stop attending church. But he wasn't sure how she would handle that change.

"Sure, I'll give you a week to decide."

"What happens if I don't have an answer in a week?"

"Then I'll choose for you," Robert said, holding the book out to Simon. "But I have a feeling you've already decided. So, before I go, please sign my book?"

"What should I write?" Simon asked, taking the book in his hands. It felt warped and made of something that looked like leather but felt squishy and rotted.

"Just your name is fine," Robert said, tossing his cigarette butt aside. "It's how I keep track of whom I have impending deals with."

"Is that what we did?" Simon asked, signing his name. "Made a deal?"

"Well, it isn't official, but yes, we did."

"Then what do you get out of this?"

"Don't worry about it. You'll find out," Robert said and walked away.

Simon watched him leave, then stared at his cigarette pack. Shaking his head, he wondered who Robert really was, since if he could produce cigarettes out of thin air, what would he do to help Simon out of going to church? He didn't want anyone hurt, but if Brandon disappeared, he could live a quiet life with Darla at his side. Simon went inside, hid the cigarettes back in the file cabinet, popped a couple of cinnamon Tic-Tacs in his mouth, then went upstairs to the living room, where Darla napped on the couch.

"I doubt I could ever live without you," he whispered, then put a blanket over her and went back down to his office.

***

Next morning, Simon approached the corner to turn left and saw Brandon walking towards him. When Brandon noticed Simon saw him, he ran to Simon's car. Simon rolled his eyes and opened the passenger side door.

"Thanks for stopping. Can you give me a ride?"

"Why do you need a ride?"

"My car broke down about a mile from your place. Can you drop me off at Marshall's auto repair, since they're across the road from your work?"

"I suppose," Simon said and wondered if Robert Bealzer had something to do with this.

"Thanks. Isn't it great how God works things out? If my car hadn't broken down and you didn't come along, we wouldn't have a chance to talk."

"Right, talk. Well, what's on your mind?" Simon said as they headed for town.

"Just wondered how you and Darla are doing."

"Things are good. If there was any problem, you'd be the first to know."

"Yeah, I guess you're right. But with Darla trying to get over Donald's death, I wanted to make sure she's okay."

"She's fine." Simon paused. "We all miss him, in our own way."

"Yes, but he was our brother. And Darla's sensitive. Just knowing Donald is in Hell because of his sin…"

"You of all people should hope God doesn't kill homosexuals for being who they are."

Brandon sputtered. "I don't know what you're talking about."

"Of course not," Simon replied. They rode is silence until he pulled into Marshall's parking lot.

"Look," began Brandon.

"Just get out," Simon said, turning the other way to avoid eye contact. "I don't want to be late for work."

Brandon got out, and the door wasn't fully closed before Simon left and then pulled into *The Novel Niche,* where he worked as the assistant manager. Turning the car off, he wondered if he still had a pint bottle of Jim Beam in the glove compartment to settle his nerves. Since when did he think Brandon was gay? Even though Brandon didn't date anyone he and Darla knew of, they never discussed it. Getting out of the car, Simon hoped the monotony of shelving and pricing books and helping customers would relax his mind.

"Good morning," Robert said as he entered the store.

"How can I help you?" Simon asked.

Simon's boss, a woman in her middle fifties named Tracy, came out of the storeroom with a box and greeted him. "After you help that customer, Simon, could you please help me set up the display for our back-to-school sale?"

"Sure. Sir, I believe the book you're looking for is over here. Follow me." Robert followed Simon and when they got to the religious section, Simon looked to make sure Tracy couldn't hear them. "What do you want?"

"To see how you're doing. Especially after your conversation with Brandon."

"How do you know about that?"

Robert winked and ignored the question. "Have you decided whom I should take?"

"Why can't you take my boss?"

"Because there wouldn't be any gain or loss to you since you get along with her. But trust me, I don't know what choice you'll make. So, I'll go since you need more time to think about it. Talk soon." Robert said and left the store.

On the way home, Simon wondered how Robert knew about his incident with Brandon. How did he know so much about Brandon, Darla, and him in the first place? Should he tell Darla about it? If so, how could he do it without sounding crazy? He decided to wait until the situation presented itself. He went inside and Darla sat at her piano, playing Mozart's twenty-first piano concerto.

"Hi honey. How was your day?" she asked when he walked in.

"It was fine. Have you spoken to Brandon?"

"He called a while ago. Said his car broke down and you gave him a ride to Marshall's."

Simon went to the kitchen for a Perrier, wished it was a beer, and set it on a table by the recliner. "Yep, I did. Why did it breakdown?"

"The mechanic said his battery died and he can pick it up tomorrow. What should we do (format issue)

for dinner tonight?"

"We can have veggie burgers and Sun Chips as far as I'm concerned. What did you have in mind?"

"I want to go out since I've been in this house all day and am in the mood for a steak with garlic mashed potatoes."

"Sounds delicious. Are we celebrating something?"

"Sort of. I finally overcame that block regarding what direction I want to take the jingle for Colgate toothpaste."

"Wonderful news, babe. You've been working on that one for almost a month, haven't you?"

"It seems like it. Let's go, I'm starving."

"Of course, my lady," Simon said.

On the way into town, Simon tapped his fingers on the steering wheel like they were listening to one of his favorite songs, but the radio wasn't on. Darla felt there was something Simon wasn't telling her, but she let it go for now so they could have an enjoyable meal out together. The timing was right since the Good Time Family Steakhouse always had buy one meal and get another meal half off on Monday nights.

"Here we are," Simon said as they pulled into the parking lot.

***

As they walked in, Simon saw Robert at the bar. He sipped a Jack Daniels and locked eyes with Simon in the mirror behind the bar, raising the glass in a toast. Simon turned to see if Darla noticed, but she stared into the restaurant.

They sat down, and the hostess handed them their menus. Simon buried his face in his, although he knew what he wanted.

"Oh honey, look, Brandon is here too," Darla said, placing her hand on his. "Should we join him?"

Before Simon could respond, a hand pulled back a chair from the table and Robert sat down at the table between them, placing his drink in front of Simon.

"Hello Simon. Good evening, Mrs. Evans."

"Excuse me?" Darla asked, her tone somewhere between polite and indignant. "Do I know you?"

"My name is Robert Bealzer. Simon mentioned you compose advertising jingles."

Darla's confusion broke to sudden relief and interest. "Oh, yes. Oh, you know Simon?"

"Simon and I spoke when I stopped at the bookstore today to see if the new James Patterson novel was in. I told him what I did, and he mentioned you write jingles. Anyway, I represent Folgers coffee and we're looking for someone to write a new jingle for us." He handed Darla a business card. "If you're interested, e-mail me some of your work in an mp3 file and we can work something out."

"All right, but what are you doing here? Shouldn't you be in a big city office building or something?"

"Yes, I should, since we're based out of Grand Rapids. But I'm here visiting my sister for a few days and needed something to read."

"Okay," Darla said, putting the business card in her purse. "Is it all right if I send them within a week?"

"That would be great," Robert said and sipped his drink.

"Hey guys, who's this?"

"Hello Brandon. Why don't you sit with us?" Darla said and scooted over.

"Sure," Brandon said and sat next to Darla, then looked at Robert. "Who are you?"

"Robert Bealzer," he said and shook Brandon's hand. "Are you here alone? Surely there's some lovely lady whom you are here with so she can join us. I don't want Darla to be the only beautiful woman I have the pleasure of dining with tonight."

"Is it a big deal if he's single?" Darla asked while she blushed.

"Not at all. How is Glen doing anyway, Brandon? Oh, never mind, here he comes now."

Brandon looked at his phone when the server came to the table.

"Hello everyone, my name is Glen and I'll be you server. Can I start you off with a beverage? Or are you all set to order your meals?"

"Yes," Robert said. "Tell you what, why don't you bring us the prime rib special with the garlic mashed potatoes and two fresh loaves of bread? Also, put this all on one check, okay? This is my treat."

"Certainly sir, I will get that in for you right away. What would you like to drink?"

"Whiskey sour for me," Robert said. "What about you Simon? Fancy a bourbon?"

"He quit drinking," Darla said.

"Really? Well, how about you, Brandon?"

"I can see you need a few minutes," Glen said and looked

at Brandon. "Tell you what, I will get your whiskey sour and bring back three ice waters, okay?"

"That would be fine, thank you," Robert said before Glen walked away. He then looked at Simon, who stared at the white tablecloth. "So, you flat out quit drinking, Simon? Not even a beer once or twice a week?"

Simon glanced at Darla, hoping she wouldn't catch his lie. "Nope. Been sober for over six months now."

"Then why did I see you leave Len's party store last week with a brown paper bag when I went to Jimmy John's?" Brandon asked. "They are right next to each other."

"I hope whatever you had was non-alcoholic," Darla said, and frowned.

"I'll tell you what was in the bag if Brandon tells us who Glen is," Simon said.

"What difference does that make?" Darla asked but watched Brandon sulk when Glen gave them their drinks. He mumbled something when Glen walked away.

"What did you say?" Darla asked.

"Glen is my boyfriend."

"What do you mean, he's your boyfriend?"

"You know exactly what it means, Darla."

"Now that you admit you're gay, tell her what you said about Donald," Simon said.

"Admit you're drinking again, and I will."

"Why don't you both tell me what you don't want me to know?" Darla asked. "How much more harm can it cause?"

"A lot more than you think," Robert said and sipped his cocktail.

"What are you talking about?" Darla asked as the food arrived and Glen passed out their meals.

"Would any of you like some more to drink?" Glen asked.

But everyone remained silent. Darla sliced into her prime rib and ate while Brandon stared at his plate, and Simon stirred gravy into his mashed potatoes.

"It looks like we're good for now," Robert said.

"Well, enjoy," Glen said and gave Brandon a worried smile.

"By the way, Darla," Robert said. "Simon and I made a deal."

"We did?" Simon asked.

"Sure, when you signed my book."

"But I thought I had a week to decide."

"You still do," Robert said. "I just want to get things out in the open."

"Hold on," Darla said. "What kind of deal?"

"A deal where Simon doesn't have to live a lie anymore and you must come with me."

"Go with you where?" Darla asked. "To Grand Rapids?"

"I didn't tell you to take her," Simon gasped.

"I know. But I've altered the deal."

"What's going on here?" Brandon asked.

"Enough of this. Let me show you who I really am," Robert snarled, then snapped his fingers. The hustle and bustle of the restaurant stopped. Servers with trays full of entrees paused in mid stride. A man's fork stopped inches from his mouth. A teenager's thumbs sat frozen over her phone while her brother stopped squirming in his seat. Even the televisions on the walls froze on the images of the sports teams they showed.

Darla, Simon, and Brandon looked at Robert, who smiled at them with an evil, playful glee revealing sharp black teeth. Coarse hair hung from his inverted triangular ears and two horns poked out from his head.

"This isn't even my full transformation," he said in a voice that sounded like he gargled with acid before speaking. "I can keep going."

"Please don't," Simon said, while Darla and Brandon looked around with disgusted amazement, then shook their heads.

"Very well," Robert said before his face contorted back

into human form. "Since I have everyone's full attention, call me by my real name. Which is Beelzebub."

"Wait. What? No way," Simon said. "You're the Devil?"

"That's right."

"And my idiot husband made a deal with you?" Darla asked.

"But I didn't know he was the devil," Simon pleaded.

"Really? You usually go around making deals with random strangers?"

"Come on Darla, you know me better than that."

"I used to."

Simon winced, then looked at Robert. "Why did you alter the deal? I thought I chose who you took."

"You expected the devil to be fair?" Brandon asked.

"I altered the deal because your bickering made me realize neither of you differ from the other people I took," Robert said and snapped his fingers. The movements, people, and noise resumed. "So, I figured why not take Darla so you can live as you want?"

"Did he tell you he wanted that?" Darla asked.

"Yes, but I have also watched him as well as the other people from your church. I've taken a few of them, too."

"So, you're responsible for the disappearances?" Brandon asked. "Why?"

"Because God and I made a deal since I'm sick of hell and tired of people not taking responsibility for their actions. And since God is tired of the atrocities done in His name, He wants me to send the hypocrites away. After I send enough away, then I'm allowed back into Heaven. Let me show you something else." He waved his hand, pointed at the closest television, and they saw the missing Shirley Peterson. The image expanded and showed Janet Henderson and Ronald Spencer. Cataracts covered their eyes while they wandered a place that looked like the last few moments of dusk under a murky, violent sky. Lucifer let Simon, Darla, and Brandon watch for a few minutes and then the baseball game resumed.

“Where are they?” Darla asked.

“In the Valley of the Blind. It’s a place in hell made for people who deny their secrets.”

“What secrets did they have?”

“Shirley and Janet cheated on their husbands and Ronald was involved with child pornography. And they denied their secrets by tithing heavily, thinking it would buy forgiveness. But Pastor Dennings lined his pockets with their money.”

“This is a lot to take.” Brandon said. “Besides, what makes you think you can go back to heaven like it was a family reunion?”

“It’s part of the deal. If I do my part, God will do His.”

“What does Simon have to do with this?” Darla asked. “Why are you taking me?”

Simon reached for her hand, but she sat back and put them on her lap. “I made the deal because I only attend church to make you happy,” he said. “It’s fine if you want to go, but I drink to calm my feelings about you going since I feel it’s a betrayal of who you are. Your parents didn’t raise you and your brothers to blindly accept what Christianity teaches.”

Darla looked at him as though he shot a dog, and her voice teetered on being angry enough to cause a scene. “So, you’re saying it’s my fault you made the deal?”

“What? No, I…”

“Was being a selfish, stupid bastard?” Darla said as her eyes narrowed and her lip trembled. “Damn you, Simon, all you had to do was tell me you didn’t want to go. I would have driven myself or had Brandon take me. Why don’t you do the decent thing and let Beelzebub take you?”

“Is that what you really want?” Simon asked.

“Yes. Unless you can tell me why I shouldn’t allow you to be taken,” Darla asked.

“Because I’m your husband and want you to forgive me.”

“I don’t know if I can.”

"That settles it then," Beelzebub said. His hands elongated into talons. The lights flickered and people stopped what they were doing. The floor shifted and flame colored light rose with the stench of sulfur. Thunder boomed and screams rose while Simon looked at Darla for an intervention.

She rolled her eyes and reached for Beelzebub.

"Wait a minute," she said. "How soon do you need him?"

Beelzebub waved his talons and everything returned to normal. "The sooner the better. Why do you ask?"

"Can you allow him and I a few last days together?"

"I had a feeling you'd do this. Fine, but if you change his (your? Confusing.) mind, I will take you. Do you understand? I won't tolerate any arguments or anything that prevents me from taking someone."

"Understood," she said, then extended her hand and winked.

Beelzebub raised an eyebrow, then raised her hand to his lips and kissed it. "See you soon," he said, then put one hundred dollars on the table before leaving.

"I can't believe you just made a deal with the Devil," Brandon said.

"Neither can I," Simon said. "Especially since he didn't have you sign his book to certify it."

"Perhaps he'll make me sign it later or your signature was all he needed. But if that's what it takes to save your stupid ass, honey, we'll deal with it later. Let's go."

"Hang on," Brandon said. "I have to do something." He went to the table where Glen took an order for a young couple and tapped him on the shoulder. Glen turned around and Brandon kissed him the way a newly married couple kiss on the night when one of them returns from being away for a long time. When they finished, Brandon, Darla, and Simon left while Glen looked at the customers with a face as flushed as a diabetic person coming out of a low blood sugar spell, then went back to the kitchen.

***

When they got into the car, it surprised Simon that Darla didn't slam the door. She sat in the passenger seat and stared straight ahead like a mannequin. Simon didn't know if he should be frightened or relieved, since he only saw her like this once before. During the first few hours after Donald died.

He knew he could try to make small talk, but what could he say to take their minds off what he did? Home felt like it was another state away and it seemed traffic moved slower than if they drove backward in a snowstorm. He almost ran a stoplight when she spoke and jolted him out of his shame. Simon sighed when they pulled into the driveway and assumed she would either watch television or play some Chopin on the piano to settle her mind. But when they went inside and settled in for the night, Darla didn't do either of those things.

"I'm going to take a long, hot bath," she said. "Where will you be?"

"Guess I'll go down to my office and figure out a way to get us out of this. I might as well sleep down there too. You deserve the bed to yourself tonight anyway, for as badly as I fucked up."

"As badly as you fucked up?" Darla said. "This is severely worse than the night you hit me, since one of us will go to hell in a few days. Do you really understand how horrible a situation you put us in?"

"Of course, I do," he said, wanting to add how stupid it was to do so, but her furrowed eyebrows, frowned lips, and narrowed eyes told him he didn't have to.

"Good," she said and nodded. "Because I asked for a few days together so we can figure a way out of this and strengthen our marriage. I mean, let's face it. This whole church thing hasn't been good for us in that regard. So, if we work something out, then we'll stop going."

"Really?" Simon asked. "You mean it?" He wanted to kiss her, but felt she wasn't ready for one yet. Especially with what he was about to say, but he had to try. "You know, we could tell Beelzebub to take Brandon. That seems the quickest way out of this."

Simon expected her to go off on him worse than before, but she looked at him like he suggested they do a pub crawl.

"I had a feeling you were going to say that," she said. "But he's the only brother I have, so let's think of a better plan, okay?"

"Sure," he said, opening the basement door. He went downstairs, then walked to the file cabinet where the bourbon and cigarettes sat like old friends.

"I doubt she'll open that door tonight," he said, then lit a cigarette and raised the bottle. "Here's to you, baby. The one thing I lived for that I've screwed over the most." He took a drink, set the bottle down, turned the laptop on, and put the cigarette in an ashtray. Darla walked across the floor above him, and it sounded like she stopped in the kitchen. He looked at a shelf in the corner where a few bottles of wine sat that they neglected to dump out since Donald gave them the wine for Christmas. The door opened, so he extinguished the cigarette and sprayed Lysol. The bourbon went back into the file cabinet along with the ashtray and he wondered why he didn't think she would be upset enough to have a few drinks as well.

She came down the stairs, went to the shelf, selected a bottle of Merlot, and walked to his desk. "What brand do you have?" she asked.

"What are you talking about?"

"Cigarettes, Simon. Where are they? You don't spray this much Lysol even after you fill yourself at the Mexican buffet, and I can vaguely smell the smoke. May I have one, please?"

Simon handed her the pack, and she took three. "Between

the hot bath, this bottle of wine and smokes, I should sleep very well tonight." She gave the pack back to him and walked back up the stairs.

"If you want more, don't be afraid to come get some," he said.

"This will be fine," she said, then shut the door. Simon took the bourbon out again and drank half of it. The alcohol led him to that place where things didn't seem so bad, and he realized Darla was the only reason he was still alive. Despite how terrible the night went, he felt she deserved a kiss goodnight for saving his ass.

When he reached their bedroom, he saw her asleep in her clothes with the empty wine bottle on the floor by the bed. She snored softly, which he found cute, but wouldn't tell her about since she believed she snored as much as she believed she farted. He wanted to kiss her, but had the coordination of a marionette, and feared he'd fall on top of her.

Darla turned over, so he lay down next to her to have better access to her lips. But sleep overtook him, and he hoped things would be better when they woke up.

"What the hell are you doing here?" Darla said when she opened her eyes the next morning. "Did you drink yourself to sleep?"

Simon didn't remember getting into bed. Especially since his mouth was dry, and he put a pillow over his eyes to block the sunlight. "Yes, I did. But I came up to kiss you goodnight until the booze overtook me, so I passed out next to you."

"How romantic," Darla scoffed, then went to the kitchen to make coffee. Simon rubbed his head and groaned, wishing the day didn't start like this. He followed her and took the bottle of Tylenol out of the cupboard above the microwave.

"Are you still mad?" He asked.

"What difference does it make? Tell me your inebriated

wisdom led to an idea."

"It actually did," Simon said, then swallowed three Tylenol.

"What is it?" Darla asked, pouring herself some coffee.

"Why don't we call Pastor Dennings? We can explain what's going on and see if he has any advice."

"I guess it's worth a shot," Darla said, handing Simon her phone. "Use mine, since you probably don't have the church's number saved."

"You know me too well," Simon said and called the church. "I also have an idea what to say, so we don't sound too crazy."

"Hello?"

"Pastor Dennings? Hi. This is Simon Evans."

"Hello Simon. What can I do for you?"

"Well, my wife and I know who's responsible for the disappearances at the church."

"Really? That's wonderful news. Who is it?"

"It would be better if we tell you in person. Are you at the church now?"

"Yes, I am. Would you both rather meet me at the police station, or should I have an officer here to take a statement?"

"It's a little more complicated than that. Can we meet at the church first?"

"Sure, I'll wait for you in my office."

"We'll be right there." Simon ended the call before they dressed and sped to the church with no regard to eating breakfast or personal hygiene.

When they arrived, Pastor Dennings met them in the sanctuary. "This way," he said and lead them to his office. "So, what's going on?" he asked as they sat. "You said you know who's responsible for the disappearances?"

"That's right," Simon said.

"Who is it?" Pastor Dennings smiled at them, but Simon bit his nails and Darla stared at the wall like they were in the principal's office. "It isn't either of you, is it?"

"No, but it's hard to explain."

"What do you mean?"

"It's not a person we're dealing with," Darla said.

"All right, so is it a group of individuals? Some sort of kidnapping ring or something like that?"

"No, it's an entity," Simon answered.

"What do you mean, an entity? I know about invisible forces because of my faith, but what makes you say that?"

"Do you have faith that the devil exists?"

Pastor Dennings leaned back in his chair and put his folded hands on his stomach. "Well Darla, you can't have God without the devil. Why do you ask if I believe in him?"

"Because he's responsible for the disappearances."

"Is this a joke?" Pastor Dennings asked. "If so, you both must have better things to do than waste my time."

"But we're telling the truth," Simon said.

"All right, let's say he is. I assume the people he took went to hell. Then again, why would he take people in the first place?"

"Because God and him made a deal," Darla said.

Pastor Dennings removed his glasses, rubbed his eyes, and sighed. "Listen to me. I have seen God in the relieved faces of struggling families when we give them food. I heard God in a mother's soothing voice to her child when they cry. And I felt God in the stillness when I pray and meditate. Now for you both to come in here and tell me that the same God who loves us all made a deal with Satan makes me believe you're the ones responsible for the disappearances." Let's pray before I call the police to arrest you two."

"Will you tell them about your stealing from the collection plate?" Beelzebub asked as he entered, wearing his Robert Bealzer disguise.

"Who are you to accuse me of anything?" Pastor Dennings asked while Simon and Darla went rigid in their chairs like children being caught drawing obscene pictures of their teacher.

"That doesn't matter, since Simon and Darla are telling the truth. I'm the one responsible for the disappearances."

"Sure," Pastor Dennings said, about to call 911. "And I'm Jonah. Get out. Now. All three of you."

"I knew he wouldn't believe you two," Beelzebub said, as he looked at Simon and Darla. "So, I'll prove it to him." After snapping his fingers, the fluorescent lights burned bright, enveloping them in a red-hot glow. Pastor Dennings gasped as heat prickled through him and an intense wind blew papers around and books fell from the shelf. Darla and Simon shielded their faces from the flying debris until the lights brightened so much they had to close their eyes. The bulbs shattered, and the floor opened while claws and talons grabbed Pastor Dennings' legs. His screams and prayers didn't last long when the nightmare appendages dragged him to hell. Beelzebub shook his head while grinding the broken glass into the floor, then looked at Simon and Darla.

"You can both look now. It's all over."

"Looks like a tornado came through here," Darla said.

"Yeah," Beelzebub said. "I rarely cause this much chaos, since it betrays the gentlemanly qualities I strive for. But it is fun once in a while. Now, can either of you explain why you came here?"

"For spiritual guidance," Simon said.

"Oh really? Spiritual guidance in what?"

Simon's shoulders tensed and he stared at the floor while he spoke. "Um, well, it's about what we're facing."

"You were going to tell him about what you're facing regarding our deal, weren't you?"

"Well, yes. But it doesn't mean we planned to cheat you."

"I suspect not, since no human would dare cheat me because of my reputation. Speaking of our deal, am I taking Brandon or one of you two?"

"Brandon," Darla blurted. Beelzebub raised an eyebrow, and Simon looked at Darla like he didn't hear her right.

"Are you sure?" Simon asked. "I thought it was my decision."

Beelzebub raised a finger and thought about it. "It is, but I'll make an exception since it's an interesting idea. And I love to watch you humans play out your dramas to get what you want. Fine, talk to him. I'll see the three of you later today," he said and left.

"So, how are we going to convince Brandon to go?" Simon asked on the way home.

"I don't know," Darla said, then called Brandon. "Hello, Brandon. How you doing?" she asked. "Good. Have you heard from Glen about last night? You have? Uh huh. Oh, good. We went to see Pastor Dennings about what Simon did and will be there soon. Bye." She ended the call and put the phone in her purse. "Brandon's at our place waiting for us."

"I hope we can think of something."

"If we don't, everything you and I have will vanish," Darla said when they pulled in and saw Brandon standing at their door.

"Well Brandon, what a pleasant surprise," Simon said when they got out of the car.

"Whatever. How'd it go with Pastor Dennings?"

"Not the way he hoped," Darla said, and they went inside. "Beelzebub took him too."

"I'd ask how many more people have to suffer because of your mistake, Simon," Brandon said. "But what you did was a good thing."

"What?" Darla asked, almost dropping her coffee cup out of shock. A few drops splashed on the floor, and she wiped them up with a paper towel. "How so?"

"Glen and I made up, and I told him I'm no longer afraid of ending up like Donald, which held me back from wanting to be with him."

"What do you mean by that?"

Brandon smiled and drummed his fingers against his legs. "I wanted to deny being gay because I was afraid of getting sick like he did."

"But people get sick regardless of who they are," Simon said. "It wasn't Donald's choice to die the way he did."

"But it wasn't only that. It was also the discrimination, threats and hatred he faced despite our defending him."

"How long have you felt that way?" Darla asked.

"I don't know. Seems like it was always there, and I didn't know how long I could keep it a secret. Funny how it took the devil to set me free."

"Consider it a favor," Beelzebub said as he stepped into the kitchen. "I'd congratulate you, but this wasn't as juicy a drama as I hoped. But that's just as well, since I'm tired of these reindeer games. So, who am I taking?"

"Take Simon," Brandon said. "He may have helped set me free, but I've always sensed that there was a part of him that despised me."

"What makes you say that?" Darla asked.

"Yeah," Simon said. "How do we know you didn't really despise yourself since you tried to hide and deny your homosexuality?"

Brandon hunched his shoulders and stared at the floor.

"You're right. I despised myself when Donald died and turned back to religion to heal the pain of losing him, but I only ended up lying to myself."

"But that isn't anything to be ashamed of," Simon said. "Looks like I did a bigger favor for you than we thought."

"It still doesn't excuse you from getting out of this," Beelzebub said. "I can't promise where you'll go because of what you did for Brandon. But the time has come."

"But I signed your book. So, doesn't that guarantee you get my soul?"

"It did. But like I said, it's how I keep track of whom I have impending deals with."

"Hold on," Darla said. "Hold on," Darla said. "How did Simon get out of going to hell?"

But now you're saying he might not go there? How did

he get out of that?"

"By acknowledging that he did a bigger favor for Brandon than he thought. Simon helped someone he secretly hated out of love, and that might make things better. But I'm not guaranteeing anything. Let's go."

They looked at Simon, expecting him to grovel or hide behind Darla. Instead, he set his mug down, put his head in his hands, and moaned before looking at Darla and Brandon.

"Before I go, please let me apologize for dragging you both into this. Darla, I realize that if I would have just told you about how I felt about going to church, none of this would have happened. I hope the last few days we had together strengthened our marriage enough that you'll always love me."

"I will always love you, Simon," Darla said, wiping her eyes. "We did the best we could."

"I know. And I have eternity to think about you." Simon reached for her as she stepped toward him, and they kissed like they were dying in each other's arms. They parted, and Darla's eyes were as red as her lips.

"All right Simon. Let's go," Beelzebub said and snapped his fingers. The coffee cups shook, splashing coffee on the table. Wind gusted around them, blowing Simon's hair and knocking his glasses off. The floor opened while the foul stench of sulfur and growls of demons filled the house. Hideous black appendages and claws grabbed Simon's legs, dragging him down. Pictures crashed from the wall, breaking the frames, and the ceiling fan fell with enough force to break the table in half. Simon's screams didn't last long before he disappeared.

Darla and Brandon looked at the damage. Brandon shook his head while Darla sprayed Lysol, then plugged in the vacuum. She swept up as much glass as she could, then turned it off and stared at Brandon. "Can you please help me clean this up?" she asked, gesturing at the mess.

Brandon grabbed the paper towel and tore a few sheets

off to pick shards of glass up with. "Well, even though Simon meant a lot to us, we're free of his mistake."

"Which he confessed to," Darla said. "So, I doubt he'll be in hell for long."

"Fair enough. But the Bible says not to trust the devil.. And since Simon made a deal with him, I wouldn't put too much faith in his escaping hell. Still, I hope none of this has shaken your faith."

She made a fist, hoping he would leave soon. "I don't know if it has or not. I could yell at the sky, asking God why this happened. But I want to know why God and Beelzebub made a deal. Pastor Dennings said nothing about that."

"It could be another lie," Brandon said. "The devil would do anything to take people."

"But after what we saw at the restaurant? How the people that disappeared were in that weird place? I doubt it was a lie."

"Guess we'll never know in this life," Brandon said before his phone buzzed. "That's Glen. He wants to meet for breakfast. Will you be okay if I go?"

"Sure," Darla said and put the broom and dustpan away. "Go have fun. Call or text me later, okay?"

"Will do," Brandon said and walked out to his car.

Darla waved when he backed out of the driveway. Though she was happy he was free, she also wanted to punch Brandon after what he said about Simon not escaping hell. She took out her phone, googled where the nearest satanic temple was, and longed to give her testimony so she could be with Simon again.

Bringing Up Lucifer

J Louis Messina

If you sleep with the devil, you'll wake up in hell.

Being a preacher's daughter, I should know. Evangelists across the world sermonized it, and that had been my life. I had sex with the devil, but I had been drugged by witches in a satanic ritual to have his baby all because my husband, Drake Stevens, made a pact with them to advance his music career. Your basic deal with the devil. Probably how most rock stars became famous.

What should I expect from a band called *The Eternally Damned*?"

I still have flashes of the beast thrusting his seed into me. Waking up in a cold sweat, I'd shudder and clamp my hand over my mouth to suppress my screams, but I'd awakened baby Lucifer again.

I offered him my breast to suckle milk. Junior's lips pinched; his teeth nipped me. Blood trickled from my teat, but I let him feed. I meant to raise him to be good, not the fiend the witches wanted him to be, or whatever foul purpose they had in mind.

Antichrist? Despot? Politician?

After my bum husband left me, the witches gave me a

hefty endowment to live on, but they controlled every aspect of my life, so I decided to kill them with rat poison. On Lucifer's first birthday, I baked a batch of cookies and a cake with poison, then mixed it in their drinks. After the witch guests left, I sat with the old Blackmer sisters across from my apartment that had groomed me for the devil's bride and double-spiked their drinks.

The oldest sister, Margaret, clutched her stomach, retched, and toppled to the floor. The other sister, Agatha, groaned, lurched to me, and grabbed my arm. Terrified she'd curse me or pull one of my four nose rings out, I stumbled backwards.

"Good for you," she said. "You'll make the perfect mother for the child."

I danced away and let her thud dead onto the carpet. I had freed myself and baby Lucifer from their slavery. After the police arrived, they assumed it had been mutual suicide. The others had died on the way home or in their beds.

With the witches out of my way, I strolled my baby daily, which the coven had forbidden, and wrapped him in blankets so no one could see his devil face. One day, I made the mistake of stopping for a rest in front of St. Timothy's parish.

"Oh, I love babies," said a priest hobbling on a cane by the carriage, having sneaked up on me. "With your permission, I shall give the child a blessing."

"No!"

I pushed him away, but the priest pushed back in, dunked his bald head inside, and uncovered Lucifer's face. Gasping, he rocked backwards. His face turned ashen and sweaty.

"It's Satan's child!" Worried his scream might attract bystanders, I begged him to be quiet and held onto his tunic, but he broke loose. "You must destroy it. I shall alert the Vatican that *it* has arrived."

Hopping with unexpected quickness up the steps and into his church, he locked the doors. Looking everywhere for danger, I hurried back to my apartment. He didn't know my identity, but I couldn't risk him finding me.

On the day of confession, I waited for the line to the confessional to dwindle. Sacred items made Lucifer fussy, if not downright cranky, so I left him at the back of the cathedral. I hadn't been in a church since I'd left home because of what my dad had done to me.

When the church emptied, I crept up to the confessional to confront the priest who had denounced my child. Jumpy as a frightened cat, I scanned the empty pews. My hands shook.

Could I muster the nerve to stop him from spreading rumors?

Swinging the door open, I froze, and we looked at each other in surprised familiarity.

"You?" the priest said.

"Just protecting my baby, father."

I stabbed the sewing scissors through his neck, yanked them out, and plunged them in again and again. Bloody and dead, he slumped back. I closed the door and crossed myself. Blood oozed from underneath.

"Confession is good for the soul."

I offered five dollars and lit two votive candles for the prayers of us both. Concealing the scissors in the carriage, I rushed out, nearly tipping over the carriage. Problem solved.

By age four, Lucifer had outgrown his red devil face, needle-like teeth, pointy ears, and a tiny tail. Looking into the blackest of eyes, one could become mesmerized, fall under their spell. On several occasions, I had found myself standing in a corner of the room for hours unaware how or why I'd walked there. What the child had done in that time, I had no idea or memory; and to be honest, hadn't wanted to know.

However, with Lucifer's metamorphosis into a conventional body, I had the desire to leave the house to shop. I hired an eighteen-year-old babysitter, someone with enthusiasm, unattached and no family, and a religious demeanor, which I thought could inspire and do Junior some good. The child had an unhealthy demanding personality. Being the devil's child, I had to train him to resist the temptation for evil. I'd read in *Kosmos Mag* that we presumed male and female traits as a matter of fact, but it was a matter of conditioning, not genetics. A boy could love a dolly and a girl a dump truck. And the devil's baby could learn goodness.

"I should be back within an hour, Tabitha," I said to my babysitter. "Instructions are on the desk. If a crisis arises, you have my number."

"No worries, Mrs. Stevens. Lucifer and I will get along famously. Children are a blessing from above."

"Please, call me Clara. We're nearly the same age."

She bounced around the room, an innocent gathering toys, like picking flowers. She dressed like one of those sixties flower girls, too, with long, flowing, multicolored dress and crowned with a rainbow bandana, which clashed with my black goth outfits.

"They love games at this age," Tabitha said, "And I know a slew of them. An hour will fly by."

"If anything happens, like really unusual, please call me immediately."

"What do you mean by unusual?"

"Nothing. Guess I'm having separation anxiety."

"That's not unusual for a young mother."

Having great misgivings, I pranced to the door and analyzed Lucifer's enigmatic black eyes. Deep in the iris I perceived malice. An alarm rang in my head.

I should insist Tabitha leave, I thought, but I resisted, owing it to my own angst at leaving him alone for the first time. Shutting the front door, I hurried to the elevator.

***

When I arrived back, night had fallen, and a crowd had

congregated outside my building. Police held the onlookers back, and an ambulance struggled its way down the busy street to join the throng.

"I live in this building," I said to an officer, showing him my identification.

"Go through that way. Best you don't see."

"What happened?"

"Some loon jumped to her death."

"Oh, how awful. Poor thing."

While the elevator rose to the sixth floor, the dread rose in me. I felt suffocated and claustrophobic. I swooned out the doors and held back my premonitions, as a dam held back water in a breach. My mind spilled over with thoughts of who might've jumped to her death. But it couldn't be.

I rummaged for the keys and dropped them and my packages. Plucking them off the floor, I shoved in my apartment key, swiped the packages, and spilled in with a whirlwind entrance.

"Tabitha! I'm back. Is everything okay?"

Please, don't let it be her.

Toys scattered over the blood on the carpet. I dumped the packages at my feet. A chill breeze caught my attention. I hugged myself for warmth. The white drapes billowed, like ghostly silk. I skipped over the fresh stains and to the open windows. Looking down, I watched the paramedics lift the covered deceased girl onto the gurney and slide her into the ambulance.

Could it be Tabitha? Why would she kill herself?

Whispers from the bedroom drew me away from the tragic scene. The curtains and my heart fluttered. Shutting the windows, I staggered to the room. My head spun. Trembling, I opened the door and slipped inside.

"Lucifer?"

Next to the bed, Junior sat on the floor playing with jacks and a ball and hummed a macabre tune. He appeared unscathed and calm, dispelling any worries he might've been injured.

I inched to him. On the other side of the bed, muttering to herself, Tabitha hunched against the back holding a bloody knife and a burnt bible.

"Tabitha? What happened here?"

"It was only a game." She repeated it as if a mantra. "A game, a game, a game."

I picked up a pamphlet at her feet, a copy of the Jehovah Witnesses' *The Watchtower*. Piecing the puzzle together, I assumed someone had come to the door to pitch their religion, which occurred a lot in this old building, and Tabitha had answered the door and let her in, for I took her as a people person, someone who loved to talk about spirituality, and it'd been the same Jehovah's girl splattered on the pavement.

I bent to help her up, but without looking my way, she stabbed the knife at me and missed until she tired and let her arm drop to her side. Grasping the burnt bible in the other hand, she examined it, as if to process what it was or why she held it.

"I'm going to be sick." Tabitha threw the bible against the wall, and ashes burst into the air. "Help me to the bathroom."

Inside the bathroom, she puked loud enough to shatter my eardrums. I imagined she had barfed her intestines into the bowl. Totally gross. When she came out, she shuffled, spent, as if she'd vomited the life out of herself.

"Come, sit on the chair," I said, leading her limp body to it. Her icy hand gave me a shock. She gripped the knife in her other hand. "Tabitha, give me the knife before you hurt yourself."

"Knife?" She looked at it, winced, and dropped it into my hand. "May I have a drink of water, please?"

"Sure." I strode back with the water, and she gulped it down. I sat in the chair opposite her. "You seem upset. Tell me what happened."

Tabitha looked at her surroundings, as if lost.

"What do you mean?"

"You said you played a game. What game?"

"We played lots of games. Lucifer has an aptitude for them. We had so much fun."

"Why were you holding the knife and bible? Was that part of the game?"

"He loves hide and seek. Found me every time. And twenty questions, he knew it in one. No child that age ever gets it in one guess. As if he could read my mind."

"He's a very intuitive child. What game did you play with the knife and bible?"

She laughed off-key, and her cackle trailed off into the distance. Her bug eyes grew buggier.

"I would never let a child play with a knife."

"Of course not. Whose blood is on the carpet?"

Perplexed, Tabitha gazed at the stain and studied it.

"It's from the girl that came in."

"What girl?"

Lucifer toddled in and played with his Legos. Tabitha curled up into a ball.

"She must've cut herself. I got her some bandages and antiseptic." Lucifer stared at her. She squeezed her ball tighter. "Then she left, that's all."

"Did she go near the window?" Tabitha pinched her eyes and shook her head. "When she left, she was fine?" Tabitha mumbled and nodded. "Was the bible yours?"

"I didn't have a bible with me."

"Then where did it come from?"

"The girl gave it to me as a present. She was so nice and friendly."

"Why were the windows open?"

Tabitha bit her fingers and gnawed on them. I fretted she might nibble them down to the bone.

"Do you need me anymore tonight?" Tabitha said, between delicious bites.

"No. Why don't you go home and get some rest."

She snatched her purse and coat and flew to the door.

"Will you need me again this week?"

"You want to come back?"

She looked over my shoulder at Lucifer.

"I'd do anything you need, Clara. For *him*."

"I'll let you know. Goodnight."

Tabitha wandered down the hallway, as if tipsy, to the elevator, and thumped impatiently on the button. After I banged shut the door, I stood as one trying to assess the damage after an act of nature; not God, for I doubt He had anything to do with the event.

Should I investigate the death of the girl who jumped to her death?

No, best to leave it alone. I had no proof that it had been the girl at the door, other than circumstantial evidence. Opened windows, a bible, and a pamphlet, hardly a conviction—although DNA from the blood could be identified.

Heading into the kitchen, I collected cleaning materials and proceeded to scrub until all traces of blood had disappeared. I washed the knife and shoved it into the utensil drawer. Good as new. It never happened. I drove the incident from my mind and started dinner. Stabbing his meat loaf with his fork, Lucifer sat at the table and chewed like a ravenous dog.

"Did you like Tabitha, Lucifer?"

"Yes. She's fun to *play* with." Pieces of meat dropped from his mouth. "I hope she comes back."

Although his response sounded more like a cat with a mouse, I decided, since he had no friends, she'd make him a good companion. I didn't ask about the episode. The police made no further investigations about the girl's death and suicide. Case closed.

When I needed to go out again, I contacted Tabitha. She showed up and charged in, as if she couldn't wait to get to work.

"Hi, Clara. I was sitting by the phone hoping you'd call. Could hardly sleep until you did. I'm so excited to babysit Lucifer again."

Tabitha exhibited a shocking change in her appearance. She wore gray matronly apparel, and the blackened circles under her puffy eyes made her look crazed.

"What's in the carpet bag?"

Tabitha lifted the Victorian style bag onto my coffee table.

"More toys I know Lucifer will enjoy."

"Educational, I hope. Never too early to stimulate a boy's brain."

"These are very stimulating."

"As long as there aren't any toys that look like guns or military weapons. I don't want him exposed to violent things."

"These are safe and childproof."

"I'll be back in a few hours, then."

Lucifer's face beamed. I couldn't fathom what his look meant. At least Tabitha would be safe from harm. But his look.

Happy child or evil incarnate? Could I correct his evil intents?

Tabitha babysat for several weeks. Each time I arrived home, I'd smell the aroma of burnt candles, but no traces of them, and she'd be on the couch reading to Lucifer, or he took a nap, and she watched television. Something was out of whack, something afoot. Call it a mother's intuition. I decided to come back early to dismiss my suspicions.

Waiting enough time for them to settle into their games, I tiptoed down the hallway, flattened my ear to the door to hear their voices. No sounds. If they had gone out, I would've spotted them. I peeked inside. Through the slit, I couldn't see any other room.

Taking a deep breath, I dove in and looked around.

No severed body parts or pools of blood, I mused. So far, so good.

Nothing amiss in the kitchen or den. The bedroom door had been closed. There was a hitch in my breathing. Lights flickered beneath the door, and a voice rumbled as deep as the ocean, but I hadn't a TV or radio in there.

Turning the doorknob, I stepped into the stench of smoke and brimstone, the smack of heat, and a room engulfed in crimson.

Tabitha levitated naked, face-up above the bed, horizontal, arms spread as on a cross, head and hair cascading down, like a sacrificial offering. Perspiration dripped off her huge breasts. Tall black candles had been lit around the bed, and a pentagram drawn on the wall above the headboard The light flickered from the foot of the bed. Flames licked and lapped the room, as if from a roaring fireplace. In the middle of the flames formed a red-faced demon. Sitting cross-legged, Lucifer spoke to it.

"Yes, father, I will."

I recognized the face that had leered at me as it had made obscene love to me; not love but pornographic lust, the grotesque face of Satan. My cheeks flushed and stung, as if I'd been slapped so many times my head chimed.

Should I stop this travesty, this horror show?

I'd read in *Kids Happen Mag* that every boy needed a father and would look beyond his faults for acceptance and love no matter how abusive. This went way beyond. Tabitha had become a willing conduit to contact his dad in hell. I wasn't sure how I felt about it. After all, my preacher dad had left when I was six, ran off with a woman from his church, and I never saw him again. I tried to contact him, but he ignored my pleas. I still longed for his love and affection.

Was this any different?

I closed the door and, without a destination in mind, roamed the neighborhood. The problem hadn't been Lucifer seeking his father. That was expected. The problem was

Tabitha, going behind my back, placing a wedge between me and my son. I'd tried to make Lucifer good, but she had led him towards evil. I wondered if the slut had fornicated with Satan. I didn't need a knocked-up babysitter and another demon child on my hands. If I fired her, I feared Lucifer would become upset and not allow it, and I'd find myself standing in a corner again. I must eliminate her.

In the next month, I made friends with a couple on my floor and introduced myself and Junior. The woman was expecting and in a nesting mood, which made her perfect for my plan. Pregnant women loved children, as if projecting them as their own.

When I arrived back to my apartment a little after 7PM, the faint odor of burnt candles lingered in the air along with the rank scent of sex. They had contacted Satan again. Tabitha's clothes appeared rumpled, her hair chaotic, and, as she'd been naked in the bedroom, she'd forgotten her bra, and her hardened nipples pressed against her blouse. The whore had slept with Lucifer's father, the devil, my groom. I felt it in my bones.

I hated her more than my husband Drake who had abandoned me. She tried to usurp my mothering, with no regard for what I thought best for my son.

"I'll see you Saturday, Tabitha, for Lucifer' birthday," I said at the door.

"Can't wait. I have the perfect present."

Once I heard the ding of the elevator, I scooted Lucifer outside and knocked on number 66.

"Hi, Ruth, do you mind watching my son for a few minutes? My babysitter left her purse behind, and I need to catch her before she gets on the subway."

"Oh, I'd love to."

"One other thing." I put sunglasses on him. "He has a light sensitivity issue. As a precaution, the doctor wants him to wear these."

"He looks adorable. If he had a guitar, he could play the

Blues."

"That's what I'm hoping to avoid."

"Excuse me?"

"Sorry, his dad that left us was a musician."

"I won't bring it up again."

Rushing out of the elevator, I raced to 77th Street and searched for Tabitha among the crowd. I weaved and jostled in and out the people, bumped and excused my way until I reached the subway stairs and hurdled down the steps.

Had I lost her?

Except for a few homeless people camped out by the grimy tiled walls festooned with graffiti, Tabitha stood alone at the end of the platform to avoid the stink of stale urine, feces, and empty needles.

I wrapped my face in my scarf and stuffed my wool cap down to my eyes. Hiding behind the pillar, cloaked in the shadows, a few feet from Tabitha, I read my watch. The subway arrived in less than a minute from the direction she stood.

The screeching rail sound whooshed from afar. The ground rattled. I stepped out. Tabitha looked straight ahead, avoiding eye contact. I trundled closer. Lights filled the tunnel, and I felt the vibrations, the warmth. Holding my arms and palms out, I ran at her and pushed. As she fell onto the tracks, a yell caught in her throat. The subway shrieked and shredded over her body and whirred to a stop. I sprinted back up the stairs.

***

Next morning, breakfast was more combative than usual.

"What've you done with Tabitha?" Lucifer said, looking at me with accusing eyes.

"She went back to Illinois to live with her parents. New York wasn't working out for her. Eat your oatmeal."

"You're lying. Did you hurt her?"

"I'd never hurt anyone. *Thou Shall Not Kill.* I'm your mommy, not that little brat."

Pouting, Lucifer slouched in his seat and folded his arms.

"I need her back."

"Why? So you can talk with your father again? That's right, I know all about you and her secret meetings. He's a bad influence. I don't want you having anything to do with him."

"You can't keep me away."

"I'll decide what's best for you." I tossed pots and pans into the sink to wash. "You start kindergarten tomorrow. I expect you to behave."

"I don't want to go to school."

Scouring the pans, I splashed water everywhere. "You'll do as I say, young man. Don't talk back to me. You need to adjust your attitude." Lucifer ran into his bedroom and slammed the door. "You can stay in there until you come out and apologize."

Lucifer was headstrong and deceitful, qualities he'd received from his dad. But somewhere deep down, he must've inherited my sweetness, my forgiveness, my kindness. If they weren't inherited, then they could be taught. I had to lead by example.

***

Like most mothers that left their precious little children off at school for the first time, I wept and felt my heart ache for him, worrying about everything.

Would the other children like him? Would he feel lonely without me? Would his psychopathic tendencies injure anyone?

When I picked Lucifer up from school, I inquired about his activities, but he refused to share anything, still moping over the loss of Tabitha and access to his father.

Would I receive a call from his teacher about Lucifer's

deviant behavior?

I didn't have to wait long.

The teacher, Mrs. Prickle, had acquired a saccharine intonation from years of teaching kindergarten kids. She sent Lucifer outside to play during our conference.

"I don't want to worry you, Mrs. Stevens." Mrs. Prickle appeared the quintessential image of a teacher: straight back, hands folded, and an apple on her desk. "I've taught numerous rambunctious boys in my years, and I'm used to their overaggressive inclinations."

"Has my boy been unruly?" I fidgeted in the chair opposite her. "He's a very willful child."

"No. Not exactly. That's what bothers me. He keeps to himself. Won't play with the other children." She put on a too big smile for even her plump face. "Frankly, the children are afraid of him."

"How do you mean? Has he done something?"

"No. Not exactly. Most kids at this age aren't used to sharing. However, anytime a child took a toy away from him, they'd have an accident."

"Do you mean he physically hurts them?"

"No. Not exactly. They'd trip and skin a knee, or fall and cut their lip, and once, a boy's shirt caught on fire."

"How? Did he have matches?"

"No." She leaned in and whispered. "Things just happened."

"Have you seen him actually harm anyone?"

"Not exactly. I'm sorry, I'm not explaining myself very well. I've never encountered such a child. There's something wrong with his eyes." She rubbed her forehead. "This all sounds absurd."

"Yes, it does." I wagged my finger at her. "If you're going to accuse my son of something sinister, you should have at least witnessed it."

"Frankly, I'm afraid of him, too. There it is." Her smile never left her face. Looking down, she adjusted pencils on her desk. “Has the child ever seen a psychologist?”

“There’s nothing wrong with my son’s mind. It sounds as if you’re the one imagining things.”

“This is a delicate situation. I hate to ask, to pry, but is his father in the picture?”

“His father left us.” I sniffed and glowered. “If you must know, Mrs. Prickle, I was raped and have a son by another man.” Starting to cry, I whisked out a tissue and wiped my eyes. “It’s a very sensitive issue.”

“I’m so sorry. I hadn’t meant to bring up such a harrowing event in your life. Most boys that have troubled minds need a male role model to set them straight. Perhaps you could convince your ex-husband to help out.”

“Never. Drake Stevens is gone for good.”

“The lead singer from *The Eternally Damned* was your husband? I adore that band.”

“Figures.” I sprang up, shaky on my feet and blew my nose. “If you’re done with your accusations, I’m leaving. I have a mind to report you to the principal. Accusing my son with no proof. This is outrageous.”

“Please don’t take offense, Mrs. Stevens.” Tottering to her feet, she wrung her hands. Finally, her phony smile collapsed, and her expression broke into a mask of terror. “I’m only trying to help. He’s a danger to society and may need to be institutionalized in a mental ward.” I fled out the door and seized Lucifer off the swings. “Think about what I said!”

***

Mrs. Prickle could become a hindrance to his education, to becoming the good person I knew Lucifer would grow to be. And a therapist may discover a problem, and they’d take him away from me.

What should I do about her? A poisoned apple? Could I dismember her and throw her in the Hudson River?

I'd become so involved with the problem, I nearly hit the car in front of me that had stopped at a red light. Lucifer and I rocked in our seat at the sudden, jarring stop, which jarred her suggestion about a father figure. I couldn't get Drake back; his guilt had driven him away, and, frankly, after what he'd done to me, I could never forgive him. I had no other man in my life, except the one Tabitha had conjured.

Was he the right man for the job? Or the only one?

When we got back home, I sat Lucifer down for a candid talk.

"It has come to my attention, Lucifer, that I may have been wrong about keeping you from your father. Therefore, under my supervision, we'll contact him again."

Lucifer's resentful looks changed to an exuberance I'd never witnessed in the child. This gave me the courage that I had made the right decision. Making a fun day of it, we shopped together at an occult shop, and I bought the candles and chalk.

That night, I summoned his biological dad, Satan.

The father of lies, my preacher dad had said, quoting John 8:44.

"Sit at the foot of the bed and turn your back." I disrobed and felt uncomfortable undressed in front of him. But if that skank Tabitha could do it, so could I. "I'm going to lay on the bed, and we can begin."

Lucifer chanted something in Latin. An oppressive heat blasted over the room. I levitated, as if hands lifted me into the air. Goosebumps rippled over my flesh. I shivered, overcome by a sexual urge I hadn't felt in over five years, Satan being the last time.

Fire erupted in front of Lucifer, and his father materialized. They whispered. I raised my head to get a better look. Satan licked his lips with his long, forked tongue. Then he rose from the fire and climbed out, naked and clearly excited by my visit.

"My bride." Satan hissed and drooled. "Go wait outside,

Junior."

"Why?" Lucifer said.

"I must have an intimate conversation with your mother."

"Again?" Lucifer closed the door behind him. "Make it quick this time."

Satan slithered to the side of the bed and caressed my breasts. "What has brought you back to me, my wife?" He trailed his long, sharp fingernail over my belly, inched further down, and twirled my pubic hair. "Do you desire a daughter?"

"No. I expect you to set your son straight." Satan waved his hand, and I lowered onto the bed. He crawled on top and wasted no time in having his way with me. I wrapped my arms and legs around him as best I could. He was as big as a walrus. "He needs a father, or else I'm afraid he'll do something wicked and be locked up."

"He understands what he must do or face the consequences. There will be no further problems from him."

Flames exploded around the bed, as if we were in a roasting pit, but nothing had burnt.

Had I gone to hell?

I panted and cried out in ecstasy, "Oh God!"

"He will not come between us."

Repulsed by his touch, I had to endure my sexual sacrifice for my son's sake.

"Place your hands here," I said. "And watch your claws."

Was Satan the embodiment of evil? Could he change? Could I change him?

I'd read in *Modern Marriage Mag* that women who married the bad boy could alter the way he behaved, his profession, the way he thought about marriage. His evil was learned, not a trait, and I had enough goodness to influence Satan into the perfect husband and father.

Was it silly to think we could picnic at Central Park as a family? Or would religious fanatics try to kill him? If anyone ever threatened our household, did we have legal ways to stop them from harassing us?

Moaning, I glanced at the sewing scissors on the nightstand. If not those, or poison, there was always the subway.

Dream Job

Terry Grimwood

New job. New start.

He was met in reception by a young woman wearing an immaculate business suit and white blouse. He felt shabby in his well-worn jacket and the best shirt he could find in his wardrobe. Money was tight. He hadn't held down a job since leaving the army.

But then, he hadn't held anything down, had he? Including his marriage.

"Lee Dartnall?" the woman said.

"That's me."

"I'm Kirsty Pearson. The office manager. Nice to meet you." He liked her smile straight away.

He was wrapped in her perfume as they rode the lift to the fifth floor. He knew her friendliness was just part of her job. He was just another newbie to be babied on his first day. Her smile was professional and meant no more than that.

Lindon's Employment Agency consisted of a maze of open plan workstations, a tearoom and a separate office for Graham Lindon himself. Toilets were shared with the other company who rented the floor. Kirsty didn't mention their name.

Lee's allocated desk was hidden away in a pen somewhere near the centre of the room. He had a view of the huge window that formed the outside wall of the space and gave a sweeping vista of London. He needed this job, badly, as much to regain his self-respect as for the money. He was divorced and alone, but at least he had been sober for two months.

He might also be suffering from PTSD. No one had checked and he hadn't asked.

"Everyone, your attention, please." Kirsty. Authoritative, but friendly.

The tapping of keys and quiet telephone conversations stopped. All eyes turned towards Lee's pen. Those he couldn't see, he felt. Odd how you always knew when you were being watched. Especially when your own sixth sense had been honed to scalpel-sharp in Iraq and Afghanistan.

"I'd like to introduce Lee Dartnall, the newest member of our team. Please make him feel welcome and support him through these first few days."

"Hello, Lee." "Hi, Lee." "Glad to meet you, Lee." Called out with surprising warmth.

Kirsty handed Lee a sheet of paper.

"Your password and userID. So, log on and I'll help you to find your way around the system."

Lee was glad that she was staying, and not only because she was going to show him what he was supposed to do.

Password accepted, up came the Lindon brand. *Lindon Employment. Careers our objective. Dreams our mission.*

Kirsty leaned in to point at the screen and there was that perfume again. "Click here, that's right. See? These are links to various job categories. Each of these takes you to a list of employers in that category who have vacancies to fill."

Her voice was a little husky.

Lee did as he was told and there they were, everything from retail to rock and roll bands.

"Now this link takes you to a separate screen. As you can

see, it's a list of email applications from our career seekers. Open one and you will immediately see which job category interests them. Read their CV, which is on the form, and try to match it to relevant vacancies. Telephone them to find out if any of the roles are suitable. That's key. You need to know what they really want, not what they *tell* themselves they want." Kirsty sounded passionate now. "If it is, call the employer and set up an interview. It's a bit clunky, a lot of companies operate entirely on-line, but Mister Lindon likes the personal touch. In fact, he normally interviews all our prospective clients, either by phone or face-to-face."

Lee glanced at the list of career seekers and wondered where Lindon found the time to run a company and interview all those people.

"You are, of course, aware, Lee, that your commission will equal ten percent of each successful candidate's annual salary."

"Yes."

The money was ridiculously good for the role, and the commission generous enough, for Lee to believe he would be able to escape from his crummy little rented flat and buy a home in London by the end of the year.

He just had to keep his demons at bay and hold on to this job.

"Oh, one last thing," Kirsty said. "You need to sign your contract of employment. It's on-line…here."

It was a monster. Lee started to read it. The usual stuff; holiday pay, sick benefits, hours…

His concentration wavered.

He blinked and dived in again. No, he couldn't concentrate, nothing was going in. It was probably fine, so he entered his name, clicked "submit" then experienced a moment of unease, convinced that he had made a mistake.

No, no mistake. This was a good job. He had fought hard to get it, put in a lot of effort researching the company and preparing for his interview. This was one of those turning points in life. And what was more, he would be helping others to change their own lives.

Kirsty headed for her own desk. No backward glance, no indication that he was anything but a work colleague. Oh well, here goes…

Lee opened the top email on his list. Sharon Miller.

"I would like to work in television; costumes or set design."

Lee scanned her qualifications. Her CV showed that she has worked as a hairdresser and then clerical assistant in an accountancy firm. Nothing relevant. This looked like a no-hoper. Lee clicked on the *Media and Performing Arts* tab on his vacancies screen.

And there it was. "Production company behind several major television shows requires costume assistant. *No previous experience necessary,* only a passion for the role."

Lee picked up the phone.

"Sharon Miller?"

"Yes?" She sounded nervous.

"This is Lee Dartnall from Lindon's Employment Agency."

"Oh, hello."

"Look, I've seen your application and CV, and I think I've found something that might interest you. I'll email the details over to you right now, okay? Just give me a moment. There. Take a look and I'll call you back in, say, fifteen min -"

"No, I've got it. It looks perfect."

"Oh, right. I just need a quick chat first, to get to know you a little. Why this particular career path?"

"Because I'm sick of working in this office. I'm sick of nine-to-five. I need to do something different, unconventional, exciting."

"I under -"

"Your web site promises that you can make any career dream come true."

"Well, yes, it does -"

"Then make this dream come true. Get me an interview."

"I'll do my best, Sharon, I promise."

Lee called the company, who sounded as eager as the client. They would interview her, on the phone, Zoom, anything, but now if possible.

Beginner's luck. Lee opened the next email, then the next and the next and each time found himself talking to a desperate client. Some pleaded with him to get them a job, others sobbed in despair. And each time he found a potential employer almost as desperate. Lee's mood changed from bemusement to delight at the steady stream of possible commissions.

Then to unease.

This was too easy. Every candidate wanted a job so badly they sounded as if they would commit murder to get it. Every company said yes to an interview.

At eleven-thirty, Lee got a call back from Sharon. She was in tears of joy, barely able to speak as she gushed out her thanks for getting her that job. They had offered it to her before the interview was finished.

Kirsty appeared at Lee's desk. "Well done, Lee." She put a hand on his shoulder. He liked that. "A success, on your first morning." She sounded genuinely impressed. "Come on, break. There's a great little deli at the end of the street. Some of us go there every lunch time."

Lee was made to feel welcome as they walked down the street to the deli. Everyone seemed interested in what he had to say. They even laughed at his jokes. For the first time since leaving the army, Lee felt as if he belonged. Like everything else that morning, it was almost too good to be true.

And did Kirsty glance at him more often than just-a-colleague should? It felt that way. There was even the occasional little smile. He knew he was being daft, but something was going on here.

The afternoon was as bewilderingly successful as the morning. Three of his clients were offered jobs straight away, no interview necessary.

So, it went. That first day, the second, the third.

He was working late. Everyone else had gone home. Oddly uneasy, he glanced towards Lindon's office. Perhaps it was time to introduce himself and thank the boss for giving him this chance at a new life. He left his workstation and set off through the maze of empty desks and pens towards Lindon's door.

Something was wrong.

Why the hell was he in combat gear? Helmet. Kevlar. He carried an SA80, its weight familiar and comforting. He wasn't alone. Others advanced cautiously on either side. They were shadows, vaguely familiar.

Remember us, do you?

Of course he did. They had been his comrades and his friends. Sergeant McDonald, tall, broad, reliable. Private Singh, easy-going, kind in his way. The sort of man who would give you his last ration, or stay with you if you were wounded, no matter how perilous the situation. Lance Corporal Goldschmidt, the clown, the joker, the cheerer-upper. Oliver, the medic. No telling how many lives and limbs she had saved with her near-emotionless quick thinking. And LeCarre, the radio operator. There had been chemistry between LeCarre and Lee, savage, lust-driven. It could never have survived the rigours of a long-term relationship.

How were they here?

McDonald and LeCarre; killed by an IED in Basra. Singh, a bloody ruin in the wreckage of a downed helicopter. Oliver, a suicide attack by one of the Afghans medics she had been training. He had cried out to his God then opened fire on the patients and staff in a field hospital where he was learning advanced first aid. Goldschmidt a bullet to the head during a fire fight in Helmand Province.

Why are you still alive, Dartnall? What gives you the right to breathe?

Lindon's office. Red light leaked through the gaps around the door.

Lee reached for the handle.

It burned his hand, but he couldn't let go. His flesh melted. The pain was excruciating. The wood of the door blistered and blackened. Someone chuckled. He looked back and saw the others, the dead, gathered in a loose arc about him. uniforms burned and blood-spattered.

They laughed, doubled over by their mirth. Their mouths were horribly, impossibly wide. Their eyes blazed with scorn.

The door opened -

He woke, disorientated and sweat-dank. He fumbled for the bedside lamp and was, for once, glad of the hideous wallpaper, vile curtains and damp odour of his flat.

On Friday, Kirsty hung around Lee's desk as he logged-off and prepared to go home. She wore her coat but seemed reluctant to leave.

"So, how was your first week?" There was a catch in her voice, as if she was suddenly shy.

"Pretty good." Now *that* was an understatement.

One of those can't-think-of-anything to say silences followed. Then Lee blurted out, "Would you like a drink before we go home?" and immediately regretted it as crass and too soon.

"Yes," Kirsty said.

She knew a bar that overlooked the river. They took their drinks out onto the balcony. Lee's a lime-and-soda, Kirsty's a gin-and-tonic. They leaned on the rail and looked out over the night-blackened water. Reflected light was sprinkled over its oily surface. They stood close. The air was cold and getting colder.

"Was it really bad out there?" she asked. "Sorry, you

don't have to answer that."

The question was inevitable. His army career took up most of his CV.

"Yeah, it was. I mean, there's friendships you won't find anywhere else. I have good memories of that, but they're bittersweet because too many of them didn't make it."

"I can't imagine how that feels, to lose people like that."

"It's the guilt that's the worst. Survivor's guilt they call it."

"It's not your fault you made it through."

"I know, but I have trouble believing it. I hurt a lot of people when I came home, including myself. This job…I'm trying to get my life together."

"Well, you've made a good start, Lee."

Hearing his name spoken softly warmed Lee to the heart.

Two more drinks, then came the awkward business of saying goodnight. Lee didn't want to go home without her, but also didn't want to push too hard.

"This has been great," he said. Great? What sort of generic, bland catch-all word was that? "I've enjoyed…you know…"

"Me too." The breeze blew a strand of hair across her face, and it was sexy as hell. Instinctively, Lee reached out and gently pushed it out of her eye. Kirsty made to kiss him, hesitated, then, without warning, backed away, expression changed from warmth to fear. "I'm sorry," she muttered, and a moment later she was gone.

Monday came around soon enough, preceded by a weekend made lonely by Kirsty's panicked exit. Her expression haunted him. It was as if she had remembered something; that she was married perhaps, or already in some long-term relationship.

It was, however, another prosperous day at the office. Lee's success rate, unsettling.

Kirsty was distant, professional and only moderately friendly. She did, however, come over to see how he was getting on.

"Does Lindon ever come out of his office?" Lee wasn't interested in his boss's work habits. The question was intended to keep Kirsty by his desk.

"He doesn't need to," Kirsty said brusquely. "We're a good team."

Then the fear was back, a brief disarrangement of her office manager's mask, and once more, she walked away.

The week slipped by.

Thursday afternoon.

The quiet routine of subdued phone conversations and keyboard clacking was disrupted suddenly by the entrance of a middle-aged woman in an expensive fur coat. She gave the immediate impression that she was used to getting her own way. There was, however, a dishevelled, slightly wild look to her. She was pale and her breath was ragged, as if she was on the verge of panic.

Kirsty was there in a moment, calm, cool and polite as she tried to block the woman's path.

"Get out of my way. I need to see Lindon. I have to talk to him -"

"I'm sorry. It won't help."

"It will. I can talk him out of -"

"You can't. Mrs Grant, Belinda, please, go home. There's nothing you can do."

"No." Belinda Grant pushed Kirsty away from herself so hard, she fell backwards onto the floor.

Lee was on his feet and across to help her before anyone else could get out of their chairs. He looked up to see Belinda Grant stride up to Lindon's office.

"Are you okay?" Lee was crouched beside Kirsty, arm about her shoulders. Others were gathered around them now.

"Yes, yes, it's all right." When Lee tried to help her to her feet she waved him away. "Stop fussing, please."

That hurt. Lee knew he had no claim on her yet felt jealous when she thanked Patel for retrieving her iPad.

There were raised voices. At least, Belinda's voice was raised; Lindon's was a low rumble Lee could barely hear. Then Belinda screamed and Lee was heading for the office. Patel and another colleague named Ling moved quickly to bar his way.

"It's okay, Lee. Really. Go back to work. Don't get involved."

The screaming and crying went on until the door once more burst open and Belinda hurried out. She was even more dishevelled than before. She stumbled and almost fell, yet no one made any move to help her; everyone seemed keen to avoid eye contact and bury themselves in their work.

But she wasn't the main focus of Lee's unease. It's what he saw when Lindon's door opened to let her out. A red glow, as if the office was on fire. He glimpsed something dark in there, incomprehensible, grotesque. Then the door slammed shut.

That red light. He'd seen it before, in his recurring nightmare…

Work resumed as if nothing had happened. A few minutes later Kirsty appeared. She brought two mugs of coffee and handed one to Lee.

"Thanks for coming to help me. I'm sorry I was sharp with you. I was embarrassed."

"That's okay. Don't worry."

"It's always a shock the first time you see this," Kirsty's spoke softly, and for a moment, Lee believed Friday evening Kirsty was back.

"The first time?"

"Nothing. It doesn't matter." She moved away, a little flustered now. Lee made to follow but changed his mind. There was nothing between them. He should let it go.

Friday night. Restless, Lee went for a walk through the darkened streets. Again and again, he had tried to convince himself that he was done with Kirsty, that he had misread the situation, but some part of him, the mythical heart where love dwelt, was having none of it. Odd how he had fallen so hard so quickly.

A woman in a parka waited outside the front door when he arrived home. The coat's hood was up so Lee couldn't tell who she was, until he was close enough to recognise Kirsty's perfume.

She didn't speak but put her arms about his neck and kissed him hard and deep. There was desperation in that kiss. Moments later they were on Lee's bed, clawing at each other's clothes, then at each other, rough and hard and urgent. When it was done they lay in silence for a long, exhausted moment.

They kissed again, slowly and tenderly this time. Lee tasted tears.

He sat up and made to put his arm about her, but she moved out of reach and perched on the edge of the bed, her back to him. She still wore her coat; he still wore his shirt. They had only shed what was necessary.

"I'm sorry," she said.

"What for?"

"I'm not being fair to you."

"Are you married?"

"No."

"With someone else?"

"You don't know who we work for, do you, Lee?"

"Of course I do."

"Do you know why you're so successful at this job?"

"I've had a run of luck."

"Luck…Yes, luck. And it will continue, Lee, until…"

"Until what?"

"The time comes for you to pay."

"Pay? No one pays their boss -"

"You'll have to pay Lindon." Kirsty finally turned to kneel on the bed and face him. "Everyone has to pay. That woman, Belinda Grant, it's why she was distraught. No one wants to face up to the consequences of dealing with Lindon. In they come, to beg and bargain and cry and scream, but there's no getting out of it. Everyone who signs up with the Agency, as a client or employee, is either out to escape the humdrum and get that dream job, or just desperate for work. They all sign and none of them reads the small print. Did you, Lee? Did you read your contract of employment?"

"I tried to, but I …" Didn't understand it? Couldn't read it without his mind wandering off in all directions?

"I did. It wasn't easy but I needed to know. We have five years then Lindon calls it in. For our clients it's longer, ten, twenty, fifty even, but it always comes to an end."

"An end?"

"We're his."

"What do you mean, *his*?"

"I'm not sure, but I've seen colleagues summoned into his office and never come out again."

"Surely, someone reported them missing."

"Who would report you missing, Lee?"

She had a point. His parents were both dead. His siblings scattered and out of touch. He had few friends who might occasionally wonder what happened to him, but nothing more...

"Why did you take this job?"

"Like I told you, Iraq and Afghanistan messed me up. Then I saw the job ad and something…"

Curled about my soul and drew me in with a promise of healing? Whispered in my ear that this was salvation?

"Same for me," Kirsty said. "Same for everyone who works there. I had an affair. My marriage failed. I was left with nothing, until this job came along. Now my five years are up. Lindon's going to open his door and call my name any day now. That's why I didn't...Lee, I don't want to put you through any hurt or grief. God, this is hard."

"You're asking me to believe that you're going to walk into Lindon's office -" Into the red behind that door, into the arms of that creature he had glimpsed "- and vanish from the face of the earth?"

"I accept it. I have to. You learn to bury it, deep down, but then you have to face it and, suddenly..."

"Kirsty, nothing is going to happen to you -"

"I'm sorry, I can't do this." She grabbed her discarded clothing and was dressed and gone by the time Lee was able to fumble his own jeans back on and follow.

He tried to dismiss it. He tried to tell himself that Kirsty was deluded. That she was trouble.

He also tried to explain away Belinda Grant's terror and the red glow in Lindon's office and the thing he had glimpsed at its heart. Then there was his run of luck, commissions piling up in his bank account. That strange, unreadable contract…

He lay on his bed, unsleeping as his mind untangled every carefully woven explanation and denial. Hours later, in the pre-dawn silence, he fell into a sleep troubled by nightmares of his death and the horror beyond Lindon's door.

Monday; a long, tense day. Kirsty stayed away from him. He felt detached, separate from the others in the office. He was distracted, unable to focus on his work.

He had to know.

He had to find out what was going on.

Lee made his excuses for staying late and waited for the office to quieten. Then he brought his employment contract up on his screen. He struggled to focus. His head ached. His attention drifted. So, he started again. He felt sick. Dizzy -

There. Gone, Slippery somehow, elusive. No, there it was.

Surely he'd misread the sentence.

Again.

...when agreed five-year period is ended, LEE DARTNALL will forfeit his soul to Graham Lindon, Managing Director of Lindon Employment, to do with as he sees fit.

A joke, surely.

His *soul?*

Time to settle this once and for all.

"Come in." A deep voice answered his knock. Like a cliche Managing Director. Public School. Authoritative.

He opened the door.

On an ordinary, if luxurious, office. Big desk of gleaming wood. Expensive fountain pen in a wooden holder. Leather armchairs. A huge scenic window showing the lights of the city.

And Lindon himself; heavy set, broad and square-jawed, wearing a pinstripe suit with matching red silk tie and pocket handkerchief.

"Good to see you, Lee." He indicated the chair that faced his desk. "How can I help?"

"It's about my contract."

Up went those eyebrows. "And?"

"There's a clause, about my..." Suddenly the whole thing seemed ridiculous. "My soul."

"You actually *read* the contract? Impressive." A chuckle, deep, warm. "But, to answer your query, yes, at the end of your five-year stint with me I will take your soul."

"I...What?"

"I believe that Kirsty has already apprised you of the fact. I don't approve of workplace romances, by the way."

"There's no romance."

"If you say so. You have five years, Lee. Five years of commissions that will furnish the sort of lifestyle you only ever dreamed about. Of course, it would be more exciting if we were investment bankers or hedge fund managers, those people can't hand over their souls fast enough, but I felt that this little corner of the business world is more discreet. And people's career dreams are just as ripe for the plucking, just as luscious and flavoursome as the cocaine-fuelled greed of Square Mile money-fuckers. So, make the most of it, Lee. Have fun. Don't tie yourself down with one pretty face, especially one who will soon be coming home to daddy."

Lee swallowed his disgust and attempted calm and cool. "What if we simply leave the firm?"

"*We*? You really are smitten, aren't you." A bemused smile. "Well, yes, you can check out, but as The Eagles tell us, you can never leave. Your body can walk through those doors, work trinkets in a cardboard box, but your run of luck will end, and your soul will still fly back to me in five years' time when a blood clot stops your heart, or cancer has its way with you." Lindon waved towards his computer. "I can tell you which it will be, if you like."

"What's your real name, Lindon?" Lee said. "Lucifer? Satan?"

"All and none of the above. I have a job to do, Lee. I'm part of the weft and weave. Without me, the universe simply wouldn't work."

"Is there a way out of this?"

"Actually, there is, but just to let you know, violence and threats don't work. I've lost count of the thrown punches, broken chairs, knives and even guns I've had to put up with." He raised his hand. Lee flinched back, expecting…he wasn't sure what. Then Lindon slammed it down onto the fountain pen. The black-and-gold Montblanc punched through his flesh.

There was red, but it wasn't blood. It glowed, like lava, and ran from his impaled hand onto the desk to dissolve into the varnished wood. All through this performance, Lindon's smile shifted from regretful to challenging.

"So how do I get out of the contract?" Lee said. It was difficult to keep his voice steady and his eyes off Lindon's impaled hand.

"You tear it up, Lee; simple as that."

"Where is it?"

"Through there." A nod towards the door behind his desk. "Feel free."

The door was a plain office type. Light brown wood, ordinary handle. Lee glanced back at Lindon, whose attention had already returned to his computer. His right hand was free again and apparently uninjured. An act. Everything about the man was an act.

This whole thing was, of course, a trick. But Lee was desperate enough to try anything. For Kirsty as well as himself. That realisation was something of a shock to him.

He opened the door.

There was…darkness, light, something that made him stumble back and gasp for breath. He slammed the door shut and backed away. What the hell had he seen in there? He couldn't remember, couldn't comprehend.

"Are we finished?" Lindon's attention was still on his screen.

"No, we haven't."

Startled, Lee turned to see Kirsty standing in the office doorway.

"What are you doing here?" Lindon said. "It's time you went home, my dear. Work-life balance and all that."

Kirsty ignored him and crossed to confront Lee. "I knew you were up to something." She reached for the handle.

"Please, don't open that door."

"It's the only way out of this, Lee."

"Make up your minds, please. I'm extremely busy." Lindon grumbled.

"Mine's made up," Kirsty's gaze was fixed on Lee as she pushed at the handle.

"And mine." Lee covered her hand with his. She offered him a quick, brave smile.

They opened the door.

For Lee, it was like stepping off a cliff.

This time there was a steep, narrow staircase. The steps and walls were made of stone, cold and dank to the touch. The light was uncertain, as if provided by flaming brands although there were none to be seen. There was something of a cliché about these stairs, as if they existed because they were expected to.

This was not what Lee had seen when he had opened the door for the first time. He might be unsure as to exactly what it had been, but there was no staircase.

Descent was single file only. Lee at the front.

The walls moved. Things slithered just beneath the surface of the stonework, worm-like, a metre long. Faces pressed outwards, mouths open, stone become flesh. Unnerving, yes, but it felt more like some London Dungeon attraction than the entrance to hell.

The staircase spiralled downwards into a pool of impenetrable darkness. Now *that* was frightening. There was no turning back, however. The darkness had to be faced.

"Are you okay, Kirsty?"

"Yes." Her courage deepened his love for her. "We can do this together."

He felt her hand on his shoulder and once more covered it with his own.

The line between the darkness and the uncertain, reddish light of the staircase was unnaturally stark. There was no progressive dimming, no gentle loss of clarity. Instead, there was a wall of black. A doorway to God knew what.

Lee took a shaky breath.

"Ready?"

"Yes."

"Go."

A step –

- and he scrambled up from the hot sandy ground and ran,

crouched low, rifle in his hands. He was not alone. There were others on either side. Felt rather than seen, obscured by the acrid smoke of the recent mortar barrage.

Stay low, zigzag. Keep moving. Objective hidden in the smoke. The terror of it loosened every part of him. He felt as if his body would crumble to bloody fragments at any moment.

Run.

Weave.

Voices.

The rest of the squad, crying out for help. Begging, weeping, pleading.

The deep thud of an explosion punched a shockwave into his chest. Then a maniac war cry, drowned by the moans of terror and agony as helpless casualties were slaughtered in their field hospital beds. Automatic fire, a grunt driven from the throat by the impact of a bullet in the chest. Over and over again. Louder, louder, until they lost coherence and became a whirlwind howl that pressed in on his ears -

Silence. An empty room. No doors. The walls, floor and low ceiling were smooth and white. Lee turned to check on Kirsty but she wasn't there.

In her own white room, no doubt, facing her own ordeal.

There were soldiers. Five of them, in field uniform, worn and battered by long, hard use. They stood at ease, their attention fixed on Corporal Lee Dartnall.

McDonald, Singh, Goldschmidt, Oliver and LeCarre.

None of them spoke but each offered Lee a humourless rueful smile. Smiles of blame, of contempt.

It isn't my fault you died. You were my friends. He spoke but no sound came. *I didn't run away and leave you. I didn't make fatal mistakes. I wasn't there when any of you were killed. You simply died in the line of duty.*

So why were they looking at him like that? As if it *was* his fault…no, they didn't hate him because they had died, they hated him because he was still alive. What had Corporal

Lee Dartnall done to deserve a heartbeat and breath? He was no better than them. In some ways he was their inferior; not as kind as Singh, or funny and generous as Goldschmidt, or cool and calm as Oliver, or courageous and safe as Pearson, or as passionate and clever as LeCarre. They deserved to be alive.

But we aren't, they say, and you are. Why is that Dartsy? Why didn't you die?

He was afraid of them. They stood, legs slightly apart, hands clenched behind their backs, caps at just the right angle. Their boots and uniforms were dusty and bloodstained. They made no move towards him, showed no aggression, just smiled their ugly, accusatory smiles.

Why them, Lindon? Lee asked. *Why not the Afghan civilians who died as collateral damage, or the men, women and children we believed, in the heat of a firefight, to be terrorists? Why not the people we murdered?*

This was a trick. There was no contract. Only their hate. Their contempt. Those smiles.

Lee forced himself into motion. His body felt heavy; his legs weak. They watched his approach then parted to form a grotesque guard of honour, McDonald, LeCarre and Oliver to his left, Goldschmidt and Singh to his right.

Lee took a breath and walked between them. The air was cold here, dank and icy. Their contempt crackled over his skin, electric shocks that burned and danced painfully on his nerves. It was the silence, the passive-aggressive toxicity that turned the air foul and sucked away his strength.

A sixth solider stepped into his path. The worst of all.

Corporal Lee Dartnall.

His hatred was deep and savage. There was no smile. He wanted violence.

He wanted a price paid. He wanted Lee Dartnall to show enough guts to do what he had failed to do, to wash away the stink of shame with his own blood.

Lee stepped up to him and stared into his eyes. His own

soul stared back at him. It was an overwhelming wall of hatred.

And he understood.

He was his own hell, formed from his own guilt and self-loathing.

He was the contract.

Lee struggled with the concept.

He only needed to pluck out its heart –

How did he know that?

He thrust his hand towards the other's chest, but it was too fast. It grabbed his wrist. and it burned. Nails tore through Lee's skin, blood flowed. Lee felt his legs buckle.

Yelling with effort, he wrenched his ruined arm free. They both stumbled, Lee backwards, the doppelganger forwards. Lee recovered quickly and drove his fist through the other's ribcage. Broken bones ripped his flesh. There was coldness as fiery as a naked flame. But he pushed on, until his fingers closed about the pulsing muscle deep inside.

He dragged it back through the razor-wire tangle of the other's severed ribs. The pain was excruciating.

When he finally wrenched it clear, the heart was already crumbling to dust. It ran through his bleeding fingers and disappeared long before it reached the floor.

The walls shattered and collapsed in a silent waterfall of broken masonry and dust. What he did hear, however, were the screams of the damned. There was fire beyond. Something vast and incomprehensible lay at its heart. It was a machine, it was flesh, it was a thousand metallic snakes twisted into a never-motionless sphere. Lee saw wheels, eyes. Its voice was a roar like the grinding of metal on metal and it dropped Lee to his knees, hands clamped over his ears. He was aware of Kirsty beside him, head bowed. She was as bruised and torn as he was.

A wave of flame swept towards them, a wall of shimmering orange and yellow that brought with it unthinkable heat. His hair burned, his skin blistered and blackened. There would be pain, any moment now, white, formless agony -

Carpet. Light. The clack of a keyboard.

Still kneeling, Lee looked up to see Lindon's intimidating desk, the leather chairs, and Kirsty, already standing. She reached down to help him to his feet.

"You're both sacked," Lindon didn't look up from his computer. "Your commissions and one month's money are already in your bank accounts."

Lee wasn't listening. He took Kirsty's hand, which was warm in his. They made for the door.

"By the way," Lindon said. "You are aware that, contract or no contract, you'll probably be mine in the end anyway."

Yes, but not yet.

Lee was alive. He had been one of the lucky ones who had made it home. He owed it to the others, to Goldschmidt, LeCarre, Oliver, all of them, to live that life. And live it, he would.

He took Kirsty in his arms and kissed her.

"Oh God, spare me the schmaltz," Lindon said.

"Go to hell," Kirsty answered.

"I'd love to." Lindon chuckled. "Oh, and shut the door on the way out, will you."

The Sunset Unlimited

James Musgrave

Bill heard the pounding at about three in the morning. It sounded like someone was hitting something against the bulkhead walls, and he got up, put on his robe, and went out into the passageway. The sound was coming from down near the coffee maker where the sleeper car attendant's room was located. Bill, a bit warily, walked toward the commotion at the other end. They were traveling fast, and the car was rocking to and fro like an old ship on the high seas. The flashing lights from the train's windows were passing over his body as he crept forward. Finally, Bill reached the door to Mary Lou's room. The shade was drawn shut with the Velcro edges, but he could still hear the pounding on the sides of the compartment. *What the hell?* The sound became increasingly louder, until it was almost deafening. Bill was afraid she was being hurt, so he pulled at the handle on the metal door. It would not budge. Suddenly, the pounding and movement stopped. The shade came apart, and Bill could see inside.

She was straddling him, and her big breasts were heaving up and down, and her ass was pounding him against the side of the bed. He was seated on the floor, and his gigantic black cock was thrust up and into the passion between her dark brown legs. As she bounced, she threw her raven-haired head back and laughed, and that's when she looked up. Bill pulled away from the door's window but not before she smiled back at him. He ran, tripping over himself, down the passageway. *Oh, my God! What have we here? It looks like our little sleeper car has a little Spanish cure for insomnia. I just might take her up on that remedy tomorrow night!*

***

One week earlier, New Orleans

Bill Daniels, high-powered software executive, stepped into line at the Amtrak station in New Orleans. He and his wife, Arlene, a college English teacher, were having problems conceiving, and so, to relax and get to know each other better, and discuss their possible options, they were going to take the final ride of the Sunset Limited, the train that had journeyed across the United States for over thirty years. However, since the current administration took over, Congress had failed to fund Amtrak, and so this route was being totally cut from Amtrak's schedule.

Bill had maintained his love affair with trains ever since he was a boy growing up in Pennsylvania, where Penn Station became his home-away-from-home, and every Christmas there was a new car for his Lionel train set. He and his father, Jake, kept a giant track layout in the basement of their house, where father and son would reenact Old West train robberies, transport weapons for world wars, and make perilous trips across the simulated deserts, forests, lakes and mountains of America.

The demise of the railroad in America hit Bill really hard. It was if a best friend had died, and now he and his wife were going to ride a funeral procession aboard the Sunset Limited. Bill told his wife, on the evening they were planning the trip, "This is the beginning of the end, honey. Even though

Europe and Asia have put a lot of money into their trains, our government has decided for us that travel by train is obsolete. What a fucking waste!"

Arlene put her arms around her tall husband's waist and pulled him toward her. "It's all about speed, Bill, you should know that. We keep going faster and faster to get nowhere. E-waste from computers, wars for oil, it all amounts to an obsession with speed. My college students are never prepared to do any critical thinking because they're so used to the speed of the Internet. They have forgotten that reading requires in-depth thinking and analysis. If they don't get the answer in five seconds on Google, it's not worth the attempt."

"Yeah, I want this trip to be an exclamation mark against our government. I'm going to send them all the digital photos and the journal that I will be keeping so they'll know what we'll all be missing from our country's history." Bill picked up the worn, blue-striped railroad engineer hat from his coffee table and pulled it down on his head. "This will be our final ride, sweetheart, and we're not going out without a fight!"

***

As Bill led his wife along the track, he inhaled the odor of the diesel fuel. He pictured himself as the conductor, waving at them, hanging out of the club car's door, his black uniform and cap pressed and neat. Bill noticed this conductor even had a gold watch chain tucked inside his vest pocket. "Greetings, Mr. and Mrs. Daniels. We have your suite ready. Watch your step!"

Bill and Arlene climbed aboard, and the conductor carried their luggage behind them as they walked down the passageway to the biggest sleeper on the Sunset Limited. Bill glanced inside the other sleepers. Not so big, but they looked fairly comfortable. Such a waste, as it will all be destroyed in a month or so.

"Good morning, Mr. and Mrs. Daniels," said the sleeper car attendant, whose nametag said "Mary Lou," but Bill and Arlene found out later she was from Spain, originally--Barcelona, to be exact--and she pronounced the city's name with the Castilian "th" sound. Bill noticed that the white shirt beneath her black uniform jacket was quite fully packed, and she reminded him of the actress, Penelope Cruz.

"I'll pull your beds down when you go to dinner," Mary Lou said, the dimples in her cheeks showing like ripe apples when she smiled. Bill made a mental note to try to be nearby some night when Maria Louisa pulled down the beds.

Bill had paid for the biggest suite in the train, and they had a shower inside the room, two beds that pulled out, and a wonderful view of the passing scenery. "We won't need to use the viewing car this time, baby," said Bill, hugging his wife. The last time they traveled by train they went by coach, and the only good observation to be had was to use the viewing car.

"I think I'll take a shower before dinner," said Bill, lifting up the two suitcases into the overhead holds. Arlene pulled the drapes shut so no wandering passenger would get a peek at her husband's nice derrière, and Bill shucked off all his clothes.

"This will be a great trip!" said Bill, as he stepped inside the shower. Bill turned the handle, so it was right in the center of the hot and cold. When the stream of scalding water hit his body, after he pulled out the lever, Bill let out a scream in spite of himself. "Shit! What the fuck?" He danced up and down and turned off the faucet.

Dripping like a wet dog, Bill pulled a large towel around him and pushed the attendant's button. A friendly chime sounded throughout the sleeper car. In about two minutes, Mary Lou was at their cabin door. "You rang, sir?" she asked, and Arlene let her inside.

"I tried to take a shower," said Bill, keeping a firm grip

on the red towel around his waist, "but all I got was a burn from the constant stream of hot water."

The attendant stepped inside the shower, turned on the handle, and the stream gushed on her arm. "I don't feel it," she said, turning the handle from hot to cold and then back again. "It seems to work fine, Mr. Daniels. I'm sorry it happened."

"That's okay, I guess I might have twisted it too much or something. Thanks anyway, Maria," he said and noticed that she smiled when he used the Spanish word for her name. "I'll let my wife try it first," he added, smiling at Arlene.

Arlene was able to shower without a problem, but when Bill stepped back inside to have his turn, the same thing happened. All he got was a scalding, burning stream of water on his skin. Arlene suggested he take it up with the conductor, and Bill agreed to do just that.

Bill and Arlene wore their old-time engineer suits to dinner the first night, and the folks in the dining car chuckled as they passed by them to their seats, rocking and rolling with the movement of the train speeding down the tracks. The waitress, a young Black woman named Bertha, was both ambidextrous and an adroit walker, who could balance her tray as the train swayed precariously from side to side. She glided up to their table and put down salads and an assortment of dressings in plastic packages. "I'll be with you in a minute," she said, winked, and took off to another table. The cacophony of voices, cutlery, sneezes and constant clickety-clack of the tracks, blended together with the odor of that evening's bill of fare to give the dining car a pleasant ambiance.

The dining car supervisor, a huge Filipino with a Fu Manchu mustache named Charles, escorted a couple to the Daniels' table. They were in their early seventies, Bill guessed, and they sat down and smiled over at their fellow travelers as they spread their napkins on their laps.

"We're riding to the end of the line. How 'bout you

folks?" asked the gentleman, a portly and balding fellow with a nervous twitch in his left eye.

"Yes, we're here for the duration as well," said Bill. "Can't you tell from our outfits? This is going to be one of the last train rides Americans will possibly ever experience." Bill tipped his engineer's cap.

"The name's Walt Iverson, and this here is my wife of twenty-five years, Marilee. We both worked for the United Parcel Service for thirty years, and that's where I found this sweet little package," he chuckled, and the rosy-cheeked, gray-haired lady at his side rolled her eyes like a teenager and smiled. Walt wore bib overalls, and his Marilee had on what looked to be a home-made gingham print dress of some kind. This was also a bit of vanishing Americana, which was quite apropos for this journey.

"We were told by some authority that our reward is coming when we arrive in the City of Angels," said Walt, a twinkle glinting in his dark brown eyes.

"Reward? What kind of reward?" Bill asked.

"Honey, perhaps the Iversons want to keep it private," said Arlene, gently prodding Bill on his elbow.

"Oh, that's okay. We don't mind. We're kinda proud that we came into the money when we did. In fact, everyone on this train has won a prize to be redeemed when they get off at the end of the line," said Walt.

"We call it the train bound for glory!" said Marilee, repeating something she probably heard at church.

"Everyone? Why, we haven't won anything. How do you suppose we were allowed to get tickets?" asked Bill, curious about the whole matter. Were he and Arlene victims of some kind of practical joke?

"Yup. We were told everybody on board is a winner," said Walt.

"Do you know Rudy Walker, by any chance?" Rudy was Bill's boss at Thor Software, and he didn't doubt that the old fart might have gone to such extremes to put one over on

Bill. In fact, to Rudy, Bill's infatuation with trains and the vanishing American landscape was quite fatuous. Rudy flew everywhere by jet, and he drove a huge Lincoln Navigator. Bill called him "Fifty-Cent" behind his back. Bill's little Toyota Prius looked like a diminutive bug parked next to Rudy's monster ride in the company's parking lot.

"Rudy Walker? No, I don't believe I do. We do know the Walkers in Galveston. Galveston, Texas," said Walt.

"No, that's not the one," said Bill, and they stopped talking long enough to order their meals from Bertha. Bill took some pictures of the old couple, and then he ordered the Cornish game hen with yellow rice, and his wife ordered the fish—Falupia, Tilapia or Palupia, some such farmed aquatic delight.

Bill was able to corner the head conductor after dinner. He was a tall Black man by the name of Richard, and he was about Bill's age, early thirties. Richard wore his black uniform like a prince of the tracks, and his demeanor was officious and grandiose. Bill looked down and could see his reflection in the young man's shined shoes. As they talked, Richard kept fiddling with his two-way, and this annoyed Bill.

"My shower seems to be malfunctioning. Strange thing is, it only runs red-hot when I'm in the shower," said Bill, feeling a bit awkward just explaining his dilemma.

"Well, you know the old saying," said Richard, his white teeth flashing, "If you can't stand the heat, then get out of the shower," and he chuckled at his own joke.

"I know it sounds ridiculous, but I was planning on enjoying my trip and taking tons of photos. Actually, what I really want to do is to write up this big report and send it to the government. We shouldn't be letting the railways go the way of the Dodo bird. We need this kind of travel for our serenity," explained Bill.

Richard hitched up his wide black belt, tucked in his white shirt on the sides, and adjusted his shiny-billed conductor's cap. "This train's on its last run, Mr. Daniels. There's no saving it from destruction. That's why all the people on it are here to receive their rewards at the end of the line. Including me and every staff member under me," he added, staring intently down at his shiny shoes, as if they held an answer to some mystery that was beyond him. "Funny thing, though, we don't quite know what exactly we're going to receive. The boss just told us to get on board and finish our trip."

"That's quite interesting," said Bill, warming to this subject instantly, "I was just going to ask you about that. We were never told about any reward for riding on this train. Why do you suppose that is?" he asked.

"I wouldn't know anything about that, sir," said the conductor, turning to go. "I'll check on your shower," he added, hurrying down the center of the car and pushing on the red door lever inside the panel indention. The pneumatic door whooshed open, and he was through it, like some kind of tall, dark spirit.

***

The next morning, as they were pulling into Houston, Bill and Arlene had breakfast with another sleeper car resident, one Roscoe Lee Hayward, from Los Angeles. He wore baggy jeans and a tee shirt with a faded color shot of John Coltrane on the front, but his blond hair was cut short, his baby face was tan, and he had a silver earring in his left earlobe. Roscoe told them he was thirty-seven, a music producer and musician. He was in New Orleans to see if he could become musically inspired. His specialties were blues, jazz, and be-bop.

However, much to Bill's chagrin, Roscoe's clean-shaven, handsomely engaging attitude impressed Arlene because she leaned forward when he spoke, showing the dickwad some of her cleavage, and she was held in rapt attention by his words. *Serves me right for flirting with Mary Lou, the Spanish sleeping car attendant.*

"I won this trip after I chanted for thirty-seven hours straight," said Roscoe, his blue eyes holding fast onto Arlene's. "I belong to a sect with over a million members in North America. You could never tell we were a sect if you saw us on the street. We chant with the *nam myoho renge kyo* lotus sutra, which, of course, is the essence of Buddhism. We call it Daimoku. Through this practice, one is able to reveal the state of Buddhahood in one's life, experienced as the natural development of joy, increased vitality, courage, wisdom and compassion."

"Hey, yeah, I remember an old Jack Nicholson movie, *The Last Detail*. Nicholson plays an old first-class petty officer who's trying to take this young A.W.O.L. sailor to the brig, and they end up at one of your group's sessions. They're all smoking pot and listening to groovy music. A little later in the movie, the kid prisoner breaks free, and as he runs he keeps chanting that sutra thing, with old Jack, huffing and puffing, right at his heels."

"Did he escape?" Roscoe asked.

"Uh, nope," said Bill, "Jack fucked him up pretty badly and finished escorting the kid to the brig," Bill smiled, relishing the look of disappointment on Roscoe's face.

"Well, karma was probably with him anyway. We can never know when our reward will come, but it sure did with me!" said Roscoe, a hint of defiance in his voice.

"Let me have one of your cards," said Arlene. "I just love jazz and the darker the blues, the better. It's so romantic that you were in New Orleans to get inspired with your music," she added.

"Yeah, let me get a shot of you next to my wife," said Bill, and he took the picture.

Back inside their cabin, on his smartphone, Bill began running through the photos he had taken so far on their trip, and when he came to the shot of Roscoe, he stopped. He was also listening to Pink Floyd's "The Wall" with his earbuds, and it was an eerie feeling when he noticed that in the breakfast pic, seated next to Arlene, was exactly nobody. Bill inspected the frame closely to see if there was a mark or some light that covered Roscoe's image, but no, it was completely empty of any human form whatsoever. He could even see the back of the chair where Roscoe had been sitting.

"Arlene," he said, handing her the camera, "take a look. This is the shot I took of you and that musical Buddha. Freaky, but he's not in the picture."

Arlene looked at it. "My, that is strange. Do you suppose he's some kind of vampire?" she said, smiling mischievously.

Bill took the camera from her, set it down carefully, and covered her body with his. "I vant to drink your blood!" he vamped, pressing his lips against her soft and tender white neck. Bill reached over, and with some awkward effort, hit the button to turn off the compartment lights.

"Maybe we should adopt," whispered Bill, as he kissed his wife with new passion.

After making love for the first time in three weeks, Bill and Arlene discussed their future.

"I want to try again, Bill. We can have a child. I know we can. The doctor gave us the go ahead, and he said all we need to do is relax and let things happen. We're both physically able." Arlene lay on her back, staring out the window at the passing lights of Gallup, New Mexico.

"What would you call what we just did; throwing out the first pitch?" Bill chuckled at his own joke.

"It's not a game, my friend. This could change our lives. We've both been too selfish. Bringing another life into the world means a lot of sacrifice and careful compromise. I think that's what we've been missing in our marriage for a long time." Arlene turned over on her side to face Bill. "I don't want to feel alone anymore, Bill. Can you understand that?"

Bill kissed Arlene again, and he believed he was finally ready for the All-Star Game.

***

The next morning, as the train was pulling into the San Felipe Indian Reservation in New Mexico, it came to a jarring stop. Bill and Arlene shot forward in their seats, almost hitting their heads on the bulkhead on the other side of the cabin.

"Jesus! I wonder what happened." Arlene stood up, brushing down the front of her dress. "C'mon, Bill, let's go see."

They both left their sleeper cabin, walked down the passageway, and entered the viewing car. Passengers were standing all around talking, trying to figure out what the commotion was outside the train. They had been having problems with the electricity going out every time they stopped, but the conductor said it would be repaired in Gallup. This was a completely unscheduled stop.

Mary Lou came into the car with news about what had happened. She looked quite unnerved as she ran her hand through her raven hair. "A woman. She was a tribal Shaman. She ran in front of our train. She was shouting at us about having demons onboard. The Chief told us she had been drinking a lot lately, so he supposes she was insane and committed suicide."

"Demons? Why would she want to kill herself over demons on this train? Doesn't sound very reasonable to me," Arlene said.

A tall man in Bermuda shorts and a Hawaiian shirt was pointing outside. "Look outside! It's the railway to hell!" He laughed, but nobody seemed to get the joke.

"Maybe the devil himself. He is onboard," a bearded Amish man, wearing a black hat and suit, spoke from one of the seats in the viewing car. He had his wife and four children with him, and they were all dressed in the 18th century Gothic attire that the Anabaptists wore.

"Yeah, sure. That's it. We're taking Satan on a vacation to California." Bill said, and he got some nervous laughs from his fellow passengers. When the train was finally cleared to continue on its journey, the passengers cast sidelong glances at each other, as they took their seats and scheduled their dining reservations. Bill and Arlene decided to eat in their sleeper cabin.

Later that evening, as the clock on Bill's cell said 3 AM, he got up. Arlene was still asleep, and he walked out into the passageway. He wore his shorts and a tee, and some new brown Crocs that Arlene had just bought him for his birthday.

He was surprised to see that the light in Mary Lou's compartment was off. In fact, there was no human noise throughout the entire train. Although they were moving on at quite a clip, and Bill could feel the usual grinding and groaning of the cars upon the old tracks, he did not see any sign of an attendant, conductor or other passenger as he made his way down the passageway of his sleeper car back toward the dining car.

Just as he was entering the dining car, he saw them through the door's window. Hundreds of lizards on the tiled floor and all over the Formica tables. No, wait. They weren't lizards. They were what Bill as a boy used to call "horny toads." Fat little lizards with two spikes on their heads, like the horns of a prehistoric Stegosaurus, and many smaller barbs all over their tan bodies. As he pushed through the pneumatic door into the car, they streaked away, falling down into the air ducts, and disappearing behind refrigerators and cabinets. When they were gone, the lights went out. It was pitch-dark, except for the passing illuminations outside the train, and Bill began to shiver. *This is odd. They never leave the lights off at night.* There was a breeze blowing down the center of the aisle, even though there were no open windows.

When Bill reached the end of the dining car, he came upon an even stranger sight. The door to the next car was locked, and a sign over the door's window read, "Private Party in Progress. Do Not Enter!"

Bill pulled the sign away from the small window. What he saw inside made him immediately drop down between the cars. The blast of wind, and the hellacious vibrations of the car speeding over the tracks, made his whole body vibrate and his teeth chatter. He lurched sideways, back and forth, and hit his head and body against the sides of the compartment. The conductor's spiel had warned them about losing a foot or toes in the small space between the cars.

Bill needed to see what was going on inside that next car, so he slowly raised himself up, until his eyes barely peeked over the door panel, and through the little window, where he could see into the next car, the black car. When he looked inside, Bill saw a human train of naked bodies glistening with perspiration and joined in the weirdest assortment of sexual positions he had ever seen in his life. In front of the line were Mr. and Mrs. Iverson, the old couple, and Mrs. Iverson had metal hoops pierced through her nipples and on her vagina's labia majora, and silver chains were running through each hoop, and the old couple was hooked up with the rest of the macabre assortment of connected bodies running behind them. Directly behind Mrs. Iverson, the big Filipino Dining Room Supervisor with the Fu Manchu, had entered the elderly woman "doggie style," and next came her husband, Walt, who was standing right beside the fat Filipino, urging him on and jangling his wife's chains as if they were bells on Santa's sleigh. Next came Bertha, the waitress, a few others he didn't know, and then at the back of the obscene conga line were Richard, the head conductor and his gal Friday, Mary Lou. Each was attached to the other with metal piercings, rings or hoops, and they were going at it like some kind of sexual three-ring circus act. They all had tattoos that decorated their naked bodies like Japanese Yakuza—dragons, lizards, scorpions, and, in the small of the lovely Mary Lou's back was the unmistaken image of the beast master, himself, Satan. The image was moving quite rapidly, up and down, and, as Bill listened carefully, he could hear heavy metal music pounding inside the black car. It sounded like AC/DC or Metallica, if he wasn't mistaken.

But it was the big sign on the wall behind the table filled with food and booze that really freaked him out. It said, "Welcome to the Natal Train of Bill and Arlene Daniels!"

The door whooshed open; Richard, the conductor, and the big Filipino grabbed Bill by his arms and dragged him inside the car. The doors shut, and Richard pulled down the Velcro shade, and the compartment was pitch dark. The train rocked from side to side, Bill inhaled the distinctive odor of sulfur, and he felt a needle being injected into his right shoulder.

***

Bill and Arlene Daniels got off in Los Angeles, California, along with Roscoe Lee Hayward. The three of them never said a word to each other as they carried their luggage off the train, pulled up the handles, and wheeled their belongings slowly down the long path leading toward the station.

They took a cab from Union Station, downtown, out to the Wilshire District, where Roscoe's music recording studio was. Inside the elevator to the tenth floor, Bill and Arlene held hands, and they kept staring at their escort. When they got out, they walked slowly down the hall, and Roscoe unlocked the double-doors to his suite of rooms. Inside it was a modern recording studio with engineering mixer, digital recording equipment, and dozens of different types of microphones.

Roscoe motioned for them to be seated on the couch

inside the studio, and he walked behind the panel of mixing controls. He took out a DVD disk and inserted it into the player. "You were right, Arlene, honey. I was inspired to write something during my trip to New Orleans. It's kind of a tune in honor of you two. You were chosen to be the couple for the New Age of the coming Kali Yuga Era. Destruction is in these days, don't you know?"

"Destruction? Bill and I are going to have a child. In fact, we may have become pregnant on our trip. We just needed to relax, that's all." Arlene took Bill's hand again and turned to look at him.

Bill frowned at the young musician. He never told his wife about the strange goings-on inside the dark car the night before and the orgy that had taken place.

A soft, bluesy jazz piece filled the room. Roscoe, the musical Buddhist, smiled over at them, bobbing his head in time to his newest composition.

At first, Bill believed Roscoe might be the leader of a sex cult. What they had experienced on the Sunset Limited was simply a private sex orgy for some weird sex group with cult overtones. He and Arlene were the crashers who were now being recruited. That made sense. It explained Mary Lou, the orgy he saw, and even the so-called "reward" at the end of the trip. Roscoe was now going to offer them their reward in the form of membership in their bizarre club.

The jazz slowly began to metamorphose into a heavy metal beat. The walls vibrated, and the doors again swung open. Every passenger on the Sunset Limited entered the room, and they were all dressed in black robes. Richard the conductor led the parade, bouncing to the beat of the music, frantically waving his arms, thrashing his head from side to side, with spittle flying from his mouth. Mary Lou followed closely behind him, and she opened her robe to reveal large breasts that bobbed along to the vibes of the metal music. Her long dark legs, with the patch of black between them, were dancing to their own insane beat, and her bare feet strutted out into the room like the Devil's own drum majorette. Gold chains bounced around her ankles and neck, and her fierce brown eyes flashed sparks from an eternal power source.

After all of the passengers surrounded Bill and Arlene, Roscoe Lee Hayward shut off the music. The steps he took toward the couple were slow, martial, and ceremonial, quite unlike the frenetic spasms of the others. Bill's forehead wrinkled, and his eyebrows turned down. *Here it comes. Now we're going to get the pitch. No way, buster. I've quit cheating on Arlene. We're going to make a family, and you cretins will never be a part of it.*

After Roscoe placed his hands on their foreheads, Bill and Arlene Daniels' bodies became rigid, like corpses. As they stared at him, they could see his musician's form change, gradually morphing into the orange-black shape of the Lord of Flies.

His two long, fleshy horns and six-foot tail writhed like snakes; his reddish-green spiked scales pulsated like thousands of serpent hearts. Frothy green slime blanketed the heavy metal throne as it grew upward through the wood floor. His fiery serpent eyes constantly moved across his dominion, recognizing only the evil acts of Man. Satan roared again, and the sticky slime from his cavernous mouth and flesh-eating teeth dripped threads of creamy elastic all over the thorny scales of his huge frame. He shook the gunk from his body, and pounded his fists against his mammoth chest, causing the room to tremble.

Roscoe's voice was a deep blast, and his body was now completely reptilian and huge. "There is a force in this world that feeds upon evil. It can be found wherever there is a human being committing an act of torture upon another; it can be found wherever soldiers are killing each other and shouting curses of vengeance and nationalistic slogans; it can be found in the adulterer's bed, and inside the serial killer's refrigerator congested with body parts; it is in the place where fury meets innocence and ignites into violence; it is in the twisted grimace of rage, in the blood of the holocaust, and it encompasses the Orwellian double speak of modern nations."

The primeval devil had shivered with excitement when his human ghouls, with their hellish souls, reported to him of the destruction of the human zygote inside the dining car on board the Sunset Limited. Now, with the replacement on the uterine wall, this last trip would forever be known as the Sunset Unlimited!

The touch of the Beast Master had filled Bill and Arlene Daniels' brains with the real truth. Inside their minds, the horrendous cerebral video of the night before began to play: *Arlene's stomach was sliced open to abort the intruding blastocyst and replace it with the Master's fetus. The mother and the useless drone were carried into the black car, and they were given injections, probed with hundreds of instruments, and, finally, an obscene passion filled their bodies like a plague of locusts descending upon the Earth. Colors became muted and then darkened to purple, everything was swollen around them, and the eyes of the watchers encircled their naked forms as they posed on the high, four-poster bed in front of them. They chanted together, "Nam, myoho ringe kyo! The master will be born! Nam, myoho ringe kyo! The End of Times has come!" Bill and Arlene fucked like swine, like goats, like spastic muskrats in conjugal love. And then, like an obscene porno movie from hell, each one of the passengers took turns fucking them. Man on man, woman on woman—it didn't matter—they were all one heaving, thrusting, and sweating pile of bodies. What Shakespeare would have called "the beast with fifteen backs." The image of the tortured prisoners of Abu Ghraib filled Bill's consciousness before he passed out for the second time. The Master's spawn was finally fertilized.*

Inside the recording studio, the heavy metal music started

again, and Bill and Arlene fell, gasping, into each other's arms. Their psyches had been polluted beyond redemption. Their soul-wrenching moans were so loud and hoarse they could even be heard above the crashing music for several minutes, until it all stopped.

Satan was left to create the final photo op for the group's website. Mary Lou, the Spanish sleeping car attendant, moved over to take the shot with her smartphone. She swept her black hair from her brow with her right hand and pointed the camera at Arlene. Her Master lumbered over to the newly impregnated woman, and he knelt down before her. With Satan's spiked scales quivering, and slime dripping from his jowls, he lowered his mammoth horned head to Arlene's stomach. Satan listened, with an acute, reptilian focus. He was listening for the first corporeal sounds of his son to come forth from the uterus of his new mother.

Unlike a human baby, this creation would form much faster, brain cells blossoming into a purplish coagulation of folded flesh, which would begin to spark evil thoughts almost as soon as they were formed. The world would soon be speeding up. Destruction would become faster. Death would increase daily, until it became a common occurrence, like the daily news. Only the father could hear it, but it was there, the first evil brain cell sparking to life. Mary Lou took the snap at the same moment when Lucifer heard the first flash of his son's brain. The proud father's head lifted, and he roared, in an eternal protestation against Heaven, as the beginning of the end of this world had finally begun.

The Haggler

Donn L. Hess

The most serious bargains, our truest promises, we seal with heart's blood. Not the blessed red, though there can be plenty of that and he likes it well enough. No, I'm talking about the thicker stuff, the ache that spills out of a chest cored by loss, the sticky pain of a hollowed soul.

He'll come sniffing after that sweet scent every time, and tonight I reek of it. It's a stink I've carried for months now.

The crickets stopped singing about a half mile back and the wind's gone still. I'd welcome a little breeze to dry the sweat running down our faces and pooling in the smalls of our backs. But I guess that's not to be, and I suppose it doesn't matter, especially not for Seb.

"You ain't gonna tell me where we're going?" he asks again, the frustration evident in his voice, though he does a good job of masking it.

"You'll see soon enough," I say.

I don't know if that's true, but it feels so. We're not headed to a place anybody knows, certainly not me. It's not somewhere that anyone could lead you to. We're going someplace a person's brought.

He mutters under his breath but doesn't argue. He's never contrary and I think that's why daddy loves him best.

Seb does as he's told. He's not too bright, but the good ones seldom are.

It's been hard to see him in the dark, to read his thoughts writ large in his expressions as I so often do. But then he pauses under a break in the trees and cool moonlight spills across his face. He looks at me with momma's soft brown eyes, looms over me with daddy's broad shoulders, and I see trust, an older brother indulging his youngest sibling.

Seb got all the looks in the family. That's why our mother loves him best.

"Are we at least close?" he asks. His eyes tell me he's confused. Annoyed, maybe, but untroubled.

"Just up ahead."

I wonder what he sees in my eyes. Perhaps nothing or perhaps he doesn't understand what he sees or doesn't care. He shrugs and forges on.

The woods shouldn't be this quiet even—or maybe especially—so close to midnight. It's as though the critters know something's going awry and they've scuttled for cover. Maybe they do and maybe they have; they're wiser than we. But even the leaves and the grasses stand still, hiding in place like they fear attracting attention. Seb's and my boots stomp the brush and the hardpacked dirt. We make three times as much noise as we should, and the ruckus feels almost blasphemous.

I don't care.

Seb swats branches out of his way, lets them snap back to lash my face and shoulders. This is as much defiance, the best insolence, his obedient soul can muster. I catch the branches on my forearms. The tiny stings feel less painful than I deserve.

We come to a clearing, a place in the forest where the narrow path we've been following crosses another, and I know we're here. My skin crawls as though trying to escape an unwanted touch. My pulse thuds in my neck and my palms sweat.

Nobody comes to this part of the woods. The creek's in the opposite direction. That's where you'll find a bit of cool on a summer's afternoon or some fish, if you're hungry. Here there's nothing to eat or take comfort from. Just thorns to scratch you and purple pokeweed berries that'll give you a deadly case of the shits if you taste them. A good nesting spot for deer, maybe, because it's too much trouble to hunt them here.

Yet I find the clearing also kind of beautiful. The trees stand far enough apart that the light from the fat full moon can paint the ground a glittering argent. Shadows from the leaves soften that gleam with a dark patina and I feel like I know this place even though I don't, even though I can't.

Even though I don't want to.

I went to a theater once, sneaking through a side door because Axel, my friend, worked there as an usher and let me in. This reminds me of that afternoon, the expectation, the uncurling of a small wickedness inside me that felt delighted with my little theft. I remember how, in the minutes before the show started, the stage looked the same way this clearing looks; empty but swollen, too, with the potential of what might happen. I almost hated it when the actors came out and the show began. I couldn't imagine the play would match the promise of that empty, waiting stage.

I almost hate now the promise of what's about to happen next.

In the middle of the glade, there's a big mound of rocks, one for each of Judas's thirty coins and then some. I'd guess every stone is just as bloody as those silver pieces, maybe more so. I don't know. I'm acting on instinct, listening to the lizard part of my brain that can tell me little more than to fight, feed, or flee. It's the part telling me now that I'm in the right place. The same, I'd imagine, as everyone else who's ever come to this clearing before me in answer to the call.

There's about to be another stone added to the pile. My

fingers twitch in anticipation.

"Is this what you wanted to show me?" Seb asks. He turns, a *what the hell?* expression splashed across his face. "A bunch of rocks?"

"They're not just rocks," I say and point to direct his attention back at the mound.

"They're not?" He frowns, looks over his shoulder at the cairn, then again at me. "What are they?"

"Offerings."

He turns all the way around to study the pile more closely. I pick up a rock of my own—they litter the ground around me like they've been waiting for this, all of them oddly smooth on one side and jagged on the other. Then I hit him with it. The blow doesn't strike as hard as I'd intended. Some last-second hesitation, the realization that this is my brother, slows my hand.

"Hey!" He whirls to face me, anger and confusion pinching his eyes and twisting his mouth. He stretches an arm behind him to feel for the bruise forming between his shoulder blades. "What'd you do that for?"

I hit him with the rock again. Harder and in the face this time. His eyes go wide with puzzlement and pain. Blood trickles from his nose.

"What? What did—"

I hit him again.

And then again.

And again.

In the movies, people make their sacrifices with knives. Maybe they plunge them into a heart or draw them quickly across a throat. But that's fast. Painless.

He doesn't like those sacrifices, the easy ones. That's not what he wants.

An offering must be more than body and blood. It has to come wrapped in betrayal and agony, loss and anguish. God understands that. He taught Cain who preached the gospel to the rest of us. Why wouldn't the Adversary expect the same?

Seb lies on the ground, now, his hands held weak and trembling in front of his face. "Why?" he asks. Or I think he asks that. It's hard to understand what he's saying.

"I'm sorry," I tell him over and over, my words punctuated by the sound of the rock coming down on his face, his chest, his gut. Thud. Thud. Thud. "I'm sorry. I'm sorry."

My brother goes limp, but my arm keeps rising and falling, mechanically, like some switch has jammed in the on position and I can't turn it back to off. I think maybe my mind goes somewhere else for a little while and I forget why I'm there, forget what I'm doing and to whom I'm doing it. It takes time to regain control of myself, to quiet everything roaring inside me and to remember why I'm here. I stop beating my brother and just kneel there, panting, his blood and bits of his skin cooling on my face. I wait for tears to come, for that unbearable welling of grief to spill out of me in chest-crushing sobs. But it doesn't happen. I'm empty, a void, and I wonder if I've at last reached the limit of my sorrow.

I know that I haven't. That's why I've come.

I stand and carry the stone, still wet with the last of Seb's life, and add it to the pile in the center of the clearing. As I set it on top, a cloud passes in front of the moon. I shiver even though the night is warm, and I'm soaked with sweat and still panting lightly from my efforts.

"Have you come to bargain?"

The voice speaks from behind me, closer than is comfortable. It sounds like a rich person talking, though I can't say why I think that. Maybe it's the tone, the complete lack of an accent. Maybe it's the vague note of boredom. But I've heard that voice before in the mouths of bankers, politicians, and salesmen. It's a voice that says, *Trust me.* And you know that you shouldn't trust it, but you also know you probably will. You know you're making a mistake and you're going to do it anyway.

I walk to the other side of the cairn because I want the pile of stones separating me from him. I know it won't make any difference, but I need at least that little bit of distance between us. I look at him and find my eyes unable to meet his, my feet shuffling in the dust. I'm reminded of every principal who's ever summoned me to his office, of my stern father slapping his belt against his palm, of a cop standing outside my car window, eyes hidden behind reflective sunglasses, citation pad in hand.

He's all these men, but none of them; beautiful rather than handsome, lovely, with delicate features and a pouting mouth. His wavy dark hair has been slicked back from his forehead but left in soft curls at the tops of his small ears and along the nape of his long, slender neck. His white shirt is heavily starched, crisp and smooth. His gray, pinstriped suit hangs with tailored perfection from his narrow shoulders. I've seen this man before, late in the evening, as I watched the silent television behind the counter at my momma's diner waiting for her to finish her shift. I've seen him in every courtroom drama, every board room soap opera. He sits behind every news anchor's desk. He's bland, but intentionally so.

He's riveting.

"Yes," I say. "I have come to bargain." I tap the bloody stone at the top of the cairn. Whether I do so to draw his attention there or to have a reason not to look at him, I cannot say.

"I brought payment."

"Hmm."

He sounds unimpressed and I dare a glance. He blinks and, for a moment, his eyes seem to reflect the moonlight and glow like a cat's. I see a sparkle along the sharp angle of his jawline and wonder if I might be looking at tiny scales or perhaps just a bit of razor stubble.

"Then how may I be of service?" he asks.

"I—I want to see him again." My voice comes out

breathy and uncertain. I clear my throat and say more clearly, "I need to see him. Please."

The "please" sounds like I'm begging and I am. There are men and women addicted to meth who live in my town. Sometimes, if they can catch you alone, they will offer all manner of terrible things in return for the change in your pocket. I find myself thinking of them with their fevered eyes and chapped lips, their pleading smiles full of loose gray teeth, and I understand them a little, their need, their helplessness.

I'm prepared to do terrible things, too.

I have done them already.

He dips his chin. Not in agreement but acknowledging that he understands the request. "This is a tall order," he says. "One I'm not sure I can help you with."

The bottom of my gut drops away and I have a hard time drawing a breath. "What?"

Have I fooled myself? Have I done something unspeakable for nothing?

"But you have to," I say. "I thought—"

"Oh, you misunderstand," he says. "This is indeed a service I offer. I can do what you ask. If I'm compensated. Well compensated. But you lack sufficient funds, I'm afraid."

Our eyes drift to Seb's body lying battered in the dirt. Flies have discovered the drying blood and now walk across his face like indifferent housewives browsing a grocery store for fresh produce. I have an urge to shoo them away, but it's a small urge that fades more swiftly than it should.

What do flies matter now?

"But I brought you—" I want to say, "my brother," but I know those words will make the horror of what I've done more real than I can bear. "I brought you Seb," I say instead.

"Yes, I see that," he says. He looks at Seb's beaten corpse the way a vegetarian might contemplate an expensive, but very rare, steak in a fine restaurant; with well-mannered disgust. He smiles apologetically. "The service you've requested is a—ah—*premium* offer. I'm afraid the price is quite dear." He looks at my face and his shoulders sag. He tilts his head. "I'm sorry. I wish I could be of more assistance."

"But I thought—" Words escape me. I won't let myself, can't let myself, think about what I've just done. I can only focus on why I'm here. "I need to see—"

"This isn't the kind of thing one usually haggles over." The reprimand is gentle but unmistakable.

"Seb—"

"Oh, yes. Of course. Forgive me," he interrupts. He offers me a small bow of apology. "I meant no disrespect to poor Sebastopol. I'm sure he was an excellent brother. Reasonably loved. Or fairly, at least." I can't stop myself from flinching at this. The smile he gives me is far too knowing.

"I'm afraid it doesn't matter, though," he continues, pausing and tilting his head in a moment of thought. "Well, no, it does, actually. The love matters. Perhaps if your mother had come to me with such an offer, or even your father..." He shrugs as if to say *We'll never know.*

I stare at him, not quite seeing. I imagine I can still feel the rock in my hand, the vibration of every blow shivering up my forearm. What have I done?

"I have a sister." The words are out of my mouth before I know I'm going to say them. "Anna Leah. She's—"

She's what? Kind? Loving? Not entirely there?

Am I truly offering another sibling? Would Anna Leah be enough? There is a reason I didn't bring her tonight.

A horse kicked my sister in the forehead eight years ago when she was only eleven. How many times had our mother asked her to step away from that animal? To stop tormenting it? Was it three times? Four? But Anna Leah loves horses, and she couldn't resist the soft chestnut fur of its rump, the silk of its swishing tail.

The horse gave her a dent in her skull as a keepsake of that afternoon, cracked her eye socket and broke her nose. My parents fixed the nose, turned it into a little button of a thing, much cuter than what she had before. I hardly recognized her.

There was nothing to be done for the eye, though. They tried. Took out a second mortgage to manage the bills. Paid for surgery after surgery.

Sometimes Anna Leah forgets who I am. But she still loves horses.

And she never has trouble remembering Seb.

"That's very generous," he says. "But I fear this is an issue of quality rather than quantity." Another bow. "Again. No offense. I'm sure your sister is a lovely girl."

"There's nothing?"

"No. I'm afraid—" His eyes drift skyward and he tickles his chin. "Well… Perhaps… maybe…" He shrugs and smiles more apologies at me. "Something else? Your current offer makes you eligible for a substantial promotion at work, say, or I could possibly help draw the interest of a young lady? Anyone you choose."

I can only stare.

"Or maybe you'd enjoy a bit of misfortune for someone you don't particularly like?" he continues. "Cancer, let's say. Pancreatic, if you're game for that sort of thing. How about that?" He tilts his head and awaits a response that doesn't come. "No?"

"No. I need to see him," I say. "Please."

He shakes his head, sympathetic smile firmly in place.

It's a smile I recognize. The last doctor my grandmother ever saw—a dentist, for God's sake—had given her one just like it. She'd come to him to have a tooth pulled. It was after she'd bitten into a pecan, gotten a bit of shell. One of her molars cracked and then later became infected. I could smell the rot on her breath as I drove her to the appointment in my rattling, rusted pickup truck. I could smell the festering stink in his examination room while I sat next to her.

"I'm sorry, but without insurance…" The dentist's gentle voice trailed off. He held up his hands. *What can I do?*

My grandmother took a tea towel from her purse and offered it to him, her hands trembling. She'd embroidered it with flowers and initials that may or may not have been the dentist's. "I made this," she said. "For you. Can you take it? In exchange?"

She'd been a fine seamstress when she was younger, even just a few handfuls of years ago. But that was before cataracts clouded her sharp black eyes and before arthritis twisted and swelled the joints of her once nimble fingers. The towel she held out to him was frayed at the edges; the white cloth stained yellow. The stitches she'd sewn were either too loose or too tight.

The dentist smiled at her with a mixture of pity and disgust, with impatience, his head swaying back and forth as though his neck was a spring twisted and set loose to slowly wind down. I'd stared at the floor as they bargained, my cheeks burning, my grandmother's words— "Please. You'll take this? For my tooth?"— like hot needles driven into my skin.

This smile, the one he gives me now, is like that dentist's, and my cheeks are on fire again.

"Please. I need to see him," I say, ignoring the shame. "Is there nothing—nothing I can do?"

He sighs. We both know I can't give him what he wants. That's already gone. To get it back, a piece of it at least, even a small one, is why I'm here.

"I want to help you," he tells me. "I do. I like you."

His eyes catch the moonlight. They glow. He shows me rows of straight white teeth. He's come closer now, close enough to touch. That isn't razor stubble at the curve of his jaw. Light reflects there, too, blue and green. Only a smattering of scales, tiny diamonds like you might see on the underbelly of a snake, but they are so beautiful. If he leans forward, across the cairn, just a little, he could touch his lips to mine. I've read in books that he seals his contracts this way, though I don't know if it's true. I know so little. If he kisses me, I think I might lose my mind, that I might start screaming and never stop. But I'll do it, if that's what he asks, because this ache inside of me, this terrible yawning emptiness, is a worse kind of madness.

It strikes me, in a moment of awful clarity, that this is all I have left now, a selection of insanities, an assortment of derangements. Will I have the luxury of choosing the manner in which I lose my mind, or will one simply be thrust upon me?

I don't know that it matters anymore.

"Maybe," he says. "Maybe there's a way."

"Tell me. Anything." I try to tamp down the fluttering in my chest. This isn't a place for a hope.

"Perhaps a custom arrangement. Not the *premium* package, of course. You don't have enough for that."

"Yes. Of course. Tell me."

"What if you could talk to him? *Just* talk to him?"

My heart thuds hard against my sternum. "You can do that?"

"I can make an exception. For you. Yes." He looks down at Seb's body. There are more flies on my brother's face now and they no longer seem indifferent. "I like you," he says.

I sob. My shoulders hitch. I can't seem to stop myself, but I am beyond caring who sees my naked emotion. "Yes." I choke on the word and then say more clearly, "Yes, please. Please let me talk to him."

"Very well. Close your eyes, then."

I do and, for a long moment we stand there in silence. "Is he here?" I ask.

"Keep your eyes shut please."

I crush the lids tight, grimacing with the effort. Black blossoms explode in the darkness.

"Very good. And yes. He's here."

I hear it then, a single shuffling, uncertain step on the hard packed dirt behind me. There's movement in the still air, or maybe I imagine that. I reach out and the night feels cooler, cold even, in that direction.

"Is it you?" I'm whispering, in fear or awe or both. A hand takes mine. The fingers long, like his mother's. I've always been so happy he took after her and not me, that he inherited her wise eyes and nimble grace and not my skillet-smacked face and wide, bear paw hands. Tears drip from my cheeks. My breath comes in strangled gasps. I know our time together is short, but I can't find the words I want to say.

The long fingers squeeze my hand. I reach back with my other hand. Do I recognize the callouses on the fingers? The scar along the edge of the thumb? I do!

Do I?

"Is it really you?" I whisper. "Please say something."

"No. You can talk to him, but he can't speak to you. That would be a *premium* package."

He says *premium* like a man poking his finger into the wound of someone he's just shot. I want to scream. I want so badly to open my eyes and look. I turn my head only a little.

"Keep your eyes closed."

A frustrated moan escapes me. I'm holding on so tightly, trying to memorize the feel of the skin, the tracery of the veins. I know this hand. I've held it before. It's him. I'm sure.

I need it to be him.

Is it?

"You know I loved you," I say. "You know that don't you? You know I love you still. So much. You know that don't you? You know that, right?"

A thumb strokes my knuckle.

"I need you to say it. Please."

The fingers pull away and the air grows warm again.

"Wait. Please. I need you to say it."

The crickets start singing again. An owl hoots in the distance.

"Wait!"

A breeze stirs the trees. It cools the sweat on my forehead, dries my shirt where it's stuck to the small of my back.

"Don't go!"

I open my eyes and I'm alone. I turn to my left, my right. I spin 'round in a circle. There's no one. I look for my brother's body. Seb is gone, too, but flies still swarm where he'd lain. Their buzz vibrates in my ears.

"Don't go," I say again, but there's no one left to hear.

I hold up my hand and still feel phantom fingers wrapped around my palm. Being here, touching him, was so much more than I'd dared hope for.

It isn't nearly enough.

I stand there in the clearing, awash in moonlight, and I know I'll be back. I'll come with my sister. I'll bring my mother and my father. Perhaps I'll marry again and bring my new wife.

I'll stand here, stone in hand, again and again. I'll bargain. I'll beg. I'll haggle.

I'll be back.

And, next time, he'll speak to me.

Horsewomen of the Apocalypse

Shannon Lawrence

Tempest's car spun out on the heavily graveled road. She fought the steering wheel, which twisted and pulled like a living thing. The entire car bucked one last time before the engine clunked to a dead stop.

When her head stopped spinning, she took in the line of trees inches from the hood. Behind her, barren land stretched out toward the distant mountains. A massive, black dust cloud rose from the ground in a fast-approaching maelstrom that sent a shockwave of fear coursing through her veins.

There was one direction to go. Straight into the trees.

Grabbing her duffel bag from the back seat, Tempest leapt out of the car and ran into the woods. Only "the woods" ended up being two lines of trees and no more. They loomed tall but merely blocked a walled mansion from the view of the road. Save for a couple fruit trees behind the walls, there were no more trees and nothing green to speak of. Everything before her appeared to be some shade of brown: brown grass, brown shrubs, brown stucco siding. Even the air held a tan haze that blocked the blue of the sky.

"Shit," muttered Tempest.

With nowhere else to go, she ran for the wall. It was

about seven feet tall. Cracks and missing chunks of wall meant it might be scalable, but a gate would be preferable. Especially if she could lock it from the other side. From what she could see, a gate would most likely be to her left, so she went that way, the duffel growing heavier in her arms with each step.

The front gate turned out to be wide open, but not unoccupied. A guard tower maybe a couple inches taller than the man inside it stood in the center of the gate. The "gargoyles" on either end of the stucco wall framing the iron gates were naked, rubicund women reclined with hands between their legs. With nowhere else to go, Tempest walked up to the guard, nodding her head toward one of the gargoyles. "Classy place. Can you tell me where I am?"

The guard, hand on his gun, looked her up and down. His face reflected the spectacle she knew she'd become at this point. Not having looked in a mirror in days, she could only guess at her level of dishevelment. She'd wrangled her knotted hair back into a sloppy ponytail, but that was yesterday, and now loose hairs floated around her face and tickled her ears. She was so hot and sweaty she could feel how red her face must be, even if she couldn't see it. Her wedding dress, once white, was shredded and filthy.

Wails and tormented screams filled the previous silence, raising the hairs on the back of her neck. The ground shook. The riders had nearly arrived.

Unwilling to wait for the guard to close his mouth and do something useful, Tempest reached into the unzipped pocket of the duffel and pulled out a gun. She released the safety with her thumb and aimed it at the guard's face before he had time to unclip his holster. "You should be a bit faster if you plan on pulling weapons on people. Move your hand away from the gun."

He did as she asked, hands trembling. He licked his lips, eyes fixed on her gun.

"I don't have time to explain, so this is how we're going

to play it. You're going to wait until I'm on the other side of this gate, then you're going to close and secure it. If you're smart, you'll be on the same side of the gate as I am. If you're stupid, you'll die horribly, and not by my hand. Deal?"

"I can't let you go in there," he said. His full body now shook, betraying the lie behind his bravery.

"Nothing you can do about it." Tempest kept the weapon trained on him as she moved sideways onto the property. Once safely behind the swing of the gate, she said, "It's your choice now. Either you come with me, or you stay out here to face what's coming."

"What *is* coming?"

"Hell's coming."

He scoffed and reached for his gun again.

Tempest switched her aim and squeezed the trigger. His shoulder jerked and he slapped a hand over the blooming bloodstain, gaping back at her.

"I don't want to hurt you, but the next one will be a kill shot." The wailing grew in pitch. "Don't you hear that?"

"I don't he— "

Trees pitched outward in a fan of splintered wood, stopping the guard mid-sentence.

"Close the gate!" she screamed. She dropped the gun, empty anyway, and turned to run toward the house, weaving through a collection of badly parked cars.

Halfway to the front porch, the stucco wall exploded, bits of hardened clay flying across the yard. Small bits pelted her, cutting the skin on the right side of her body.

The front door opened. A large man, pale, hair-covered belly flopping over loose shorts, peered out, eyes squinting. "What's all this noise? Who are you?"

Tempest plowed into him. Together, they fell into his foyer, landing hard on the marble floor. She climbed off him, no time to be disgusted by the muggy wetness of his skin and locked the door. "Do you have weapons?"

Shaken, he looked up at her. "What?"

"Weapons. Do you have weapons? Anything we can use to defend ourselves."

"No, why?"

Tempest sighed. Was she the only one who could hear the cacophony accompanying the riders? "There are some bad, bad…people, I guess, coming our way. They've broken through your wall. They will bust into this house any second. We need to defend ourselves. Is anyone else here? The more hands the better."

Outside, rapid shots rang out.

Tempest closed her eyes.

A man's scream rose, falling away abruptly.

The guy in front of her stood up, eyes round. "What was that?"

"I assume it was your guard. I advised him to come with me. Right now, I'm advising you to work with me to get ready for them, so you don't die screaming like him."

He stared between her and the door.

"Listen, what's your name?" When he didn't answer, she hit him on the arm and raised her voice. "Hey! You! What's your name?"

"Kevin."

"Okay, Kevin, is there anyone else here right now?"

"Yeah, there's some people."

"How many?"

He thought for a moment. "About eight."

"Okay, do you have yard tools, like a hatchet, an ax, large clippers, a saw, anything?"

"The gardener has some supplies in the garage."

"Take me there."

He led her to the garage, his flip-flops making suck-n-slap noises as he walked. It was the cleanest garage she'd ever seen. "Over there." He pointed toward a corner on the other side of a red convertible.

"Figures," she muttered. Moving around the nose of the

car, she discovered a large pair of garden shears, a push mower, a shovel, and a weed whacker. Not much to work with, but as far as she'd seen, there was no garden. Must be in the back where the fruit trees had been visible. She gathered up everything except the mower and went back inside, Kevin following her. "Can you think of anything else we might be able to use?"

"Maybe some stuff in the kitchen?"

She sighed. "Where is everyone? Maybe they've got weapons."

A slurred voice rang out from another room. "Hey, Kev, get back in here, you ol' perv!"

With a glance at Kevin, Tempest went in the direction of the voice, pausing in the kitchen long enough to put down her duffel and the tools. As she walked down a long hallway full of artsy pictures of men and women in leather fetish gear, lower voices tiptoed down the hall. At the end stood a large, black door, partially open. Someone walked past the doorway.

Outside, the screams and wails had paused, which meant the riders had, as well. Whatever reason they'd stopped wouldn't last long. The silence scared Tempest more than the noises had.

She stepped through the doorway only to be greeted by a roomful of sex toys and partially clad people. There were six people in casual loungewear dressier than Kevin's shorts, and two people dressed only in black leather and vinyl. These two were each in incredibly compromising positions that Tempest didn't have time to analyze.

"What the hell is this?"

"A work party."

"A *work* party? What do you do for a living?"

"I produce porn."

Much to her horror, Tempest had led the riders to a den of iniquity that would probably juice them right up. No wonder they were chilling outside. They were probably sucking it up.

"Well, don't make me search everything. Is there anything actually useful for defense in here? Pretty sure we can't use vibrators or handcuffs to fight these things off."

"Who the hell is this batty twat?" asked a British man in loose, white cotton pants and a tight t-shirt that showed off his wiry musculature.

"Who I am doesn't matter. Why I'm here does." Tempest looked over at the man and woman strapped to various devices. "Will someone loosen those restraints and get them out of there?"

"Okay, honey," drawled a fake redhead with a Texas accent, "we give. Tell us why you're here or quit busting our balls."

Kevin answered before Tempest could. "She said there are bad people outside who want in. I think poor Duke is dead."

"Aw, not Duke," said a twenty-something with her hair up in pink-dipped pigtails. "I was hoping he could play later."

"You know that's not allowed," Kevin said.

"Doesn't matter now, does it?" asked Tempest, certain that with these people around she was now more likely to die than she had been before. "Hey, Kev, why don't you see if any of these nice people have weapons?"

He moved over to a trunk at the base of a four-poster bed. The sheets were black satin and visibly stained. When Kevin pulled out a variety of whips and floggers, she just shook her head.

"I guess…bring them? We need to get back out there. Anyone else have something you can use to defend yourselves?"

The wailing kicked up again. It sounded like a million people were pounding on the outside of the house. The ground shook, items fell off the walls. The shattering of glass sounded in another room. In the bondage room, chains rattled, and something started vibrating in one of the trunks.

“They’re getting bored,” Tempest said.

Kevin followed her, calling, “Who got bored?”

Tempest checked the gas on the weed whacker and found it to be mostly full. “I don’t really know who they are. They’re just the riders. They’ve been following me for days.”

“Why don’t you call the police?” He picked the phone up off the counter and held it out toward her. “I can call them if you want.”

“I tried that. In California, in Nevada, in Denver. The police don’t take it seriously; they think I’m a crank. If they do show, they die.”

“If the police die, what makes you think we can fight them with a weed whacker and a bullwhip?” Sweat had broken out on Kevin’s forehead and upper lip. His Adam’s apple bobbed with each swallow. “I’m calling the police anyway.”

“Go for it. You’re just killing them.” She opened drawers, pulling out a meat tenderizer and some knives. “Where are your pots?”

He opened a lower cabinet and gestured toward it.

“Awesome.” Tempest pulled out the larger frying pan. “I wouldn’t have thought you cooked.”

“I don’t. I have a cook.”

“Ah. Porn must pay well.”

“You bet.” He picked out a cast iron pan she’d missed.

“Ooh, that’s a good one!”

“Listen, have you ever done porn?”

She held up the skillet. “Stop right there. Arm up.”

The party guests ambled into the kitchen, the two leather bound ones now on leashes and crawling on all fours. The Brit held the woman’s leash, while a gorgeous amazon of a woman who hadn’t spoken yet held the man’s. Both the leashed man and woman were in amazing physical shape. If anything, they were the two who might be able to put up a fight. Of course, they didn't look much like fighters right now with red rubber balls sticking out of their mouths.

The pounding stopped, as did the shaking, but the sounds of torment continued. Tempest realized that she'd finally grown used to them. Sort of. After days of hearing people being tortured, she assumed in hell, they'd lost their power over her. The first day, her ears had bled. Ever since then, it had caused her heart palpitations and made her feel as if she were on the brink of insanity.

Now nothing. They were just sounds. Awful sounds, but sounds, nonetheless. She wasn't sure that was a good thing.

"Find something to fight with!" she yelled. The guests, still showing no sign of concern, tromped over to the counter where Tempest had laid everything out. They plucked up items, oohing and aahing over them. The redhead picked up a pan and slapped the ass of the leashed woman with it, creating a resounding *clang* that made Tempest wince. The leashed woman moaned.

A man with massive buck teeth, a comb over, and a cheap suit picked up the hedge clippers and giggled. "I've got friends who would totally party with these. Not my thing." He dropped the hedge clippers and picked up a knife. "Now this I can do things with. Yummy things."

A horse whinnied, joined by others. Their whinnies built until they resounded like thunder, shaking the house yet again.

Hooves thundered on the front porch, growing louder.

Tempest prepared herself the best she was able, sucking in a deep breath.

The door burst open. In rode a chestnut horse, thick blood coursing down its flanks. The armored female rider atop it held a mace aloft and let out a guttural yawp before charging at Tempest.

A chorus of shrieks sounded from the party guests, who scattered uselessly.

Tempest grabbed the weed whacker and pulled the cord.

It didn't start.

She yanked again, repeatedly. It sputtered but wouldn't start.

Tempest looked up in time to see the chestnut moving toward her.

Kevin yelled and ran toward the red rider with the cast iron pan in his right hand, the meat tenderizer in his left.

The rider swung the mace. It clanged against the cast iron and sent Kevin flying into the opposite wall, where he crashed to the ground and fell unconscious.

The redhead dropped the pan, picked up the clippers, and ran forward now, her high heels clacking across the kitchen tiles. She stopped at the edge of the tile and chucked the clippers at the rider. They stuck into the horse's chest and vibrated momentarily before sagging downward and falling to the ground.

Tempest continued pulling at the weed whacker, looking around for the next closest weapon.

The rider passed Tempest and took out the redhead with a single swing of the mace, which lodged in her chest. One of the woman's breasts flattened, a sack full of clear liquid slapping onto the floor. She looked down in shock, eyes wide, then brought a hand forward to touch the mace. Pulling her hand away, she looked at it as if it would give her answers.

Apparently bored with the show, the rider yanked at the mace. It resisted at first, well attached, but finally sucked loose with a series of wet sounds. Broken ribs jutted out of the woman's battered chest. Her heart pulsated visibly behind a cage of jagged bone.

The rider swept the mace once more, this time burying it in the redhead's face. Her hair puffed out on either side before she fell to the ground, face a shattered mess of bone and blood.

Tempest closed her eyes and pulled one more time. The whir of the weed whacker sent a brief, sweet taste of relief through her.

Then she opened her eyes, and the fear returned.

The rider had returned to her position before the front door. Her face was demonic. She had multiple goat-like eyes across her forehead and cheeks, but no nose. Her mouth opened as a giant black hole full of sharpened teeth, three tongues protruding as she screeched. Metal-plated armor covered the top and sides of her head, continuing down her entire body as if it were her skin. Every movement she made sounded of battle, human screams surrounding her, metal clashing with metal.

From behind the red rider two more riders burst through the front windows, coming abreast of her. The second horse was pitch black and scrawny, its rider so skinny Tempest would never have known she was female if it weren't for the sagging pockets of flesh on her chest. Dark, soulless eyes stared out of sunken orbital sockets, and she held no weaponry, only hole-filled rags swathing her body in places. Sickened groans surrounded her, adding to the horrific chorus of human suffering.

The third rider sat atop a pale tan horse infested with fleas. Ragged patches of hair bracketed raw, pink flesh covered in bug bites. This rider's eyes stood out at the end of stalks, and when she opened her mouth, flies sprang out and circled her head as pus dripped from her nose and mouth. Her clothing appeared to be moth-eaten. The sound of human retching warred with the buzzing of flies, making the cacophony complete.

Behind Tempest, several of the party goers continued to scream and run around in utter chaos. The Brit attempted to sneak past the riders toward the door, his back pressed to the wall. Without moving any other part of her body, the blackened rider extended her arm, grabbing his throat in her hand, elongated fingers wrapping completely around to overlap each other.

Instantly, the Brit's cheeks sunk in, his body withering

before their eyes, graphically illustrated by his tight shirt. He gasped in one breath and slumped to the ground, bones rattling against each other upon impact.

Bedlam broke out. Everyone scattered in different directions, seeking any form of egress, some of them grabbing weapons off the counter. The amazon woman grabbed the shovel and stood beside Tempest. Now holding the hedge clippers, the knife abandoned, the buck-toothed man stood on the other side of Tempest.

Buoyed by the addition of fellow fighters, Tempest ran forward with the weed whacker, swiping it across the red horse's throat. Dark, clotted blood slithered down its chest, plopping onto the floor. The horse didn't make a sound.

Buck-tooth ran up beside the pale rider and jabbed the clippers into her belly. She screeched, maggots falling from the wound and pelting the ground. He pulled the clippers back to strike again, but the pale rider grabbed him and lifted him until their mouths met. He screamed into her mouth, making her cheeks puff out.

Then something changed. His screams stopped, turning to pained grunts. His cheeks writhed as if something, or some *things*, tried to escape.

The pale horse pawed at the ground.

Buck-tooth's stomach swelled outward, finally bursting. Out poured what looked to be thousands of grasshoppers.

The pale rider dropped Buck-tooth and rode past the others into another room, where fresh screams sounded.

Tempest swept the weed whacker toward the red rider, but it merely dented her armor. The only part of the rider exposed without armor was her face, but when Tempest aimed there, the rider batted it away with the mace. The weed whacker flew end over end, broken in half, the blade still whirring just enough to slice through the wall and stick there.

As Tempest turned to run, the amazon smacked the black rider with the shovel, letting out a guttural yell. The rider's head bent to the side, neck broken, but rode forward. The black horse's chest struck the amazon, who spun to the side, but caught her balance. The amazon raised the shovel again, but the black rider caught it. Shovel held in one hand, the black rider shot her arm out and eviscerated the amazon as quickly as she had the Brit, liquids bursting from the woman's flesh in an explosion of viscera.

Tempest got to her bag and pulled out a shotgun. Her ammo was low, but she had two shells. She'd used her only bullet in the handgun earlier to wing the guard. No time to reflect on her bad choices now, Tempest turned, cocked the shotgun, and fired at the red rider.

Part of the red rider's face disappeared, her blood thick and clotted like the horse's. It dripped like sludge, sliding along her armor. Still, she came forward, mace spinning through the air.

Tempest dove to her side. The mace hit her ankle, pain blasting up her leg. She hit the ground worse than she'd planned, scraping up her palms and forearms, and slamming her shoulder hard.

The two previously leashed guests ran up to Tempest, each grabbing one of her arms to pull her to standing. They fled with her down the hall toward the black door, lifting her up as best they could so she didn't have to put weight on the bad ankle.

Behind them, hooves pounded down the hallway.

Reaching the door, they clambered inside and slammed it shut.

"What are those?" the man asked.

Tempest sunk to the ground. "I don't know."

The woman picked up a black, latex, thigh-high boot and ripped the high heel off it. "Put this on your injured foot. It'll be tight like a pressure bandage."

Tempest did as she asked, wincing as she struggled to remove her shoe then get the boot over her ankle. Sharp pain radiated out from the injury, but she got the boot on and zipped it up. The pressure hurt more at first but brought some relief after a moment.

Something hit the door with a thud then slid down it.

They all stared at the door in trepidation.

Blood seeped under it, soaking the carpeting.

"We have to get out of here," Tempest said. "I don't suppose either of you have keys to one of those vehicles out there?"

The man went over to a rolling plastic storage tower and opened the top drawer. From there, he pulled a pair of jeans and a set of keys. The woman ran over to join him, opening another drawer to pull out her own clothing. They dressed quickly, her in a sundress, him in the jeans and a t-shirt. Both put on shoes before the man moved back toward Tempest, where he held out a hand and introduced himself. "I'm Ben and this is Laurie."

Tempest took his hand and shook. "Tempest. Now let's get the hell out of here."

The sounds of battle had slowed outside the door. Any minute now, they'd come searching the rooms.

Tempest went to the bed and pulled off the top sheet, wrapping it around her arm. She went to the nearest window and slammed her elbow through it, shattering the glass. Once she'd cleaned the remaining glass from the frame, she ran to another storage container and dug through it, pulling out anything that looked halfway likely to use for defense. She handed the woman a giant, solid vibrator with a pointed tip, wondering who the hell used anything this sharp without seriously injuring themselves. She found a set of chains for the man and grabbed a long, flexible whip for herself.

She gestured for the other two to go first. They moved quickly, climbing out the window.

Tempest watched the door, which started to bulge. The window clear, she headed for it, throwing a leg over the sill.

The door slammed open behind her. The black rider ducked to get through the doorway, arm extending toward

Tempest.

Tempest fell backward out of the window, slamming into dry, dusty ground. It knocked the air out of her, but the arm overshot her, hitting the man who'd bent to help her.

Tempest kicked out at the creature's arm, knocking it away from him. Still alive, but weak, he fell beside Tempest, his bones visible through his sagging skin.

The two women helped him to his feet and stumbled toward the front of the house. He felt fragile under her palm, like he'd lost all fat and muscle. Even his bones felt hollow.

A window in front of them burst outward, glass flying onto the hard-packed dirt, along with the pigtailed girl. She'd been ripped to pieces, her body twisted in crazy angles. Her eyes were missing.

"Go, go, go," chanted Tempest, darting around the body.

"The Toyota," Laurie said. It wasn't too far. In fact, it was the closest to the house. A shiny blue, it beckoned them forward with a hint of safety. Laurie held her keys out and pushed the fob's button to unlock her car. The headlights flashed in response.

Tempest shot a look toward the front door. "I hope they didn't see that."

They waited, shooting looks toward the front door and behind them.

When no riders came for them, they shuffled toward the Toyota. Tempest held Ben up against the side of the car while Laurie opened the back door to let him in. Together, Tempest and Laurie shoved him in and shut the door. Tempest climbed in the front passenger seat while Laurie ran around to the driver's side.

It didn't take long for Laurie to start the car with a smooth growl from the engine. Laurie backed up and maneuvered around the other vehicles, driving over the downed iron gate. Once on the open road, she punched it, accelerating away from the massacre behind them. "Where should I go?" she asked Tempest.

"I don't know the area. Any ideas?"

Ben answered weakly from the backseat. "There's a military base nearby. Maybe there?"

Tempest nodded. "Sounds good to me. Do you know where it is, Laurie?"

"Yeah, we passed by it on the way here. It's not too far."

Snores sounded from the backseat. Tempest turned to check on Ben, finding him slumped over, head on his own shoulder. "It's probably good he's sleeping. He looks like he was two seconds away from dying."

She settled back into her seat, putting her seatbelt on, and laid her head back. It had been days since she'd slept. Days since these riders had killed her fiancé and all their friends and family at her wedding in San Diego. It felt like she'd traveled around the globe since then, but at least the constant running had kept thoughts of her losses at bay.

The riders had come down the road in Old Town like Wild West outlaws, side by side, slow, purposeful, like the opening of an old western. No one had paid any attention, thinking it was part of the affectations of the tourist trap.

Just as the minister asked, "Do you, Tempest, take this man—" the horses had broken into a gallop, running through the seated guests as if they were nothing but blades of grass. A swarm of pests had come on like a storm; clouds of flies, a flood of rats. As these beasts covered the guests, eating through their flesh in seconds, the red rider threw fireballs that bowled through those running, lighting them on fire. Her parents met the hands of the black rider, shrinking to nothing but bones and skin, hands grasped in their final seconds.

"Stop, in the name of the Lord!" yelled the minister, holding her hands up as if that would stop the riders. She wore a white, lace dress, heavier and more formal than Tempest's own wedding gown, which was a gauzy summer dress sewed by her grandmother, who now lie on the ground, rats eating their way through her stomach while she fought to get them off her.

The red rider threw her head back in a laughing motion, but only screams of agony exited her open mouth, her three tongues waving in sadistic glee. She drew a small hatchet from her back and tossed it, end over end. It struck the minister in the head, sending her flying backward through the flowered arch they'd erected just that morning.

Colin put his arms around Tempest, and they backed away. Only there was nowhere they could go, nowhere the riders couldn't get to them. The riders had circled them, forcing the nearly newlywed couple to a scraggly, thirsty tree. When their backs were to the tree, the black rider came forward and extended her arm to Colin's head. Before her eyes, Tempest's new husband-to-be shriveled to about a third of his normal size, his eyes the only recognizable part of him, staring longingly at her until they emptied and rolled back in his head.

Only then did his body hit the ground.

Those eyes would haunt her into eternity.

Alone, Tempest had shot through a space between the riders, racing to the main street. A man hopped out of his car, leaving it running while he ran inside a restaurant with his large, red insulated bag. Tempest had done the only thing she could. She'd jumped into the car and taken off, running for her life.

Thinking about it now, was she really running for her life? It had been ripped out from under her. She had nothing to return to even if she could get away from these fiends. Her husband, parents, grandmother, everyone had died back there, their bodies left to rot on the hardened earth of the historic town in San Diego.

She'd driven to a nearby police station and run inside, thinking she'd be safe, that they'd save her. But their guns had been useless against the riders. Even so, she'd gathered up the weapons she was able, putting them into a black duffel bag she'd found on one of the officer's desks. While the riders had been busy emptying the police station of anyone living, Tempest escaped in the same car, driving as far as she could, stopping only to seek help that quickly died for trying to aid her.

Everyone she'd met since then had died.

Lost in her thoughts, she didn't notice the dissolution of the quiet in the car. It wasn't until something struck the trunk that she sat up, gasping at the abrupt interruption.

Laurie looked in the rearview mirror. "Shit. Shit, shit, shit, shit, shit."

"Does this car go any faster?"

"I've got the pedal to the floor. This is what we've got."

Tempest turned to Ben. "Wake up! We're going to need some help."

He didn't answer. She reached over the seat and nudged him, fingers sinking into his flesh. His body toppled over, hitting the soft seat with a dismal crunch. He didn't appear to be breathing.

Panic enlivened every nerve in her body. She grabbed the chains he'd managed to hold onto, wresting them from where he'd wrapped them around his arm. Laurie had set the vibrator in the center console once they'd gotten on the road; Tempest grabbed it and wrapped the chain around it, twisting the base until it vibrated.

Laurie looked over. "What do you plan on doing with those?"

"I have no idea." She rolled her window down, undid her seatbelt, and climbed out, sitting in the window frame. The car felt much faster with the wind beating against her face, pushing her ever loosening hair into a jig that occasionally slapped her in the eyes like tiny, painful needle pricks. She wrapped her legs around the seat to hold herself steady, pulled the chain out, and spun it over her head like a pathetic, vibrating lasso.

The riders sped behind the car, the horses not looking at all fazed by the speed they'd reached. The red rider looked angry, the pale rider sad, and the black rider pained, but they held steady on their steeds, gaining on the car as if it stood still.

Tempest spun the vibrator twice more then released it in the direction of the riders, praying it would hit one of them.

It sailed uselessly through the air to land on the road.

She pulled it back, twirled it once more.

This time when she released it, the vibrator flew true, knocking into the head of the pale rider. She fell back behind the other riders, shaking her head.

Tempest worked to pull the vibrator back toward her, the chain vibrating.

About halfway to the car, the chain stopped vibrating. The vibrator had fallen.

She pulled the chain toward her anyway, figuring she could still do damage with the metal links. Hand over hand, the chain slowly reeled in.

The riders grew closer.

Tempest panted at the effort, still pulling.

The red rider leapt, soaring through the air to land on top of the Toyota. The roof crumpled inward. The vehicle swerved.

Tempest tightened her legs and tried to lower herself back into the car, but the damaged roof prohibited her from getting inside. All she could do was hang on.

The car continued to swerve.

Tempest felt her legs slipping.

The red rider looked down at her, eyes locked on hers and slowly lifted the mace.

Tempest reached into the car and tried to find the handle.

The swerving car straightened out abruptly, sliding off the road.

The red rider spun the mace.

Tempest closed her eyes, waiting for the end.

Then everything was chaotic motion: spinning, tumbling, impacts, pain. So much pain. She felt weightless for a few seconds and opened her eyes in time to see the ground rushing up to meet her. She slammed into the dirt and rolled into high grass.

The car flew by her in a fiery ball, and only then did the sounds of metal against rock break through Tempest's eardrums.

Heat licked at her as she lay there, looking up at the sky, unable to breathe, reeling from the pain. Then there above her, a white horse stood. It was pure and bright against the darkening sky, almost glowing in its luminescence. It bent down and nudged her with its nose. Tempest placed a hand against the velvety muzzle and whispered, "What are you doing here?" It hurt to talk.

It nudged her again, harder this time, and gently took her hand in its mouth, its teeth barely denting her skin. It pulled her up to standing then knelt down before her. She slumped onto its back, unable to fully mount it with her broken body. The horse stood anyway, and walked calmly toward the other three horses, their riders once more whole upon their backs.

Together, the four horsewomen rode off into the sunset, leaving fiery destruction in their wake, just as they were meant to do.

Hand of the Damned

Chase Hughes

"Are you sure that's them?" she asked; her face cast in the violent glow of the streetlamps. The truck was parked under the overpass just ahead.

We had accidentally seen it while driving towards a meeting with one of the other associates. I had Vinney stop the car and turn the lights off. If the men in the truck noticed, neither of them showed it.

I regarded the orange truck. The back half was rusting, with holes going through, showing bits of the detritus in the bed. The back windshield was cracked and covered in fading stickers. The rest was the faded color of rotten pumpkins. An Alaskan license plate stood stark yellow in the dim light.

"Yeah," I growled, "I am sure." Vinney looked from me to the truck and tapped her fingers on the steering wheel.

The sound of shuffling cloth came from behind me. Cross grabbed my shoulder, "let me take them out." He shoved a pistol in the space between Vinney and I, shaking it to show off the reflections on the chrome. His finger was wound dangerously around the trigger.

I pushed his hand away and opened the door. "Put that

thing away, fool. I'll do it." Exiting the car, I reached my hand into my pocket.

***

The timing had been perfect for the pizza. I had pulled up to my decaying house at the same time as the pizza delivery guy did. Paying him, I went inside with a fresh six pack of beer and the pizza. I settled into my living room and turned the tv on. There was a rerun of some old boxing match that I had been looking forward to. A knock came from the door. I took a drink of my beer, ignoring it, but it sounded again, harder. Begrudgingly, I got up from my armchair and walked through my kitchen to the door.

Just as I reached the door, the knock sounded again. The door almost jumped from the force of the slams and an uneasy feeling tore through my stomach. Ignoring this, as I had been expecting rough company anyway, I opened the door. Two men stood looking back at me, their faces shrouded in balaclavas. There was an awkward moment as the two men and I stared at each other. The taller of the men, a brick wall whose shirt was too tight, had his knuckles raised as if readying to knock again.

He looked at his knuckles and then back to me. His decision came fast, the fist becoming as a blur as it struck out and into my nose. I sat down hard onto my floor. Warm blood flooded from my nose, filling my mouth and down my chest. "What the f-" I began to say before my mouth was painfully stuffed with the barrel of an old-fashioned revolver. The metal sight split my lip and chipped my front teeth. Stars were still swimming in my vision as pain exploded from everything on my face.

"Shut up and stand up," Brickwall said, lifting the gun in my mouth so that my face angled upwards. He kept it painfully shoved into my mouth as I attempted to stand up through the waves of dizziness from the punch. Once on my feet, I thought about raising my hands but decided against it.

"We hear you are an associate of our dear friend, Mulner," the other one said. I hadn't gotten a good look at him, and he stood somewhere off behind me. The sound of his feet pacing back and forth on the sticky linoleum of my kitchen seemed to echo in the kitchen. I tried to turn my head to get a better look at him, but the gun was shoved further into my mouth, causing me to gag.

"As I was saying," the shorter one said again, "your friend, Mulner, took something from us and we are here to take it back." I wanted to say I didn't know a Mulner but couldn't with the gun shoved halfway to my ass. They would have known it was a lie but anything to stop them from hurting me anymore. The sound of his feet came closer; I could feel his presence behind me. "My friend here is going to remove the gun from your mouth and then you are going to tell me where my briefcase is. Don't feel the need to lie, Mulner told us it was here on his way out."

The gun came out of my mouth fast, the sight catching the backside of my front teeth. Sharp pain shot through my mouth, and I felt certain that all my teeth had shattered. Gags ripped through my body, and I bent over, retching. After coughing for what seemed like eternity, I put my hands to my face to try and stop the blood from pouring down my nose. "He left it in my closet," I said, my voice thick and strange sounding.

"That was quick," Brickwall said, his tone slightly judgmental.

I shrugged, "you guys could have gotten it out of me without breaking my nose." There wasn't a world where I would have taken a beating for anyone's random items, especially someone like Mulner. He had marched in here earlier that day, much like these two clowns, and demanded I store this junky looking briefcase. With a heavy hand on the pistol in his waistband, he had threatened me not to even think about the briefcase.

"Where is this closet? Show us," the shorter one said. He must have motioned because Brickwall raised the gun again and flicked the barrel for me to turn around. "You lead us there. Go straight to the closet and get on your knees. Don't reach for anything, don't look at anything. Just walk."

Not wanting to test their patience and get myself hurt further, I followed their instructions. I figured they didn't mean to kill me because why wear the stupid masks otherwise. We walked through my living room, and I took the chance to eye my pizza sadly. Then we went through my room and into my closet. I kneeled on the ground and put my hands behind my head.

"It's in this cardboard box next to me," I said calmly. A boot slammed into my back, propelling my head forward into the closet wall opposite me. Stars, that had faded, exploded back into view. I cursed and fumbled around. A fist caught me in my eye as I turned. My body hit the floor, and my consciousness ebbed.

The sounds of the two retreating out of my closet came to me. Anger flooded into me, the pain giving way to the adrenaline and a thirst for revenge. There had been no reason to escalate and attack me, I had complied with them easily from the beginning. There was a shotgun, always loaded, that I kept at my bedside table. I rushed out and grabbed the gun before running after the men as they slammed the front door shut.

I practically broke my front door, shouldering it open and bringing the shotgun up to fire. They were in their orange truck and looked at me. The truck spewed a black cloud and tore from my driveway. I noticed the yellow Alaskan license plate as I lowered the shotgun. Cursing, I went back inside to clean my wounds and make some calls.

***

The street was dark, most of the ambient light coming

from a flickering streetlight directly in front of the truck and the overpass overhead. The sound of traffic on the overpass filtered down occasionally. The parking lots surrounding us were empty and nothing else moved in the night. The two in the truck appeared to be bent over something, using the light from the lamp to inspect it. I turned back and looked at the car, hidden partially by some bushes.

Looking back to the truck, I toyed with the pistol in my jacket pocket and quickened my step. I paused as I neared the back windshield. The truck bed was full of trash and crushed beer cans. Taking a deep breath, I took my gun from my pocket. I raised and fired into the silhouette of the driver's head. The glass punctured and the head slumped forward, blood spraying the windshield. Instantly, I swung my arm and fired twice more into the figure in the passenger seat. Blood ran in droplets down the windows and windshield. Both figures lay slumped, one over the steering wheel and the other against the passenger window. I took another deep breath and rubbed my ruined nose.

With the pistol still ready, I opened the driver's door and inspected the two. Brickwall had been driving. The briefcase was in between the two. Putting the pistol back in my pocket, I pulled Brickwall out of the car, where he slumped to the asphalt. Blood poured thick from his head. I stepped over his body and closed the briefcase.

Just as my hand wrapped around the briefcase's handle, another hand wrapped itself around my wrist. The hand was red.

I yelped and jumped back. The pistol caught in my pocket as I fumbled at it. "You don't know what you're doing," the short one said, through the gunshot wound to his forehead. "Don't do this, don't do this, don't do this." Each time he repeated this phrase, his voice went up in pitch and volume. Soon, he was just screaming as his body thrashed in its seat.

"Fuck you," I said, pulling the trigger until the gun stuck

back on its slide.

***

I threw the briefcase down on the bed as we filed into the cheap motel room. It was the common layout of cheap rooms: two disgusting beds, a small TV forty years past its lifetime, and a Petri dish of a bathroom. The room smelt faintly of cleaning chemicals and old cigarette smoke. Both of the comforters on the beds had questionable stains. It wasn't luxury nor was it supposed to be, just a place to hole up and figure out our next moves.

Everyone sat as far apart as possible. Vinney sat in the desk chair, playing with the small pad of paper. Cross jumped in the bed nearest the bathroom and lounged against the backboard, digging in his pockets for a cigarette. Charley acted as if he didn't want to be in the room and stood by the window, playing with the curtains.

I put the briefcase down on the bed closest to the door and sat next to it. It was just a brown briefcase, heavily scuffed and stained. Didn't look like something that had been worth three lives, but all that really mattered was what was inside. I felt a ping of sadness over Mulner, but it quickly faded. He was an asshole and had it coming.

"What's in it?" Cross asked, lighting a cigarette as he regarded the briefcase. The disgusting scent of smoke filled the room.

"Fuck if I know," I said as I inspected the briefcase for a few more seconds before tearing it open like a child on Christmas morning. Flashes of drugs or stacks of cash flicked through my mind as I pulled the top half open. My excitement died when all I saw was a green felt bag, covered in white serpents and a man with two wings. "What the hell is this?" I said out loud.

Charley looked over my shoulder at the bag. "That's weird," he said, "looks kind of religious or something."

Vinney laughed, "the thought of Mulner and anything religious is hilarious." Charley just shrugged at her and went back to the window.

The bag was about the size of a closed fist, the green felt hiding any details of what might be inside. I picked up the bag, the felt soft against my fingers. Snakes wrapped around the green felt and in the middle of the bag, a man with wings stood out in stark white. It wasn't heavy but the object inside was hard. I thought maybe a gem or diamond. Whatever it was, it had various bumps and ridges.

A feeling of anxiety, of deep dread, washed over me. My stomach felt weak, and my legs shook. I had to fight to not drop the green bag. The room suddenly felt colder. The sound of Cross crossing his arms startled me and I took a deep breath. My hands were trembling. I felt like I was standing on a precipice.

Another deep breath and then I grabbed the white string that held the bag close and pulled the knot loose. My feeling of anxiety increased as I looked at the darkened hole. A maw, waiting to take me in and end my life, seemed to be staring back. Opening the hole further, I looked inside. Immediately, I shouted and tossed the bag onto the bed.

It had been a hand. A human hand with the skin of dark arterial blood. Black horns – maybe scales – grew from the knuckles and in between the fingers like warts. The fingers were bent and twisted, arthritic in their appearance. Deep black veins ran just under the skin.

Charley stepped back and said, "what did you see?"

Before I could answer, the bag began to move, twisting and thrashing on the bed like the flopping of a dying fish out of water. Cross, on the opposite bed, scooted further away and flung his cigarette towards the bag. "What's moving in there?" he asked, his voice scared.

The opening was facing me, and in the darkness, I could see the fingers moving like legs of a giant tarantula within its burrow. Coiling to strike at prey that happened to walk by. A red finger tipped with a black fingernail and giant black scale on the first knuckle, stuck out of the bag. The appendage rubbed at the comforter of the bed, as if testing the waters.

The rest of the hand followed. It stood on its fingers like some demented spider and spun around. A fully black eye near the thumb looked out unblinking. It was the eye of a shark. Soulless and unfeeling. The lights flickered and the four of us started screaming. More voices joined ours, continuing as our voices died out. These were pained and terrorized, coming from everywhere all around us and nowhere at all.

Trying to make the screaming stop, I grabbed the hand and tossed it across the room. The skin was rough and burning to the touch. It flew across the room and hit the wall with a dull thump, falling into Cross' lap on the opposite bed.

Cross screamed and tried to flick it out of his lap, kicking his legs out wildly. "Why'd you throw it over here?" he screamed. The hand scurried up his torso before the fingers wrapped themselves around his throat. His screams became thicker and higher pitched. "It's biting me, oh God!"

Blood began pouring from his neck from where the hand thrashed. Cross tried to pry it off himself, but its nails dug deeper into his skin. Tears streamed down his face as blood began to pour from his mouth.

I ran across the room and grabbed the hand, using both of my hands to pry it off Cross' neck. As it came away, the fingers dug deep enough to tear the skin and peel a section off. A current of blood washed over my arms and the hand as it finally came away. A large gaping wound was in the middle of Cross' throat.

Vinney was beside me, the green bag held open. Cross lay dying on the bed, reaching out for us with weak arms. The hand instantly turned on me, its strength surprising as its fingers wrestled for control. I turned it around to see a blood-stained mouth, sporting sharpened black teeth and a gorging tongue. Another black eye looked up from just under the pinkie.

"Put it back!" Vinney shouted next to me, swinging the open bag at the hand. I cried out in pain when a fingernail started to dig into the skin between two of my fingers. The skin of the hand began to grow hotter, and a deep hiss escaped from the mouth. Just as one of the fingers touched the bag, a resounding 'NO' came from everywhere in a tidal wave of pressure. The shockwave sent Vinney and I flying back from the hand. The nightstand between the beds broke as Vinney fell on top of it.

Suddenly, the hand was in control, and I could not physically drop it. The mouth smiled; the tongue wet its red lips. I wanted to let go, to throw it, to get it away from me but my hands were locked around it, even as the heat turned my skin red.

My throat grew hoarse with screaming. "Help me, oh fuck!" I shouted.

A flash of light and the hand had disappeared. The burning moved from my ruined hands to my face. I fell to the floor, writhing as I clawed at the intense heat on my face. Through my hands, I spotted Charley. He was standing at the door and looking at me fearfully. Suddenly, the door shut, and he was gone.

Vinney's face loomed over mine. "It's in you," she said, horrified, "it's in your face." Her eyes had an animalistic look to them, wild and terrified. The screaming moved from in the room to all within my head along with a pressure so great that I thought it was going to burst.

I felt her hands pawing at me, my hands clawing at my face. Could feel the heat burning my face and then I couldn't.

***

I was somewhere else. My eyes felt screwed shut, the lids refusing to open. As I wrestled with opening my eyes, I felt a great heat all around, as if I were in an oven. The bottoms of my feet screamed in pain as the hard floor radiated intense heat. All around me, screaming started, grew in intensity and volume, then decreased and stopped. There were many different voices coming from all directions. Finally, I tore my eyes open.

I was in a cave. The cave was a small round enclosure, with one entrance just in front of me. A light radiated from the entrance, a red light that cast over dark mist swirling within the room. The walls around were blackened and charred. Niches were cut in randomly, with small white things overflowing from the cutouts. I neared one and saw that they were human skulls, with most having their jaws screwed open as if still screaming in death. It was an auditorium of death. Some were too large to be human. Thousands surrounded me.

Something moved in the entrance, a shadow temporarily dimming the room as it passed. A sick curiosity took over me, overpowering the want to just curl up near the wall of the cave and wish for it to be over. Crouching low, I edged towards the entrance and peeked around the corner. A great heat radiated into the room from the entrance.

A sight of pain on such a magnitude that my brain couldn't comprehend what I was seeing. It was as if I was viewing the world through a foggy glass. Finally, I got a clearer view and immediately wished I hadn't.

Large creatures, a fusion of arachnid and humanoid features, laughed and cheered as they drove large crowds of people towards a lake of fire. They entered the lava as if going for a swim and the screaming multiplied as more were forced in. Others were dragged out, skinless and thrashing, towards large machines. All around there was torture, there was endless pain. All around there was fire.

Something was behind me. I could feel the presence as soon as it appeared. The skin on my back burned hotter as the air around grew more stuffed and choked. I didn't dare to turn around and face this new threat. Suddenly, a language filled my ears, coming from all around and within me. I couldn't make out any individual words within the sounds of metal grating and bones breaking. Only a feeling, a feeling of rage, hatred, and lust all flooding together.

A flash accompanied the feeling of falling. I was somewhere different but instantly recognized my surroundings. The overpass, with the little orange truck under it. Something moved within the cabin of the truck, something with too many legs, fighting to escape. An unnatural glow came from beyond the overpass as the city burned, great plumes of smoke escaping into the night sky. It was raining a thick oily liquid. I looked up to corpses dancing from rope as their fat burned off their bodies and their screams formed harmonies of terror.

I got the feeling that this was a prophecy, a vision. Something that was being promised. Something unstoppable and inevitable.

***

"Wake up!" Vinney said, shaking my shoulders violently. Pain still seared hot on my face, but the screaming had finally stopped. Vinney's face was just over mine, pale with fright and speckled with small droplets of blood. She backed away as I sat up. I took a few heavy breaths and then stood up.

Cross lay dead, his face frozen in a pained grimace. He looked so young. Regret filled my stomach for inviting him along earlier that day. All he had wanted to do was prove himself to me. Now he lay dead in some run-down motel.

"Jesus," I said as I turned my gaze back to Vinney, "where the fuck is the hand?" The hand going towards my face played on repeat in my head. It was a blessing that I wasn't laying in death with Cross.

"It's in your face," she bawled, covering her face with

her hands. "What the hell. We need help. What are we doing." I took a step toward her, but she backed up. "Stay away! It's in your face. Jesus, it's spreading! Your eyes!"

I turned to the open bathroom door and caught my reflection. A gasp escaped me, and I ran towards the mirror. A red imprint of a hand covered my face. I pinched at the skin, which was giving off heat as if burning. The skin wasn't covered in something, it was as if the skin itself had been stained red. Where a finger covered my eye, the sclera had gone extremely bloodshot.

Without warning, a retch escaped me, and I puked over the bathroom counter. Tears broke loose from my eyes and dripped to the ruined counter below me. A pressure increased in my skull, a presence that was not mine trying to override my subconscious and take over. "Get out of my head," I begged, "get out, get out." A rage took over me, a strange rage that felt more like a hunger. A scream escaped me, and I punched the mirror until it shattered. Blood poured from the cuts to my knuckles.

I surveyed the room as I left the bathroom. Vinney had covered Cross' body with the other comforter and was now sitting on the other bed, rubbing her face with her hands. She looked at me fearfully as I left the room. "What do we do? Oh, God, what do we do?"

Charley's face looking down at Vinney and I as we struggled with the hand before he left replayed in my mind. "Find Charley," I said, "how dare he leave us, the little ass. Then, we find a priest or something about my face."

"The priest should come first. Charley did nothing wrong, he's just a scared kid," Vinney said, defending the man who left us for dead. I didn't feel like getting in an argument at the moment and said nothing, just looking at the blood staining the cloth that now lay over Cross. Something stirred deep within. A disgusting hunger emanating from my stomach. Another retch threatened to escape, and I turned away.

I opened my mouth to talk but a knock sounding at the door cut me off. It was followed by a quick succession of three more, all equally loud and commanding. Vinney and I stared at each other then looked to the body on the bed and the mess of a room.

The knocks came again, violent enough to shake the door. "Let me in, Newsome." I recognized the voice immediately and my feelings of anxiety increased. I forgotten that I had told him to meet us over here.

Vinney got up and walked to the door. She turned the knob and slowly opened it. A foot lodged itself in between the door and the frame as soon as the space opened. A second later, the whole door was thrown open, sending Vinney to the floor. A cop more bear than man came through the doorway. He looked down at Vinney, around the mess of a room, especially on the corpse, before turning his eyes towards me. The feeling of a deer caught in the headlights worked over me.

"Rough night?" he asked, shutting the door with a bang behind him.

"Renner, we can exp-" I started but he held up his hand.

"I've already dealt with one of your messes tonight and now this shit," he said, gesturing to the room. "You've given me a lot of shit but tonight takes the cake." He pulled out a cigarette and lit it. After blowing a large cloud of smoke straight towards me, he continued, "you left those two boys in the truck alive, you know that? They were still screaming when I pulled up."

"That's impossible. I- I killed them," I said, shocked. "I shot them both in the head."

"You calling me a liar?' The threat of violence filled the room. I shook my head vigorously. "Good, what's up with your face? Your lady friend over here hit you?"

I turned away from him, "yes."

He continued, "not that I care. All of this covering for you cost. I want my money tonight."

"I can't do that, Renner," I replied, "I need a few days to get it."

"Oh, you can't do that? Really?" A swift sound, something being pulled from a plastic sheath. Vinney gasped and whimpered. I turned to see Renner standing over her with his pistol heavy in his hand. "How much you paying her?"

"Nothing. I just need a few days, I'll get you your money, please calm down," I said, my voice approaching a shout. I was too afraid to move in case he decided to turn the pistol on me.

Renner shook his head but didn't answer me. Instead, he flipped the pistol and slammed the grip hard into Vinney's forehead. A wet thump echoed throughout the room. She fell limp instantly. The giant reared his arm back and struck her head again. Blood poured from her deflated head. Renner kicked her; she didn't react.

The enraged cop rounded on me. "You are next if you don't produce my money in the next fifteen seconds, Newsome."

My eyes kept drifting to the blood oozing from Vinney's head. The warmth radiating from it, the promise of fulfilment. The deep thirst returned. "I don't have anything for you," I said, distracted.

"Eyes on me, asshole," Renner said. "I don't have time for your bullshit."

The pistol was now pointed directly at me. My focus wouldn't shift from Vinney. Even with the fear of the pistol, my mind wandered to the blood. My breathing grew shallow, and I felt like I needed a drink. "I- I…" I stammered.

Renner noticed the briefcase on the bed. Keeping the pistol trained on me, he walked over and examined it. "I, I, I," he mocked, "what was in the case? Whatever it was, give it to me and I might let you live."

Rage, terrible and bright, filled me. I charged Renner. He fired but if it hit, I felt nothing. Slamming into his body was like running headfirst into a brick wall. The cop barely moved, grabbing my face with a meaty paw. He released it as soon as his palm touched the burning red skin of my face. Crying out, he retreated a step as he shook his hand.

Using the opportunity of the second where he shook his hand, I opened my mouth and jumped for his throat. My teeth found purchase in the meaty skin of his neck, and I bit down hard. Warm blood filled my mouth as Renner screamed. His hands grasped at my back and head, but I bit down harder and shook my head around like a rabid dog. His screams became gurgles and resistance ebbed.

We fell to the floor, on top of Vinney's corpse. The hunger took over and I tore chunks off with passion, swallowing lustily. I lapped at the blood, never feeling satiated. Eventually, I stopped and stood. Blood covered the room. The corpses lay brutalized.

I looked at my hands. Red skin ran up my arms, shallow black veins pulsing with the sustenance I just received. Black scales popped from my knuckles and ran up my arms in two rows.

A new world was coming. Retribution, revenge. A world to stomp and make mine.

I smiled and resumed my feasting.

There Will Come Chaos

KT Bartlett

When Detective Trey Holton arrived at Beulah Jessop's house, she was sitting in a folding chair in the front yard, a shawl wrapped around her despite the mugginess of the late morning.

"About time you got here. I called over an hour ago." A table sat beside her. She'd set out glasses and a pitcher filled with dark liquid. "Want tea?"

The oldest resident in Clineville, Beulah spent most of her time telling everyone that her land backed up to a haunted part of the woods, that evil lurked just behind the scrub.

Holton shook his head. "No, thank you." He wasn't sure it was tea. "Let's just get to why you called."

Beulah nodded, leaning back in her chair. "Seen an opening into this world, like a chasm. I think it's the devil."

Holton had no interest in investigating the occult. But now he would have to try to make sense of whatever biblical mumbo jumbo she came up with.

A mosquito buzzed his neck, and he reached to swat it away. "The ground opened up and the devil walked out?" He tried to keep a straight face. "Ms. Beulah, that sound like something that could really happen?"

Beulah crossed her arms and squinted at him. "You're just like everyone else. Stupid and blind."

"Ms. Beulah—"

She put up a hand. "No, you go on and laugh. I know what you all think of me. But I know how the devil works."

"Is this the devil with a forked tail or the one with the scythe?"

"Devil don't carry no scythe." Her voice trailed off, and she frowned at him. "And he don't come here himself. That's not how he works." She leaned forward. "He sends out his demons, his tricksters to do his bidding. It's a cycle. He only needs to sow a little chaos, then it will take hold and build, like a chain of events. You'll see."

A bead of sweat ran down Holton's face. He wiped it away. "What do you mean?"

Beulah shook her head. "Do you have ears, boy? I just explained how the devil works." From beneath her shawl, she pulled out a book. "Take this. You'll see what I've seen. This cycle's just getting started. There will come chaos."

The book was an old leather-style journal with a strap wrapped around to secure it. Parts of the material had been nicked and worn. Holton took it and nodded to Beulah. "Just call the department if you have anything else you want to tell us."

This wasn't the first time he'd had to deal with Beulah. Since his time as a rookie, she'd called in to report tales of haunted woods. But there were others who told similar stories. Back in the 1960s, there'd been some religious nut who'd claimed he was possessed by a demon when he killed his family. Then in the late 80s, a group of six boys went camping, only to be found the next morning mutilated and strewn across the grounds. No evidence of who did it or why was ever found. By the early 2000s, reports of devil worshipers circulated in the surrounding towns.

In the last few years, a group of local reporters had written an investigative piece on the haunted history of the area, hoping to uncover something sordid. All they found was a pattern of tragic events that happened every twenty years or so.

Though the reporters interviewed Beulah, they couldn't make sense of her stories. Holton figured she'd lost any sense of reality long ago, but as he walked back to his truck, all he could focus on was one question—how was he supposed to be on the lookout for the devil?

***

Mitch Phillips rode his Ninja out to the winding roads in the piney woods. The trees lining each side of the road towered above. Deep woods lay behind them. He liked losing himself in the intoxicating isolation.

Technically, he was late for work. His boss, Chuck Donnelly, would tear him a new one for it, but Mitch didn't care. The job at Chuck's Auto Shop was barely tolerable anyway. Mostly, he just cleaned around the shop. Mitch figured if he was going to get in trouble anyway, he may as well make it worth it, which is why he decided to take the long way.

As he took a curve in the road, the back wheel slipped a bit. He cranked the handlebars and straightened the bike with ease. The winding roads of the piney woods could challenge any rider, but these roads made him feel more alive than he ever did doing anything else.

As he turned onto FM 152, smoke curled up from the engine. "Shit."

Before the acrid smoke could choke him, he pulled over, turned off the bike and stepped away. He figured the engine was overheated.

Now he'd have to call Chuck. He took out his phone and dialed.

"Chuck's Auto." Chuck's gruff voice was unmistakable.

In the background, the high-pitched whir of a hydraulic drill cut through. Mitch winced and took the phone away from his ear.

Before he could answer, a flash of heat blew up around him, creeping under his shirt. The ground underneath his feet trembled. In the distance, he heard what sounded like metal scraping against metal. Turning around, he scanned the area but saw nothing.

He ended the call and walked backwards down the road a few steps. Then, a bike rounded the corner and headed toward him. A shimmer surrounded it, making it look out of focus. Thinking his eyes were blurry from the heat, Mitch rubbed them, then squinted and watched as the bike approached. Flames seemed to surround the rider. The heat of it reached out to him as the bike came closer.

It was old and in good condition. Black and chrome, it had a lean, mean look. Black saddlebags were attached to the back. Mitch figured it was some type of Harley, a real bike compared to his Ninja. The rider pulled up to Mitch, killed the engine, and took off the helmet.

Black hair so dark it gave off a blue tint flowed out and hung down just past her shoulders to tanned muscular arms. She wore a sleeveless shirt, and her tattoos flexed as she gripped the handlebars. On her right shoulder there was a long, thin dagger with blood trickling down one side and dropping just past the tip above her elbow. Three dragonflies with wings of fire stretched across her left arm. The earrings that dangled from her ears were the shape of feathers. She wore what looked like painted-on jeans. Her black boots had a snake design that wound up to her knees. His reflection showed in her dark sunglasses.

Mitch struggled to speak. "Your bike…"

"You like it?" When she spoke, her voice was deep and smooth. She took off her sunglasses and eyes of deep shadowy green stared at Mitch. "Wanna ride?" She gestured her head to the space on the seat behind her.

"Uh, I was just headed to work."

"You always walk to work, baby?"

He chuckled. "No, my bike overheated."

The edges of her eyes tightened slightly. Saliva pooled in Mitch's mouth. He swallowed hard.

"Get on." She held out the helmet to him.

He looked back at his bike. "Uh, I can't just leave it here."

A smile crossed her lips. "Baby, where we're going, you won't need that piece of shit."

"I ain't looking for trouble."

When she spoke, the words rolled out of her mouth like billows of smoke. "You ain't got to go looking, baby."

***

Holton sat at his desk trying to read the book Beulah had given him, but he hadn't been able to get past the first few pages. A woozy feeling set in and made the words look bleary on the page.

"You okay?"

The voice startled him. Brianne Sims, the admin for the Sheriff's department sat on his desk, smiling at him.

He turned to face her. "Yeah, I'm just tired."

She nodded, then pointed to the book. "What's it about?"

"The devil, I think."

"Ooh, fun reading. Is that bizarro Beulah's?"

He turned to the inside cover and showed her the label. "I got it from Beulah, but it looks like a personal journal for Mamie Hendricks. You heard of her?"

Brianne shook her head. "No." She took the book, examining it. "This is so cool. How old do you think this is?" She turned to a dog-eared page and studied it. "Oh God. I remember this story from when those reporters wrote about it. Listen, "'May 6th, 1883. Just as I said, there was no miracle—thirty women all pregnant at the same time? It was a sign of things to come.'"

Holton leaned back in his chair. "She sounds just like Beulah."

"Yeah, but it gets worse." Brianne traced her finger along the page. "'They didn't believe me when I told them my vision. They called me "crazy Mamie," but I saw their death because the devil showed it to me. Pastor Hughes was the first to know I was right. He found his pregnant wife lifeless on the floor, blood seeping from her eyes and nose. In two days, the rest of the women were also dead, all just weeks before their due dates.'"

Holton stood, groaning as he did.

Brianne set the book down. "What's wrong?"

"Now I've got to go back out to the Jessop property and ask Beulah why she gave me that book. In the meantime, would you see what else in the book jogs your memory?"

"Hmmm, you're asking a history buff to read a journal from the late 1800s?" She smiled at him. "Yeah, I can do that."

As he walked out of the department and to his truck, exhaustion almost took over. He couldn't shake the feeling that something had been set in motion.

***

Mitch realized he hadn't thought any of this through as they drove down a narrow, winding road. A pit grew in his gut. *Goddamn, she's probably taking me to meet a bunch of other biker bitches who'll beat the shit out of me.*

They passed signs denoting private property, but they drove past them and pulled up beside a small lake that was flanked by tall pine trees. The rider pushed down the kickstand.

Before getting off, Mitch removed the helmet and scanned the area. It was isolated, and they were alone.

The rider tapped his leg, and he got off, setting the helmet down on the seat.

She swung her leg over the seat and stood facing him. Taking off her sunglasses, she leaned against the bike. "Do you fish?"

"Uh, not since I was a kid. Anyway, I ain't got a license." He smiled but couldn't tell if she was joking.

The corners of her mouth turned up a little. She turned away and walked to the back of the bike. Opening one of the saddlebags, she plunged her hand in and pulled out a revolver.

Mitch's breath caught in his throat, and the pit in his gut deepened. "What's that for?" He heard a tremble in his voice.

She held up the gun and pointed it at him. "Fishing." Then, she offered him the grip.

He paused a moment, unsure. Then he reached out a hand and accepted it. She took his other hand and led him toward the water's edge.

"What you want me to do with this?" He gestured with the gun.

She stepped in close to him, holding his gaze. "I want you to fish, baby."

His shoulders tensed. "I never fished with a gun."

He barely got the words out before she moved behind him, putting her hands on his hips, guiding him closer to the water's edge. Her touch seeped through his jeans and into his skin.

Standing behind him, she positioned the gun in his hands and wrapped her hands around them. "It's easy. Just look, aim, and fire."

The gun erupted. Water, blood, and fish parts splashed out onto Mitch's jeans. His ears rang from the sound of the blast. She shoved him aside, squatted down, reached in the water, and pulled out what was left of the fish. When she stood, she held out the fish's head with a trail of remains.

Mitch recoiled. "Goddamn, get it away." He backed up, almost tripping over his feet. From behind, he heard a truck pull up fast.

"Hold your fire!"

Mitch wheeled around to see Detective Holton getting out of his truck, gun drawn and aimed at him.

Holton lowered his gun. "Mitch? What are you doing with that gun?"

Mitch had been two years behind Holton in school, and though they never ran in the same circle, they knew each other. Mitch was glad to see the detective.

The rider stepped forward. "He shot a moccasin." She held up a long, dead snake.

Mitch scrunched his eyes closed, then open. Just a second ago, she was holding a fish head.

Holton nodded. "Those things are bad news."

Mitch looked at Holton, then back at the rider.

Holton placed his gun back in its holster, a puzzled look on his face. Mitch thought he might ask the girl who she was. But as Holton started to speak to her, she tilted her head and smiled.

Holton grimaced and shook his head, then froze in place. When he looked at Mitch, his eyes were glazed over. "Right now, I need to get to Beulah Jessop's. By the time I come back around, you two need to be gone. You're still here, you better be ready to show me a permit for that gun."

Mitch nodded. He wanted to tell Holton he needed help, that he wanted to run away from this woman, but his mouth would not move. He looked at her and their eyes met. She shook her head so slightly; he wasn't sure she'd really done it.

Mitch watched Holton get back in his truck and drive away.

***

"Ms. Beulah? It's Holton," He stood on the porch, knocking on the door. "I need to ask you about the book."

When no reply came, he knocked again. "Ms. Beulah?"

Tension grew at the base of his skull and dripped down his spine. Something wasn't right. He pulled his gun from the holster, backed down the steps, and walked toward the back of the house.

Yard stakes with windchimes and crosses littered the yard. Dreamcatchers hung from low tree branches. Overgrown weeds snaked across the ground. Holton scanned the area, but didn't see any movement.

A storage building sat in the back. Holton made his way through the maze of yard décor toward it. As he rounded the shed, he saw her. Beulah Jessop was tied to a post, positioned like a scarecrow. Her eyes had been carved out. Bloody holes gaped forward.

Holton stumbled backwards, almost losing his balance. "No…"

From his pocket, his phone buzzed. He pulled it out and answered. "H..Holton."

"It's Brianne. I haven't finished the journal yet, but there's something weird about it. There are a lot of handwritten accounts that talk about 'the two,' like two people. Somebody is a witness to the stuff that happens or will happen. As best as I can tell, the other person is a kind of harbinger—that's like a forerunner. Something that comes before…. Holton, are you there?"

His breath came fast, but he couldn't answer.

"Holton, what's wrong?"

He tried to steady his voice. "That's what Beulah was." It came out hollow.

"I don't think so. Mamie writes about witnessing things like what Beulah did, but there is something else that is the harbinger. Wait, you said Beulah *was*…Holton what happened?"

A dispatcher's voice broke through the radio on his belt.

"All available units. 10-80 at 12th and Lowel, location Chuck's Auto Shop. Mass casualties." As he heard it from the radio, it echoed in the background on the phone.

Something didn't seem right. *An explosion at Chucks*? He looked again at Beulah's body. Images of Mitch with the woman at the lake flooded his vision, and he knew he had to go. "Send someone here to secure the scene."

"Holton…"

"And send CSU. I've got to get to Chuck's."

***

Mitch wished Holton would come back. The woman stared hard at him and tossed aside the snake. She nodded toward her bike and motioned for him to follow.

Not moving, he watched her. "You ain't even really that pretty," he said, his voice just above a whisper.

Turning back, she stepped to him and leaned in close. When she spoke, her breath brushed across his lips. "You don't want pretty, baby."

The breeze blew her hair, making it flow like silk.

"What's your name? I don't even know that," Mitch said.

She turned, walked to her bike, and got on. "Call me Miranda." She held up a finger, flexing it, motioning him to her.

A click in the back of his mind told him he should stay put, but he felt himself walk to the bike and climb on behind her.

They drove into town. Evening sunlight cast a shadow across the buildings. They passed by Chuck's Auto Shop. As Mitch turned to look at it, Miranda extended her arm and pointed to the building. Light flooded Mitch's eyes, but as he tried to turn to see what it was, Miranda sped up and made a sharp turn onto a side street. Waves of heat rushed around him. His ears clogged, and all he could hear was the sound of his own breath.

They drove on to his house. He wasn't sure how Miranda knew the way. Maybe he forgot he'd told her.

They parked and got off the bike. Miranda unzipped a saddlebag and pulled out a smaller bag. "Anybody else home?"

Mitch shook his head, trying to clear his ears. "Bingo night. My mom won't be home till real late."

Miranda smiled at him, her green eyes piercing into his.

Inside, in his room, she closed the door and turned on the radio and scanned for some music. Nothing more than static and the occasional, "Amen, brother, won't you come," sputtered through. She flicked off the switch and sat down on the bed, setting the bag beside her.

Standing by the door, Mitch wondered if this was a moment of no return. Somewhere in his mind, he felt a nudge to open the door and run. But all he could do was watch her.

Reaching down, she pulled off her boots. Then she leaned back on her elbows and extended her neck back until her black hair pooled onto the pillow.

Mitch watched her, his breath loud in his ears.

She leaned over, opened the small bag, and pulled out a flask, then tossed the bag aside. She unscrewed the flask and held it out to him.

He stepped forward, grabbed the flask, and took a swig—his tongue registered Jack Daniels. He swallowed hard, choking down the stinging liquid.

She watched him and smiled as he struggled. He held the flask out to her and wiped his mouth with the back of his hand.

Miranda held up a finger and flexed it. "Come on baby." Her voice was deep and smoky. It snaked into his ears.

Goddamn, yes, was his only thought.

***

When Holton arrived at the scene, it was a blurry mix of ambulances and fire trucks. He felt his sense of dread growing. He'd replayed in a loop what had happened at the lake with Mitch. Holton hadn't known the woman there and couldn't figure out why he hadn't questioned her.

He parked, but didn't get out. Lowering his head, he tried to clear his mind.

A knock on his window startled him. Sheriff Banks motioned for him to open the door.

Holton got out, taking in the scene. Chuck's shop was a black shell of what it had been. Parts of the building scattered across the road. Smoke and flecks of drywall floated up.

"Holton, you okay?"

He walked toward the smoldering building. "Mitch Phillips in there?"

Banks took off his hat and wiped his forehead. "That kid that cleans the shop? Don't know yet. We got body parts everywhere. It's going to take some time to wade through it all. Match heads with bodies."

"What happened?"

"Massive explosion. Don't know how many casualties. Waiting on the report from the fire chief. Not sure if it was an accident at this point."

Images of people on fire and writhing in pain flashed in his mind like warning signs, but Holton didn't know what he was seeing. He shook his head to clear his eyes and grabbed Banks' arm. "But no sign of Mitch at all?" His voice sounded strained.

Banks studied him. "Holton, what the hell is going on?"

Holton felt an urge to tell Banks what Beulah had told him, that this could be the work of the devil, but his phone rang. Thankful for the interruption, Holton turned from Banks to answer it.

"Holton, I finished the journal." Brianne's voice was excited, though she whispered. "I think I know what the harbinger is. It's in an entry from 1900 by someone named John Harlow."

"John Harlow? Is he the harbinger?"

"He was like Mamie, a witness. The harbinger is something different. They seem to have something to do with the tragedies that happen."

"How?"

"I'm not sure yet, but they're connected to hell in some way."

"What did you find about witnesses?"

"Not much, just it's a horrible, tormented existence. They're plagued with images of hell, death, and destruction. As much as they try to help, most people don't believe them."

A sharp pain seared across his temples. Thoughts of Beulah on the post flashed in his mind. He put a hand over his eyes, trying to force the image to pass, but it morphed into one clear thought. Holton's chest tightened. "It's Mitch. I think Mitch Phillips is the next witness."

"Mitch Phillips? Are you sure? From what I can tell, the witnesses are pretty moral people, like the good citizen type. Not that Mitch is a bad guy, just there's not much to him."

"I can't explain how I know, but I saw him just before I went to Beulah's. I got the feeling he wanted to tell me something, but I was too focused on finding out about that book." Quickly, his frustration grew. He looked back at the shop.

"Okay, if it is Mitch, then tell him to look out for a woman with dark hair," Brianne said.

Holton's stomach fell. "What?"

"The witness after Harlow, Malcolm Caswell, wrote about a woman with black hair. Then after that every witness has mentioned a woman with dark hair. That's since 1940. I don't know yet what their purpose is."

Immediately, Holton knew. He'd seen that woman with long black hair. She'd been holding a dead snake.

***

The morning sun peeked from behind heavy curtains. Mitch laid still with his eyes closed. He took in a breath and tried to clear the fog from his brain. Opening his eyes, he scanned the room but didn't see Miranda. For a moment, he wasn't sure if yesterday was real, but then he noticed the bag on the floor.

He tried to recall the events, but he couldn't pull them together. *Goddamn Jack*, he thought. He sat up and ran his fingers through his hair, trying to pull out some memory from the day before. All that came to him was flashing lights and fish heads.

Then came a knock at the front door. "Mitch, you there? It's Holton. Please, tell me you're there." The detective sounded rattled.

Mitch wanted to call out to him, but Miranda swung open the bedroom door. She stepped in, grabbed Mitch's jeans from the floor and tossed them at him. "Get dressed. We're on the move."

He stood and put on his jeans. "I've got to tell my mom something. She'll—"

Miranda grabbed his arm. "No, baby. She's not going to do anything." She gazed into his eyes.

Ice settled in his chest, and he felt his head nod.

Miranda tossed him a shirt, then grabbed her bags. She tilted her head, motioning him to follow into the hallway.

From outside, Holton pounded on the door again.

They crept past the front door, to the kitchen, and out the side door. Once outside, Mitch paused, but Miranda grabbed his hand and pulled him to the bike. They climbed on and Mitch felt the bike rumble alive underneath him. As they pulled onto the street, he looked back expecting to see Holton. Mitch wasn't sure how they were able to get away from him.

They rode again into town, toward Chuck's Auto shop, but as Mitch crooked his head to see it, Miranda turned onto a side street away from the shop. All Mitch could see was the burnt husk of a building. He felt like he should react, jump off the bike, but he just sat there.

It was early and traffic was light, but in the distance, Mitch thought he saw Holton's truck. He wanted to wave, signaling to make sure Holton saw them, but when he tried to lift his arm, it wouldn't move. The only thing Mitch could focus on was Miranda.

She pulled the bike into the parking lot of a corner store and parked. Stepping to her saddlebags, she untied them and slung them over her shoulder. "Come on, baby."

Mitch got off the bike and followed her inside. A girl behind the counter—Suzy, according to her name tag—looked up at them. Mitch thought he remembered her from high school, but she didn't seem to know him.

Miranda stepped up and placed the saddlebags on the counter. She reached into one and pulled out the gun they had used at the lake. She raised the gun and aimed at Suzy. With her other hand, she pulled out a wadded-up canvas bag and handed it to Mitch. He wanted to scream at Miranda to stop, but his voice felt trapped in his mouth.

The bag, though empty, felt heavy.

Suzy reached a hand under the counter, like she was trying to find a panic button, but Miranda cocked the gun and held it up to Suzy's face. "Uh-uh, baby. Open the drawer."

Shaking, Suzy opened the drawer and pulled the cash from the slots. She handed the money to Mitch.

Miranda gestured to the tray with the gun. "Don't forget this."

Suzy lifted the tray and pulled out a pile of cash, twenties, and hundreds, and gave it to Mitch. Without thinking, he placed the money in the bag. His mind couldn't catch up with what was happening.

Miranda reached out and put her hand around Mitch's and squeezed his hand closed around the bag. She shifted her eyes to his and pushed the bag toward his chest. "Meet you outside, baby."

The momentum of her push made him take a few steps backwards. He was almost out the door when Miranda held the gun up to Suzy's chest and fired two shots.

Miranda turned and followed Mitch out before Suzy had fallen all the way to the floor. Mitch stumbled the rest of the way out of the door and into the parking lot, still clutching the bag.

"What the hell?" His voice didn't sound like his own.

Miranda stepped outside and stopped short. Turning to Mitch, she looked into his eyes, lifted the gun and fired one shot straight into his belly.

Mitch dropped the bag, and his hand rushed to his stomach. He looked down, shocked, to see his blood splattered on his shirt. His breath rushed out and he crumpled to the ground.

Miranda walked to Mitch and knelt beside him. He felt her reach to his forehead and trace a finger in a circular shape, but he couldn't tell what it was.

***

Holton had to find Mitch, talk to him, warn him. He stood outside of Mitch's house, pounding on the door.

From the side of the house came the rumble of a bike starting. Holton pulled his gun and started toward it, but as he rounded the house, there was no bike.

Then from behind, he felt a rush of heat, felt the rumble of an engine. Still, he saw nothing. He shook his head hard to clear it, but when he opened his eyes, all he saw were images of the black-haired woman killing Mitch. He rubbed his fists against his eyes as Beulah's words about the devil came to him again—*He means to cause chaos here.*

Holton felt frozen in place, but when his vision cleared, he forced himself to go to his truck. As he got in, his radio reported "…10-31 at the corner market on Pine Street…." *Crime in progress*, he thought, *I've got you now.*

Muscle memory kicked in. Without responding to the call, Holton flipped on his flashing lights and drove toward Pine Street.

His mind went back to the scene from Beulah's. He'd seen what happened to her, and he knew he'd failed her. He couldn't let Mitch suffer the same fate. Or worse.

Veering into the lot, Holton scanned the parking lot but knew he was too late. There Mitch lay on the ground, lifeless, blood pooling around him.

In the background, sirens sounded.

Defeat gripped Holton as he got out and walked to Mitch. He leaned down and felt for a pulse, knowing there was none. "Ah, Mitch, I'm sorry."

From behind he heard a loud scraping sound, like metal on metal. The ground beneath him trembled. He stood, spinning and pulled his gun.

The black-haired woman was walking toward a chasm that had opened in the ground. It kicked up a fog of acrid dust. She turned to look at Holton.

He tried to aim his gun at her, but his arms wouldn't move. "I know what you are."

The woman shook her head, a smile spreading across her lips. When she reached the edge of the chasm, she climbed down into it. Her hair flowed like silk. Just before she disappeared, she tossed her sunglasses up. They landed beside Mitch.

From behind, Holton heard Mitch stir. He turned to see Mitch sit up and put on the sunglasses. His movements shimmered, like they were out of focus.

Panic gripped Holton. He'd been wrong.

Mitch wasn't the witness. He was the harbinger.

Holton tried to step back, but his mind flooded with

visions of death and chaos. They came fast, folding into each other. He saw Mitch standing on a hill, a line of bodies behind him, eyes carved out. He saw bodies writhing in pain at Mitch's feet. Holton groaned from the impact of it. The weight of impending tragedy dropped him to his knees.

As Mitch walked to the bike, Holton reached up a hand to him. Mitch paused. "You see? Now, it begins." His voice came out like billows of smoke that snaked into Holton's ears.

Mitch started the bike, the engine roared, and he drove away.

Holton could only watch, a witness to the chaos to come.

Girls Who Love the Devil

Sarah Oechsle

The Sorrel Mountain Renaissance Faire was not a Ren Faire so much as a gathering of nerds who wanted to dress up, do drugs, and fuck each other. That's what Jake told me when he invited me. He swore I couldn't miss it. The *girls*, he'd said, his eyes rolling back in his blocky, acne-scarred head. The Faire was just out on some old guy's land, so there were no hotels around. Everybody camped. People set up bonfires and spent the whole weekend drunk on mead or high on mushrooms. Cringey as the whole thing felt, if *Jake* could get laid there, then I would be fighting girls off with a stick. Who was I to turn down free pot and even a slim shot at easy pussy?

We turned off the main road and gravel popped beneath the tires of Jake's Forester. It was a hot summer weekend. Perfect weather for girls who like to run around mostly naked. Bad weather for Jake. I could smell him already. His thinning mop of hair was plastered to his forehead even with the sun still behind the trees. Jake was one of those guys that you know isn't a virgin, but the notion is still a little baffling. At our Sunday night D&D group, he played a barbarian half-orc in some nod to his enormous size and, I think, his unfortunate looks. Jake was *really* into that sort of shit. I mean *really*. He LARPed at the city park every Thursday. Fought with a foam sword and went by Drazan Blackwall. Drazan. Blackwall. So, you can imagine that when this guy calls something a "fuckfest," I'm listening.

"Holy shit."

The woods peeled back, and the campground was all around us—Coachella for nerds. Everything was green in that way it gets in late June. The grass was still wet and sparkling. Jake steered us through a jungle of tents and RVs. Some Jake-looking guy with an airstream and a death metal tee shirt raised a beer to us from a lawn chair. His wife was sunbathing topless on a Celtic-knot beach towel.

"Holy shit," I said again. "Did you see her?"

"I told you, man," Jake said, waving to let a group pass in front of us. A pirate even shorter than me, and a chubby girl with elf ears. I smirked as a flabby Witcher jogged after them. Freaky, maybe, but I doubted this place would turn into the drug-fueled orgy Jake promised. But I'd never have tagged along if not for Jake's drunken insistence that it was Woodstock for horny nerds.

It took us forty minutes to find a spot big enough for Jake to open up the back of his Forester, behind a circle of Winnebagos flying identical red and black flags. In the center of them was a huge pile of wood and cardboard. Preparations for a bonfire later that night.

I clutched my sleeping bag to my chest. "You didn't pack a tent?"

Jake just laughed. He hadn't even brought food. Just a fold of cash, a cooler of beer, and a flask of Johnny Walker. After a few minutes, he crawled from the back hatch of his Forester in full costume–a fake leather vest and knee-high boots. He had a nerfed-out war-hammer strapped across his meaty chest. A helmet with Viking horns on it. Drazan Blackwall, in the flesh.

I glanced around to make sure we were alone. I didn't

want girls–or anyone for that matter–to think I was like Jake. I like games and anime as much as the next guy who didn't peak in high school, but all this dress-up and play-pretend stuff was too asinine for me, and Jake had that basement-dweller look that repels pussy like bear mace. I wondered how much walking around with him was going to hurt my chances.

He looked me up and down in my tee shirt and jeans.

"You want to change in the car?"

I looked down at my Demon Slayer tee. "You didn't say I needed a costume."

"Garb," he corrected with a snort. He crawled back into the Forester on all fours, and I tried not to look at the ass crack peaking from his waistband. After a few seconds of rifling around, he came out with a bundle of brown fabric and tossed it in my direction. "Got this on Amazon in case you didn't have anything."

It was a cheap, polyester monk's robe. The medieval-looking kind. Only this one was wrinkled to all hell, damp from sitting at the bottom of Jake's duffel bag. It came with a rope belt and a big, plastic crucifix. I shook my head. "No way, dude."

Before Jake could say anything, he fixed his gaze on someone over my shoulder. I turned to find a man hovering too close behind me. He wore a green cloak fastened around his neck by a plastic dragon pin. The hood was pulled over his face, casting him in shadow, but I could still see his red-rimmed eyes fixed on me.

I took a startled step backward. He was muttering something to himself. Twitchy, like a guy who's about to ask you for spare change. But there was something more than that. It was those eyes, I think. They were wide with fear. Like he'd just watched someone die.

"Did you see what they're burning?" he asked, too quietly. I opened my mouth, but he seemed not to notice. "Bibles. They're burning Bibles."

I raised an eyebrow. Jake had come to stand at my side, looking smugly down at the guy.

"Who?" I asked.

The man raised a trembling finger to the stack of logs in the center of the next camp. There were no books that I could see. And it certainly wasn't burning.

I shook my head. "I don't think so."

"Look at the flames," he hissed. He stooped so his face was inches from mine. "They're purple and red. Devil colors." His breath smelled like vomit. His eyes were even more frightening up close. The huge, dilated pupils gave them the look of two black pits. I staggered backward and Jake started to laugh. The man looked up at him with an unreadable expression and said, "Protect your friend. There are demons here. Can't you see them?"

"Yeah man," Jake gestured to the nothing around us. "And the gnomes, too. Watch out or you'll step on them."

The man gave no indication that he'd heard Jake, but he walked off. His head swiveled back and forth as he cut through the other campsites. I wondered if he thought gnomes were following him. I rubbed my hands on my jeans to hide their shaking.

"What the fuck was that?"

Jake chuckled, "Some guy tripping balls. You've got to pace yourself better. What a moron."

I stared after the man, but he'd disappeared in the labyrinth of campsites. I was still clutching Jake's balled-up monk's robe. I held it out and grimaced. I'd worn my best jeans, and my shirt was one a buddy said made it look like I had abs. How was a brown tarp going to help my odds?

"Trust me, man," Jake lowered his voice, "it's not going to be fun if you don't play along."

A jeep rolled by us, flying a red and black pentagram banner from the roof. A girl in a corset and a pair of huge demon horns hung her arm out the passenger window. She leaned out as she passed.

"Did a guy come by here? Green cloak?"

Jake laughed and pointed in the direction the man had gone. "Said he's seeing demons."

"Well," the girl gestured to her plastic horns and gave Jake a simpering smile. She was cute, and her dark eye makeup and demon costume gave off an enticing, slutty look. Like a priestess of hell.

"Great helmet," her friend shouted to Jake from the open back as they pulled past us. I felt a stab of jealousy. I'd never been a ladies' man, but I wasn't half as nerdy as Jake and knew for a fact I was better looking. The one thing Jake had on me was his absurd height, but I figured he lost a lot of those points with his width, bad hairline, and general ugliness. I had good hair, and the few girls I managed to amuse into overlooking my stature always told me I was cute.

The message was clear. I put on the robe.

It was only late morning, but Jake had us take two shots each before we left the campground and headed for the Faire. I kept tripping over my robe as we headed up the hill, shooting Jake a pissed-off look whenever I did.

They stood in line at the entrance gate, beneath a pair of huge wood-and-foam stone parapets. The crowd was a mix of costumes and regular people—some families, even. My stomach churned a bit from the whiskey and the sight of screaming kids. It was crowded, and despite the theater-set Tudor facades, it didn't look much like the Renaissance. Huge guys with axes. Slutty fairies. Fifty-year-old women dressed as belly dancers. A couple of guys in those huge Game of Thrones fur cloaks, despite the heat. It was already steaming hot, and the smell of cooking meat and french fries hung smokey in the air.

"I want to grab a stein with my old Pathfinder group," Jake said as we hit the wall of a crowd. "They usually meet at 'the dragon'."

"The dragon?" I echoed as we fought our way past a

makeshift stage. A small crowd had formed, blocking much of the path. I was trailing behind Jake when I heard a voice call out.

"Hey, little buddy!"

It was too much to hope he wasn't talking to me. The carnie was bent over in a corny stockade. I bristled as he went on.

"Hey, holy father. I don't think they make those robes in dwarf sizes."

I gave an awkward little laugh. Across the square, the carnie's partner was selling water balloons filled with red paint. $5 a throw. A few people had partaken already. The carnie's jester's hat was knocked crooked, and his shoulder and left hand were splattered with crimson. I tried to push through the crowd after Jake, but the man called again.

"Nice crucifix. Want to see mine? It's bigger."

Beneath the smear of red paint, the man's eyes were wild and bloodshot. I wondered if he was on the same shit as the man from earlier. But he seemed too cogent. And a little too toothless. I figured it was meth, and turned to look for Jake again, but the carnie went on. His voice was lower, and the lilting, clownish tone had suddenly gone out of it.

"You're going to die tonight," he muttered.

The words ran like a cold finger down my spine. I stopped dead, eyes darting to the faces around me, searching for some sign that they'd heard him, too. Before I could meet anyone's gaze, Jake grabbed my arm. Over my shoulder, the carnie disappeared behind the crush of tourists.

"Did you hear that guy?" I asked, once we were clear of the bodies.

Jake didn't even look at me. "It's just one of those acts trying to get you to buy a throw. Like a dunk tank."

I felt the whiskey turn in my stomach again and wondered if I was going to throw up. "No, I mean… did you hear what he said?"

"He's a professional asshole. You should hear the stuff he

shouts at chicks."

I was trying to stammer out a better explanation when I caught sight of another devil-girl in the crowd. This one had pink horns and one of those barmaid-type outfits that lifted her tits up practically to her neck. I managed to catch her eye, and when she saw my robe she broke into a girly little smile. I smiled back, but Jake was pulling me toward a cluster of picnic tables, and she quickly disappeared.

"The Faire is basically just the pregame," he explained as we joined the end of a line. I scanned the crowd for the girl, but she was gone. "Hope you like beer."

I had two steins with Jake's friends at "The Dragon." They were all guys except for one skinny, pale girl with a bullish nose ring. She was dating two of the other guys or something. I sat in silence and stared up at the dragon: a huge, animatronic lizard with scales of red and gold foil. Its eyes glowed, and every fifteen minutes it spewed propane fire from its nostrils.

"You on acid?" the nose-ring girl asked suddenly. I hadn't seen her walk over.

"No," I said. Nobody had offered me any. I took a drink of watery beer.

"This place is fucking crazy on acid," she added. She was smiling at me. I didn't like looking at her. After a beat of silence, she added, "Jake said it was your first Faire."

"Yeah."

"Is it what you expected?"

"Nah." She gave me an expectant look, so I added, "The costumes are pretty cool."

"Garb." She was still smiling. She'd dressed up as some kind of generic maiden but with a ring of plastic, purple flowers around her head. Ill-fitting elf ears poked from under her hair, but her own jutting set made them stick out at a ridiculous angle.

"I like your… garb," I lied.

She gave me another gummy grin. "I like yours. Very

cool."

"Getting a blessing from the father, Tal?" one of her boyfriends called over. I took a step away. She didn't seem to notice.

"Never," she laughed. "Hail Satan."

Afternoon came slowly and steamed like a greenhouse, but nobody seemed to care much. The drunker the crowd got, the more they noticed my costume. A pair of wasted lady vampires asked me to bless them. They smelled like beer and plastic. I'd muttered something and held out my crucifix for them to kiss. They actually did it. After a couple more beers, the crowd was stinking. It was past three. Jake's ugly friend had gone off with the boyfriends and Jake returned with a couple of turkey legs and a paper cup of fries. We dozed in the shade.

"Forgive me, Father, for I have sinned."

I sat up on my elbows, peering drunk into the sun. Her face was spinning a little, but I recognized the Jeep girl from that morning. Her box-dye black hair was braided into two pigtails. Red, plastic horns jutted from the crown of her head in crazy, goatish swirls. She was pretty enough that I impulsively ran my fingers through my hair.

"How long since your last confession?" I answered. Was I slurring? She had a purring smile, and her body was a little plump in the way some guys like. Maybe I did, too. Maybe I was drunk.

To my surprise, she laughed. *Really* laughed. She looked me up and down, as though trying to assess something. I felt my face growing hot.

"You're not a narc or anything, right? The costume's just a bit?"

I sat straighter. "I'm cool."

This seemed to satisfy her. She nodded to where Jake was sprawled on the grass, his gut rising and falling as he snored. "Is that your friend?"

I nodded reluctantly. She smiled. Was she flirting with

me? It was too hard to tell with a head full of beer, and I'd made the mistake before. She went on.

"I saw you guys at camp earlier. Anything good in that cooler?"

I thought about lying, but my answer sputtered out before I could come up with anything good. "Just some beer and liquor."

"That's perfect," she said. "Me and my girls are joining forces on the west edge of camp. By the woods. You know it?"

"Sure," I lied.

"We've got mushrooms and a shit ton of weed, but nobody brought enough booze. You guys wanna join up?"

For a moment I wondered if she was fucking with me. I half-expected to spot her friends laughing from their hiding place. I looked at Jake again. Maybe he hadn't been talking shit all this time. The thought had my heart pounding. I tried to play it cool.

"Are all your girls sinners, too?"

To my surprise, she let out a bright, barking laugh. "Worse," she said. "We're demons. That alright with you, *Father*?" The way she said it might have made me hard if not for all the beer. And I could smell Jake.

"Maybe I'll get you to repent," I added. It was a stupid line, so I tried to glaze over it quickly. The situation was precarious. I'd somehow just gotten fabulously lucky. I could blow the whole night if I said the wrong thing. "I'm Aiden."

She gave me an up-and-down look. Instinct made me stretch myself taller. "I'm Delphine," she replied after a beat, flashing another smile. "See you tonight, Brother Aiden."

As she turned to go, I saw she had a little devil tail sticking through a slit in her skirt. I shook Jake awake.

"What?" he grumbled. His breath reeked.

"Dude. That devil-girl just invited us to party with them tonight."

Jake heaved himself upright, rubbing his eyes. "Devil-girl?"

"Those Satanist chicks from earlier. I think she was actually into me."

He slapped me on the shoulder, knocking me off my balance. "See? What did I tell you? And my buddy said the devil worshippers throw crazy parties. Girls who love the devil are fucking wild."

After a few blurry hours, we returned to our car and watched the lights of campfires spring up across the advancing darkness. When the sun disappeared, Jake carried the cooler through camp and I puffed on a cigarette behind him, hoping it would still my spinning head. The taste alone brought me back to reality long enough to notice the revelers all around us. We headed in some general westward direction where I could make out thumping music and the psychedelic glow of Halloween lights.

After several minutes trudging through pot smoke and tire tracks, we found ourselves at the back of a huge crowd. A hundred people were gathered around some animal pen where a stack of jumbo Jenga blocks stood ready to topple. Beneath the tower, a topless woman was swaying. Staggering drunk. Beyond her, a man on a stage barked cruel encouragement while the crowd laughed. Some homely blonde next to me in a ranger's tunic shouted at the top of her lungs.

"Six!"

The mic man laughed, "Come on, folks. You think she can count that high?"

"Strip Jenga," Jake breathed into my ear. "They set it up every year."

The topless woman looked like she might collapse before the Jenga tower did. It was only the thought of Delphine's grin that kept me from wanting to stay and watch.

"Flash the crowd!" the mic guy belched. The woman must have pulled a six.

The devil-girls had set up on the west edge of the campground, just where Delpine said they would be. Jake dropped the heavy cooler, and it hit the grass with a thud. I gawked at the size of the "demon" camp. It was its own festival. They'd erected makeshift walls of chain link and chicken wire. The entrance was a banner pulled taut between two tiki torches. Something red was scrawled on it in those illegible death metal letters, giving the impression of a seeping wound.

The bouncer at the entrance wore a black bull mask over his head. Through it, his deep-set eyes had the bloodshot look of a practicing stoner. He was the size of Jake but with arms as big around as my skull, and his minotaur head had an upside-down cross branded into it right above the eyes. He looked us over as we approached, his gaze lingering on my plastic crucifix.

"Uh… Father Aiden?" I tried. "Delphine invited us."

The minotaur looked down at me with a disaffected sneer. Jake opened the cooler to show we hadn't come empty-handed. The bouncer raised an eyebrow and shrugged.

"And?" he grunted again. He had a voice like a grave digger or a death metal singer. Jake caught me by the arm and turned me around.

"Dude, fuck this guy," he whispered. "Let's go back to the strip show."

I pictured Delphine and shook my head, instead slipping a last, crumpled $20 from my billfold. The bouncer was chatting with a couple of pirate queens who'd arrived. He stepped aside to let them in, then slid back into place and crossed his huge arms as I approached again. I held out the bribe and he stared at it for a breath before snagging it and stuffing it into his front pocket. He still didn't move, and for a fraught moment, I worried he had just stolen the money. But he stood stone still as we skirted awkwardly around him and into the camp.

Beyond the entrance, everything was red. It felt like another world. A huge bonfire threw shadows across the clearing, and they twisted into monstrous, thrashing shapes on the circle of tents and RVs. A crowd flailed to screaming music from a palette stage, so loud I couldn't think. The thumping of the bass and the roar of the singer's voice shook the ground. I felt my chest cavity ringing; struggling to rise and fall as though it were being struck with a mallet. Everyone was decked out in purple and crimson wherever they weren't in head-to-toe black. Someone had clawed a crooked pentagram into a sheet metal wall and splattered it with red paint.

Like a curtain backdrop in a theater, the forest rose dark and deep behind it all. It was a dense, summer wood. Nasty—all blackberries and kudzu running like a slime down the trees. I felt a tug on the end of the cooler and Jake was on the move again, leading us toward a table where the denizens of hell had stacked all their booze.

"I'm gonna try and score some coke," Jake must have said, but I wasn't listening. I stared past the band where a throne of skulls was propped up on cinder blocks above the stage. Satan presided over his domain, spiked, leather boots spread wide, sculling Miller High Life from the can. Without the horns or the bare, red-painted chest, he would have looked like some guy who worked at 7-Eleven.

When I looked back, Jake was already gone. Delphine seemed to appear out of the smoke. She didn't notice me at first. I tapped her on the shoulder, and she turned lazily to face me.

"Hey, I remember you," she said, offering me a drowsy smile. I felt a stab of disappointment. "Want?"

She shoved something toward me, and I took it before recognizing the feel of a vape in my hands. I could taste her spit on the mouthpiece. The weed hit hard, so fast it undid all the work of my cigarette. To my surprise, Delphine didn't disappear. She stood beside me, staring at the stage and swaying invitingly back and forth to the music. I didn't dare try to dance. I didn't want to look like an idiot and, besides, the lights were spinning. I worried I'd just resigned myself to puking in the kudzu rather than shooting my shot. That was, until the crowd parted for another devil-girl and Delphine became invisible.

She was the most beautiful woman I'd ever seen outside of movies or porn, though I couldn't have said why. She had the sallow, hollow-eyed look that girls have when they aren't wearing any makeup. It must have been her lips that did it for me—fat, flowering things. Strawberry red. They puckered into a smirk when she saw me staring.

"This is my sister, Lilith," Delphine explained. I knew already they weren't real sisters. Lilith was taller. Taller than me, anyway. And she didn't have Delphine's flushed, overstuffed look. She was blonde, with sunken eyes in the brightest blue I'd ever seen. Blue fire. I couldn't look away.

"Hey," Lilith said over the noise of the music. Maybe it was the weed, but her voice caved my chest in. Low and cruel. I wanted her so bad I was stammering. She just smiled. "You're cute. Want some mushrooms?"

I nodded furiously. It was a terrible idea. I was so drunk I couldn't remember where Jake had gone, and only a couple of puffs away from being cross faded enough to vomit. But what was I going to say, no?

Lilith took my hand, and it felt like I'd touched an electric fence. The crowd parted around us, all eyes on her as she squirmed through the wall of stinking bodies toward the stage. We came out right next to the speaker. I could feel the bass guitar in my bowels. Lilith was above me now, and I looked up straight into the crotch of Satan. She leaned on the arm of his throne, whispering in his ear. His eyes found me and a twitch of humor floated across his scowling, trailer-park face. This Satan guy was even bigger up close, and I was getting the sinking feeling that Lilith knew him well.

I stood before the throne. Lilith's breath was in my ear. A

grin in her voice.

"He likes your costume."

"Thanks," I shouted. I'd forgotten I was even wearing one. Delphine had seated herself by Satan's other arm. He was a big, meaty guy. A1. Not like Jake. I was grateful he didn't stand up.

"He wants some mushrooms," I heard Delphine say in that prodding voice. A handful of other devil-girls had gathered around the throne, too, watching me with vacant eyes. They looked coked out of their minds—pupils huge as dimes. I thought about asking for some of that instead, but Satan was already fishing around in a duffel bag.

What he handed me was definitely not mushrooms—or at least not the kind I'd taken in my grandma's empty house. It was a little disk—like a big pill. I looked down at Satan's big, sweaty hand and wondered what he did 364 days of the year that made his palms so rough. Delphine was looking me up and down. Lilith was frowning.

"What do you want for it?" I asked, hoping I could refuse on account of an empty wallet. Then Satan's dull, black eyes were on me. His voice was raspy the way girls like.

"He doesn't have to take it, Lil," he said, with paternal admonishment that made me want to clench my teeth. Then he broke into a crooked, meathead smile, pressing the pill into my palms. "But for a man of God, this one's on me."

I'd tried. At least I could say I'd tried. The pill tasted like chalk and dirt, which I hoped meant it really was mushrooms. Some girl with bright pink hair and bull horns handed me a Miller High Life.

The next hour was a blur. We were standing at the back of the crowd, again. This new girl, me, Lilith, and Delphine. A joint smoldered between Lilith's long fingers. Her nails were a chipping cherry red. She passed the joint to Delphine and exhaled a puff of smoke into the air between us.

"How do you know Satan?" I asked. It was meant to be a joke but didn't come out as one.

Lilith shrugged her bony shoulders. “Me and my girls have been coming here for years.”

The question came out before I could stop it. “Have you fucked him?”

Lilith laughed out loud. A surprising sound. Candy-sweet and vicious. “Of course I have.”

“Jealous, holy father?” Delphine cooed. Her friends seemed to be multiplying, though it was hard to tell most of them apart as drunk as I was. They all had the same plastic horns. The same Halloween vampire teeth. I had a passing memory of Jake and thought to glance around for him in the crowd. He liked death metal, I think.

“What’s wrong?” Lilith asked. She laid her arm across my shoulder, and I could feel her nails graze the back of my neck, erasing the very notion of Jake.

“Nothing. Just looking for my friend.”

She smirked, then reached through the smoke and grabbed me by the chin. Her eyes had begun to take on a sort of glow—icy against the neon red of everything else. I recognized the over-saturated look from college basement trips.

“Your friend is fine,” she said, and I believed her. “Probably off having more fun than you.”

“Yeah, Father. Maybe you should step it up?” Delphine echoed.

Lilith never looked away. She narrowed her eyes, those lips twitching into a wicked smile. “Yeah, Father. Want to step it up?”

I wasn’t sure what they meant but I knew the answer was yes. I said a tiny prayer to Jake—thanking him for this damned costume. For inviting me to this place. I couldn’t believe it. I *hadn’t* believed it.

“I’ve always wanted to kiss a priest,” Delphine added, looking up at me through her dark lashes. I felt a flush rise up my neck. My eyes darted to Lilith. I didn’t want her to think I was choosing Delphine—not if she was on the table.

Was she on the table? Were any of them? If I could only pick one, I wanted Lilith. My heart felt like it might explode out of my chest.

I was tripping for real now, watching Lilith look from Delphine to the others. I could swear I saw the air move around her, as though she'd unfurled a set of invisible wings. "You girls ready to head to the after party?"

I didn't know where we were going, and I didn't care. Lilith threaded her fingers through mine while Delphine clung to my other arm, leading me toward the wagon circle of RVs. For a breath, I thought they might be taking me inside, but then we pushed past the porta potties toward the line of dark trees. The other girls trailed behind, stumbling and laughing. They were all grins, and the shrooms gave their smiles an otherworldly look. Suddenly they were all beautiful. Every one of them perfect. Their horns gleamed all shades of bronze and black, like dragon skin. Their eyes danced red and purple and gold.

The music faded as the wood surrounded us. Blackberries caught at the sleeves of my robe. The world smelled fresh and spiced with the acid scent of summer. Kudzu clung to every branch, parting as Lilith led the way into the dark. I breathed and the trees breathed with me, undulating pleasantly as the shadows between the trunks started to spin. I could feel Lilith's hand on mine. The bodies of the other girls brushing past—softness ruptured here and there by clawing brambles. Fragrant and womanish. Skin-smelling. The music was gone. I didn't know how Lilith and the others knew their way in the dark, but I let them lead me until an orange glow appeared through the trees, and we stopped.

Like an animal, I could smell it before I saw it. Fire. A shrieking bonfire. In my psychedelic haze, it raised its head up like a dragon, one thousand reptile tongues lashing at the night air. There were bodies in the clearing already—dancing. Flailing to no music. Or had my mind erased all sound in favor of touch and smell and taste? Taste. I could taste the smoke in the air. And then the cloying strawberry flavor of Delphine's lip gloss. My lips parted for her tongue. The taste was foul and exquisite. Tequila and blood.

"Here?" I asked, but I did not stop her. I couldn't. Her saliva was hot on my tongue. I looked up as she trailed her mouth down my neck. Lilith was watching us, smiling, silhouetted against the fire. Her face was a shadow, but her eyes were glowing electric blue. Her teeth were bright as moonlight. In the mirage of flame, her body was a hundred different shapes. Her hips moved with the music, widening and thinning as she twisted in time with the fire. Her hair hung wild around her naked shoulders, and her horns drew further into the sky as she moved, sharpening and glowing at the ends like a branding iron.

Delphine withdrew her tongue, and Lilith took me by the hand, leading me to where the others were dancing. Twenty–no, one hundred devil-girls. Moaning and weeping and laughing with the music of the fire. I might have been frightened. I *should* have been frightened, but then fingers were lifting up my robe. Delphine's was nipping at my neck again. The ground was warm and soft as a mattress. The dragon breathed its fire breath across my skin.

"Who are you?" I managed to ask the unfamiliar girl I saw fumbling with the button of my jeans. She smiled a sharp-toothed grin but didn't answer. Something compelled me to add, "I'm not really a priest."

"I know, Father," she purred.

I started to say something else, but then she took me into her mouth and the thought fluttered up and away into the black sky. They were singing now. A wild, wailing noise from everywhere and nowhere. The trees. The grass. The fire. It was coming from the fire. I tried to open my eyes the way one does in a dream. To suddenly see the world as it is. Lilith was standing over me. She'd changed. She'd grown taller. Her horns were the color of bleached bone, glowing hot where they sprung from the burning tissue of her scalp. She was the most beautiful thing I'd ever seen.

"Do you want me, Aiden?"

The answer pried its way out with vicious fingers, leaving my throat ragged as though I'd vomited. "Yes. God, yes."

She laughed a sharp, wicked laugh and shook her head, then knelt down to straddle me. It seemed I had a hundred hands on me. A dozen mouths. Lilith crawled forward. I could feel her skin burning through my shirt. She ran a long, serpent's tongue over her puffy lips. Those lips. Fat and dripping red like overripe fruit. I needed to touch her, but I was held fast. There were more hands than there should have been. Muddy, earthen hands. The scream-singing grew louder. The air was choked with black smoke. Lilith's face hovered above mine in the haze. She smiled and those lips parted to a row of razor teeth.

I tried to scream but the sound was lost in a plume of black smoke. She plunged her teeth into my neck. The feeling was ecstatic. Religious. Her body gave a shudder before she came up for air, crimson blood–my blood–dripping down her chin like an animal. Eyes like blue fire. I couldn't have moved if I'd wanted to. I didn't want to.

"Aiden!"

The fire popped and hissed and screamed. Lilith snapped in the direction of the voice, bloody teeth bared and snarling. A ridge of black feathers bristled up her naked spine. Then something struck her. Her head cracked sideways, and she screamed again, this time reeling back and lashing with all ten claws. The other girls scattered like a flock of crows; their singing turned to angry shrieking. The ecstatic feeling was gone with them, and I was overcome with rage, scrambling upward and barreling toward their attacker. *She's mine. She's fucking mine.*

It was Jake, wielding a branch the size of my whole leg like a baseball bat. Drazan Blackwall, in the flesh. He dropped the log and caught me by the shoulders. I swung at him, and he swung back, catching me on the cheekbone and dropping me. The rage went out of me like a smothered flame. Jake went for the log again and Lilith—or what had been her—gave another furious shriek. She unfolded a pair of huge, shadowy wings, batting embers across the clearing. The fire simmered low and electric blue.

The horror of it hit me then, even in the haze of drugs and whatever spell I'd been under. A monstrous, demon thing. Hell on Earth. Lilith looked back and forth between us and I knew I was about to die. I didn't notice pissing myself. I braced to run. To try and escape its razor claws before it tore into my back and got its teeth in my throat.

Then it shrugged, gave a little snort–almost like a laugh– and beat its wings once, twice, three times before disappearing into the black trees.

Jake tossed the branch aside and fell to his knees, panting so hard I thought he might keel over and die along with me. I couldn't feel the wound in my neck yet, but I could feel blood pouring down my shoulder, soaked up by my Demon Slayer shirt. Jake reeked of sweat and weed but I'd never been so happy to see anyone in my life. He huffed and puffed.

"Jesus… Aiden..." he panted, looking at my neck. I felt for the wound and found it oozing and flaking with burned skin. That's when I started puking. I retched beer and turkey leg into the grass until nothing else came up but hot, stinging bile.

"The devil-girls–" I groaned, but I couldn't finish. Already the memory was fading like a nightmare.

"What the hell happened?" Jake said, stepping closer to look at my neck. "Jesus, man. Was somebody on bath salts?"

I gave him a strange look. "What? No, it was… You saw…" I trailed off. The bonfire had cooled, now no more than a circle of stones overgrown with kudzu, like it hadn't burned since the 80s. I touched my neck again and winced with pain. "I think I need to go to the hospital."

"No shit, dude."

I couldn't stand. Every limb was trembling violently. I smelled like blood and piss. Jake finally managed to catch his breath and rose.

"Come on," he said. He took my hand and pulled me to my feet in one easy motion. I took a staggering step forward and almost fell again.

"What happened to your costume?" he asked as he hoisted me over his shoulder. I was too sick to be embarrassed. Just grateful he was strong enough to carry me. I looked to where my monk's robe had been cast into the fire, burned away to ash. All that was left on the grass where I'd fallen was my plastic crucifix.

"It's called garb," I coughed.

Jake carried me into the woods.

The Colors that Shine

Mariah Southworth

A soul is a beautiful thing. It shines out in the blackness of the void like a faceted star, brilliant and glittering. Humans on the other hand, are ugly. They are like oysters—rough and uncouth on the outside, but holding inside themselves treasure that they never see and don't fully appreciate. Also like oysters, humans taste good with garlic and butter, but we're waxing poetic about souls at the moment, not culinary delights.

Some demons like their souls to be pure and clear, like fine diamonds. Xilacque is like that, the snob. She's encouraged many a suicide cult, just to snag the pure souls of children from the fanatical masses. She practically drips with white light when she goes out. Baltholious too, loves a pure soul, especially those falsely condemned, though at least has the good taste to pair them with the blue-black souls of their executioners.

Personally, I find the pure souls boring—I love the rainbow oil spill of colors brought on by sin; the sheen and texture of the tortured and the suicidal. I want my souls to have *life.*

Humans can't see souls. I often wonder how they stand living in their world without seeing those brilliant lights shining through themselves, like the sun through stained glass. A human without a soul is an ugly thing, but *with* one there is nothing in all the planes of existence to rival their beauty.

I was going through my collection of souls when I felt the call of an incantation. Whatever mortal had made it had down their homework—all the proper patterns and offerings were there. I picked my head up, grinning as the incantation pulled at me. The timing could not have been better—I had a party to attend, and was finding my current collection of souls outdated and boring. It was a very important party—the annual Ball of the Damned, where fashion trends were set and lives were ruined. I needed some new finery to adorn myself with if I hoped to compete with Xilacque's gaudy display.

So I gave into the call, letting the incense and the words wrap around my essence and pull me through dimensions. With any luck there would be something beautiful in store for me.

The fire and smoke roared up inside the circle of chalk, faintly pink from the blood mixed into it. Black as a tire fire, the smoke settled back into a modest cloud, and my bright yellow eyes peered out from within its heart.

The woman before me glowed with a subtle beauty. Her soul gleamed like white crystal struck through with rainbow facets of fear and grief; a moonstone carved with hopelessness. I let my gaze crawl over her, drinking in the glory of her tortured innocence. She would make a lovely, contrasting centerpiece on a necklace strung with jet-black sinners.

She gazed up at me, hallowed eyes sunk into her thin face. She seemed neither shocked nor ecstatic that her summoning had worked, though this was her first time calling a demon. I needed no trick to tell that—the required "virgin" blood simply meant that the source of the blood needed to have never been used for occult purposes before. Even the lowest imp in Hell could sense that the blood used for the circle had been her own.

She was not old, but she was not a child either. I could not gleam much more about her from just her appearance. A human is a human—they all look more or less alike, and I would need to get inside her head to really know her. The circle of chalk prevented that. Instead, I let my attention drift to the immediate room—a squalid, ill-lit chamber with peeling wallpaper and a faint smell of mold wafting up from the carpet. A single, old mattress sat in one corner and a bookshelf made from boards and cinder blocks in the other. The chalk circle, I noted, had been drawn on a large piece of cardboard held down with rocks. Though the room was tidy, it reeked of despair and long hours of fearful, silent crying. A desperate room, though unlike the woman kneeling in front of me, it had no soul for its despair to give color to.

I broke the silence first. "Well?" I asked, ready for the negotiating, the barter, the wheedling.

She looked at me steadily, her thin lips parting. "Save me," she said softly.

I stared at her for a moment. No caution, safe guards, or fey double-talk. There were a million ways I could interpret such a simple plea. It would have been laughable had it not been so surprising.

"From what?" I asked, more amused then intrigued at this point.

She closed her eyes for a moment, then opened them again. "From the man sleeping in the other room."

Oh, *oh,* better and better. Was I to see the person who had painted those colors on her soul? A connoisseur of finery such as myself did *love* to meet the jeweler.

"Very well," I said gravely, hiding my enthusiasm. "But it will cost you a soul."

"Done," she said.

She didn't even *try* to argue—but then, she had no way of knowing how beautiful her soul was. "And," I said, pushing my luck, "I will need out of this circle."

She closed her eyes again. "Do what you must."

This was going to be so much fun.

***

Francis gradually woke up in his trophy room, frowning at the uncomfortable cold. He brought a large hand to his face and rubbed his eyes, then sat up in his recliner. The television in front of him was still on, but the muted baseball game had turned into late-night news. He groped around for the remote and shut it off. Francis shivered, then scowled. Laura had been screwing around with the thermostat, there was no other explanation for the cold.

Francis got up and scanned the room, with its glass-fronted cases full of gold and silver trophies. He had been a star athlete—he had gone to college on a baseball scholarship, and scouts had come looking at him. Then a motorcycle accident put his wrist out of the game, and here he was.

Francis wasn't bitter though. Well, not anymore—not that he admitted to himself, at least. In his mind, a bitter man wouldn't zealously worship the past the way he did, treating his old trophies and memorabilia like divine gifts from god.

Take his baseball bat, for instance—the bat that he had hit three back-to-back home runs with, the bat that had gotten the attention of the scouts. The bat that sat on its own little pedestal. The other night when Laura had brought him dinner, she had bumped into it. That was how Laura had gotten her latest batch of bruises. You'd think she'd know better by now, but as Francis had told her, sometimes you just couldn't train out innate ineptitude.

He'd phrased it just like that too—he had gone to college, after all. Fantastic words just flowed out of his mouth. Laura, dumb, uneducated little twat, had been a starving musician when he'd found her, barely able to keep herself off the streets.

And how did she repay him for his love? By turning the god damn heat off.

Francis stepped out of his trophy room, eyes on the hallway thermostat. When he arrived at it, he was surprised to find that the heat was still dialed to seventy-five. He scowled at it, tapped it, then cranked it up to ninety. Hopefully it wasn't broken—Francis considered himself a handy kind of guy, which meant that if something broke, he took out his hammer and nails and shored it up with a piece of wood. If something couldn't be fixed with a hammer and nails, well, it would be a long time before it got fixed. The rest of the house was evidence of this—there were several holes in the plaster that had been there for years, back when he still hit the walls instead of Laura. They had a dishwasher, but it hadn't worked in half a decade. Laura, Francis often joked, was the dishwasher, and when he said so she smiled at him with dead eyes. She had at least learned to laugh at his jokes.

The thermostat hadn't been turned down, which meant that Laura had been a good girl after all. Francis sniffed and looked up and down the hall. It was about time that he forgave her for the baseball bat. In other words, he was horny. He wanted to screw her before her new bruises faded—not that he would ever hit her if she didn't deserve it, he wasn't a monster! He just liked the way seeing them during sex made him feel.

"Baby doll," he called jovially.

No answer.

"Laura!" he barked.

Laura didn't come.

Francis frowned, then shrugged. That didn't mean anything—she could be asleep, after all. He'd wake her up and scare her a bit for not listening, and then she'd be extra grateful and fawning when all he wanted to do was make love.

He made his way down the hall. She'd be in her own room, of course. She wouldn't dare sleep in the master bedroom without him. It was important for Laura to have her privacy. Never mind that "her" room was barely bigger than a walk-in closet, had no real furnishings or comforts. Never mind that he often came bursting in unannounced, or the fact that the room was mostly used as a punishment, so that he could send her there when she displeased him. No matter the details, the room was hers, and he should be praised for being so thoughtful as to give her anything of her own when the house was in his name and paid for with his salary.

Francis turned the corner of the hallway and stopped short.

"Laura? What the hell are you doing?"

Laura continued to ignore him and stayed standing in the corner with her back to him. She wore one of her long pale nightgowns; silken, cool and lacy—Francis wouldn't let her wear anything that wasn't pleasing to him, even if it was cold and uncomfortable. Her dark head bowed low and her shoulders shook ever so slightly, like she was trying and failing not to cry.

Francis bristled—he didn't like to be ignored, especially not by Laura, who, by all rights should worship the ground he walked on. He still *wanted* her, but now she would have to work *very* hard to prove to him that she wanted it too.

"Laura," he growled, closing the distance between them with heavy footsteps. "Are you being a bad girl?" He clapped his heavy hand on her little shoulder and spun her petite form around. She looked up at him.

Something was wrong with her eyes.

Laura's lips pulled back in a sneer. "*This* is him? Tuh—he looked so much worse in your memories, darling," she drawled.

Francis stared at her for all of three seconds, shocked more by her lack of cowering than her nonsense words. He jerked his hand up and sent her sprawling with a resounding smack.

Laura caught herself on the wall, just barely avoiding hitting her head against the wood and plaster. Her shoulders began to shake again, and Francis bared his teeth in a savage snarl. She knew better then to cry in front of him. "Suck it up," he snapped. "Or I'll give you something to cry about you little…"

He trailed off as Laura straightened and threw her head back, black hair spilling over her shoulders and face as she laughed and laughed, her arms swinging limp as a string-less marionette.

Heat flooded Francis's face and neck, turning them a bright, beet red. "What the Hell is so funny?" he demanded, hands bunching into fists. "Shut up!"

Laura kept laughing.

Francis hadn't heard Laura laugh in a long, long time, but he didn't remember it being like this—deep and wet, with a manic reel to it, like carnival music echoing in an underwater cave. "I said shut up!" he yelled, pulling his fist back and swinging at the gentle curve of her jaw.

Thwak.

Francis stared at Laura's long, elegant fingers wrapped around his fist. Those fingers *used* to play the violin. Not anymore—not since Francis had broken her instrument over his knee three years ago because he couldn't stand the screeching anymore. Now her long musician's fingers had caught his punch without her even looking at Francis.

I giggled again with Laura's mouth—I couldn't help it. I was having *so* much fun, and we had barely begun.

Francis couldn't grasp the significance of little 110lb. Laura catching his punch. "Why you little bi—" he started.

Laura's head rolled up and he stopped mid-word. *Now* he could see what was wrong with her eyes. They glowed sulfur yellow from her sunken sockets, the hellish light drowning out her pupils. Laura grinned and tightened her grip. "Oooh… this is the bad wrist, isn't it?" she cooed.

Crunch.

Francis screamed as his wrist bent backwards, pain shooting up his arm like nothing since that long ago, fateful motorcycle accident. Laura let go as he stumbled backwards, cradling his hand against his chest.

"Francisssss…" Laura hissed through tight teeth. "Oh, Francisss, Francisss, Francisss, what did you do to Lllaurra?"

He looked up, face red and sweating. "Laura…" he gasped, half question, half demand.

"Oh, no, nnnnooo." Laura said, smile widening past the point of normal human flexibility. "Laura's stepping this one out," she said, arms swinging loosely at her sides. The hallway light flickered and the already low temperature took a dive. "Oh, but I can see her memories, I can see it all, the way you shaped her and painted her. Oh *Francisss…"* She leaned in. "You're so *colorful* Francis."

Unexpected as it was, Francis wasn't stupid. He was able to put it all together and realize just how screwed he was. You could see that moment in his face—all the red drained away, leaving him pale and sweating. His eyes widened like an animal's caught in the headlights, and he took one hesitant step back.

Laura crouched like a cat ready to spring.

Francis turned and ran.

I cackled with Laura's voice and sent my darkness flooding through the house.

Francis made it to the phone in the kitchen. He even managed to hit 911 without any light to see by—one-handed too, that broken wrist certainly wasn't helping him. It only rang once before the other line picked up.

"Hello, you've got to help me, my wife has gone crazy and—"

He froze as the sound of sobbing came pouring out from the phone.

"Please, I'm sorry Francis, I'm sorry, it was an accident..."

"L...Laura?" he asked. The sobbing continued, slowly getting deeper, until it wasn't Laura's voice anymore. *"Please, please no..."* sobbed Francis's voice from the phone.

Thwak.

Thwak.

Thwak.

A loud, rhythmic thumping came from the hallway, getting closer and closer, louder and louder. Francis shot a frightened glance behind him and dropped the sobbing phone. He bolted for the living room, heading for the front door. He ran right into the dining table in the dark, but he managed to make it out of the kitchen with only a bruise.

The thumping stopped.

Francis froze, heartbeat loud in his ears. Suddenly he didn't know which way the door was—panic and darkness had erased all sense of direction.

He took a tentative step to the right, then another, hand out. He touched brick and jumped back, cursing. He had almost run into the fireplace. That at least gave him a better idea of where he was, and he made a quarter turn and stepped quickly towards the front door.

He screamed and fell as forty-two inches of maple wood sent a crack through his right shin bone.

Francis shrieked in agony, and for good measure Laura brought the bat down on his left knee.

I turned the lights back on. Francis, pale, sweating and screaming in pain, looked up to see little Laura in her white nightgown, slowly swinging his precious trophy bat up and down, lightly smacking her free hand with the smooth, pale wood. Her eyes glowed candlelight yellow.

Laura grinned and Francis moaned. "Please, please, no," he sobbed.

The smile faded from Laura's face and she cocked her head. "Laura wants to talk to you," I told him.

Through the pain and fear, Francis's eyes brightened. "Please, yes! Let me talk to Laura!" he begged with all the desperation of a drowning man.

The yellow glow faded, leaving behind Laura's own brown eyes, only slightly bloodshot from smoke. Laura, the real Laura, looked down at the pitiful broken figure of Francis groveling on the floor.

"Please, Laura," he begged. "I don't know what that was, but please, I need help."

"Hello Francis," she said coldly. "It's good to finally see you afraid of something."

His eyelid twitched. Even in the teeth of agony and terror, her disobedience enraged him. "Laura…" he said, voice low. He paused and swallowed. "Laura, please, you're not going to kill me. I love you, you know that."

"I know," she said, voice barely a whisper, eyes glancing away from his face. She folded in on herself, collapsing under the weight of his stare. The hands holding the bat began to shake.

"You're the most important thing in the world to me," he said hurriedly, tongue tripping over itself. "It will be better Laura, you know that. I'll be better. Please, Laura, I need an ambulance."

She didn't move.

"Laura," He said, voice gravelly with impatience and pain. "Be a good girl and put down the bat. Put it down."

She looked at him, looked at the bat, and with a shaking hand she put it down. Francis let out a rattling sigh.

"Good, now—"

Laura walked over to the dusty fireplace and picked up the hatchet that waited there. She turned back to him, eyes hard, axe heavy in her hand. "Good-bye Francis," she said.

Her eyes didn't turn yellow again until after the first few swings.

***

The smoke came pouring back out of Laura's mouth and eyes, driving her to her knees. Once outside of her, I extended clawed hands to collect the shining soul stuff that had been flung from Francis's body with each swing. I had killed him so I got to keep him—those were the rules, and why I hadn't let Laura have those last few swings.

By the time Laura recovered from my exit and looked up, I had the black rainbow of Francis's soul in my hands, its radiant colors finally free from the gross bulk of its body. It would look dazzling back home, in the darkness of the void.

"Here is my payment, as agreed," I said, glancing down at Laura. Lovely, lonely, abused Laura, kneeling in the congealing puddle that had been Francis an hour ago. Red sanguine now tinged her shining moonstone soul. It looked even more beautiful than before. "Do call me again next time you need help, my dear," I purred. "I think we work well together."

I left her there to clean up the mess. She was a smart woman, I could tell that much from being in her head. She could handle Francis from here, and I had a party to attend. Francis' soul would look magnificent pinned to my lapel, and I would have a titillating story to share over the hors d'oevres.

Of course, could have taken Laura *and* Francis. They would have looked nice in the same piece together; abuser and abused. But Laura deserved more than that. I saw such potential in her, such capacity for darkness. She would be a centerpiece in her own right, given more time to sin. Call it an investment in beauty. Maybe I would not be the star of the Ball this year; maybe Xilacque's innocent baubles would outshine my new soul.

But there was always next year, for me to bring Laura out.

Oh, how her colors will shine.

El Diablo's Cocina

Terry Campbell

The blazing afternoon sun beat down mercilessly on the small black sports car as it made its way down the lonely stretch of highway. Black was not a wise choice of color for a car when driving through the unforgiving deserts of southwest Texas.

Inside, Kurt and Marsha Watkins said nothing. They were both well aware of the heat; there was no point in either of them voicing the obvious. It would only mean another argument, and the sweltering atmosphere already had their respective nerves on edge. To add to the discomfort, the air conditioner wasn't working, and the steady hot breeze from the open windows offered little comfort.

Marsha glanced at Kurt, his skin slowly melting before her eyes. She saw tiny droplets of perspiration forming on his forehead. He smiled weakly at her, and she returned it with an equally forced smile. Marsha reached down and, without thinking, turned on the air conditioner, as if blindly hoping some act of mercy had laid its healing hands on the stricken unit.

No luck, of course.

And so, the heat from the relentless Texas sun continued to broil them slowly like some tasty morsels inside a giant microwave oven; relief seemed to be nowhere in sight.

The road stretched endlessly before them. They hadn't passed another car for the last hundred miles, or so it seemed, let alone a gas station. And they were getting low on fuel. It was as if the rest of the world had simply disappeared, leaving them alone to cook in the desert. Marsha considered for a moment the unlikely act of nuclear war, the heat and radiation slowly drifting south to Mexico. Then, realizing the absurdity of such a thought, she dismissed it, pressing an already damp handkerchief to her sweaty brow.

She looked at Kurt. "Kurt honey, do you think we maybe took a wrong turn somewhere? Shouldn't we have reached the border by now?"

"I knew I should've taken that left turn at Albuquerque," Kurt replied jokingly. Marsha wasn't laughing. "No, I'm sure we're going the right way. Robert said to take the Infierno exit and stay on the highway."

Marsha nodded and looked out the window, watching the same rocks and cactuses that she was sure she'd watched a hundred miles back. She turned her attention to the road ahead. Nothing but black asphalt.

"Too bad Uncle Willy's souvenir stand was a bust," Marsha referred to the glimmer of hope a series of billboards fifty miles earlier had given them, promising everything from cold beer to desert fish to two-headed rattlesnakes. But the building had been boarded up and long forgotten, just as everything seemed to be in this God-forsaken countryside. Uncle Willy had apparently retired to Florida a long time ago. "I'm not too sure about some of the things they were claiming, though."

"Hey, I'd have watched human sacrifices if it meant sitting in an air-conditioned building," Kurt added.

They both had a good chuckle over that.

Suddenly, Marsha perked up. In the distance, she could make out a shape through the waves of heat shimmering up from the hot road.

A building.

"Kurt, look." She was unable to control her excitement over possibly finding life in this remote land. "There's a station or something. Let's stop and ask for directions."

Nodding, Kurt pulled into the dirt parking lot, stirring up a great cloud of red dust. The two opened the doors and stepped out onto the loose gravel and were immediately taken aback by the searing heat. There was no trace of wind, and the air was extremely oppressive; it clung to Kurt and Marsha, making their clothes feel several pounds heavier. Kurt stooped to check the car's tires. For a moment, Marsha thought they were smoking, but she decided the "smoke" was simply the dust they'd stirred up. She heard the engine hissing and popping, a vehement response to the torture to which they had subjected it.

"Jesus Christ, it's hot," Marsha gasped.

"It's hotter than Hell," Kurt responded.

"I can't imagine Hell being much hotter than this," she agreed, pushing her hair back from her face. Whatever style she'd given it that morning had been stripped by the oppressive temperature and her sweat.

Kurt and Marsha approached the run-down building. It had seen the effects of the brutal weather as well: Much of the paint had cracked and peeled, the wood warped and splitting., and many of the fascia boards along the eave were either missing or hanging by a rusted single nail. A sign hung from the porch by a rusted chain.

It read: *"El Diablo's Cocina."*

The windows, those that weren't broken out, were adorned with various Spanish words and childlike paintings of horned creatures. Painted in big red letters across one window was *"El Chile Mejor De Todos Del Sudoeste."*

There, in the porch's shadow, a Mexican man sat snoozing on a lopsided bench, a sombrero balanced over his face.

Kurt and Marsha studied the scene for a moment. Finally, Kurt spoke up. "I take it this is a restaurant."

"How do you figure that?"

He pointed at the hanging sign. "*El Diablo's Cocina* means 'The Devil's Kitchen'," he said. "But it's worded wrong."

"What do you mean?"

"Well, there's no apostrophe in Spanish," he exclaimed. "Instead of saying 'The Devil's Kitchen', they would say 'The Kitchen of the Devil', or in Spanish, *'La Cocina Del Diablo'*."

"How do you know that?" Marsha was seemingly amazed.

"I took two years of Spanish in high school."

"And you remembered *that*?"

"Well, yeah." Kurt was somewhat embarrassed.

"Were you a geek in high school, then?" Marsha teased.

Kurt play-slapped her gently across the face and playfully grabbed her in a headlock. She pulled away, laughing.

"So, what's the rest of it say, Mr. Mexico?"

"Honestly? I have no idea."

"The Devil's Kitchen, huh? Well, that would explain all those weird paintings on the windows."

As Marsha's words left her lips, a man came from the dark shadows of the porch, screaming and shouting in Spanish.

"No! No! Vay se! Vay se aqui! No es bien! Es maligno! Es maligno!"

The man was dressed in black and white, the garb of a Catholic priest. A tarnished silver crucifix dangled from his neck, and he clutched an old, yellowed Bible in one hand. He pushed Kurt and Marsha back toward the car, crazily looking over his shoulder at the same time.

"No! No! Vay se! Hay muerta en aqui para se!"

Kurt grabbed the priest and shoved him backwards. The priest's heel caught a protruding board, spilling him to the floor. He quickly picked himself up and held the crucifix out towards them. Eyes wild, he spat out more Spanish gibberish and turned to run, stumbling from the porch to disappear in a cloud of thick dust.

Nonplussed, Kurt breathed heavily as he watched the priest flee like the very devil himself was on his tail. The encounter had been quite unexpected.

Marsha took his arm. "Are you okay?"

"Yeah. I'm fine," he assured as he watched the priest's figure grow smaller and smaller as it vanished off into the horizon. "Let's go in."

"Hey . . . *Gringo*."

It was the man who had, up until then, been snoozing. He held the sombrero up over his brow, squinting against the glare of the sun, and he spoke in a low, deliberate voice. "Señor, pay no mind to the priest. He is *muy loco*."

The man smiled. He was missing several teeth. A fat, green fly lit on the tip of his nose. He didn't seem to mind.

Kurt and Marsha nodded apprehensively. The man nodded in return and placed the sombrero back over his face, scaring away the fly.

Kurt and Marsha entered the restaurant, the rusted hinges of the door screaming in the silence. It was equally hot inside, but at least there were ceiling fans. The dining room's decorations were somewhat akin to what one would expect to find in a Mexican-style restaurant. Huge pots containing large cactuses sat along the walls, which were finished in stucco and painted a dirty off-white color, the edges trimmed in bright festive colors. That was about it for the normal decorations.

The rest was quite bizarre.

A large glass aquarium sat in the center of the room, inside it, a live Gila monster. Small white mice wandered nervously about the tank, awaiting their destiny. Along each wall stood statues of what was apparently the Devil in various poses. Mystical masks lined the walls and devil marionettes hung from the ceiling, swaying and dancing in the warm breeze from the fans. Kurt and Marsha looked at each other, exchanging confused, but amused, glances.

"Table for two, señor?"

Kurt and Marsha jumped. They had not heard the waiter coming up behind them.

"Yes, two please," Kurt answered.

"Right this way, señor."

"Everyone speaks pretty good English here – except for that priest," Marsha whispered.

The waiter placed them at a table between two statues of the Devil, the outstretched arms hovering over the seats. Two devil-faced masks glared down at them from the walls. Even the ashtray bore the Devil's face.

"Is this good, señor?"

Kurt looked at Marsha. She couldn't help looking over her shoulders, aware of the arms poised directly over her head. It made her nervous, but she motioned that it was okay.

"Yes. Fine, thank you."

The waiter handed them each a menu. A devil face blanketed the front cover.

"Can I get you a couple of *cervazas* while you are deciding?"

"Yes, two beers," Kurt said. Marsha mouthed *show-off.*

"Certainly, señor." The waiter disappeared into the back.

Marsha crossed her arms across her breasts, as if she were cold, though it was still quite hot. "This is a weird place," she said, looking around nervously. "A lizard. There's a goddamn lizard eating rats in the dining room."

Kurt took her hands. "I think I've got it figured out."

"What?" she asked.

"It's a theme restaurant. A bizarre one, mind you, but still. You know, like a sports bar has sports equipment as decorations. Or the Hard Rock Cafe has music memorabilia.

The Devil's Kitchen. It's all part of the atmosphere they're trying to convey."

"But why the Devil?"

"I read somewhere that Mexican Catholics fear the Devil to such an extent that they may try to cope with it in strange ways. Maybe this is their way of coming to terms with their fears."

The waiter returned to the table, bringing two frosty mugs of beer. "Are we ready to order?"

"Oh, I'm sorry. We haven't even looked at the menus. We were busy discussing your motif."

"So, what's good?" Marsha asked the waiter.

"Oh, but may I suggest the chili. It is our chef's specialty. He uses special herbs and spices indigenous to these parts, and a unique blend of six hundred and sixty-six peppers. It is very hot, but if you like spicy foods, you will love it."

"I didn't know there were that many different peppers in the world," Marsha marveled.

Kurt and Marsha looked inside the menus and were confused by what they saw. One word—chili—graced the page in big bold letters. Kurt cast a wary eye to Marsha. She rolled her eyes.

"It says *chili*."

"Si, señor."

"That's *all* it says," Kurt said.

"That is all we serve," the waiter answered.

"But what if I don't want chili? I mean, it's over a hundred degrees outside. I don't want anything that hot."

"But, señor. Around here, everything is hot."

Marsha began to giggle at Kurt's inability to argue with the waiter. He gave her a dirty look, and she put a hand to her mouth to stifle the laughter.

"Two bowls of chili then, señor?" the waiter asked.

"Evidently so." Kurt sighed and leaned back in his seat, still looking at Marsha sourly. She began to snicker again.

"Trust me, señor. You may think you don't want chili now but wait until you taste it. You may never want to eat anything else."

The waiter began to laugh, his merriment building up from a soft chuckle to a wave of hysterical cackling as he walked back into the kitchen area. He disappeared behind swinging, stainless-steel doors.

"Relax, Kurt. You're hungry, aren't you? God knows how far we'd have to go to find another restaurant around here."

"I guess you're right."

She took his hand and squeezed it. "Of course, I'm right. You'll *love* the chili."

* * *

The waiter was right: Kurt and Marsha thoroughly enjoyed the chili. The blend of herbs and spices and all those peppers had culminated in a culinary delight. There was an odd but pleasant taste to the chili, almost an afterthought. And hot, damn was it hot. They must've gone through three pitchers of iced tea. Before they had realized it, Kurt and Marsha had knocked off four big bowls of chili between them, and still did not feel gorged.

Kurt leaned back and let out a loud satisfying burp. "Excuse me."

Marsha smiled at him. She suddenly felt very passive, very peaceful, almost like she was drunk. She wondered how just one beer could've affected her when diluted by a sea of chili and iced tea. She looked across the table at Kurt. He had that same dopey look on his face that she knew must be evident on hers as well. His eyes seemed to be glazed over. She had heard stories of the potency of Mexican beers, but this was hard to believe.

Kurt took her hands and squeezed and patted them lovingly. “That was absolutely the most enjoyable, delicious meal I have ever had.”

Marsha nodded in agreement. “We must ask for the recipe.”

The waiter returned with a bowl of after-dinner mints. “How was the chili? Did I not tell you it was excellent?”

“Yes. Perfect. The chili was absolutely perfect,” Kurt praised.

“Yes. Splendid,” Marsha added. “I *must* have the recipe.”

The waiter looked surprised, almost insulted. “Oh señora, but I am sorry. I cannot give you the recipe. It is an old family recipe, passed down through many, many generations.”

“But I must have it. I’m hooked. I *need* it,” Marsha pleaded.

“I am so sorry.”

Marsha looked at Kurt, her eyes begging for help.

“We’ll pay you for it,” Kurt said. “How much do you want for the recipe?”

The waiter smiled apologetically. “I am sorry señor, but it is not for sale.”

“Not for sale? Oh, c’mon. Everything has a price.”

The waiter’s eyebrows rose, and then he held up his finger as if suddenly struck with an idea. He rubbed the bristly whiskers on his chin and pondered in silence. Marsha chewed her lower lip, an act she often did when nervous, and glanced eagerly from the waiter and back to Kurt again.

Finally, the waiter spoke. “Perhaps there is a way. But the price is very high, *very* high indeed, señor.”

“Money is no object.”

“Oh, but it would not cost you money, señor. It would cost you your souls,” the waiter said, matter-of-factly.

Kurt met Marsha’s eyes. They each looked around the dining room as if to confirm the other’s thoughts. She nodded to him in understanding. It was all part of the restaurant's act.

Kurt looked back at the waiter. "Deal."

"Excellent," the waiter responded. "One moment, please."

The waiter disappeared and shortly returned with two objects in his hand, which he laid on the table in front of Kurt and Marsha. He held a small, sharp knife in one hand and two quills in the other. Kurt picked up one of the objects and inspected it. It seemed to be crafted from some sort of thick parchment, dimpled and slightly opaque, its edges framed with what appeared to be chicken bones. An odd smell permeated from the material, and there were small black hairs protruding from the surface in random spots.

Kurt held the parchment where Marsha could see it and read. "I, the undersigned, with Pancho Garza Guadalupe Felipe Miquel Perez as witness…" He paused to glance at the waiter. The waiter smiled, revealing gold caps. Kurt continued, "Do hereby forfeit all rights to my soul, and in addition, do sign all aforementioned rights over to Satan, the great and evil one, the eternal Lord of Darkness."

Kurt laid the paper back down on the table. "Everything seems to be in order," he said. "Let's have the pen."

The waiter's grin widened. "Your hands first, please," he said, holding the knife, its sharp blade gleaming in the incandescent lighting.

"What?" Kurt stuttered, astonished.

"You must sign in your own blood."

That was it. Kurt had had enough. He slammed his fists down on the table, making Marsha jump, and stood up. "Now wait just a goddamn minute here! This is carrying this 'theme' thing a little too far! You're not going to cut me with some dirty knife that's been God only knows where and make me sign some bullshit fake contract with the Devil in my own blood!"

The waiter snatched up the papers. “Fine, señor. Have it your way. No signature, no recipe.”

“*Kurt*,” Marsha said sternly.

He looked at Marsha; her eyes were burning, intense. She wanted the recipe. She *needed* the recipe. He needed the recipe. *They* needed the recipe.

The waiter stood silently, patiently waiting. Kurt ran his fingers through his sweaty hair and sat back down.

“Your hands, please,” the waiter repeated.

Kurt and Marsha extended their arms and placed their hands palm-up on the table. The waiter took first Kurt’s, then Marsha’s, and made a quick clean cut on the index finger. A small dot of bright crimson appeared.

“See. That was not so bad, eh?” the waiter said, handing them each a quill.

They dipped the sharpened tips of the feathers into their pinprick wounds and signed the papers in a nervous, cryptic pattern at the bottom. They then laid the quills down on the table and looked up at the waiter.

“*Bien. Bien.* Very good,” he said happily.

He picked up the contracts and disappeared once again into the kitchen.

“You’d better make this chili as good as the chef did,” Kurt threatened playfully, wiping blood from his fingertip.

After a few minutes, the waiter returned.

“Excuse me, señor, señora. The chef wishes to meet you and give you the recipe personally.”

“Oh, great,” Marsha said, standing up.

“Well, this should be interesting,” Kurt mumbled.

Kurt and Marsha followed the waiter through the double doors.

“This way, please.”

The kitchen was filthy, and it was hotter, *much* hotter, than it had been outside. Dirty pots and pans, caked with dried, rancid food, were piled high on the countertops. The walls were discolored by years of grease build-up. The floor was covered with spills that no one had bothered to clean up for what must have been decades. The whole scene made Kurt and Marsha regret having eaten anything made in such a squalid place.

"When's the last time the Health Department was here? This kitchen is disgusting," Kurt complained.

"Do not worry, señor. The chili was not cooked here. The chili is cooked in the basement," he assured.

He pushed open a single stainless-steel door and a searing wave of heat almost knocked them over. A spiraling stone staircase disappeared down into darkness.

Holding the door open, the waiter said, "This way please." He took a flickering torch from a sconce inside the doorway, and Kurt and Marsha entered.

The heat was unbearable. Clothes clung miserably to the couple's bodies, soaked through with sweat. An odd, overwhelming odor hung in the air; Marsha detected the faint, rotten smell of sulfur. They continued down the stairs, the shadows cast by the torch dancing an eerie waltz on the cavernous walls.

At last, a faint light began to appear from the depths of the basement, growing brighter as they made their way into the subterranean depths. The waiter placed the torch into another sconce and stopped.

"We are here," he said.

The waiter stepped into a passageway that spread out into a huge cavern. Great stalactites hung from the ceiling above. Shelves holding thousands of jars lined the walls. Eerie displays of light cast by the flames in the center of the room played across the damp, slimy cave walls. In the center of the room sat a huge, blackened iron pot atop a roaring inferno. The rank odor of sulfur hung heavy in the air. A crude wooden staircase curved around the circumference of the steaming pot, ending in a leaning shaky platform. Standing atop the platform was an awesome spectacle: A giant humanoid figure, its skin a deep, boiled crimson color, stood stirring the massive pot with a great iron pitchfork. It wore a dirty, smeared apron and a large chef's hat. Great, curved horns protruded from the hat. A long flowing forked tail whipped lazily about behind it, and the sounds of its huge cloven feet on the boards echoed ominously throughout the cavern.

The creature sat the pitchfork aside, wiped its great clawed hands on the apron, and reached for the two signed documents.

"Ah, Mr. and Mrs. Kurt Watkins," the thing hissed, its breath visible as a heavy, stagnant vapor. It studied the papers, dwarfed in its huge hands and looked down at Kurt and Marsha. "Welcome to Infierno, otherwise known in your language as Hell. I do hope you enjoy your stay and, please, feel free to have as much of my chili as you like."

THE END

OTHER HELLBOUND BOOKS

www.hellboundbooks.com

Satan Rides Your Daughter

In our spine-chilling homage to the late, great Dennis Wheatley and the inimitable Hammer Horror films spawned from his works, HellBound Books presents twenty superlatively satanic stories guaranteed to have you fearing for your very soul?

A whole host of Hell's denizens skulk within these pages, waiting with growing impatience for brave of heart - or the relentlessly foolhardy - to make their otherworldly acquaintance, so please, do venture inside.If you dare?

Featuring hellish tales from: L. G. Merrick, Henry Myllylä, Alan Derosby, A.K. McCarthy, Brian James Lewis, C. C. Parker, Chisto Healy, Leo J. Winters, R.C. Mulhare, Henry Myllylä, J.B. Toner, Glen Damien Campbell, Nathan Blake, Gerald Dean Rice, Ricki Whatley, Carlton Herzog, Len M. Ruth, Vivian Kasley, Carson Demmans, Mark Towse, and Alexander Marai.

Notes of Discord

These Squatters Are Going To Rot!

In the late eighties, the Lower East Side of New York City rippled with turmoil. It was the city against the poor and destitute, it was punk versus skin versus hippy.
All of it had a soundtrack, call it drunk punk, call it what you would, the LES throbbed with a new generation of punkers pushing the boundaries. Underneath it lay an evil that even the headline writers of the Post could never have imagined.
An unearthly evil that twists the will, an evil that an up and coming punk band will never forget.
An evil that will never forget them. *Notes of Discord*, part coming of age story, part personal memoir, and all horror novel. A book with lots of punk rock, and even more full-on bloody bits.

Anthology of Horror

hor·ror
/ˈhôrər/

A literary or film genre concerned with arousing feelings of horror.

Rest assured, HellBound Books knows what scares you!

Skulking around in the deepest, thickest, darkest shadows of our authors' imaginations lies a whole host of terrifying tales to scare you witless and stir your greatest fears and, dear reader, we have compiled twenty-one such short stories for that specific purpose within the beautifully crafted pages of this very tome!

So, dig in – we dare you – and do remember to leave a light on…

Featuring short tales of terror from: Cory Andrews, Kathrin Classen, William Presley, John Schlimm. K.L. Lord, Jane Nightshade, K. John O'Leary, Dante Bilec, D. H. Parish, Whitney McShan, Keiran Meeks, Josh Darling, Paul Lonardo, Martyn Lawrence, Eric J. Juneau, Terry Campbell, Brett King, Sophia Cauduro, Christina Meeks, Kody Greene, and HellBound Books' very own James H Longmore.

The First Time I Saw Her

Heart-stopping folk horror to keep you out of the woods!

Anna and her mother are on the run after a tragedy shatters their world. A stranger has offered them protection in a private community hidden deep in the woods, and Anna and her mother have no choice but to abandon their life and belongings to take refuge until they can figure out their next move.

But the woman who helped them may not be what she seems, and the safe-haven community has its own secrets ... and its own dangers.

Anna is no ordinary girl, though. She can perceive things others cannot, impossible things. Now thrust into an unfamiliar setting with horrors unfolding all around her, Anna must figure out what she is and what she is capable of before she loses what little she has left of her life.

A HellBound Books Publishing LLC Publication

www.hellboundbookspublishing.com

Printed in Great Britain
by Amazon

58274054R00219